Large Print Set
Setlowe, Richard.
The Black Sea

WITHDRAWN

The Black Sea

This Large Print Book carries the
Seal of Approval of N.A.V.H.

The
BLACK SEA

RICHARD SETLOWE

Thorndike Press • Thorndike, Maine

Library of Congress Cataloging in Publication Data:

Setlowe, Richard.
    The Black Sea / Richard Setlowe.
        p. cm.
    ISBN 1-56054-330-2 (alk. paper : lg. print)
    1. Large type books. I. Title.
[PS3569.E78B57   1992]   91-42229
813'.54—dc20   CIP

Excerpts from "Tao Te Ching" by Lao-tzu, translated by
Stephen Mitchell, copyright © 1988 by Stephen Mitchell,
are reprinted by permission of HarperCollins Publishers.

Thorndike Press Large Print edition published in 1992
by arrangement with Houghton Mifflin Company.

Cover design by James B. Murray.

The tree indicium is a trademark of Thorndike Press.

This book is printed on acid-free, high opacity paper.

For David and Iris,
Whose cruise aboard the Odessa
planted the first creative seeds

Yet mystery and manifestations
arise from the same source.
This source is called darkness.

Darkness within darkness.
The gateway to all understanding.
  Tao Te Ching

Contents

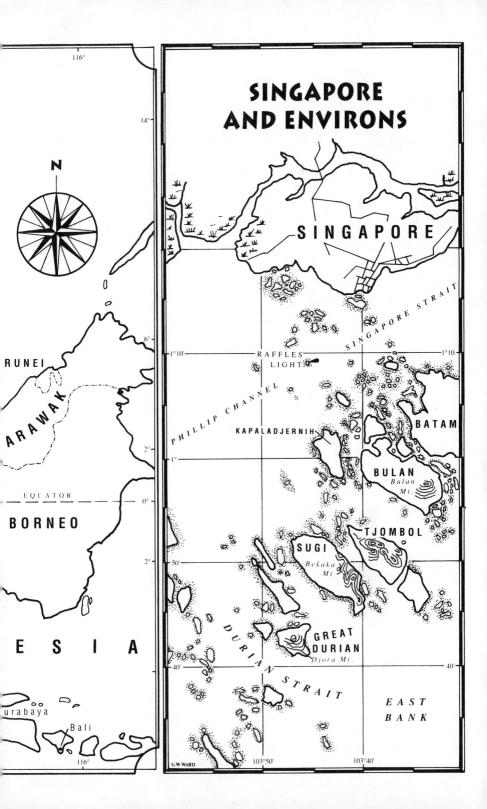

Part I
On the Northeast Monsoon

1. A Package for Raffles

The coolie stood on the pedals of the bicycle rickshaw, furiously pumping the *becak* through the ghostly, white-walled canyons of downtown Singapore, as if he were being goaded by demons. But the only occupant of the cushioned rattan passenger seat behind him was a lidded wicker basket.

The heavy monsoon rains that had swept the city earlier in the evening had ceased, but at one o'clock in the morning the air was still so thick with moisture that Singapore appeared to be under water. The pale concrete cliffs of high-rises cut off the northeast wind but not the drizzle that fell like detritus raining on the bottom of the sea from the ocean above. The streetlights along Bras Basah Road wavered and diffused. The scattered room lights still burning in the Westin Stamford Hotel hung in the night sky, growing dimmer, dimmer, dimmer, blinking, and finally dissolving away in the distant high mists that veiled the building's seventy-three-story summit. Lightning pulsed in the cover of cloud that shrouded the city.

The coolie's sweating face and bare arms and legs reflected a moist, oily gleam in the street lights, and his T-shirt and shorts stuck to his body. Still standing on the pedals, he careened around the corner at Beach Road at full speed. The *becak* lurched alarmingly, as though for an instant it might overturn. The coolie froze on the pedals. His head twisted about, and he stared with a bloodless, terrified face at the wicker basket.

It swayed slightly on the seat a moment but stayed fast, held down by the weight of whatever was inside. The rickshaw man continued to stare at the basket, then cautiously turned back to his pedaling. It was a strained, desperate movement, as if he were at once terribly frightened of jostling the basket again but was pushing to go as fast as his heart and legs could drive the *becak*.

He suddenly braked and turned, this time infinitely more gingerly, into the curving carriageway of the old Raffles Hotel. With its worn, gray cobblestones and Victorian portico, the Raffles was an anachronism amid the relentlessly modern skyscrapers, a storybook throwback to colonial times. Two other bicycle rickshaws were parked just outside the entrance of the carriageway, their drivers both curled up in fetal positions in the passenger seats. The Sikh doorman, sweltering in the humid heat in his long coat and turban, stood guarding the hotel entrance, his erect, rigid stance disguising the fact that he was all but asleep on his feet at that hour.

The coolie warily eyed the Sikh. Then, with the same strained, gingerly movement of frantic haste, he lifted the basket by its handles and very quickly slid it onto the faded red carpet that ran from the curb to the marble steps. Then he leaped back onto the bicycle, and the rickshaw bolted off, careening back down the cobblestones.

The doorman started awake, but the *becak* was around the corner and out of sight before the Sikh shouted after it. The big turbaned man shuffled to the curb and bent over the basket, the sort of woven lidded affair in which snake charmers keep their cobras.

He cautiously eased off an edge of the lid. A circle of polished white cloth caught the overhead light. The Sikh lifted the lid off.

His rheumy eyes stared in puzzlement at a naval officer's cap with a foreign gold crest and band. He fingered the shiny black leather bill, then tipped it up, toppling whatever it rested on back against the basket, revealing a shock of black hair, a broad, white-skinned forehead, eyes of lifeless amber glass, blood-smeared nostrils, and a tortured mouth.

The Sikh gasped and staggered back,

gagged by the sour, metallic stench of blood, congealed in a thick puddle at the neck of the severed head.

2. *Maggi Chancellor Takes a Cruise*

Liz Schneider was, at fortysomething, a testament to the mesmerizing power of sex deployed by a clever woman, and Maggi Chancellor, ten years younger and an associate professor of Asian Studies, regarded her with no mean degree of envy. Even in the air conditioning of the ship's saloon a fine moistness highlighted the ripe flesh of Liz's breasts, making them seem still succulent.

"But why, darling, are we aboard a *Russian* ship?" Liz Schneider cooed.

The expression on Alan Schneider's face told Maggi that he was being asked that question for the dozenth time.

"The Society felt a Russian ship would add another dimension to the cruise," Maggi answered.

"But this is a voyage to the exotic isles of the *Java Sea*," Liz proclaimed with an extravagant sweep of her jeweled hand. From the gesture and the theatrical lilt in her voice, Maggi guessed that Liz had drunk abundant champagne at the sailing party in Singapore. "This is *Joseph Conrad* country. Or Willy Maugham's world, to be a bit more modern. We should be on a posh P and O liner. Or on some *scurvy* tramp streamer with a *drunken, sweating* Dutch captain who's just reeled aboard after a *debauch* with *seamy* native girls." Liz relished each innuendo, and the hushed vibrato of her voice caused men at adjacent tables to lean forward to overhear what it was that had so excited her.

Alan Schneider winked at Maggi over the rim of his champagne glass. "Yes, that's the ticket," he exclaimed enthusiastically. He apparently enjoyed his wife's performances almost as much as she did.

The waitress — dressed as if for a Ukrainian wedding in a starched, flowered blouse, red doublet, and a glittering, high-crested cap — stood at his elbow waiting for the order.

Did they really still dress like that in Russia? Maggi wondered, or only in Russian restaurants and aboard Russian cruise ships. She smiled and shook her head at the waitress, "No more, thank you."

"I mean, this is all very *glasnostic* and all that, but where's the *romance?*"

"I'm afraid, darling, it all ended with World

War II." Schneider glanced at Maggi. "Russian cruise ships have taken a great deal of the local luxury trade away from the British and Americans' lines. They even shuttle between Melbourne and Sydney taking Australians to the Polynesian Islands. Give a capitalist enough caviar, and he'll choke on it. Isn't that what Lenin said? Or something to that effect."

All the while he spoke, Schneider was preparing a tidbit, heaping silver spoonfuls of the Beluga caviar on a small slice of black bread, then fastidiously adding delicate pinches of chopped onion, egg, and capers.

Liz sighed. "After all the sacrifices Daddy made in the *Big War*. Bedding big-busted Australian girls in Brisbane, rolling around in the coconuts with native girls on Nouméa. He was quite nostalgic about World War II."

The wicked tongue that had been the delight of Washington soirees and columnists was apparently scandalizing faculty dos at Stanford now that Schneider had moved from the State Department to academia.

There was something contagious about Liz's glamour. Maggi wondered if Schneider himself had seemed half as attractive with his first wife. He now held the hors d'oeuvre up to Liz's lips. She closed her eyes like a child taking a communion wafer and savored the offering with a rapturous expression. "Oh, darling!" she exclaimed finally. "Let's supper on caviar and French champagne the whole cruise."

Schneider sipped from the crystal flute. "It's Georgian actually, but they're getting quite good at it." He glanced about the lounge, and his remark appeared to take in the plush upholstered beige and coral chairs, the rich carpeting with its geometric Persian design, the teak paneling, and the fluted art deco columns that rose to the low ceiling and blossomed into petals of recessed lights. The cruise ship *Black Sea* was more like a luxurious private yacht than an ocean liner.

A Russian officer in a white tropical uniform with black and gold epaulets strode into the lounge. It was the young blond officer with the cleft chin with whom Maggi had chatted briefly at the sailing party. Vladimir Korsakov. He hurried straight to a far table, as if intent on official business.

"What will your lectures cover?" Maggi asked. "The changing geopolitics of this area?"

Schneider nodded. "I think it's vital that *they* understand it." He indicated a table at which the respective presidents of Lawrence Technology and the WestPac Corporation were huddled. "In the sixteenth century the Portuguese explorer Pires said, 'Whoever is

21

lord of Malacca has his hand on the throat of Venice.' The players have changed, but this is still one of the most strategic areas in the world."

"You've become so professorial," Liz murmured in a throaty voice. "It's exciting."

"I thought power excited you."

"That was in Washington, when you were Secretary of State, darling. In Palo Alto my libido reverts back to my schoolgirl crush on certain professors." She turned to Maggi. "I went to Radcliffe just as they began to *integrate* with Harvard." Her lips curled about the word, suggesting something lascivious.

At the far table, where the ship's captain was entertaining guests, the Russian officer Korsakov bent and whispered something in his ear. Captain Khromykh immediately stood, appeared to make hasty apologies to his guests, and rushed out with Korsakov in his wake.

Liz studied the departing uniformed figure and favored Maggi with a small conspiratorial smile and an arched eyebrow, a woman-to-woman appreciation of an attractive man. Schneider, fussing with another canapé of caviar, did not notice the exchange.

The other woman studied Maggi a moment. "You're really much too young to be a professor. You look barely old enough to be a graduate."

Maggi smiled politely. She was actually an associate professor, but she never corrected anyone on that point. "It's my genes. Or delayed puberty. But I really am old enough."

Liz now glanced down at Maggi's left hand. Her eyes lingered several moments on the milky white area at the base of her ring finger, which sunlight had not touched for ten years.

"And how long have you been divorced now, dear?"

"Only a few months."

"And now you're running away to sea."

"Really, Liz," Schneider protested.

She slapped her husband's hand. "Hush. Maggi and I are going to become great friends on this cruise, aren't we?"

Maggi smiled back.

"We should discuss these things. After all, Maggi is our ultimate authority on Indonesian shadow puppets and Balinese burial rites, and we have a scholarly obligation to know where she's coming from in the cosmic scheme of things."

"It was, as you said, a schoolgirl crush on a certain professor." Maggi tried to make it sound light and bubbly as Liz had, but even her own ear detected the pain in her voice.

23

"Anyone we know?"

"Bryce Chancellor."

"Yes, of course. I didn't make the association," Schneider said.

"Do I know him?"

"I don't know. You may have met him, dear. He's really one of the two or three leading scholars on Southeast Asia in the United States." He looked back at Maggi with interest. "He brought you into his business, did he?"

The assumption had once enraged Maggi, but she had learned to suppress that anger. "Actually, I came here originally in the Peace Corps. I was right out of college, assigned to a *kampong* on the east coast of Malaysia. I met Bryce later in graduate school."

"The *Peace* Corps!" Liz exclaimed. "Oh, ask not what your country can do for you but what you can do for your country." She regarded Maggi with tearful, shining eyes, as though she might cry in another moment.

Schneider noticed it. "Perhaps it's time to turn in," he suggested gently. He rose.

Maggi rose also. Schneider, once the Secretary of State, now held the Konosuke Matsushita Chair of International Economics and Policy at Stanford. Rising seemed somehow appropriate.

Liz stood up, and with that simple motion,

a bit vague and unsteady, drew all eyes in the saloon to her.

Schneider handed his wife a last tidbit of caviar on black bread. "The Russians claim it absorbs the alcohol."

"Then why do the Russians have such a drinking problem? They're worse than the Irish." Liz smiled at Maggi, as if apologizing. "My father, rest his soul, was Irish. So I can say that without prejudice. And with personal authority." She abruptly walked off toward the lounge door, holding herself with a formidable steadiness, as though she keenly felt how much champagne she had drunk but willed herself not to sway.

At the door she paused and turned back to Maggi. "When we get to Jakarta, we'll go shopping for shadow puppets." Her eyes widened, as if plotting a great intrigue, but Liz Schneider was really requesting that Maggi accompany her.

"It's a date," Maggi answered enthusiastically. She knew her place in the academic pecking order.

The speedboat crouched behind the channel buoy so that any faint radar echo its wooden hull or powerful engine might bounce back would be hidden in the radar return of the buoy itself.

The men in the boat waited, as they had waited for a dozen ships before this one. The Indonesians smoked *kreteks,* and the sweet, spicy smoke of cloves hung in the heavy, wet air. The glow of the cigarettes was the only light. Tengku Haji Azhar could not make out the men's features, only the faint gleam of moist brown faces and bare, sinewy arms, the oily, metallic shine of knives and gun barrels. The Bugis chewed his betel nut and noisily spat the bloody juice over the side.

Tengku frowned. He had gathered a motley pack of cutthroats — greedy, ravenous men. He would have preferred more devout, faithful men, rather than this unholy alliance. But each man in the boat had done this many times before, and Tengku needed their experience, their skill, their courage.

And he needed their swords. He felt the weight of his own *parang* in its sheath on his back. It had been his father's and his father's father's. It was a sharp, righteous sword. In his belt the butt of a Colt .45 cut uncomfortably into Tengku's stomach, but if he had to shoot, he would take Mahmud's AK-47. Each of the seven men in the boat had an automatic rifle, either a Russian AK-47 or an American M16, but each also carried a long knife in a sheath at his side or slung across his back. He had known these men most of his life; only Yusof and Mohammed had ever killed a man.

Tengku checked his watch again. The ship was late. If it had left Singapore late, it would speed up to make up time on the open sea, but it must still slow down to thirteen knots to navigate the channel.

His legs were cramped from the prolonged crouch, and Tengku shifted his weight. His knee struck one of the slender bamboo poles that ran the length of the boat and thrust out several feet ahead of the bow. The ends of the poles were lashed to steel hooks, swathed in burlap to muffle the noise of grappling. These men knew how to plant the hooks from a bucking, speeding motorboat and then scamper up the poles like monkeys climbing after the sweeter fruit at the top of the tree. Such an act required greedy, ravenous men. Ravenous for money, power, or God. Tengku had promised them all three.

Tengku saw the forward and aft masthead lights first, distant beacons hovering like stars above the inky sea. Then the red port sidelight and the green starboard lamp followed, the soft yellow glow of portholes, and finally the massive, ghostly bulk of the cruise ship itself, plowing up a phosphorescent wake.

"Ikan gantung kucing tunggu!" Tengku whispered. The fish is hung, the cat waits. It was an old Malay proverb, but to the men in the boat it was a call to battle. They grunted in acknowledgment. The speedboat's engine coughed to start, then settled back to an asthmatic idle.

The ship sailed by, showing a broadside of bright lights from the upper-deck lounge and the portholes of scattered cabins. The telltale funnel swept past, spotlighted and glowing in the night like a sail, a towering white cone with a broad red band on which was emblazoned a golden hammer and sickle.

Tengku pointed a powerful lamp across the channel at the opposite buoy a mile away and flashed three times. *God . . . be . . . praised.*

A pause of only a second or two, and then three answering flashes. *God . . . be . . . praised.*

"My brothers," Tengku announced, and the dark heads in the boat all turned toward him, "death is a treasure when we are martyred for the Almighty. The winds of Paradise are blowing."

The engine exploded to full power, and the speedboat leaped after the Russian cruise ship like a panther pouncing from its hide.

★ ★ ★

Maggi was much too restless to sleep this first night out at sea. Her small cabin was absolutely claustrophobic, one of the few aboard without a porthole. As a nonpaying tour guide and secondary guest lecturer, she had been given the most inexpensive accommodation aboard the *Black Sea,* an interior cabin on the main deck. She fled it for the sea air of the promenade.

In the passage she met her next-door neighbor, a tall, white-haired gentleman in his late sixties, a Mr. Benjamin. He was still nattily turned out for the sailing party in a well-tailored blue blazer, white slacks, and foulard tie, and his long silvery hair fairly shone with brushing and grooming. Maggi had chatted with him briefly when she had first checked aboard that afternoon. He was a pleasant, chivalrous widower, retired, traveling alone, and painfully lonely for company. He walked with the aid of an elegant Malacca cane, and unlike the debonair puff of patterned silk in his breast pocket, the cane was not merely for style. Mr. Benjamin had an air of fragility about him, the timidity of movement of an elderly man recovering from a recent serious operation.

"I'm going on deck," Maggi greeted him. "The sea air is supposed to be invigorating."

"Oh, I don't think I'm quite up to *invigorating*," he said with a soft laugh. "*Recuperating* is about as much as I can handle right now."

Maggi laughed with him. From their few snatches of conversation, Maggi rather liked this elegant, elderly man, with his polite, almost courtly manners and gentle, self-effacing humor.

On deck the warm, humid air was balmy rather than invigorating, yet there was an exotic incense in it that stirred and excited Maggi, standing alone in the dark. It teased up poignant memories of the younger, wildly romantic girl who had shattered both Malay taboos and U.S. government regulations to make love on the beach and swim naked in the moonlight in the same sea over which she now sailed. That had been more than a decade ago, another time and, sadly, perhaps another girl.

Maggi stood on the Lido deck just outside the main lounge and watched the distant lights of Singapore die out like smothered embers. The sky was overcast and the air itself so thick with moisture it seemed to swallow up whatever light there was.

The cruise ship was now navigating through a strait between dark walls of islands. Maggi leaned over the rail. Both ahead and

behind the ship, dark hulks now rose up, blacker masses against the pitch-dark sea and sky that totally blocked out the lights of Singapore, as if drawing a curtain about the ship. The only beacons in that darkness were an occasional red, white, or green flashing light on the buoys that marked the channel.

Was she really running away to sea, as Liz Schneider had quipped? Fleeing the suffocating groves of academe, the pity and tolerance of colleagues, and especially Bryce and his new protégée. Berkeley was not big enough for the three of them, especially since they all had a taste for the *rijstaffel* at the same Indonesian hole in the wall.

Perhaps if she had really loved Bryce, she would have been devastated by his affair or scratched the freckled Eurasian bitch's eyes out, but in truth she had felt almost relieved by the discovery. It had been her excuse finally to leave Bryce and take a leave of absence from Berkeley. The opportunity to organize the cruise for the National Oceanographic Society and be a guest lecturer had been a godsend.

A sudden movement near the stern startled Maggi out of her reverie. A Russian sailor in a white uniform materialized like a ghost out of the shadows. He moved quickly to the rail, as if alarmed, and leaned out.

He hung that way for several moments, frozen, intently peering down into the inky sea, then suddenly bolted upright. He swatted at his neck, as if he had been stung by a ferocious hornet, staggered back, then keeled over, his body convulsing on the deck.

Maggi dashed toward him. Her first thought was that the sailor was having an epileptic seizure. She vaguely remembered first aid instructions about pillowing an epileptic's head so that he wouldn't bash his brains out, and prying his teeth apart to keep him from biting off his tongue. She folded the light sweater she had carried on deck into a pillow and bent over the sailor. Something in his throat glinted in the light emanating from a cabin porthole a few feet away. Maggi reached to examine it. Her hand froze, then recoiled back in horror as she recognized the delicate polished bamboo shaft protruding from beneath the man's jaw. It was a blow gun dart.

She stared at it in amazement. The sailor's body jerked, his head twitched, his foot kicked once, and he lay still. Maggi did not dare touch the dart. Its poison had been incredibly potent and fast acting.

Not knowing what else to do, she cushioned the sailor's head with her sweater. His eyes were open in a frozen, glassy stare and his mouth gaped. A wave of nausea swept over Maggi, and her knees buckled with sudden weakness.

There was a muffled bumping noise from the promenade deck directly below. Instinctively Maggi crouched back against the ship's bulkhead, away from the lighted porthole. She had no idea what was going on. But there was a dead sailor with a dart in his throat at her feet, and whoever had killed him was now on the deck just below her.

She dropped down to her hands and knees, and, making one movement at a time, pausing a moment to listen each time her hand or foot slid on the hardwood deck, she crawled along the narrow promenade. She inched past the swimming pool, still lit up for the sailing party and giving out a shimmering, watery light through its glass-walled windbreak. Maggi felt exposed and dropped flat against the deck and squirmed on her belly until she was once again in the shadow cast by the upper-deck bulkhead.

A furtive scrambling noise stopped her. It came from farther back near the stern. She crawled to the rail. Hoping that here in the shadows a few inches of her dark auburn hair would be invisible, she took the chance to peek over the rail.

At first she did not see anything, but then

a movement on the rail below her caught her eye. As Maggi watched, a hook, wrapped in some dark cloth, reached up and looped over the railing. A few moments later a man's head appeared. He looked about anxiously, and then with a movement quick and agile as a panther's he sprang over the rail and onto the deck. His bare feet hardly made a sound as he landed. He immediately unslung a rifle that was strapped to his back and swung it in an arc about the deck, as if he meant to spray with bullets anyone who intruded on him.

He held this pose a moment, then bent over the rail and waved to someone below him. In a beat another hook looped over the rail and a second man leaped onto the deck. From their wiry builds, dark complexions, and the shadowed features Maggi glimpsed, she guessed the two were either Malay or Indonesian. Like the first, the second man unslung a rifle and covered the deck. Then both disappeared into a corridor beneath Maggi as a third and then a fourth man scrambled aboard.

Maggi dropped back from the railing. She bolted down the deck, now abandoning any attempt to hide, slammed through the first door into the starboard verandah, and burst into the lounge. "Pirates!" she cried in alarm.

She looked about frantically. There was no one there. The tables had been wiped clean, dirty glasses collected, ash trays emptied. Even the bartender who had been idly polishing glasses behind the pale teak counter when she had left the room a half hour before was now gone. Maggi was utterly alone.

She whirled about in a momentary panic, expecting to be attacked from any quarter in a second. She had to warn whoever was running the ship. She remembered seeing steps outside leading up to the ship's bridge on the deck above. She collected herself and fearfully retraced her steps. She crept back outside onto the wooden promenade deck, carefully easing the door shut behind her so as not to make a sound.

The ship still glided silently through a corridor of dimly seen dark islands that now seemed more menacing than before. Maggi could scarcely catch her breath. Once again she inched forward along the narrow promenade that ran about the ship three decks above the water. Every hair bristled with fear. It was not the physical presence of the now unseen pirates aboard that terrified her so much as the knowledge that any moment a dart might shoot out of the shadows and stab her with a paralyzing, fatal poison.

The stairs leading to the ship's navigation bridge on the deck above were little more than a ladder. The leather heels of the Ferragamo pumps she had worn to the sailing party rang out on the metal rung like an alarm bell. She stopped, removed her shoes, and climbed rapidly on tiptoe. The raised studs on the rung, meant to prevent slipping on the wet metal, bit painfully into her now bare feet.

The bridge was several levels above the main deck, and Maggi was dangerously exposed. She bit her lip and scaled the torturing steps as swiftly as she could. Broad rectangular windows on three sides gave the bridge a sweeping 270-degree view of the sea. Inside a young Russian watch officer in a white uniform with black and gold shoulder boards stared out to sea, while next to him a sailor in a blue T-shirt stood at the wheel, steering the ship.

Exploding with relief, Maggi flung open the door and rushed in. "Pirates!" she gasped out. "They're climbing aboard. They've got guns. They killed one of your sailors."

The Russian officer whirled about. It was Vladimir Korsakov. He stared at her with an odd, fearful expression, then glanced immediately at something behind Maggi.

Maggi spun about. A pack of pirates

crouched against the rear wall of the bridge, all pointing the muzzles of their assault rifles at her.

One pirate sprang at her. All Maggi saw was the flash of light off the four-foot blade of his *parang*. Maggi was hypnotized by the gleaming sword, swaying toward her like a silver serpent with a malevolent life of its own, independent of the wielder.

A white-clothed figure suddenly moved between her and the blade. "No! You swore no one would be hurt," a Russian-accented voice shouted urgently. The young officer Vladimir faced the swordsman.

"I not hurt lady. Only stop that she run from this place and make alarm." The pirate thrust the long blade of the *parang* between Maggi and the door, creating a razor-edged barrier, to make his point. He spoke in lilting Malay-accented English. He merely glanced at Maggi, then focused his attention on the Russian officer, studying him intently. There was a fierce, palpable tension in his stance, as if in the next moment he might strike Vladimir Korsakov dead.

The pirate suddenly smiled, but the small, tight twist of his lips conveyed neither humor nor mercy. "You are brave man," he said. The cadence of the words did not signal a compliment but rather a problem that had unexpectedly revealed itself. "Gallant." He nodded at Maggi, not really looking at her but merely acknowledging her as the object of the gallantry.

The Russian said nothing but stood braced, as if expecting a blow. Maggi had the sense that the guns were all now pointed at him.

She noted with surprise that the swordsman wore the distinctive white cap of the *haji,* a Malay Muslim who had made the pilgrimage to Mecca. He seemed almost ritually dressed in a spotless white shirt and trousers, except for the butt of a .45-caliber automatic thrust in the gold silk sash about his waist. The three swarthy gunmen now flanking him were dressed like local fishermen in torn, stained T-shirts, shorts, and batik head scarfs.

"A brave man," the *haji* commented to the others in Bahasa. "He puts his body between the sword and the woman."

The others grunted in response.

"Honor should be marked," the *haji* said in English. The sword suddenly flashed up and over Maggi's head — she felt the whip of air on her cheek — and struck Korsakov in the face.

He cried out and staggered back an instant before Maggi herself screamed. The Russian reeled back against the window of the bridge, his hand pressed to his cheek. Blood ran through his fingers, drenching his white jacket. His wide, astonished eyes stared at the Malay.

The *haji* stood with his arm outstretched, holding the hilt of the long sword with his fingertips, sighting along the blade at the Russian. The blow had been so quick and deft that there was no blood on the cutting edge. "*There!* Now you have a mark to show your bravery. People will know you are gallant."

There was terror in Korsakov's eyes. Maggi saw it and was herself afraid. The *haji* had complimented the Russian officer by scarring him for life, but the blow had been so lightning quick, so skillful, yet so contemptuous that there was no doubt that had the whim possessed the pirate, he might have lowered the blade mere inches and cut off Korsakov's head. Even the other pirates appeared intimidated by the action.

The Russian helmsman cowered next to his officer, the sailor's dark eyes flitting from Korsakov's bloody face to the sword, all the while his mouth working convulsively. He looked as if he were about to bolt from the bridge.

"*Mind your helm!*" The pirate barked the order in English at the sailor with such authority the latter immediately whirled about and seized the ship's wheel with both hands, staring through the windshield at the sea ahead. Even Korsakov was startled by the command.

The pirate turned to Maggi and studied her. He was unusually tall for a Malay. "Who are you?" he demanded.

"My name is Maggi Chancellor."

"She's a passenger," Korsakov suddenly interjected.

"Ah," the pirate nodded, as if that were all the description necessary. "You go to your cabin," he ordered. He turned to one of the gunmen. "Ahmed, take the *memsahib* to her cabin," he ordered in Bahasa, using the old colonial term of respect for a European lady. Apparently either the fact that she was still dressed in her pastel silks for the sailing party or Korsakov's gallantry had given her *memsahib* status.

"His wound. He's hurt," Maggi protested.

The pirate leader looked from Maggi to Korsakov, and he studied the bloody face. "The blood will run until the wound is clean. Then the blood will stop." Something in his pronouncement frightened Maggi, as if it embraced much more than the slash on Korsakov's face.

He turned back to Maggi. "You must stay in your cabin until tomorrow afternoon.

40

Everyone must stay in cabins and below deck, or people will be killed." There was no threat or menace in his voice. He seemed to be conveying a timetable that was as preordained as the change of the tide.

The pirate named Ahmed grabbed her arm to lead her from the bridge. Korsakov was too dazed and intimidated to interfere this time. As she moved through the doorway, Maggi heard the pirate leader say to the Russian in a concerned, almost friendly voice, "You must keep wound clean. Infect very fast in tropics. Wound in head very dangerous. Very dangerous. You get fever in brain and die."

When they reached the main deck, Maggi spoke to her escort. "Ahmed — is that your name?"

He looked at her suspiciously. He was a small, gaunt, narrow-shouldered man, shorter than Maggi.

"Do you speak English?" She decided it was best to keep her knowledge of Bahasa a secret until she knew what was going on.

"Yes, I speak English," he answered in a hissing accent, as though offended by the question. The Malays spoke pidgin English to the Chinese and Indians who dominated the trade and business of the area. It was their common lingua franca, but it was often incomprehensible to anyone else.

"Who are you?" she asked.

"We are messengers of God."

"What do you want?"

There was a beat of silence, then he prodded her with the muzzle of his rifle and ordered, "You go to cabin."

In the corridor to her stateroom a pirate in fisherman's rags was standing guard, cradling the wooden grip of his rifle. He leered at Maggi, and when he smiled a gory drool like blood oozed out the corners of his mouth between blackened teeth. "Aaaah, you've got a pretty one there," he said in Bahasa to Ahmed.

"Yaw, but I think Tengku wants her for himself."

"Oooh." The bloody mouth worked itself into an obscenity. "Does he want her to serve him here or in Paradise?" The dribble and the blackened teeth were from the narcotic betel nut the man chewed.

"Everywhere." Both men laughed. "Key!" Ahmed demanded from Maggi.

He carefully unlocked the door, then violently kicked it open and sprang into the room with his gun pointed, as if to blast anyone there. He peered into the darkened space, then flipped on the light switch.

"You sleep alone?" he asked, after he had

swept the empty room.

"Yes."

The dark eyes now examined Maggi in an openly sexual appraisal, and then, quite suddenly, he exited the cabin, slamming the door behind him.

"You stay. Tomorrow afternoon," he ordered through the closed door.

She heard the two men outside exchange a few words she could not make out through the door paneling; then they laughed.

Maggi's knees wobbled, and she gripped the desk chair for support. Her legs trembled, and then her entire body began to shudder, and she could not stop.

3. The Boat People

On the northeast wind came wails and cries in Vietnamese, "*Tiep, tiep,*" the sound elusive and faint, like the plaintive whimpering of small birds. "*Tiep, tiep.*"

Commander Henry Stewart leaned into the gusts across the port bridge wing of the United States guided-missile frigate *Stephen Decatur,* his lanky frame hanging well out over the bulwark, and listened intently. The ship was three hundred miles due north of Singapore in the Gulf of Siam, and Stewart could smell the Mekong and its delta just over the eastern horizon. The fetid ripe scent of the jungle and the cloying stench of the night soil fertilizing the paddies were familiar and poignant. But then he caught an elusive acrid whiff of cordite and the garbage stink of bodies putrefying in the tropical sun, and he knew the smells were not borne on the northeast monsoon but had seeped up from memories that, like the scars along his ribs and belly, were forever seared into his flesh.

The plaintive cries were also a memory teased up by the soft warm winds blowing now across the South China Sea. Stewart had heard and smelled them often at this time of night in less likely places — Al Kuwait Bay, off Athens, San Diego, Norfolk — these ghostly echoes and stenches from his nightmares.

He looked away from the black sea and gazed through the window into the wheel-house of the *Decatur* just behind him. Beside the helmsman the diminutive officer of the deck stood, intently peering through his binoculars at the sea to port. Lieutenant junior grade Tram Nguyen was another of the ironies that seemed to have brought Stewart's life full circle in twenty years, back to the

44

South China Sea.

Again he thought he heard faint cries of distress, unearthly wails on the northeast wind. *"Tiep, tiep."* Stewart stared into the blackness of a cloud-shrouded, starless night and then down into the phosphorescent bow wave that swirled beneath him like a phantom, struggling to separate what was immediate from what was memory.

"Captain, the forward lookout reports he hears cries or voices to port."

"What?"

Nguyen was on the wing beside him. The junior officer repeated what he had just said.

Stewart leaned out over the rail, straining to hear. *"Tiep! Tiep!"*

"That's Vietnamese for 'Help!' sir. 'Save our souls.' "

The stricken sound of the officer of the deck's voice made Stewart turn. In the dim light he could not make out the expression on the young Vietnamese's face, but the tension in his stance, coiled for flight, brought Stewart immediately into the here-and-now.

"I'll take it, Tram." He strode onto the bridge. "This is the captain. I have the deck and the conn. Left full rudder. Engines ahead one-third; indicate three knots."

The helmsman at the ship's control console repeated the orders.

45

"Mr. Nguyen, call away the rescue and assistance detail and commence a searchlight search to port. Let the forward lookout guide you. He's got a lot sharper ears than I have," Stewart advised.

"Aye, aye, sir."

Stewart stared out but saw nothing except the black velvet curtain of a misty midnight sea and sky. The shift of pressures rather than any visual reference told him that the ship was wheeling to port. A moment later he heard the change in the turbines and felt the subtle adjustment in the propeller pitch as the frigate slowed.

"Away the rescue and assistance detail. Rescue survivors port side." Bosun Thomas's Alabama basso profundo boomed out of general announcing speakers throughout the 453-foot warship.

The searchlight on the signal bridge directly behind the wheelhouse snapped on, shooting an incandescent thousand-watt beam of light to port. A few moments later the amidships light also blazed. The beams swept from bow to stern, then back again, crossing and separating in an inky void that reflected back only a black choppy surface.

Stewart paced the bridge, leaning over the bulwark of the port wing to scan the sea, estimating the wind, peering astern at the phosphorescent arc of the wake.

On its third pass the forward light picked up something pale and ghostly about a half mile away. The amidships light swung onto it.

Stewart peered at the bobbing object in the water, then strode inside the bridge. "Mr. Nguyen, take charge of the rescue detail." Stewart towered over the junior officer, but for a moment their eyes met, and he saw the anguish in the young man's. He knew what was out there. "They'll need your help," Stewart added softly.

"Yes, sir." Nguyen bolted from the bridge.

Stewart turned to Ensign Leonard Fine, the junior officer of the deck. "Have communications send an immediate message to ComSeventhFleet that *Decatur* has spotted a sinking native craft, and we're proceeding to rescue survivors."

"Aye, aye, sir. A fishing boat?"

"No, it's not a fishing boat." The entire hull of the boat was below water, but the thatched roof poked above the surface on bamboo poles. In the glaring white light of the spots, that sloping thatched roof had a sharp familiarity. It was another image from Stewart's nightmares.

He gave the orders to back down and maneuvered the ship to a stop far enough away so that the frigate's wake would not swamp whatever fragile buoyancy still kept the craft afloat. Through his glasses he saw a dozen survivors clinging to the sunken boat. A few waved feebly at their rescuers, but even in their exhaustion there was something tentative in the gestures, as if they weren't sure if they were hailing friend or foe. Their cries and wails now clearly floated up over the water.

In the bright searchlights Stewart could make out the submerged hull. From its size and configuration he estimated that there should have been at least twice as many passengers. What the hell had happened to the rest?

Lieutenant Commander Charles Robinson, the *Decatur*'s executive officer, suddenly lurched through the door, his massive, muscular bulk momentarily filling the frame. The red bridge light gleamed off the executive officer's dark face, still moist with the sleep sweat of the tropical night and the dash to the bridge. He looked momentarily chagrined to find Stewart already there, binoculars about his neck.

"What's up, Captain?"

"Boat wreck — "

Before he could brief the XO the bridge telephone talker interrupted. "Captain, the whale boat's in the water. Proceeding to pick up survivors. The officer says they're calling out in Vietnamese."

"Boat people!" Robinson exclaimed.

Stewart nodded. "Trying to run six hundred miles of open ocean in a twenty-seven-foot flat-bottomed riverboat."

The cries had, at the first sighting, hung over the water like the weak, pathetic mewing of kittens, but then the unmuffled roar of the whale boat's diesel drowned out the sound, until the boat was upon the wreck and the coxswain cut the engine. The survivors were now ominously quiet.

They were still alive. Nguyen could see their eyes, glittering like bits of anthracite in the brightness of the searchlights. But the survivors could not see the sailors in the boat. Their blinking, salt-caked eyes could make out only silhouettes and ghosts against the blinding light that had suddenly burst out of the blackness of the night.

"Hey, grab her!"

The huge boatswain's mate Freeman bent down into the water and plucked up a woman, apparently middle-aged but a slight, frail child in the giant's arms. "Easy there, *mama-san*. We got you." He swung her aboard as if she were the weight of a doll and set her down with a surprising gentleness in the boat. "You're safe now — safe with Uncle Sam."

The woman stared up into the fleshy black face, shining in the incandescent light with a sheen of sweat and sea spray. Her eyes widened with astonishment, and her blistered, swollen lips broke open in a strangled croak, *"Hoa Ky."* American.

The cry had a strangely prayerful sound that ripped at Nguyen.

"Hoa Ky!" the woman repeated in a louder cry. American! The word rippled over the water, murmured from survivor to survivor through cracked, oozing lips and shattered jaws. *"Hoa Ky."*

The electricity of it galvanized the survivors. They stirred, then splashed and reached out their arms, now crying out with supplicating hands, begging deliverance. The shrill cries and moans smacked Nguyen with the fullness of their agony and desperation and ripped tears from him.

Without a command from the boat officer the crewmen immediately began tugging and hauling the survivors into the boat.

"Hey, spread them around. Both sides," the coxswain yelled. "On both sides. You'll swamp the boat."

Nguyen was stunned by their appearance.

Their faces were scorched by their exposure, and one woman's nose was shattered, smashed to one side of her face. They moaned and sobbed, too exhausted and shocked to form words through split, puffy lips.

In the unearthly glare of the *Decatur*'s searchlights, Nguyen felt he was reliving a nightmare. The boatswain lifted in the gaunt, ragged bodies and Nguyen hauled at an arm or leg, deliberately splashing himself, so that neither Freeman or the others would notice that he was crying all the while.

There were half a dozen survivors left in the whale boat when Nguyen first realized it. He pulled a half-unconscious girl into the boat and then stared at the others still clinging to the gunwales and poles of the sunken craft.

"Hey, they're all women!" the sailor next to Nguyen suddenly exclaimed. "Where are the men?"

The women had tied themselves to the wreck with rags, sleeves, and tails of their clothing. As the big American sailors tugged them aboard, the soaked cloth simply disintegrated, shredding their blouses, leaving their shoulders and breasts exposed. The women were too near shock to notice, or to care if they did, but a sailor solicitously draped wool blankets about their shoulders.

51

Nguyen bent over one of the older women. "Where are your men? What happened?" he asked in Vietnamese.

She looked up at him with glazed, uncomprehending eyes.

He repeated the question.

The woman blinked, and a light of comprehension gleamed there for an instant until they widened into a wild-eyed insanity that brought forth a shattering scream of pain, as though her heart had been ripped from her.

"Jesus, Lieutenant, what did you say to her?"

"Where the hell are your men?" Nguyen shouted.

A girl tied to one of the bamboo roof posts was either dead or comatose. Freeman and Nguyen pulled her away and lay her limp, half-nude body on the boat bottom. She was about thirteen, the same age as Nguyen's sister, with a sweet, pretty face and little buds of breast. From the way her arms and legs had splayed out, he was certain she was dead.

Freeman shook his head. He covered the girl with a blanket, hesitated, then gently tucked the blanket under the fragile chin, as though by not covering her face he might somehow still coax her back to life.

★ ★ ★

Stewart studied the wreck through his binoculars. All the survivors appeared to be women, except for a few children he had spotted clinging to the bamboo uprights.

"XO, call down to sickbay and double check that they're all standing by. Have cots ready for about a dozen survivors, mostly women. And make sure we have people on deck with towels and blankets," he ordered the executive officer.

"Aye, aye, sir."

Stewart never lowered his binoculars nor took his eyes from the rescue. "Then call down to the mess decks and have them cook up a kettle of rice and lots of hot tea."

"I imagine they'll be ready to eat anything."

"Their stomachs won't take 'anything.' "

The whale boat appeared to have picked up the last of the survivors, just as the overhead speaker crackled. "*Decatur*, this is *Decatur One*. We've picked up all the survivors clinging to the boat. We'll make a quick circle around the wreck to see if we can spot anyone else, then head right in. Some of the women are in pretty bad shape."

Stewart grabbed the radio telephone. "*Decatur One*, this is *Decatur*. Roger. We'll have corpsmen standing by. Out."

"Who's that on the boat?" Robinson asked.

"Nguyen."

"He speaks the language?"

Stewart nodded grimly. "That's how he got out. By boat. He and his family. They were slowly starving to death on jungle snails and coconuts on the beach in Malaysia when the relief agency finally got to them."

"Captain, the helo reports it's manned and standing by for take-off," the telephone talker sang out.

"Tell them to stand by but not to start engines until we know what the hell's out there."

Stewart looked down into his executive officer's troubled face.

Anticipating him, the XO said, "With your permission, Captain, I'll go on deck and take charge of the survivors."

Stewart nodded. "Very well."

It was going to be a long night without sleep, and he plotted his next moves. Ensign Fine, the junior officer of the deck, looked confused and nervous, as if he half expected Stewart to take a bite out of him. He had been aboard only a few weeks, and he had never been alone on the bridge with the captain. "Ensign Fine."

The ensign started. "Yes, sir."

"Get Lieutenant Balletto up here to take

over Nguyen's watch. Nguyen is going to have his hands full down below. Then notify all rescue stations to stay on station. We're going into a search pattern. Do you know how to plot out a search pattern?"

Fine looked stricken. "Yes, sir, I'm pretty sure."

"Get Combat to plot it." Stewart studied the status board that logged the current wind conditions. The monsoons were always from the northeast this time of year. "A standard expanding square pattern along the axis two-six-five, using our present position as the center. The range of the searchlights is about a thousand yards, and we'll use that as the initial leg. We'll get under way as soon as the whale boat's aboard."

"Aye, aye, sir." Fine looked relieved and dove for the phone to get Balletto on deck.

The whale boat pulled up alongside under the forecastle's portable davits. The survivors were much too weak to climb a cargo net or ladder, so, one by one, they were strapped into stretchers and lifted up onto the deck. Finally, when there were only a few left in the whale boat, it was hauled aboard, their fragile weight making little difference.

From the bridge wing Stewart watched the big boatswain Freeman lift a half-naked girl out of the boat and gently lay her down onto the deck, a surprisingly tender gesture for the burly man, as though he were handling a piece of crystal he was afraid might shatter. He looked down at her, and then his head rocked from side to side and twisted up as if in pain. In the glare of the searchlight Stewart saw the anguish and grief in the shining wet face, and a terrible rage.

"Captain." Nguyen reappeared on the bridge. His uniform was stained and sopping wet. "The XO told me to come up and brief you, sir," the young Vietnamese said in a deadened voice, totally without inflection. "The refugees are from Vinh Long on the Mekong River."

All Stewart remembered of Vinh Long was the support ship bristling with 40-mm. guns anchored in midriver and the cacophony of patrolling Seawolf helicopters and patrol boats constantly taking off and arriving. Neither the people nor the city on the Mekong had etched an image that he now could summon up that distinguished it from Ben Tre, Binh Thuy, or My Tho.

"Their engine failed about two or three days out, and they were just drifting when a Thai fishing junk found them. That was yesterday. The Thais gave them food and water and took them in tow. Last night the fishermen got drunk and insisted all the

Vietnamese men go aboard their boat. To drink, talk, they said. The men didn't want to go, but the Thais had guns and knives and forced them. They were robbed. The Thais took everything they had, except for the clothes they were wearing. Then there was screaming, gunshots. The Thais threw all the Vietnamese men overboard. If they tried to crawl back onto either boat, the fishermen stabbed or shot them.

"Then they dragged all the women aboard the fishing boat and raped them. All the women were raped except one old lady with gray hair and the children. A thirteen-year-old was raped several times." Nguyen's voice was a monotone, completely devoid of expression.

Stewart felt the rage building within himself, a fire that started in his chest and spread to his limbs, causing his legs to tremble.

"This morning the fishermen forced the women back into their boat, all except three of the younger women, whom they kept aboard the fishing junk. Then they chopped holes in the boat, scuttled it, cut it loose, and left it to sink with the women clinging to it."

"That was this morning?"

"Yes, sir."

Stewart sprang to his chart table, then cursed the navigational chart on which the ship's course was plotted. By now the Thai pirates could be anywhere along one hundred miles of coastal villages or ten thousand square miles of the Gulf of Siam or the South China Sea.

He turned back to Nguyen. "How are the women?"

"The men killed were all their husbands, sons, and fathers. Some were beaten badly. They tried to fight. One looks like she has a broken jaw, another has a broken nose. Two were cut with knives. The thirteen-year-old is dead. The women tied everyone to the boat when it didn't sink all the way. It was a wooden hull."

Outside the bridge the fore and aft searchlights swept together, blazing in an incandescent white cross over the black sea, then moved apart in their sweeping arcs. Stewart couldn't stop the tremor in his legs. He rubbed his eyes and forced himself to concentrate, calculating back in time. It had been over twenty-four hours since the refugee men had been butchered or thrown overboard without life jackets. Those who might still have been alive had by now drowned, bled to death, or been devoured by sharks.

Stewart studied Nguyen. He looked as if he had aged ten years since leaving the bridge. When the Vietnamese junior officer had first reported aboard, Stewart had assumed from his education and mandarin bearing that his had been one of the families that had jetted out of Saigon before the fall, their suitcases stuffed with bullion and designer clothes. The story of his escape had only come out, and then reluctantly, during their long passage to the Persian Gulf. "Are you going to be all right?" The captain unconsciously put a trembling hand on the young officer's shoulder.

Nguyen seemed to regard neither the gesture nor the question unusual. "I'd like to stay with the women if I can. They need a translator."

Stewart nodded. "Do everything you can." Then in a softer voice he added, "Whatever you have to do."

The small, almost delicate figure of Nguyen quickly moved through the hatch, leaving behind a large puddle where he had stood in his drenched khakis. Stewart stared at it. In the red night light of the bridge, the puddle gleamed like a pool of blood.

"Should we continue the search pattern, Captain?" Lieutenant Balletto inquired.

Stewart slowly looked up, then silently nodded. There was no hope of finding any of the refugee men, but he would find the Thai pirates. "Launch the helo," he commanded.

Part II
The Darkening Dawn

4. Yee Baiyu Investigates

By a formidable act of will Yee Baiyu, a frail man with a delicate stomach, forced himself to study the head — the sallow, bloodless cheeks, the prominent aquiline nose, and especially the murky brown eyes that were forever fixed on a horror only they saw. Yee bit down hard to keep from gagging, as his stomach heaved and threatened to erupt up through his throat.

"You don't have to look at the bloody thing, you know," Ballinger scolded him.

Yee swallowed hard. "I may learn something by examining it."

"I can damn well tell you what you want to know without your throwing up all over my autopsy room."

Yee felt the hot rush of blood to his cheeks in shame.

"That's not the reason you want to *examine* the bloody head."

Yee turned to the tall, gaunt pathologist hovering over him. "What is the reason?"

"*Bushido*. The Samurai used to force their sons to attend public executions, especially decapitations, and then at night the boy would have to go to the execution ground alone and leave a personal mark on the mounted head. It was to test the lad's courage," the Englishman said in a querulous voice. "The Japs used to do similar nonsense at Changi, and you're doing the same damn bloody thing."

The old man had been a British army doctor imprisoned at Changi during the Second World War. "I'm sorry if my investigations offended you," Yee said. "I thought it was part of my job."

The old man grunted and nodded. "No apology necessary, old boy. What do you want to know?"

Yee knew the question seemed foolish, but he had to ask. "What killed him?"

"Chopping his head off would do it, of course. There are no other indications of bruises, wounds, or violence on the head or face."

"What if he were shot or stabbed in the heart, and then the head — " Yee groped for a word " — taken?"

"Of course, we can't very well tell without the rest of the fellow, can we? That sort of trauma would affect the brain the same as if his head were lopped off when the bugger was alive." Ballinger spoke around the cigarette that habitually dangled from the corner of his mouth, as if it were as natural a feature as the old Englishman's guardsman's mustache, a thick gray bristle that was stained almost yellow from constantly filtering cigarette smoke.

"Have you run any toxicological tests?"

"They're under way now." Ballinger nodded toward a stainless steel centrifuge the size of a television set in the corner of the laboratory that emitted a quiet electric whir. "Are we looking for anything in particular?" Again the querulous note crept into the old man's voice.

"I don't know. I rely on your expertise in these matters. Alcohol, drugs, poisons. *Anything* that tells us something. Can you estimate how long he has been dead?"

"From the lividity — that purplish discoloration there in the left cheek — the rigidity of the jaw muscles, the general state of decomposition, I would make an educated guess of more than six, less than twenty-four hours. I could extract some vitreous fluid from the eye and check its potassium level. It goes up after death at a known rate, and I could narrow the range somewhat closer for you."

Yee nodded, fearful that the medical examiner might extract the fluid then and there, and his stomach surged again.

"Without the rest of the body to test for

core temperature or the stomach contents to see when his last meal was eaten and what it was, we must use our head, what?"

Ballinger took a puff on his cigarette and squinted at Yee through the smoke. There was a mischievous gleam in his eyes. "However, he was killed first and then the head lopped off by a man who handled a sword like a samurai," the pathologist said off-handedly.

"How do you know that?"

"The neck tissues are exsanguinated, not at all as bloody as they would be if the fellow had been decapitated when he was alive and in the pink, so to speak, and the carotids pumping quarts of blood to the brain. A live and functioning head is, quite literally, very bloody. That's why any head wound, however superficial, bleeds like hell. But the stump is relatively clean. Most of the blood in the brain had already flowed back into the heart chamber, pooled elsewhere, and started congealing by the time the head was lopped off. Here, have a look."

Ballinger suddenly grabbed the head by the ears and tilted it back to expose the bloody pulp of the stump with its severed white tendons and blue ganglia.

Yee's stomach exploded.

"In the parts can, damn it." Ballinger

66

shoved a plastic garbage can at him.

Yee still had the presence of mind to grab at the can and thrust his head all the way into it before vomiting.

When he stopped retching, he deliberately kept his head low, partly in shame and partly to allow his head to clear and the dizziness to pass. Yee glanced up at Ballinger, who was regarding him with amused tolerance, then down into the plastic bag that lined the can. His tear-blurred vision focused on the obscene mess at the bottom of the bag, and he suddenly realized with horror what "parts" meant in an autopsy lab. His stomach exploded again.

"Here, use the sink in the corner to wash up," Ballinger said, not unkindly, when Yee had finally finished retching. "I suppose you had better get used to this sort of thing."

Yee washed his hands, then splashed cold water on his face and rinsed his mouth.

Ballinger handed him a fresh towel. "Let's go to my office. I think we've had enough *bushido* trials for the day."

The old Englishman limped badly, lurching down the corridor on a left leg that was either crippled or artificial. In the gleaming white plaster and stainless steel modernity of the new forensic science institute, the medical examiner's office was something of a museum with its battered oak desk, swivel chair, and scarred cabinets dating back to the prewar colonial period. The old Englishman slumped into the chair and lit a fresh cigarette from the glowing butt of his last. He caught Yee watching him. "Yes, of course, the damn things will kill me. But the smell of strong tobacco is preferable to the stench of putrefying flesh. In this climate, aside from the occasional well-refrigerated tourist, most of the chaps are pretty ripe by the time I get them to cut up."

Yee did not want to offend the medical examiner by implying disapproval of his addiction. "Stout English incense," he remarked.

Ballinger laughed, but the old man's laugh sounded like a hacking cough.

"You said something about how the head had been . . ." Yee hesitated, not wanting to use the expression "lopped off," of which Ballinger seemed so perversely fond, ". . . removed."

"Yes, a remarkably clean cut. No jagged edges, tears, crushed vertebrae. A razor-sharp sword, I would imagine."

"A very powerful man did it, then."

"Not necessarily. It's in the speed, you see. There used to be a Jap major at Changi, something of a *kendo* master. They never let the enlisted men or even junior officers do that sort of thing, you see. The lower ranks were only allowed to execute people by using them for bayonet practice or with a bullet to the back of the head." Ballinger's voice and gaze trailed off, but his was not the silence and withdrawn look of a victim reliving horror, rather that of an old man recalling a curious bit of history in which he had once had a part.

"Of course, we can't entirely fault the Japs, can we?" he suddenly continued. "Taking heads is an indigenous custom in this area, isn't it? Our white rajahs supposedly put an end to it in the nineteenth century, but our behind-the-lines chaps revived the practice in the war, paying the natives bounties for Japanese heads."

"It was more recent than that," Yee said.

Ballinger looked sharply at the younger man. "The emergency up north, you mean?"

"Is that when you developed your . . . expertise?"

"I was sometimes called upon to make positive identifications, yes."

"Of Chinese."

"They were the communists, weren't they?"

"Not all of them."

"Well, it was difficult in an attack for our

Dayaks to tell one Chinaman from another."

The Dayak headhunters of East Malaysia had been brought in as commandos by the British army and paid bounties for the heads of known communist leaders. British mercenaries quickly joined the Dayaks in bounty hunting. A cousin of Yee's mother had been one of the victims of mistaken identity, the inability to tell one Chinaman from another.

"But this head is Russian, isn't it?" Ballinger said rather quickly.

Yee nodded and was silent, suppressing his outrage. The pathologist, he knew, was basically a kind man. He was not responsible for the atrocities of a history he himself had barely survived. The Englishman now considered Singapore his home, and after independence in 1965 the doctor had chosen to become a Singaporean, a citizen of the newly declared island-nation of Singapore.

"What do you make of it?" Yee asked. "I mean, as a crime."

Ballinger nodded and pursed his lips, pleased to be asked for his opinion outside the realm of forensic pathology. "It's an act of political terrorism, of course."

"Why do you say that?" he asked.

"That's why *you're* here at this ungodly hour, and not a police detective, isn't it? The head of a Russian naval officer, his

70

gold-braided cap neatly on his head, his sea book and identification assiduously placed in a plastic baggie to protect it from the blood and rain, is deliberately dropped at Raffles, that edifice of old colonialism. Someone is telling us something — something rather outrageous I should think. But I just don't know what it is. Have you received any other communications."

"None."

"What do the Russians say?"

"We haven't notified them yet. I'm on my way to their embassy now." Yee stood to leave. "I wanted to have as much information as possible."

"I'm afraid I haven't been able to tell you very much." Ballinger extended his hand.

"You've told me a great deal. We just don't know what it means yet."

Yee was almost out the door when he turned back. "What did you mean before, in the autopsy room, when you said I had better get used to 'this sort of thing'?"

"There'll be more, you see," Ballinger said offhandedly.

"Why do you say that?"

The old Englishman shrugged, and his face held no expression other than resignation.

5. The Pirates of the Singapore Strait

Maggi fearfully paced the six feet of powder blue carpet between her bed and the door to her cabin, then suddenly stopped and stared at the white phone on the night table by the head of the bed. Who could she call? Who was there to warn, and what could they possibly do?

Alan Schneider.

She quickly found his number in her notebook and tremulously lifted the receiver, terrified that the bloody-mouthed betel nut addict outside her door might hear the noise and bang in to investigate.

The phone sounded ominously quiet. It was the first time she had used the shipboard phone, and she did not know whether it had a dial tone or not. She softly pushed the number of the Schneiders' stateroom. There was no electronic chirp when she dialed, no ring on the other end. The phone was dead. The pirates had already disconnected the room phones.

Who the hell were they? What did they want?

Maggi fought to suppress the panic and

terror that was now building within her like a fever. She willed herself to think. Hers was the last of four inside cabins on that deck. She might try to communicate with the stateroom next to hers by rapping on the wall. But that was Mr. Benjamin's room, and the fragile old gentleman was not someone on whom she could rely at the moment. His illness might be more serious than he made out. Maggi was totally isolated.

She threw herself on the bed in despair, then immediately sprang up again and tiptoed to the door and listened. There was no sound outside. She turned the knob very slowly. The latch made a soft metallic click as it drew back. In the absolute stillness it sounded like the clang of an alarm bell in her ears.

She held her breath, listened again, and, hearing nothing, slowly cracked the door and peeked out.

Inches away the swarthy face of the guard leered back at her. The blood of betel nut juice dribbled from his mouth. He pointed the muzzle of his AK-47 at her head and laughed. "Bang, bang."

Maggi slammed the door and threw the inside bolt.

It was several minutes before she stopped shaking, still longer before the terror faded and she began to think rationally again. Damn it, she was supposed to be the academic expert on board. It was the irony of the situation that appalled her. *Pirates!* Maggi had actually prepared a lecture on the sea brigands of the straits; she thought it would titillate the passengers to learn that in the 1990s they were cruising through a time warp of pirate-infested waters.

Maritime muggers regularly waylaid the cargo ships and tankers passing through Singapore, slipping aboard in the middle of the night to loot the ships' safes and rob the unarmed crews. There had been hundreds of such incidents in recent years, but the pirates had never attacked a passenger liner before.

Historically the area had always been a profitable hunting ground for pirates, who originally preyed on the wealthy traders sailing between China and India. The fifth-century Chinese writer Fa Hsien had a run-in with them while traveling from Ceylon to Java.

Fleets from the Philippines — each made up of hundreds of great sixty-man war canoes, propelled by banks of oars and armed with cannons — had regularly ravaged the South China Sea like locusts. An eighteenth-century Malay chronicler, Abdullah the Teacher, wrote: "No mortal dared to pass through the Straits of Singapore. Jins and Satans even were afraid, for that was the place the pirates made use of, to sleep at and divide their booty."

The Bugis buccaneers from the Celebes Islands, prowling in black-sailed schooners, also made Singapore their base. When the British East India Company's Stamford Raffles landed in 1819, he found the banks of the Singapore River strewn with hundreds of skulls.

The pirates were suppressed by the cannons of the English frigates, but not rooted out. Like an ancient plague they had festered in the backwaters and mangrove swamps, while the Royal Navy, the Gurkhas, the Queen's Own Highlanders, and Crown Colony police patrolled the coast.

In the 1960s the British, their empire bankrupt, had gone, and the scourge had once again broken out, the brigands grown more daring and savage. In the Peace Corps Maggi had heard horror stories of coastal villages looted and slaughtered, of victims, their hands tied behind their backs, executed at close range with shotguns and submachine guns, small children along with their parents. At sea the pirates had at first attacked the small trading craft, the *kumpits* and *padangkangs* that carried copra and produce from Indo-

75

nesia to Malaysia and took back cigarettes and manufactured goods in exchange. In the 1980s the heavy traffic of giant container ships and modern supertankers threading the narrows of the Singapore Strait and the Malacca Strait between Sumatra and Malaysia became easy prey.

Maggi did not now consciously review her meticulously researched lecture notes — the two-thousand-year-old history of South Seas marauding that she had read as romance in the dusty book stacks of the university library, the escalating current statistics. These facts and figures absorbed in bookworming afternoons at Berkeley had now materialized as the blood-drooling bandit just outside her door.

In the space of minutes she had seen one man killed horribly with a poison dart and another disfigured for life on a whim. How many others on board had since been murdered, mutilated, or raped by the pirates?

Suddenly Maggi felt alone and very frightened. When she had first checked aboard, she had been delighted that she was bunking alone; she would not have to share her cramped, windowless inboard cabin with a stranger. Now she would have been grateful for the companionship of another woman, someone with whom to talk and share her fear. What had been luxurious privacy a half hour earlier now was a terrifying solitary confinement.

She listened very carefully, her ears straining to pick up the slightest telltale noise, but she heard nothing, not even the movement of the guard outside. The cruise ship's staterooms were curtained, carpeted, and wood paneled to give them the quiet privacy of a luxury yacht. The ship was still running. Maggi could feel the steady vibration of the engine and movement of the hull plowing through the sea.

She pictured the pirates now going through the ship, plundering the passengers cabin by cabin. She had already faced their open leers, overheard their coarse jokes about using her sexually. The specter of a vicious rape now terrified her.

For the first time in years Maggi *needed* Bryce. Her ex-husband's overbearing presence had become insufferable, but now it would be a shelter under which she could hide. She felt absolutely vulnerable, helpless.

She wondered what Bryce would do if he were here. He would pace, bluster, alternately rage and rant until Maggi might wish one of the pirates would shoot him. That is what he had done in Surabaya during their summer study two years before, when a bureaucratic

77

foul-up had brought down on them a squad of scraggly Indonesian troops and a greedy lieutenant who had held them up until he had been suitably bribed. Bryce's blustering had almost turned a routine *baksheesh* into a bloody brawl. In the end, to save face the Indonesian had demanded, and gotten, triple the rupees for which he originally would have agreeably eased their way. No, even as alone and badly frightened as she was, she might survive better without Bryce.

But working with him had instilled in her an academic discipline. She began to take detailed notes of everything that had happened. It was more than the first rule of the ambitious researcher. In the Peace Corps it had been her way of coping with the fear and loneliness of the strange Malay village into which she had been dropped. Those journals of cramped scribbling by oil lamp in a thatched hut in Kampong Kuala Besut had eventually become her graduate thesis.

She opened the closet, retrieved her canvas and leather Gurkha bag, and took out her notebook. Now she recorded all her observations and impressions over the past hour, as quickly as she could recall the images and snatches of conversation. She noted the military tactics of the pirates, the almost ceremonial dress and sword of the leader, his white *haji* cap. No sooner had she jotted them down, forced her mind to focus on the details, than they took on an even darker, more ominous look. These were not the common seagoing gangsters of the Singapore Strait. They were cutthroats, certainly; but something more ambitious, possibly more dangerous, than amphibious armed robbery was taking place.

A shout and a burst of gunfire exploded outside Maggi's cabin. She sprang to her feet, the notebook sprawling onto the floor, then froze. The shots reverberated through the passageways and decks of the ship.

"No body leave cabin," a voice shouted just outside her door in barely comprehensible pidgin. "No body leave cabin." There was another explosion of gunfire just outside her door. The sound was deafening. In the reverberation she heard a terrified cry, then a door slammed.

Maggi was petrified. Her first thought was that the pirates were running amok, massacring passengers. At any moment the maniac in the corridor might burst through her door. The bolt from which she had drawn comfort only minutes before now looked ridiculously flimsy. A vicious kick would rip it from its mountings, shattering the door. A burst of gunfire would disintegrate it.

She looked about desperately for a place to hide. The space beneath the bed was just high enough for her to squeeze under. If she crawled in the pirates might not find her right away and might forget that she was there. She dropped to her hands and knees.

"This is Captain Khromykh, the master of the *Black Sea*." A speaker in the stateroom suddenly boomed on, startling Maggi almost as badly as had the gunfire. "We have emergency situation. All passengers must stay in rooms for safety first," the voice continued in a heavy, rumbling Russian accent that was deepened by the speaker's bass. "I repeat. All passengers must stay in rooms for safety first." The speaker clicked off abruptly.

Maggi remained on her hands and knees on the floor, her head cocked expectantly toward the speaker, waiting for more information. The announcement abated her panic. For the moment, some sort of order still appeared to be in place. She suddenly felt embarrassed, cowering on the floor, half under the bed. But what had the gunfire been about?

She crawled across the carpet to the door and warily pressed her ear to it. She could hear no sound outside. "This is Captain Khromykh." Again the sudden, disembodied voice booming into the room startled Maggi, as though the Almighty had caught her in a transgression. "Armed men are boarding ship. Leader says no one hurt if we cooperate. Gunfire was warning shots. No one hurt. Please passengers stay in cabins until we say you leave." Again there was a click and then an ominous silence.

No one was hurt, the captain said. Maggi had seen a sailor murdered, another's face slashed to the bone. She crawled onto her bed and hugged the pillow to her, her knees drawn up in a fetal position, pressing her back against the wall in the far corner of the room away from the door. The scribbled pages of her notebook lay on the floor, and a disturbing bit of academic trivia, teased up by terror from a dark, forgotten note, flashed through her mind: The word *amok* was originally a Malay term, describing a psychic disturbance, acute depression followed by an overwhelming desire to murder.

Maggi stared at the door, waiting.

6. A Mother's Pleading

At first light the guided-missile frigate *Stephen Decatur* launched its two helicopters. Stewart squinted into the glare of the sun breaking over the eastern horizon, now matted with puffs of purple clouds, as the first Seahawk, its twin turbojet engines shrieking, lifted off the pad on the fantail and swept off in a steep bank to the north. The other chopper, its rotor blades folded back, was towed by cable out of the port hangar.

This far from land it was chancy to operate both of the aircraft at the same time in the event one went down or fouled the deck so that the other could not get aboard. But even with both airborne and searching, Stewart had no realistic hope of finding any survivors. Still, they might find the pirates. Before the women had collapsed, Nguyen had coaxed a description of the Thai fishing junk from several of them. Painted red, with a high stern and uncluttered bow with no fish hanging out to dry and no nets in the water, as it lay waiting for another easy catch of refugees, it would be distinctive enough to spot.

As soon as the helos were airborne, Stewart

set Condition Three as a preliminary to bringing the ship to General Quarters for battle. If the Seahawks found the junk, Stewart was determined to board and capture it and bring the pirates back to Thailand to be hanged. During the predawn hours he had pored over the regulations concerning piracy on the high seas. Then he ordered the ship's .50-caliber machine guns, which had been stored away in the armory since their departure from the Persian Gulf, broken out and mounted on stanchions on the frigate's forecastle.

"We've got to hit them before they get within the Thai or Malaysian twelve-mile limit. Knock out their steering and power with the 76-mm., have the chopper sit on them, and keep their heads down with the 50s until we're aboard."

"Captain, they still have those three women aboard," Robinson said. It was an objection, and he twisted his blue and gold Annapolis ring nervously with his thumb.

Stewart regarded the executive officer with flat, expressionless eyes. "And do you think these butchers will hesitate one second to cut those women's throats and throw them overboard once they know we intend to board them? We've got to keep them busy worrying about the junk sinking or burning down around them."

"We don't have the authority to engage them," Robinson persisted.

"I have the authority to blow them to hell!" Stewart shot back in a charged, angry voice. He studied his executive officer — the dark, troubled face and thick neck, the chunky, powerful body. Because Robinson was so obviously the ex-jock, it was easy to forget he was an Annapolis grad and an officer on the fast inside track to promotion whose first commandment was Protect Thine Ass. Stewart had graduated from a different school.

"I am the authority," Stewart pronounced. "Under navy regulations and international law. This is piracy *jure gentium.* A crime against mankind. We have an obligation under international law to apprehend them."

He turned away from Robinson. The rage Stewart had felt earlier was still a searing flame in his belly. He had not slept in thirty hours, but he felt neither fatigue nor any desire for sleep. The rage stoked him like adrenalin. He had drunk too much coffee. He had the wardroom attendant bring him a cheese sandwich and a glass of milk for breakfast to soothe the acids burning his stomach.

The sun came up brilliantly, and the frigate

knifed through the calm blue tropical water at twenty knots, a sparkling spray flying from the bow wave.

The first helicopter returned to the ship after four hours. It had made an area search to the northeast along the coast of Thailand over 150 miles from the *Decatur* but found no sign of the pirates. It refueled and took off again to expand the search pattern to the east, deeper into the Gulf of Siam, before the *Decatur*'s second Sikorsky Seahawk returned from its hunt to the south.

"Captain, Doc Blowitz." The junior officer of the deck handed Stewart the telephone.

"Cap'n, a couple of these women just aren't going to make it if we don't get them to a hospital soon," the voice on the other end immediately announced. "Doc" Blowitz was the chief hospital corpsman, the senior of the two enlisted corpsmen aboard who were the entire medical staff for the 203-man crew. "The kids, the lady with the broken jaw, the one with broken ribs, the old *mama-san*. They're in shock. We've got them on intravenous feedings, and we're doing all we can. But they need a real hospital with real doctors, ASAP."

Stewart realized with a pang of conscience that he had not checked on the rescued refugees since they had been winched aboard on stretchers. "What do you need?" he asked.

"We need nurses," Blowitz stated. "I mean it, sir. These women have been raped, brutalized in ways we don't even know. We've cleaned some of their wounds, kept them hydrated, put some on sedation to rest, but we have to be very careful on that or they might go into shock. But they won't let us near them to treat them — even if Dennis and I really knew what we were supposed to do in the case of rape. We're just reading it from the book. We really don't have that kind of experience."

"What about Lieutenant Nguyen?"

"He's terrific, sir. He keeps talking to them, and a couple of them seem to trust him, but they're still not going to let him touch them." Blowitz was silent a beat, then said, "Oh, damn it, Cap'n, you ought to see that thirteen-year-old." His voice broke.

Blowitz had been a medic with the marines in Vietnam, and he had years of specialized training to handle the emergencies that might erupt on a ship at sea a thousand miles away from the nearest doctor. He didn't shake up easily.

"Any other problems, Doc?"

"Just that little girl, sir."

"What little girl?"

"The thirteen-year-old."

"What about her?"

"Her mother doesn't want her buried at sea. She's crying and pleading."

"Christ, we can't keep her body aboard."

"Cap'n, please talk to her. Mr. Nguyen will translate for you." Stewart did not want to see her. He had seen enough ravaged, bleeding, and broken Vietnamese for a lifetime. But as commanding officer he should personally check on the survivors. He noticed that Robinson was watching him closely.

"I'm coming down there, Chief."

The sickbay was three decks below the bridge. It held only two beds, so the crew compartment just forward of it had been cleared out for the Vietnamese women, with the displaced sailors doubling up elsewhere.

The women were all lying in the bunks with blankets over them, either in drugged sleep or staring out of blank, empty eyes. Blowitz was fixing an intravenous feed on one, and Nguyen sat by another, holding her hand and talking softly in Vietnamese. As soon as the junior officer saw Stewart, he stood and came to attention.

Stewart waved him at ease.

The woman by Nguyen stared at Stewart, then crawled out of her bunk and hobbled toward him, moving with evident pain, on the verge of collapse, as if she were drawing from a well of strength that had already been drawn bone dry. She clasped her hands in supplication, begging Stewart for something, crying in Vietnamese, her entreaties feverish.

"What does she want?" he asked Nguyen, unhinged by the woman's anguish.

The woman suddenly quieted and looked from one officer to the other with wide, desperate eyes that had been blackened and bruised by a blow. She might have been in her early thirties, but the tragedy and grief now indelibly cast in her face made her seem aged.

"She wants to take her daughter's body with her, sir. Bury her ashore, so that she'll be near her. She was beaten trying to protect her daughter, and raped. Her husband was one of the men killed. The body is all she has, Captain. It's very important to her." This time Nguyen's voice had an animation in it, an emotionally charged pleading that it had not had when he had first briefed Stewart on the bridge hours before.

Stewart stared at the young officer. Like Stewart, he had not slept, nor had either of the corpsmen who now flanked him. "What did the girl die from?" he asked Blowitz.

The chief corpsman shook his head. "Shock, exposure, possibly internal injuries and bleeding. I can't really tell." He too looked up at Stewart with a certain supplication. "We can keep the body all right, Cap'n, until . . . No problem. She's just a little thing." With that his voice quavered again, tears flooded his eyes, and, embarrassed, he turned his face away from Stewart.

When he turned back after a moment, Stewart was staring into the flat, expressionless eyes of a man who could kill. "Are we gonna get these scum bags, Cap'n?"

"Do you want to keep searching for them or get to a hospital?"

Blowitz shook his head. "We've got to get these women to a hospital, sir."

The chief hadn't hesitated. He had his priorities straighter than his commanding officer did, Stewart thought. "Okay," Stewart nodded. He gazed about the compartment once more. "Let me know if you need anything else."

He left the sickbay and headed for the bridge to call off the search for the pirates and plot a new course.

7. Spycraft and Pirate Tactics

Yee Baiyu sat in a small office in the embassy on Nassim Road intently studying the man opposite him behind the desk. Yuri Yevshenko undoubtedly had Mongolian blood in his ancestry. It was there in his sleek, straight black hair, the narrow slant of his dark eyes, more Asiatic than European, as Lenin's had been, and the prominence of his cheekbones. He was a handsome man, and on the streets of Singapore one would assume he was a native Eurasian rather than a Russian.

"We were, of course, notified when he missed the ship's sailing," Yevshenko said. His English was almost without an accent.

"But you didn't notify our police?"

Yevshenko shrugged, and his smile was charming, a worldly amusement playing on his lips. "A sailor," he said. "They get a little drunk, find a beautiful Chinese girl, and they miss their ship's sailing. It happens occasionally — not very often, but it happens. The next day they show up at the embassy with incredible stories."

"Unless they've defected."

"Never in Singapore," Yevshenko said,

shaking his head. "A few times it has happened in New York, New Orleans, Southampton, but not here. It is too . . . *exotic.*"

"The man was an officer?"

"Yes."

"What was his position aboard the ship?"

"He was the purser." Yevshenko was volunteering nothing without being asked.

"This is a position of great trust and authority on a ship."

"Yes."

"What are his duties?"

"He is in charge of accounts, finances, the general business of the ship."

"He has more business ashore than the other officers?"

"That is my understanding."

"Do you think robbery was involved?"

"That is a possibility."

Yee waited for Yevshenko to say more, but he didn't. "Was anything missing from the ship?"

"Not that we know of."

"The ship delayed its sailing over an hour."

"Yes. The captain was naturally concerned."

"So you knew the purser was missing last night?"

"Yes. The captain informed us, but, as I said, we assumed it was something . . . trivial."

Yee paused again, waiting for the Russian to add something. "Mr. Yevshenko, the government of Singapore considers the murder of a Russian citizen in our country the gravest possible business," Yee said in his sternest voice. "We expect your full cooperation."

The Russian glanced at the business card Yee had given him. "I assure you, Mr. Yee, we have told you everything we know."

"Are you in contact with the ship?"

"Not since it sailed." Yevshenko frowned. "Perhaps they're having radio difficulties." He gave a small, apologetic smile. "Sometimes our Russian-made electronics are not as reliable as the equipment made here in Singapore."

Yee remained silent. The top floor of the embassy, he knew, was a warren of radio and microwave receivers, tape recorders, teletype machines, and electronic eavesdroppers — the roof a spiky forest of antennas — with which the Russians intercepted satellite communications, monitored half the world's shipping and warships that passed through Singapore, and spied on the banking and business calls and computer transmissions of the Pacific Rim.

"We'll try again to contact the ship with our embassy transmitter." The Russian waved Yee's card. "I'll call you if we speak to them."

Yee could tell instinctively when someone was lying or withholding information, but he could discern none of the telltale tics — the breakout of a bead of sweat, the evasion of the eyes, or the quickening of a pulse in a temple vein — in Yevshenko's expression.

"We would like the body returned as soon as you've completed your investigations," the Russian said.

"We have no body. The man was decapitated. We have only his head." There was a streak of perversity in Yee's nature that gave him a tweak of satisfaction to watch the blood drain from the Russian's face.

Yevshenko watched through the window as Yee walked across the courtyard outside. Yee was a small, slender man, delicate even by Chinese standards. But there had been nothing delicate about his questioning, none of the usual deferential politeness toward diplomats with immunity. Yee seemed to sense as soon as he entered that Yevshenko was not a Foreign Office bureaucrat, the second secretary, as he was titled on the embassy roster.

Yee got into a waiting blue Mercedes, which immediately pulled away. He had a driver. Yevshenko again studied the card. Even the lowest Oriental official always presented his business card with all the ceremony and grave formality of an ambassador presenting his credential to a head of state. In that gesture Yee had been no different, yet his card simply read:

> ### YEE BAIYU
> *Office of the Prime Minister*
> *Republic of Singapore*

They had not sent a policeman, but who the hell was Yee Baiyu? How much did they know?

Yevshenko stood a moment, frozen, absorbing the horror. *It had begun.*

The supervisor of the port operations center was a plump, moon-faced man, and he once again studied the business card Yee had presented him, as if trying to figure what authority Yee might have over him. He shook his head impatiently. "The ship should be halfway to Jakarta by *now*. It's really out of our jurisdiction."

"Are they out of range?" Yee asked.

"No, the UHF band should reach them easily. And a ship like that is equipped with satellite communications."

"Then use the satellite radio," Yee ordered. The inspector looked startled by the sudden tone of command in Yee's voice. Yee glanced at his watch. "It is not too early for one of your superiors to be in the Port of Singapore Authority. I will call him, if necessary."

The moon face made a little deferential bob. "That won't be necessary, Mr. Yee. We're happy to be of service to the Prime Minister's office. We'll try to contact the ship by satellite." He pivoted on his heel and trotted to the radio console.

The port operations center resembled an airport control tower and, in fact, similarly directed the vessels arriving, embarking, tying up, and anchoring out in Singapore harbor, monitoring them on radar. The radio and radar transmitters were located on the historic lighthouses — Raffles, Horsburgh, Bedok, Sultan Shoal — safeguarding the sea lanes into Singapore, but the operations center itself was downtown, more than a kilometer from the marina, perched on the twentieth story of Tanjong Pagar Complex. Yee turned and gazed out the wide observation windows that circled about him from east to west. As far as his eye could see, and beyond, there were a thousand ships.

Yee took great pleasure in the panoramic view, especially at that time of the morning, when the mist, tinged with pink by the rising tropical sun, still hung on the sea,

95

veiling the tankers, oilers, cargo haulers, tramp steamers, lighters, and bumboats, concealing their rust, grease, and flaking paint, transforming them into a dream seascape.

The harbor was Singapore's reason for being, its history, its source of wealth, and its destiny. The island perched at the southern tip of the Malay peninsula, where the great land mass of Asia shattered into the 1,500 islands of Indonesia. Here the five-hundred-mile-long Strait of Malacca debouched into the South China Sea, creating the shortest sea route between India and China. The point on which Yee now stood at the mouth of the Singapore River was sheltered from the northeast monsoons in winter and the southwest monsoons in summer, and the breakwater of islands to the south formed a superb natural harbor.

Even the winds blew to Singapore's unique good fortune. Thirty-one-sail Indiamen from England and lateen-rigged Arab dhows had once ridden the southwest monsoon winds, and in January and February junks from China and Siam and three-masted American clipper ships blew in on the northeast winds. In September and October the winds had driven the Bugis schooners and *prahus* of the East Indies, laden with spices and hardwoods. It had been just a Malay fishing village in 1819, when the British East India Company bought the land from the Maharajah of Johor and built a trading post. Singapura quickly became a thriving entrepôt, the crossroad of East and West, where cargoes were warehoused, traded, and transshipped.

Yee's great-great-grandfather had arrived in 1860, one of the horde of starving refugees from the famines of Fukien indentured to work in the Malay tin mines to the north. The Yee ancestor had been locked in the hold of a junk until his passage was paid off by the labor contractor, and then he had had to work a year to buy his freedom to sweat, or starve, someplace else. Like the other Chinese *sinkeh*, he had never returned to his impoverished homeland.

By 1963, when Malaysia declared *merdeka*, its independence from Britain, the Crown Colony of Singapore was three-fourths Chinese. Two years later the small island-nation of Singapore was handed its own *merdeka* from Malaysia. Only the tremendous wealth of the port allowed the new city-state to survive, and then prosper.

Supertankers from the Middle Eastern oil fields hauled the crude east through the strait to Japan and the west coast of the United States, and giant container vessels transported California produce, Japanese automobiles, and Korean textiles west to the Suez Canal and Europe. As the nations on the Pacific Rim boomed into economic superpowers in the 1980s, Singapore became the most heavily traveled waterway and the richest port in the world.

"Mr. Yee, we can't contact the *Black Sea*." The agitated voice of the port operations center supervisor startled Yee out of his contemplation of the harbor.

"What is it?"

The moon-faced man shook his head and looked deeply disturbed. "I fear the ship has run into trouble."

Yuri Yevshenko left the small, cramped office and hurried through the marble foyer of the Russian embassy to the elevator. Several floors up he stepped off into a windowless anteroom. With a special key he unlocked the gray steel door that in turn opened only to reveal a second door a yard beyond the first. A button concealed in the floor released that door into the Rezidentura, the KGB's inner sanctum within the embassy.

Just to the left of the entrance two female clerks logged the message traffic. On the wall of the secretariat were posted pictures of known Singapore surveillance agents and their auto license numbers; a second board posted the photos and license numbers of identified CIA personnel. Neither Yee nor his car was listed. *Who was the Chinaman?*

Yevshenko had to be careful. The local internal security force had originally been organized and very well trained by the British Secret Service; now independent, spunky little Singapore had developed a wily Oriental tradecraft of its own. Bondarev, Anatoli Larkin, and Mironenko had all been caught with their fingers in the fortune cookie jar and been expelled.

One of the traffic clerks — a beefy blonde — noted Yevshenko lingering by her and smiled up at him anxiously with a bright-eyed, almost feverish coquetry. She was the wife of the residency's Line X officer, a technician who spent little time at home, as he skulked about Singapore, Malaysia, and Thailand stealing industrial and scientific secrets, invariably from Chinese-owned companies that subcontracted electronic and computer components for American and Japanese manufacturers. Yevshenko smiled politely at the neglected wife and strode off down the long corridor.

To his right was a large office space where two dozen case officers translated documents, studied, and wrote reports in cloisters like monks in a monastery workroom. Indeed, an eerie, almost monastic silence pervaded the entire Rezidentura. Double walls, ceilings, and floors encased the entire area; music and electronic signals pulsed through the surrounding space to confound any bugging devices. The few windows that broke the sense of claustrophobia were made of a special soundproof opaque glass. The KGB residencies in Tokyo, San Francisco, Washington, and London were all alike in layout and operations; this bureaucratic cookie cutting supposedly increased security.

Yevshenko's office was the most spacious, with wood paneling, a broad conference table, and a comfortable sofa. He immediately grabbed the phone on his desk and punched a number. "Have you contacted the *Black Sea*?" he barked in Russian.

"No, Colonel. We've tried every possible frequency. They're simply not answering."

"Repeat your calls every fifteen minutes."

"Yes, Colonel."

Yevshenko crossed the office to a black lacquer cabinet set against the inside wall. Inside the cabinet, embedded in the concrete of the wall, was a safe. He spun the combination, yanked open the heavy steel door, and withdrew the plain, white business envelope the ambassador had received that morning.

He hefted the envelope in his hand, as if

trying to estimate its weight. How extraordinary to be in a country where the mail was so secure and dependable that even terrorists use it. He thrust the letter into the inside pocket of his suit jacket, left the room, quickly retracing his steps through the residency, and took the elevator to the eighth floor. There he identified himself into a wall speaker, and the six-inch-thick armor-plated door swung open from the inside.

At that time of day there was both an armed guard and a cipher clerk on duty in the Referentura, manning the secret satellite transmitters and cryptographic machines. Yevshenko stepped in. He would observe the protocol of briefing the ambassador later; he had to notify the Kremlin immediately.

"The *Black Sea* is not responding to any of our radio calls."

"Is it possible the ship's radio is out?" Yee interrogated the port operations supervisor.

He shook his head vehemently. "They have several radios; we've tried all the channels. We must contact the ship's agent. They may have run into difficulty."

"What kind of difficulty?"

The supervisor shrugged wearily, "Two ships were attacked by pirates last night in the strait." He made a sweeping gesture to indicate the channel to the south that ran between Singapore harbor and the chain of Indonesian islands. "We can't be everywhere," he complained. The port supervisor sounded harassed, angry, at the edge of his patience, and pointed down to a marine police boat working its way through the harbor. "At any moment we have two dozen boats on patrol, more at night, but we can never catch them."

"Why not?"

The supervisor looked suspiciously at him. Yee saw the sudden distrust in his eyes and understood it. Singapore's problem with pirates had steadily escalated with its prosperity. The situation had become critical. The controlled press of Singapore seldom reported it, but the Japanese Foreign Ministry, the Hong Kong Shipowners' Association, the American President Lines, and a host of other major shipping companies and governments had demanded that Singapore put an end to the piracy.

The International Maritime Bureau had singled out the Singapore Strait as the danger area. It was the focal point for five hundred shipping lines, linking all other world ports. Six thousand vessels pass through, heading both east and west, each month. But now seamen were afraid to crew aboard Singapore-bound ships. The Port of Singapore Authority was under siege. The supervisor feared for his job.

"I'm not here to investigate pirates," Yee reassured him. "I know you and the marine police are doing everything that can be done." He shook his head with sympathy, one conscientious civil servant to another. "Do you think the *Black Sea* had trouble with pirates?"

The supervisor pointed to the radio operator. "We have a special VHF channel just to report attacks and warn other ships. But we haven't heard anything from them."

"Last night?"

The supervisor shook his head. "By the time we do hear, it's always too late. The raids are so quick the rascals have disappeared before we can get a patrol boat there." He gestured in frustration. "Or they're out of our jurisdiction. Most of the attacks occur in Indonesian or international waters." He pointed angrily across the strait to Pulau Batam, a low-lying Indonesian island of mangrove swamps and jungle larger than Singapore but almost uninhabited.

"The Phillip Channel into the Strait of Malacca. That's the biggest trouble spot. The throat's only 1,400 yards wide, and the pirates are like flies there. But we can't conduct patrols there because it's Indonesian. The

Indonesians say *they* patrol it. But it's six hundred miles from Jakarta. It's not their shop being robbed."

The supervisor was Chinese, and his accent suggested that his ancestors had come from Shanghai, a dialect incomprehensible to Yee, who spoke the Hokkien of his father. It was one of the paradoxes of the Chinese of Singapore, who had come there in successive boatloads from different regions of their sprawling homeland, that the port operations man and Yee had to speak English to each other to communicate.

"The pirates are Indonesian?"

The supervisor shrugged. "They don't show the captains their passports. Indonesian or Malay, what's the difference? They go back and forth in their boats. They fish where there are fish, smuggle goods to where they get the best price, and pirate where there are no police. They stick the captain of a container ship with a *parang* and make him open the ship's safe. They get thirty thousand United States dollars. How can they spend that much in Indonesia? They come here to Singapore. Borders mean nothing to *them*, but *we* can only work on this side of the lines."

"A *parang*?" Yee questioned.

"*Parangs,* bayonets, machetes, always

the long knives."

"They use *parangs?*" The traditional three-foot-long Malay swords. Yee had patiently listened to the supervisor's litany of complaints, but suddenly he was alert. He had not told the man why he wanted to contact the ship or about the severed head that had been dropped at Raffles that morning.

"A few carry guns, but mostly the big knives. The shipowners don't want firearms aboard their vessels, because they are afraid the pirates will then get bigger guns and everyone will start shooting. Then a tanker will blow up. A Russian sailor was stabbed when he tried to fight off four of them, but so far there has been very little violence."

"How do they get aboard?" Yee asked cautiously.

"They always attack ships that are fully loaded and low in the water, so that there is the smallest freeboard between the water line and the deck. They climb aboard in two seconds and head straight for the captain's cabin." The supervisor now seemed eager to impress Yee with his knowledge of the pirates' tactics.

"Don't the crews see them?"

"They always attack in the middle of the night when everyone is asleep. The lookouts never see them until there is a *parang* at their throats. The pirates hide their boats in the mangrove swamps and the islands, or behind buoys. Small, fast speedboats with big outboard motors. The big ships have to slow down to navigate the narrow channels, and then the rascals maneuver directly astern into the ships' radar blind spots."

Yee shook his head in amazement. "What are they after?"

The supervisor shrugged. "They are professional thieves. They want money or anything they can easily sell for cash — jewelry, watches, cameras, radios, expensive clothing. Perhaps this time the rascals carried off the *Black Sea*'s radios. We'll try to contact the ship when they dock in Jakarta" — he glanced at the sheaf of papers in his hand — "tomorrow morning."

Yee stared out at the harbor, but his eyes did not focus on the fleet of merchants anchored there. Instead he thought of the ship now somewhere over the horizon, of pirates who attacked giant computerized cargo vessels, of *parangs* and the head of a Russian merchant marine officer. Each was like a tossed yarrow stick that touched and interconnected with other sticks in a pattern that foretold the future in the *Book of Changes*. But Yee could not read this pattern of sticks, or their prophecy.

8. The River Gorge

The pirate with the black teeth, drooling blood, shoved the muzzle of his assault rifle against Maggi's throat, choking her, forcing her head down into the pillow. A half-dozen pirates crowded about the bed, and Maggi, gasping, breathed in the rank, sweating stench of them. The pirate chieftain took off his white haji *cap with a studied, ceremonial gesture and leaned over her. Maggi saw the flash of light off the sword an instant before she felt the cold blade against the flesh of her leg and then the needle point sliding up along her bare thigh, along her belly. She screamed.*

"This is Captain Khromykh."

Maggi bolted up from the bunk, her eyes wide with terror, glaring wildly about the stateroom.

"For safety first, it is necessary all passengers stay in cabins, please." The heavily accented, all but incomprehensible voice boomed from a hidden speaker in the ceiling. "Stewards bring food to cabin for nourishment. If you have medical problems, please say to steward." The announcement clicked off abruptly.

107

Maggi stood reeling in the middle of the floor, confused, trying to separate the empty stateroom now about her from the terrifying images of filthy, half-naked pirates poking her with bloody knives. It took several moments before she oriented herself, since she had never awakened in this room before. She was still shaking and drenched with sweat from her nightmare. She glanced at her watch. It was a few minutes after nine. It seemed inconceivable to her that she had fallen asleep. Gradually she separated the facts of the previous night from the phantoms of the nightmare. The sailor in his agonized death throes, the pirates scrambling aboard, the white-capped chieftain with his razor-edged sword, the black-toothed, drooling betel nut addict with an assault rifle outside her door — those were a reality. The ragged, savage crowd about to rape and murder her were — she glanced fearfully at the door — for the moment at least, phantoms of a nightmare.

She glanced at her watch again to convince herself that it was really morning, slowly looked about the stateroom, and cursed aloud the lack of a porthole. The sight of daylight, the morning sun over an azure sea, might reassure her that the nightmare was over. But locked in this claustrophobic, windowless room with its Spartan furniture, she felt that at any moment she might suddenly be grabbed by blood-smeared, clawing hands and brutally plunged back down into that nightmare.

But the real terror was apparently still going on. She tiptoed to the door and listened with her ear pressed against it. She did not hear a sound. The captain had warned the passengers to stay in their cabins, and she was not going to open the door, peek out, and come nose to nose with Bloody Marty again.

It was quiet, ominously so. If the pirates were systematically looting the ship cabin by cabin, they should have been done by now. She glanced at her watch once more. They had been aboard over eight hours. What were they up to? Maggi could feel the engine vibration and the motion of the ship under her feet. *Where were they going?* The original schedule had called for them to sail all day and dock in the port of Jakarta on Java the next morning.

She plunged back into her Gurkha bag for her maps, spread them out on the floor, and traced the ship's route with her finger. They should be about a third of the way to Java, she estimated, somewhere in the Lingga archipelago between Sumatra and

Borneo. If they were still en route. If they had changed course, they might be anywhere — either the west or the east coast of Malaysia, Sumatra, the wilds of Borneo, or halfway to Vietnam. Singapore was the busiest port in the world specifically because it was the hub of so many shipping lanes.

There was a sudden knock on the door. Maggi was startled, then very frightened.

The knock was repeated. It was a polite, undemanding knock. "It is the steward, Miss Chancellor. We have some food for you." He had a strong Russian accent. "Are you all right?"

Maggi rushed to the door, ecstatic to hear a friendly voice, unbolted it, and flung it open. A sallow-faced man in a short-sleeved white shirt and a black bow tie stood alongside a room-service cart. Just behind him the pirate, drooling betel juice, held his automatic rifle, its muzzle waving in their direction. This time Maggi had the scholarly presence of mind to note that the rifle was a Russian AK-47.

The steward held out a tray with a roll, cheese, and slices of papaya, watermelon, and banana. "Would you prefer coffee, tea, or milk?"

The absurdity of the question under the circumstances almost made Maggi laugh, but the expression of abject fear on the steward's face stopped her. "Coffee, please."

"Yes, very good." He lowered his eyes to pour the coffee. The cup rattled in its saucer in his trembling hand, and he placed it on the cart to steady it. "Are you all right?" he asked in a whisper.

"Yes, I guess."

The guard watched them with a menacing suspicion, the gun barrel tracing their slightest movement.

"The officer Korsakov, on the bridge. He was hurt. Do you know how he is?"

The steward shook his head and busied himself arranging the cream and sugar packets. The man's fear was contagious. Maggi wondered what might have happened to terrify him so.

"Where are we going?"

"I don't know."

"Too much talking," the guard suddenly barked. He prodded the steward painfully with the muzzle.

The steward was so badly frightened that he yelped and almost threw up the tray. Maggi grabbed it. "Find out medical problem," he pleaded with the guard. "Medical problem."

The guard grunted. "She medical problem?"

The steward was sweating heavily. He

turned slowly to Maggi. "Do you have any medical problems?" He enunciated each word for the benefit of the guard.

"No, I'm all right, thank you." She gave the steward a faint, encouraging smile. "But please check on the man in the next cabin, Mr. Benjamin. He's elderly . . . an old man, and he has just had an operation." She too spoke each word carefully, not just to pacify the guard but so the steward would understand her.

He nodded. "Mr. Benjamin in the next cabin."

Then the door slammed shut, leaving Maggi in her solitary confinement once more. She had not thought of food, but suddenly she was ravenous. She wolfed the bread and cheese and then quickly drank the coffee while it was still hot. She thought of saving the fruit until later, since she didn't know when they might be fed again, but nervously picked at the papaya and banana slices until they too were gone. At a thought she rebolted the door, then sat on the bed to wait.

She realized that she did not know what she was waiting for, and whatever she imagined only increased her fear. On a nervous impulse she again seized her notebook and scribbled, "The most terrifying thing about breakfast, other than the fear of the steward — he was actually quivering at moments — and the guard constantly threatening us with his Russian AK-47 rifle, was its very routineness and efficiency, the inquiries about our health. The pirates, if indeed they are pirates, are not thieves in the night who have come to loot the ship and passengers, then leave. Then who are they and what do they want?"

It was Bryce who had trained her to identify the make, model, and origin of the small arms that the police, local militia, and army carried — to differentiate the sinister-looking black American M16 with its carrying handle from the Russian AK-47 with its solid wooden butt and grip — and to spot the aircraft that flew overhead or were parked on the fields that they bounced in and out of. In the volatile Third World of Southeast Asia, weapons were concrete signs telling which way the political winds were blowing and what the governments' priorities really were.

Bryce had been a lousy husband, domineering, insensitive, condescending, and ultimately unfaithful, but the son of a bitch had been a great teacher, a demanding taskmaster with an enthusiasm for his field that had become, for Maggi, an infectious passion. And he was a world-class scholar, extraordinarily well read, and a tireless, probing

113

researcher. He was a pompous ass, petty, impossible to live with, but he was not a phony. His ego demanded protégées — invariably young, attractive graduate students — and that vice was certainly not unique in academic circles. Maggi had been one of them. But she had not been the last.

The discipline that Bryce had taught her had become a mixed virtue. Had she been less disciplined, less devoted to her work, perhaps she might have endured her marriage for only a few years rather than ten. In her notebook he had once written, "A bivouac in the tropical rain forest is endured until staying there becomes unendurable, the leaving less painful and less destructive than staying." Then after that note she had scribbled, "It is like marriage." A week after that entry she had left Bryce.

Now she was finding out what it meant to be truly, terrifyingly alone.

It was several hours later that Maggi felt the engines suddenly change speed, or rather the hum and vibration that pervaded the air of her stateroom like white noise now made a shift in frequency. Then she thought she felt the ship turn, but confined in the windowless cell of her cabin, she could not be sure. She sat tensed, every muscle and sense straining to register what was happening.

She rose and stood in the middle of the room, listening, expectant. For a long while nothing further happened, and then the engine changes became more definite and frequent, as though the ship were maneuvering rapidly. Suddenly the engines were still, and a palpable shudder came through the floor, ran up Maggi's legs, and shook her, as if she and the vessel were one in their fear of what might happen next. The silence now was disorienting, frightening, as if a constant wind that one no longer heard had abruptly blown itself out.

Maggi remained standing in the middle of the room, waiting nervously, for several minutes. Nothing further happened, and she sat down again, now sensitive to every noise and vibration. The speaker clicked on, a low background hum indicating that someone was about to talk.

"This is Captain Khromykh. All passengers and members of the crew assemble on promenade deck on bow of ship immediately. No one hurt. Please leave stateroom and assemble on bow of promenade deck immediately." He then spoke in Russian, possibly repeating the message, but Maggi did not understand a word. Then the speaker clicked off.

Maggi was frightened. For an instant she thought again of hiding under the bed. Perhaps they were being summoned to their massacre. But that made no sense. In just a few seconds her overriding emotion became curiosity. She wanted to know what was happening, where they were, and what the leader of the pirates had to say.

She unbolted the door, cracked it open, and tentatively peeked out. The bloody-mouthed guard was not in sight. She took a step, stuck her neck out, peered down the corridor, and found herself staring into the frightened face of a middle-aged man two cabins down. He started at seeing Maggi.

"My God, what's happening?"

"I think we're being hijacked." She was surprised by the calmness in her own voice.

"*Hijacked!* My God, by who? The Russians?"

"No, they're prisoners the same as we are."

The man looked at Maggi with suspicion, as if he wondered who she was. Behind him she saw the frightened face of a woman in her fifties, probably his wife. Other cabin doors along the passageway now opened, and the passengers warily stepped out and looked at Maggi and the man. "I think we should go on deck," Maggi volunteered.

"Do you think it's safe? That gunfire and

that terrible little man."

"It's probably as safe as standing here." She didn't want to stay there in that closed corridor discussing the situation, but she waited a moment or two for Mr. Benjamin to emerge from the cabin next to hers. When the tall, white-haired figure did not appear, she knocked on his door. "Mr. Benjamin."

There was no response. She tried the knob, and the door opened. The small cabin was empty. Had the old man moved on deck so quickly?

She climbed up the ladder and onto the open promenade. To her amazement the first thing she saw was a sheer wall of natural rock and earth in front of her. She leaned out over the railing. The steep river bank ran as far as she could see forward and aft. Frightened passengers were now emerging onto the promenade, urged by a Malay armed with an M16 in the rear to move forward to the bow.

As Maggi stepped out from under the overhang of the Lido deck into the open, she spotted other armed Malays on the raised bow and on the bridge above her, but her astonishment at the surroundings overcame her fear of the pirates.

The ship was in a narrow river gorge. Limestone cliffs rose up on either side, climbing higher than the ship's mast about a hundred yards ahead, where the river twisted, creating a stone wall that blocked any further view. Where Maggi stood, the river was about seventy feet wide, giving the ship a tight squeeze of no more than ten feet on either side. Steep, heavily rooted mud banks rose almost to the level of the deck above her, and there the jungle burst up from the mire. Great barked pillars lined the shore, reaching up into a steamy twilight where their thick branches formed a vaulted arch two hundred feet over the river. The lush canopy of feathery mengaris and red belian leaves shut out the sunlight, casting the river and the ship in perpetual shadow. The ship was moored in the midst of a primordial rain forest.

The extraordinary passage of the ship had frightened the birds and monkeys and stilled the cicadas, and the jungle all about was eerily silent, breathless.

From her spot on the bow Maggi could not see downriver in the direction from which the ship had come, but heavy hemp lines, the thickness of her arm, ran out from the bow and were tied about massive tree trunks on both banks, securing the liner. She was shocked to see a platoon of armed men, more than a dozen lined up on each bank. They stood several feet back from the river, each cradling a rifle, shotgun, or automatic weapon, so dark and still in the shadows of the great trees that she had not seen them immediately. Most wore the dirty T-shirts and shorts of workers in Southeast Asia, but a handful wore sarongs and bright head scarfs, and their torsos were bared to reveal intricate tribal tattoos, as if they were dressed for a ceremonial welcome.

"What do you make of all this?" a man whispered at her elbow.

It was Alan Schneider. He had his arm protectively about his wife, Liz, who was pale but not nearly as fearful as the other passengers, who now pressed all about them, cramming tightly up against one another, instinctively seeking protection in the herd. Schneider looked all about, sizing up the situation with eyes that were as probing as they were wary. Maggi was somehow reassured that there was no air of panic about the man. She wondered if the pirates had any idea that they had bagged the former American Secretary of State.

Suddenly a shout went up from the men on the river bank. They raised their guns above their head in a salute, shook them, and cheered.

Maggi spun in the direction of the salute. The Malay in the white *haji* cap stood on the port wing of the bridge, two decks directly above. He waved his sword over his head, acknowledging the cheers.

An unearthly tongue-trilling ululation sprang from a man on the bank and was quickly picked up by the others. The high-pitched wail quavered through the still, thick humid air, a primitive cry that resonated with the jungle and river. It struck a primal chord of terror in Maggi, a terror she felt move like a wave through the other passengers pressed about her, their panic mounting. The moment before it exploded into a mindless, screaming stampede, the *haji* raised both hands above his head, and there was immediate silence.

He stood motionless on the bridge, a commanding figure in white, who appeared to Maggi to grow in stature with each beat of silence. He suddenly waved his sword overhead and shouted, *"Allah akbar!"*

"Allah akbar!" shouted back three dozen voices. They raised their guns overhead, and the cry became a chant, *"Allah akbar! Allah akbar!"* their weapons working up and down, as though pumping out the cry.

Allah akbar. God is great. Maggi understood what was being chanted, but she was as confused as the other passengers who stood uncomprehending and intimidated about her.

The *haji* again held up his hands for silence. He stared down at the cowed passengers and Russian crew members as if noticing them for the first time. The Russians' uniforms identified their jobs aboard — the officers in white four-button suits, crewmen in blue T-shirts and work pants, waitresses in white peasant blouses and red doublets, cabin attendants in blue blazers, cooks in white chef's caps and jackets.

"You are prisoners of war," the *haji* suddenly shouted in heavily accented English. "This is a revolutionary war against the superpowers of the right and the left. We are not against the American or Russian people. We are against the oppression and injustice of your imperialist governments."

He paused and peered down into the crowd, as if searching to see if he were being understood. "You will not be harmed, but you must obey. You must not leave the ship. There is no place to go. Only the jungle, the crocodiles, the sharks."

He stopped again and studied the crowd. For a fleeting second he made eye contact with Maggi, seemed to study Schneider, and then his attention shifted. "We are merciful. Humanitarian. Every day one prisoner go free. One day American. One day Russian. We take to Singapore. Today we take old man who is sick. We are humanitarian. But you must obey. No trouble. Now you eat." He stepped back from the railing, and as abruptly as he had appeared on the bridge, he disappeared.

"What were they chanting?" Liz Schneider asked in a hushed voice.

" 'God is great.' It's a common greeting among Muslims in this part of the world. It may not mean any more than that."

"Their idea of 'howdy' sure scared the shit out of me," Liz said.

Schneider turned to Maggi. "What do you think? Have we been hijacked by the local holy warriors?"

She shook her head in frustration. "I don't know. I thought they were pirates, but now I don't know what the hell's going on." The crowd on deck lingered there, milling about and talking in secretive whispers in English and Russian, completely confused as to what to do next.

"Who's their leader in the white cap?" Schneider wondered aloud.

"The white cap means he's a *haji*, someone who's made the holy pilgrimage to Mecca. But a *haji* wouldn't act this way."

"To where else has he made a pilgrimage, I wonder?" Schneider asked in a quiet but cutting voice.

The harsh shouts of the guards interrupted them. The guards appeared to be trying to separate the passengers into two groups, prodding them with the muzzles of their guns. The middle-aged Americans stood rooted with terror, while the guards shouted what sounded like "You miss goat" and "Yugocaban" at them, getting increasingly angry. One viciously poked a woman with his rifle. A male passenger, obviously her husband, grabbed the rifle and grappled with the guard. Two other guards rushed at them, guns cocked to fire point blank into the crowd.

"No," Maggi screamed and ran to intercept them. "What do you want?" she pleaded with them in Bahasa. "We'll do what you want."

The guards were startled by the young woman suddenly thrusting herself in front of them, beseeching them in their own language.

"What do you want us to do?"

"Half should go and sit down to dinner. And the others should go back to their rooms," he said gesturing excitedly. "We spoke to them in English, and they are not obeying. They refuse to move."

Maggi instantly understood the problem. "You speak English beautifully," she said in

Malay, using the polite form of address, *saudara,* which literally meant "brother." "They speak American, which is different from your excellent English." "You miss goat" and "Yugocaban" apparently translated into one group must go eat and the other go to their cabins. To add to the confusion, the Malay gesture for "come here" was the hand extended, palm downward, which meant to the passengers "stay put."

Maggi repeated the instructions to the passengers and Russian crew members. "Please, it's just a misunderstanding. The guards are trying to get us all fed and safely back to our cabins. Please cooperate, and for God's sake smile at them as you go. And no one will get hurt." She knew that the loss of face and dignity of the guards had to be salvaged; otherwise they would regain it by beating the passengers, or inciting even worse bloodshed. She turned and smiled at the guards with a slight nod of her head.

Several of the passengers followed her lead and smiled nervously, as they filed off the deck. After a half dozen had passed, first one and then another of the guards smiled back. Maggi was only slightly reassured.

Schneider patted her on the back as he passed. *"Well done,"* he said emphatically, then in an urgent, lower voice whispered,

"We have to talk. Please sit next to me in the dining room, if you can. Or I'll try to get to your cabin."

Maggi hung back until the last of the passengers and crew had left the deck. It occurred to her that she was probably the only one of the 230 on board, Americans and Russians, who spoke the language of the area. She moved to go to the dining room, but a guard suddenly gripped her arm.

"Tengku wants you." His tone of voice and his nod made Maggi look up. The *haji* stared down at her from the bridge directly above. His dark eyes shone with an almost preterhuman brightness, like the eyes of a jungle cat, and an indecipherable smile played on his lips that sent a deep chill through Maggi.

Part III
The Second Man

9. The Dutch Woman

"What happens to them now?" Stewart asked the Dutch woman.

The *Decatur* was tied up to a quay on Bidong Island on the east coast of Malaysia. The Vietnamese women were being carried down the gangway on stretchers to a truck waiting at the end of the pier. Each stretcher was borne by four or five sailors carefully carrying its frail burden, easing her off the gangway and onto the bed of the truck so that there were no knocks or jolts.

"They'll get medical attention, of course, and then, when they've gained strength, we'll try to resettle them. As far as I can make out, they're all widows now. God willing, some will have relatives that have already been resettled and will take them in. Most, I fear, will just rot away in the refugee camps. Nobody wants them anymore."

The Dutch woman was an official with the United Nations High Commission on Refugees. She spoke fluent English, but the harsh way she spat out "rot away," as if clearing her throat of some disease, chilled Stewart. But more disturbing was the saddened resignation, rather than outrage, with which

129

she had examined the women when she first came aboard, and now the efficiency of her handling their transfer.

"You deal with this sort of thing often?"

The Dutch woman nodded slowly. "Our last report counted almost 3,000 murders, over 4,500 women raped, and 1,100 abducted." She clicked off the statistics in a listless voice, as if to give them more energy might cause her unbearable pain.

"The women kidnapped by the pirates — three of these were — what will happen to them?"

The Dutch woman shrugged. "When they are done with them, they will be murdered or sold into bordellos in Thailand, if there is money to be made. They used to keep the women on Kra Island for the fishermen to use at their pleasure, until we discovered it. Sometimes we just find one of the kidnapped women stranded on a beach, or a kind fisherman will bring them in."

She turned to Stewart. "You called them *pirates*, as if they were professional cutthroats." She shook her head. "They are simple fishermen. The refugees always tell us that it is simple fishermen who have attacked them." She gestured with a lean, brown leathery hand, taking in the sea to the east and north where the Gulf of Siam debouched into the South China Sea. "For centuries the Malays, Thais, Vietnamese, Cambodians have all fished these same waters. They are very old enemies. One fishing boat might attack another just for its catch. Now Vietnamese refugees, carrying all the gold and valuables they can smuggle out, and their women are the catch." Once again she said it totally without outrage, as if it were a sad and dangerous fact of life, like sharks. "Half the refugee boats that arrive here have been attacked. A few years ago it was almost 80 percent. But how many boats, thousands of people, were just sunk out there and disappear completely that we don't know about? We only see the survivors."

"And now we're responsible for them," Stewart said.

"Oh?" The porcelain blue eyes looked at him curiously.

"An old Oriental custom. If you save a person's life, you are responsible for them. You have interfered with destiny."

"Ach, yes." The Dutch woman nodded, and her lips curled in an ironic smile. Her skin was tanned like leather and deeply etched about the eyes and mouth, and her hair a faded yellow color, like a once bright cloth that had been washed and hung to dry for too many years and was now turning gray.

Had she been a man, she would have been handsome, but for a woman she was too severe looking. Stewart estimated that she was about his own age, and he had a vision of how she had looked before her wide China blue eyes had been seared into a permanent squint, when her skin had been cream and her hair the color of a ripe lemon. He would have been in college or a junior officer then, and he would have been dying to meet her.

It was a strange, bittersweet, deeply lonely thought, the kind that had increasingly plagued Stewart of late, but it was healthier than the rage that had been burning his gut for the past twelve hours.

The Dutch woman hefted the large leather briefcase she was holding. "There's over five thousand here," she said with wonder in her voice, holding up the navy payroll bag.

"The crew took up a collection." The wardroom had fattened it with a contribution from the mess fund. "They'll spend more than that their first night ashore in Singapore."

"I will send you an accounting of what each woman gets," the Dutch woman said in a precise voice.

"Please. I think we'd all like to know how the women and kids are making out and what happens to them. There are other

132

ways we may be able to help back in the States."

The Dutch woman studied him, the blue eyes intense and probing, and then, as if sensing Stewart's discomfort, she broke off her gaze and turned to the truck. "That young officer, he is Vietnamese also?"

Nguyen was supervising the loading of the stretchers. He knelt by one of the women, holding her hand, talking to her. Stewart could not hear him or see his face, but something in Nguyen's stance told him he was reassuring the woman, comforting her.

"He and his family got out by boat," Stewart said. "They washed up somewhere around here. They had to fight the coconut crabs for the fallen coconuts and ate them both to survive. He finally got to high school in the United States and won a scholarship to study engineering at Stanford."

"Y-a-a-a," the Dutch woman exclaimed in a long breath, then nodded her head as if confirming something. "God's work," she said. "Very mysterious ways." The sudden expression of awe seemed to ease the deeply cut lines of her face.

Stewart was suddenly aware of a sailor standing silently at his right elbow. It was the duty radio watch messenger holding an aluminum clipboard. He saluted smartly when Stewart recognized him. "Operational immediate message, sir."

It was probably the confirmation from Seventh Fleet headquarters to hunt down the pirates. Stewart excused himself to the Dutch woman, signed for the message, and quickly scanned the paper.

FROM COMSEVENTHFLEET
TO USS DECATUR
SUBJECT: REFUGEE OPERATIONS
1. AS SOON AS REFUGEES DE-
BARKED PROCEED TO SINGAPORE
AS ORIGINALLY TASKED. DO NOT
REPEAT DO NOT ATTEMPT TO
ENGAGE PIRATES. DISCONTINUE
SEARCH AND PURSUIT.
2. FORWARD ALL AVAILABLE
INTEL TO COMMANDER ROYAL
THAI NAVY, SONGKHLA.

Stewart was furious. He wanted to lash out and smash something.

"Is anything the matter?" the Dutch woman asked in a disturbed voice.

He had momentarily forgotten she was there. His eyes focused on her, and he saw his own fury reflected in the sudden fear in her crinkled blue eyes.

10. The Pirate Chieftain

The dark eyes that now intently studied Maggi had a sultry, heavy-lidded quality. The white *haji* cap and the handsome, high cheekbones framed the extraordinary eyes in a way that made them almost hypnotic.

"You are always in the midst of trouble," he said in Bahasa. "Do you cause the trouble I wonder, or are you drawn to it like a deer mouse to fallen fruit?" He smiled at Maggi, flashing even, unstained teeth, but the smile did not reassure her. Malays had a smile for every occasion, even executions. His sword stood leaning against the arm of his chair, as if at his right hand for instant use. She had seen him slice the face of the young Russian officer Vladimir Korsakov with it merely as a gesture. She was terrified of this man, and she felt her legs tremble.

They were in the ship's lounge, which the pirates had apparently commandeered as their headquarters. A handful of armed guards with automatic rifles loitered against the walls, and three henchmen sprawled on couches clustered about the *haji,* who sat imperially in an encircling rose-colored armchair as if it were a throne. The richly furnished lounge with its Oriental carpeting and fluted ivory columns — now empty except for this Malay *haji* and his court — conveyed the atmosphere of a barbaric sultan's chamber.

"You speak Bahasa very well. How did you learn it?" He used the polite form of *you*, literally meaning "sister." In Bahasa his voice had a lilting quality that was lost in his awkward use of English.

"I studied and worked here for several years." Maggi was being deliberately vague. The fact that she had once worked for a United States government agency, even one as altruistic as the Peace Corps, might be seized on by radicals as spying for the CIA.

"Where did you study and work?"

From the inflection of the question, Maggi wondered where they were. The size and great height of the trees about the ship indicated that they were in a primeval rain forest. For all she knew, they might be somewhere on the west coast of Borneo. "It was a village north of here, on the east coast of Malaysia."

"What was its name?" The sloe eyes still held her, as if the *haji* himself believed that as long as he looked into her eyes, she could not lie.

"Kampong Kuala Besut."

"Ah," the *haji* nodded, but his eyes narrowed. "What was your work there?"

"I was doing a study for my degree. And I taught children in school." She smiled to indicate that it was a small thing that she did. "I also helped the village set up a business to export their handicrafts." It was all true, although her formal graduate work had in reality come after the Peace Corps stint.

Maggi stood during the interrogation — she had not been invited to sit — deliberately keeping her arms at her side, her fingers, now absent of a wedding ring, curled out of sight.

The *haji* silently stared at Maggi, as if he did not quite believe her. What she had told him did not add up.

Maggi saw the look and added hastily, "I was studying for a doctorate. I am a professor in East Asian Studies." Devout Muslims traditionally had reverence for scholarship.

The *haji's* eyes did, in fact, widen in surprise. "You are a professor?"

"Yes, at the University of California in the United States." Maggi attempted to stand taller to give herself an authority she did not feel at the moment.

"What is your name, please?"

"Dr. Margaret Chancellor."

The *haji* turned to one of the guards. "The

passenger list," he ordered in English. He studied the printout.

Maggi spelled her name to assist him. For a moment she wondered if he could really read the English names or if it was an act to preserve face.

"Dr. Margaret Chancellor," he repeated. "Guest Lecturer?" He read off her title as if it were a question and looked back at Maggi.

"I am to give lectures on the places the ship visits, the history and customs of the people, lead the tours."

The *haji* turned and smiled at the three men grouped about him, as though this were a point of some importance. He shook the papers of the passenger list. "The tour guide is a professor at the University of California. That tells you how fat these tourists are." The Malay word *gemuk* meant more than "fat"; it also conveyed prosperity, wealth, and position.

The other pirates nodded and grunted in agreement.

He again studied Maggi in that disquieting way. His eyelashes were unusually long and lush, almost feminine, softening the predatory look in his eyes. "As a professor, you have studied our language and the ways of the people . . ."

"Yes." Maggi nodded vigorously, then realized that he had not finished.

"Perhaps as an 'ichthyologist' studies the habits of fish in order to increase the catch or a 'botanist' studies the rain forest to better lumber it?"

"No," Maggi protested, "I study them as an ancient and beautiful culture from which we in the West can learn." The *haji* had used the English terms *ichthyologist* and *botanist*. His Malay was not the Bahasa of the fishing *kampong*. It was educated, almost courtly.

"And do you study our religion?"

"Yes," Maggi said, suddenly very wary.

His silence demanded more.

"I have studied the Quran," she added, pronouncing the name of the sacred book of Islam in the reverent Malay.

"*Allah akbar,*" the *haji* pronounced.

"*Allah akbar,*" Maggi agreed. God is great. It had always seemed to her a rather non-denominational profession of faith, a greeting to which she had been comfortable responding when she had lived in Kuala Besut.

"*Allah akbar,*" the group about them murmured dutifully.

Once again, the *haji* glanced at the other pirates who flanked him. Then, with an imperious wave of his hand, he indicated that Maggi should sit in the upholstered white

139

easy chair to his left. She hesitated. "Please sit," he commanded.

Maggi immediately sat, carefully folding her hand demurely in her lap and arranging her feet not to point at any of the pirates, a gesture considered rude among the Malay.

Once again he studied Maggi before speaking, but the lushly lashed dark eyes now seemed softer, less suspicious. "I am Tengku Haji Azhar," he announced, introducing himself with a certain grave formality. "I have studied at the university in Kuala Lumpur. This is Ahmed, my cousin," indicating the small, gaunt man at his right hand who had escorted Maggi from the bridge the previous night and now regarded her with narrowed eyes, "Yusof, he studied at the university also, and Mahmud." The sweep of his hand introduced the two men seated opposite Maggi. "I speak English," he said as though making a decision. "We all do. But it is awkward for us to communicate with the passengers, and especially the Russians."

"Yes, of course," Maggi nodded. "The Americans speak a different dialect than the universal form of English spoken in this area. And the Russians speak very little English." To speak badly meant a loss of face in the Far East. The Malays in particular put great value on eloquence.

Tengku smiled, apparently pleased with her answer. "You will be my translator, my spokesman," he announced. He again glanced at the others, as if for confirmation. Watching them now, Maggi realized they were not his henchmen but his subchieftains, his advisers, and with a subtle look here, a nod there, they had concurred, except, perhaps, for Ahmed, who continued to study her with mean, suspicious eyes.

"This is a good thing," Tengku pronounced. "It will prevent misunderstanding between us. But more important, it will prevent bloodshed, as we just saw on the deck." The others, except for the distrustful Ahmed, appeared satisfied with the arrangement.

Maggi sat stunned. These terrorists — or whatever they were — were going to use her as their agent to control the passengers and crew. Obviously they were not ordinary pirates who planned to loot the ship at their leisure and then leave.

"Who are you? What do you want of us?" she asked almost in a whisper.

"We are the Party of God." The fervor in his voice made Maggi involuntarily shiver. "We have accounts to settle with the Great Powers."

"We're hostages?"

"We do not mean to harm you. You are

here to guarantee the good faith of your governments."

"What do you want?"

"Our God, our independence, our manhood."

It was a strange pronouncement, not at all Malay but more like that of an Arab radical in its rhetoric. Maggi wondered where this Tengku Haji Azhar really came from and what he wanted.

"You said you will let one person go free each day," she ventured carefully.

Tengku nodded. "One day an American, one day a Russian."

"Did someone go today?"

"Yes." He again read down the passenger list.

"Mr. Benjamin," the man named Ahmed answered.

Her next-door neighbor. "An old man with white hair?" Maggi asked anxiously.

"Yes, long beautiful white hair. He was the first," the *haji* responded. "He was a sick old man. It would be very difficult for him."

She had an image of the tall, obviously frail, courtly old man, the painful walk supported by the Malacca cane. "Where is he?"

"We took him to Singapore. Everyone, we take to Singapore. We show our righteousness."

That was why the steward had asked if anyone had medical problems. Maggi had told him to check on Mr. Benjamin. Perhaps she had been partially responsible for his release. If so, she was grateful to the *haji*. Maybe his intentions were humane.

"I will help you in any way I can. May I move about the ship?"

"Everyone may move about the ship. Except at night. You all must stay in your cabins." Tengku shrugged and smiled. "It is for your own safety. Some will try to escape, and the jungle is very dangerous."

"How long will we be here?"

Tengku shrugged. "God knows. He will tell us when we need to know." Once again he consulted his cohorts with a glance.

"What do they want?" Alan Schneider demanded.

"I don't know. I asked, but he was pretty abstract. He talked about God, independence, and manhood."

The former Secretary of State nodded, as if Maggi had given him a specific answer. "But they're bargaining for something very concrete."

"What makes you say that?"

"Their promise to let one person go each day. And they're starting with people in ill health. As a practical matter, of course, it prevents the most fragile of the hostages from dying on them. But it demonstrates their humanitarian concern and delays an armed assault to rescue us until they get what they want."

"*Rescue* us? Does anyone know where the hell we are? Do you?"

"We're less than a day's sail out of Singapore," Liz Schneider said hopefully. They were her first words since Maggi had entered the Schneiders' stateroom. She had sat silently throughout Maggi's account of her meeting with the pirate chieftain and her husband's pointed interrogation.

"We could be anywhere!" Maggi exclaimed. "Sumatra, Borneo, Malaysia, or several thousand islands between. Could you see where we were going through the window?" The Schneiders had one of the most expensive, Type AA cabins, at $7,575 per person, opening on the promenade deck, almost directly above Maggi's windowless Type D cell.

"All I saw was the sea, a jungle coast, and then we were upriver."

"Surely they're searching for us now," Liz insisted.

"But will they find us?" Schneider mused. He paced to the porthole and peered out, but the view was almost completely cut off by the high river bank a few feet away. "Did you see the sky when we were on deck?"

Maggi shook her head. "The jungle canopy totally covers the river at this point."

Schneider nodded. "A search plane directly overhead couldn't even spot us. Somebody meticulously planned this operation. What do you think, Dr. Chancellor, is the headman up in the lounge behind it all, or is he just the field commander?"

The question had never occurred to Maggi. "I just don't know."

"Did they mention me?" There was a flash of fear in Schneider's eyes.

"No."

"Anything to indicate that they knew I was aboard?"

"No — wait . . . at one point the *haji* waved the passenger list at the others and said something about the importance of the people."

"What did he say exactly?"

"He said the tourists were . . . *fat*. I mean it was a Malay word that literally means 'fat,' but it conveys wealth or position. You'd use it to describe an official or wealthy merchant."

"Well, we certainly have a lot of *fat* cats aboard," Liz remarked.

Schneider shot her a look, but he was clearly relieved that he had not been singled out. "You say this . . . Tengku Haji Azhar is educated?"

"He made a point of telling me that he had studied at the University of Malaysia. Since he was impressed by the fact that I am a professor, I think it was a status thing with him. His Malay is educated, even if his English is marketplace."

"An unusual background for a pirate," Liz interjected.

"But not one for a terrorist," Schneider said. "They're invariably university dropouts the world over. Was there any sign that any of them have been to Libya or Tehran?" he asked.

Maggi shook her head. "No, but he's made the pilgrimage to Mecca. That's what the *haji* in his name means. It's sort of a title. It's not uncommon for a Malay. Tens of thousands go every year. Even though they're one of the most distant Muslim countries, they actually have the highest per capita rate of pilgrimage. Even in the small village in which I worked in the Peace Corps, at least a third of the Muslim men, even teenage boys, had made the *haj*. But a Malay *haji* wouldn't do such things."

"Mecca was also where the ayatollah recruited for his Islamic revolution," Schneider speculated, "and from the few words we heard on deck, this guy certainly is spouting the party line."

"Well, what should I do?" Maggi snapped, suddenly exasperated with Schneider's seemingly endless analysis. He reminded her of her ex-husband with his interminable dissections and pronouncements.

The question seemed to surprise Schneider. "You'll do whatever he damn well says," he answered harshly. "This isn't a job offer. There are no options here. Our lives, even your own, now depend on what you do. That much should be obvious from what happened on deck."

Schneider played with his mustache, and his eyes took on a shrewd look. "What a canny Oriental this *haji* is. You're a godsend to him, and he seized it immediately."

"What are you talking about?"

"He's got 135 American passengers and a Russian crew of — what?"

"About ninety."

Schneider nodded. "Right, 225 foreigners he has to control. His English is undoubtedly adequate, but he's subtle enough to know it will lose him face. So now he has a spokesman, or better yet a spokeswoman, one who speaks the language in which you say he is quite eloquent. And, what's more, you're a professor, someone who has obvious status. My bet is that he won't ever say a word to us. Everything will be conveyed through you. He'll stay as aloof as an Oriental potentate."

Maggi was silent. The fear she had felt earlier had not abated one bit. But one of Schneider's remarks troubled her. "Why is it better that I'm a woman?"

"He doesn't feel threatened by you. If you were a man, especially an older man, he would be giving you the power."

"This is a hell of a time to be chauvinistic, darling," Liz suddenly interjected.

Her husband shot her a nasty look, then turned back to Maggi. "It's also a subtle insult to us, isn't it? You're the expert here."

"Yes, he would think that way," she said quietly. That was the reality of the position of women in the Muslim world.

Liz looked back and forth from Maggi to her husband, then suddenly stood and seized Maggi's left hand and examined it. "I really don't think your divorce should be finalized quite yet," she said in a conspiratorial tone. "Do you have your ring?"

Maggi shook her head. "I thought about bringing it, but then I felt like such a hypocrite. If I put it on, you know, for protection. I was going to be with the group

148

most of the time."

"Well, darling, this is definitely not Berkeley, and you're going to need all the protection you can get." Liz suddenly slipped off her own wedding ring, held Maggi's left hand, and started to put it on.

"I couldn't take yours."

"Don't worry," Liz said with a mischievous smile, "I always travel with a spare. And I put on my cheap one before we went on deck, just in case they started a collection for their cause."

"What the hell is going on here?" Schneider asked. He looked genuinely confused.

Liz turned to her husband. "A little personal survival technique for ladies traveling abroad. There are still countries where saying you're a divorcee is regarded as little better than announcing you're a whore. And I believe we're in those latitudes."

Maggi nodded. "I kept my left hand covered the entire time I was talking to him. I felt I was suddenly in the Dark Ages."

"He didn't ask?"

"Not yet, but he will. How do I explain my traveling alone?"

"Maggi dear, you are *not* traveling alone," Liz said in a sugary voice. "You are traveling with your dear, dear cousin Liz." She gently took Maggi by the shoulders, leaned forward, and kissed her on the cheeks. "Our mothers were sisters, and we've been practically sisters our whole lives, haven't we?"

Maggi was astonished at the instant inventiveness with which Liz concocted the story.

"And we are traveling together with my very uninteresting albeit handsome husband the academic." She turned brightly to Schneider. "Darling, name something you can teach that these rogues wouldn't possibly be interested in."

"International econometrics."

"There!" Liz said enthusiastically. "Aren't you clever? I haven't the vaguest idea what it means, but I'm sure it would put me to sleep."

She turned back to Maggi and searched her face with deeply serious eyes. Beneath the blithe chatter there was fear. Fear for her husband. Liz had not forced her wedding ring on Maggi out of generosity. She was offering her a subtle form of protection in return for Alan Schneider's anonymity.

"They may already know he's aboard or recognize him. One of the passengers or the Russians may say something."

"But we needn't volunteer it."

Maggi nodded. "His politics are certainly something that should be kept in the family."

Liz's smile expressed her gratitude. She now turned, cocked her head, and studied her husband. "I've always loved your mustache. It's so distinguished — *distingué*, really. Only the most handsome of the foreign secretaries and secretaries of state — Anthony Eden, Dean Acheson, that sort — can really wear one. People are *always* making the comparison," she said in an aside to Maggi. "But darling, in this equatorial heat and humidity, don't you think it would be more comfortable to be clean-shaven? It would give you a whole different look — more youthful, I think."

Schneider smoothed his mustache with the tip of his index finger and nodded thoughtfully. He looked from his wife to Maggi. "Be very careful. All our lives are at stake here," he said quietly. "But you're now in the most dangerous spot of all."

11. An Emergency Notice to Mariners

It was an awesome sunset. Banks of great thunderheads roiled on the horizon to the south over the South China Sea, and to the west a few scattered white columns rose up somewhere beyond the lush green coast of Malaysia. The cloud shattered the light into shards of pink and magenta that thickened to blood red and deep purple somewhere over the Road to Mandalay.

Lieutenant Commander Charles Robinson, the executive officer of the *Decatur*, stood on the starboard wing of the bridge and framed the sunset in the view finder of his Nikon. He positioned a rocky island in the bottom left of the picture to balance the flaming clouds in the upper right. What he really wanted in the foreground was a fishing junk, but the *Decatur* had not passed another ship in quite a while. If he waited any longer, he would lose the extraordinary colors of the equatorial sunset.

He clicked off several shots, varying the exposure an f-stop on each photo. Over his years in the navy Robinson had become quite a good photographer. Originally it had become a way of sharing his travels away from home with his wife and three children. He was a dutiful letter writer, but he was not comfortable writing down his thoughts, his impressions of places. But the split-second freezing of an image seemed natural to him. Perhaps it was a carryover from football, where the instantaneous perception of patterns, and anticipating them, had been as necessary to the ex-Navy halfback as his explosive power and speed.

It was quiet on the bridge, and Robinson thought of having someone take his picture against the Malaysian sunset, but then immediately rejected the thought. He could never balance the light on the coal blackness of his face against the dazzling sky. His wife had filled three albums with what she called "eyes and teeth in exotic settings," before he learned to use an electronic flash for a fill-in. Besides, Stewart was also on the bridge, and Robinson did not feel comfortable even distracting the signalman, who was sipping coffee and loitering by the chart table with the quartermaster of the watch, by asking him to take his picture.

The XO was a stranger on a strange ship. Robinson had joined the *Decatur* in the Persian Gulf just three weeks earlier. He had spent five days being briefed by the previous executive officer, who had then been flown ashore to Bahrain by helicopter, and the *Decatur* had immediately separated from the Joint Task Force Middle East to sail back independently to San Diego. It was not uncommon for a ship's executive officer or captain to be relieved on station at the very end of the deployment. It allowed his replacement to get acquainted with the ship on the easy homeward-bound milk run back to the States.

But after three weeks aboard the *Decatur* Robinson was still not comfortable around the frigate's commanding officer. There always seemed to be a wall around Stewart. It went beyond the isolation of command, of his being "the man." Even now the captain stood by himself on the opposite wing of the bridge, staring east into the thickening blue-blackness rushing toward them across the South China Sea.

Robinson couldn't get a fix on him. To the eye the CO was tall, lanky, and loose-limbed, his movements as unhurried as his speech, a flow of Tidewater born in Richmond and cultivated at the University of Virginia. He had the manner of a Southern aristocrat, a man to the manor born. That alone was enough to set the executive officer's teeth on edge.

Robinson had blasted his way out of the Chicago ghetto, through pile-driving, slugging Southside high school football into Annapolis. He was black and an All-City halfback, and in 1974 Annapolis had needed both attributes. Allowances had been made for his grades; tutors had helped him grind through math and science. But it was more than the gulf in their backgrounds that made

Robinson now hesitate to approach Stewart.

The man seemed to be in a state of barely controlled rage. His anger at not being able to pursue the Thai pirates had been almost irrational. On the departure from Bidong Island he had stiffly stalked the bridge like a loose rocket about to explode, snapping out each command with the ominous crack of a percussion cap. But the bigger, more devastating explosion had not occurred. When the ship had cleared the harbor, the captain had secured the special sea detail, turned the conn over to the officer of the deck, and retreated silently to the port wing of the bridge, where he had remained. At his exit through the hatch, everyone on the bridge had exhaled in one collective breath.

But the executive officer was disturbed. A commanding officer, especially one with Stewart's experience, should have been more in control of himself. Seventh Fleet's orders to proceed to Singapore made perfect sense. The chances that the *Decatur* — then tied up in Malaysia unloading the refugees — could track down the pirates hundred of miles away and thirty-six hours after they had disappeared were slim. The task was best left to the Thai navy and police. But Stewart's anger had not accepted that logic. It was a fever that fed on itself. Something was going on with the man, and Robinson had no clue what it was.

By this time tomorrow evening they'd be at anchor in Singapore harbor for two days' liberty. Until then Robinson, as second in command, had damned well better keep a weather eye on the captain. He rubbed the blue stone of his class ring nervously against his meaty palm, then sauntered across to the port wing. "Anxious to get home?" Robinson asked cordially.

Stewart didn't answer.

"It's been a long cruise," the XO persisted.

"Christ, you just came aboard."

"I mean for the rest of you," Robinson said defensively. So much for cordiality.

Lieutenant Marty Mitchell, a tall, harassed-looking man, approached the captain. Behind the horn-rimmed glasses the engineering officer's brown eyes looked forlorn.

Stewart regarded him with suspicion. "Problems?"

"Yes, sir, we have a casualty to the compressor in the number one air-conditioning plant. We'll have to shut it down."

"How long to repair it?"

Mitchell took off his blue baseball cap and rubbed his scalp. In his early thirties, he was already half bald. "We can't do it aboard, sir. We'll have to take it to a machine shop when we get to Subic."

"Can the other two a.c. plants handle the load?"

"They should be able to, sir, but we'll be running both compressors day and night. And we're keeping our fingers crossed that number three lasts to Subic. The seawater injection temperature is 92 degrees, and the bearings are hotter than normal."

"I know," said Stewart, with a nod of appreciation for the problem.

The *Decatur* was returning from a deployment to the Persian Gulf, six months of intensive operations and steaming in hot, confined waters. Things were beginning to break down.

Robinson followed Mitchell back inside the wheelhouse. A messenger from radio central scrambled up the ladder, toting his aluminum clipboard, and looked about.

"What do you have?" Robinson asked.

"Emergency Notice to Mariners, sir."

It was probably a storm warning for the South China Sea. "I'll take it." Robinson signed for it and read:

BLACK SEA, 333-FOOT SOVIET FLAG PASSENGER LINER, IS UNREPORTED ON VOYAGE FROM SINGAPORE TO JAKARTA. LAST

COMMUNICATION AT 181630Z
MAR. NO INDICATION OF
DISTRESS AT THAT TIME. LAST
KNOWN POSITION SEAWARD END
OF SINGAPORE DEPARTURE
CHANNEL. ESTIMATED COURSE
123 TRUE, SPEED II KNOTS. ALL
VESSELS IN THE VICINITY OR
TRANSITING THE AREA
MAINTAIN A SHARP LOOKOUT
AND REPORT ALL SIGHTINGS OR
UNUSUAL DEBRIS TO PORT OF
SINGAPORE AUTHORITY.

Robinson handed the dispatch to the officer of the deck.

Stewart stood on the starboard wing, out of place in a natty civilian suit and foulard tie his wife, Charlotte, had bought for him, and peered down on the forcastle, as the crewmen unloaded the Vietnamese women, bleeding, naked, plaintively wailing, "Tiep! Tiep!"
The muscular black boatswain's mate Freeman bent down and lifted a woman. He held her up in his arms so that her bared thighs and pale breasts were harshly exposed in the incandescent glare of the searchlight. It was a white woman, not

158

Vietnamese, and her head hung back over his arms, slack in death, the woman's long auburn hair loose and tumbling almost to the deck, her blue eyes open, now staring up at Stewart. It was Charlotte.

Stewart sat bolt upright in the bridge chair with a start, then wiped the sleep from his eyes. In the darkness of the wheelhouse there was no easy reassurance that it had been just a nightmare, and he sat very still, trying to shake off the horror of the image. He felt like weeping, but he never did. The rage never quite left him; it was always there, an angry mercy that checked his tears. He swiveled about, blinking at the red-illuminated dials on the control console, orienting himself.

"Any contacts?" he asked in a subdued voice.

"No, sir, not since the one we passed an hour ago," the shadowed figure of the officer of the deck reported.

Stewart's back ached. Falling asleep in the bridge chair invariably tortured his spine. He lurched to his feet and groped for the ladder leading down to his cabin directly below. He should stretch out for the few haunted hours he had left before reveille, even if he did not sleep again.

"Captain's departed the bridge," the boatswain's mate of the watch bawled out.

159

12. Strange Fruit

"No one saw who left the shopping bag?"

"No, Mr. Yee. There were too many people." The policeman was a young, slender Chinese. The white patent leather chest belting over his blue uniform reflected the rainbow colors of the neon and fluorescent lighting all about them, as the policeman pointed to the tide of pedestrians surging along Orchard Road and Scotts Road and flowing in and out of the Dynasty Hotel. Even at eleven in the evening the sidewalks were jammed.

This was the apex of the city's "Hotel Alley." Next door on Scotts was the Singapore Hyatt Hotel and across the road the Holiday Inn. A few doors down on Orchard was the Hotel Mandarin, and in the other direction the Singapore Hilton. All about the gleaming new alabaster and crystal towers of tourism clustered the airline offices, shops, and restaurants that catered to Singapore's five million tourists each year.

The Dynasty Hotel itself was a thirty-three-story octagonal pagoda with a classic pointed, green-tiled Chinese roof topped by a red finial like a cherry. The imperial-style canopy over the entrance formed a pavilion, which contained a sidewalk cafe fronting on the corner of Orchard and Scotts. It was here that the package had been dropped. Yee Baiyu looked about and felt a piercing chill in his bones in spite of the humid, eighty-degree warmth of the evening.

"Who found it?" he asked.

"A bus boy picked it up and stored it under the sink in the kitchen. He was saving it for his break."

"What? Was he planning to steal it?"

The policeman was pale and shaken, but suddenly he looked as though he wanted to laugh. "No, sir, he was planning to eat it."

Yee stared at the young officer, who was obviously enjoying his confusion and horror.

"It was in a sack of durians."

"Durians!" Yee was appalled. The durian was a local jungle fruit about the size of a small melon. The outer skin was green and spiky, but it was the cheesy flesh inside that caused civil insurrection, fistfights, and divorces. To Yee, it smelled like an open sewer. But to durian lovers the odor was earthy, sensual, the taste of the flesh like almond custard, the sweetest of ambrosias. The fruit's distinctive stench was offensive to anyone but the addicted durianophile. It was sold only in open-air markets and banned by law

from hotels, airports, buses, and taxis. But passionate gourmets like Yee's own mother carted bundles of the heavy, highly perishable fruit miles from the market to their home to gorge themselves. As a child, Yee had been the only one in his family who hated the fruit. When his mother cut one open, the boy had had to leave the cramped apartment to get away from the smell. But its rank odor hung about the kitchen for days. Fortunately the fruit was so expensive that his family could not afford to splurge often. To this day Yee, a fastidious man, had never overcome his revulsion for the smell of the legendary fruit.

He shook his head at the irony of it; whoever had left the package with its all-pervasive stink had known that it would not go unnoticed for long in the jammed, bustling pavilion with its constant traffic of tourists and shoppers. "Which table did the bus boy find this . . . *fruit* on?"

The policeman led Yee just a few steps. "This one."

The table was at the edge of the cafe, and anyone entering or leaving the hotel or strolling in the evening crowd along Orchard might have dropped it. "Where is the bus boy now?"

"We're holding him in the kitchen. He's

162

an Indonesian here on a work permit."

Yee nodded, but for a brief moment he found that information disturbing. Why? Singapore had a labor shortage, and it brought in workers from the neighboring country to do the dirty, low-paying jobs that the now prosperous Singaporeans, mostly ethnic Chinese, no longer wanted.

Several of the plainclothes detectives were laughing about something but immediately quieted when Yee entered the kitchen. The bus boy was a low-browed, swarthy Indonesian in his twenties, but he looked very pale, as if he had been sick. He seemed stuffed into his starched white busing jacket, which was a size or two too small for him, and he sweated heavily despite the kitchen's air conditioning. A uniformed policeman stood on either side of him.

On the stainless steel counter was an object about the size of a large durian, now covered up by a batik cloth. Everyone in the room appeared to be avoiding looking at it, as if to stare would be an unforgivable breach of etiquette. Instead their eyes fluttered everywhere else, at the ceiling and floor, the row of knives and cleavers for chopping vegetables, and now they fluttered to Yee as he entered.

One of the uniformed policemen, a Chinese,

stiffened to attention as he saw Yee. The other, a Malay, merely looked at him curiously. A plain white canvas shopping bag also lay on the steel counter.

"Is this what it was in?" Yee asked, picking it up.

"Yes, sir. He says it was covered by that cloth on top. It's all where it was when we came in."

"He doesn't speak much English," the Malay volunteered. "He's only been here a few months from Sumatra."

"Can you talk to him?"

The Malay nodded. "Yes, sir." The Bahasa Malay spoken in Singapore and the Bahasa Indonesian used across the straits in Sumatra were the same language.

"What time did he find the bag?"

"At about 10:30. He brought it in here to keep it, until his shift was over at midnight."

"Didn't he look inside?"

The Malay questioned the bus boy, who answered in an excited voice at great length.

"He said he was too busy. He just took a quick look under the cloth. All he saw was the durians . . . until he dumped it on the table there. He was going to give one to one of the waiters who had a date after work tonight." The Malay grinned at Yee.

"When the durians come down, sarongs go up."

The fruit was reputed to be a powerful aphrodisiac. The Chinese said that the durian was *yang,* containing great heat, whereas all other fruits were *yin* and cooling. Yee's father had told him that in the jungle tigers fought over the fallen fruit.

"Was there anything else in the bag?"

"Yes, sir, the jackfruit's under the cloth," one of the plainclothes men said. The other detective guffawed at the reference, then covered his mouth.

Yee was astonished that they could make a joke about such a horror. Now all eyes in the room were on Yee. He hesitated to lift the batik cloth. The rancid, foul stink of the durians escaped from under the cloth and permeated the room, despite the air conditioning. The smell brought to Yee the image of his mother's and father's flush, sweating faces, teasing him, his father holding out the cheesy white lump for him to take a bite, as the boy fled the house.

Ballinger suddenly hobbled into the kitchen. Yee was surprised to see the old Englishman. The medical examiner's eyes immediately focused on the batik-covered objects on the table, then glanced up at Yee. "I told you there'd be more," he said.

Ballinger's nostrils twitched, and he sniffed the air. "Durians," he snorted, as if more offended by the foul-smelling fruit than by the grisly thing that lay under the batik. Without ceremony Ballinger yanked off the cloth. "Aha, what strange fruit do we have here?" The spiky green-skinned durians somehow resembled the severed heads of alien beings, lying there alongside the human head.

It was face down, and all Yee saw was the mane of long, silvery white hair, so at first glance he could not tell if it was a white man or a woman. But he saw now why the detective had callously joked about its being a jackfruit, which was larger, more mild, and known locally as the "white man's durian." And with the black humor there occurred to Yee the certainty that whoever had left this package was not some foreign terrorist but a native, and one with a diabolical knowledge of Singapore.

Next to the head was a plastic bag. Yee carefully lifted it with his handkerchief. Inside was a thin blue booklet. "An American passport," Yee said aloud, opening it. An identification card slipped out of the passport and fell on the table. Yee examined it and compared the name on the I.D. with that in the passport. He handed the card to Ballinger.

"It's a ship's boarding pass," the pathologist said with a note of puzzlement in his voice.

Yee studied the passport photo of a handsome elderly man with a mane of white hair. "The American's name is Benjamin. Martin Benjamin. And he was a passenger on the *Black Sea*."

Part IV
The Eye of the Day

13. The Poetry of the Malay Language

Maggie stood on the bow of the *Black Sea* gazing upriver. Fifty yards ahead the jungle drew back from the water, and the vaulted canopy of leaves overhead broke open. There the sunlight on the rippling stream was dazzling, bursting so suddenly into the twilight gloom of the rain forest that the landscape seemed an illusion, the artificially lighted scenery of a stage viewed from the real but darkened world of the audience.

At that point the river narrowed and the high, steep, root-woven earth banks were abruptly transformed into limestone, a rock-walled gorge that rose into distant lush green mountains. A waterfall spilled out of the high jungle, tumbling and disappearing into the mists that veiled the canyon and river ahead.

In that patch of sunlight where the jungle shade ended, before the canyon walls rose up high enough to cast their own shadow on the water, a kingfisher now plummeted into the river, a sudden bolt of blue and yellow that splashed and then winged up again. A pair of enormous long-tailed hornbills, dark and majestic, sailed across the pale blue sky. A cloud of butterflies, so thick and wide Maggi could see it from fifty yards away, floated along the sunlit river edge like an enormous orange flower fluttering on the breeze.

"It is a taste of Paradise," the tall man next to her said, as if reading her thoughts.

She turned to face Tengku Haji Azhar, and the presence of the pirate chieftain beside her jolted her back.

He leaned over the rail and stared straight ahead, as if no less enchanted with the view than she had been, then pointed upstream. "The river here is very fast, especially during the rainy season. It cuts through the rock like a saw. *Here,* before it spreads out in the soft earth, the river is still deep and narrow, and the trees touch overhead. Here, where the mountain marries the jungle, it is a special place, a sanctuary. The sun cannot see us. The sun cannot spy on us."

He smiled at Maggi, and in that brief speech he reminded her what a simple and instinctively poetic language Bahasa was. The expression for "sun" was *mata hari*, literally meaning "the eye of the day." The eye of the day cannot see us, he had said. It cannot spy on us. The word for "spy" was formed by repeating the word for "eye," *mata mata,* implying an eye that sees more than it should. He had simply described how nature had conspired to form this special sanctuary, and he had created a poem.

He smiled at Maggi, not smiling at his own cleverness but at his pleasure in this special place where the mountain marries the jungle. "Do you know where we are, Professor?" he asked.

She shook her head. "I have no idea. I was locked in my cabin when we came here. I couldn't even see out the portholes."

He nodded. "You are in the midst of the ancient kingdom of Srivijaya. From here my ancestors commanded the sea from the Philippines to the Bay of Bengal for almost a thousand years." Maggi was drawn in by the sudden intensity in the dark eyes. "My ancestors were great men of the sea. They sailed here on the southwest monsoons from India to trade, but they stayed, taught the people their ways, married the daughters of the soil, and mixed their blood. This became the Srivijaya."

Maggi nodded. The ancient kingdoms of Southeast Asia, from Angkor Wat in Cambodia to the Majapahit of Bali, were referred to by Western historians as "Indianized states." During biblical times the Indians had arrived not as military conquerors but as traders and adventurers, then priests, scholars, and artists. They had, in effect, conquered with trade, art, and religion, first the Hindus, then the Buddhists, and finally the Muslims. The influential Indians married into the local ruling families, and their courts developed into Indian aristocracies.

Tengku himself was unusually tall for a Malay, and broad-shouldered, but with the graceful, boyish slenderness and narrow hips that many of the Malay men kept. He had prominent cheekbones and a strong, more defined nose than most Orientals. A handsome man by any standard.

Maggi must have been staring at Tengku, because he suddenly asked, "You look at me curiously. Why?"

Maggi was flustered. "It's just that you are, well, taller . . ." She stumbled over the words. Asian men were very self-conscious about being shorter than Europeans, but Tengku stood a head taller than she.

"Ah, yes!" he exclaimed, as if seizing the clue in a mystery. "I am taller. Do you know why?"

Where did a Malay pirate chieftain with Brahmin features fit in? The question was more than academic. Maggi framed her answer to make it as flattering as possible. "The great ancient Indian poems called Malaysia the Golden Peninsula. And the rulers of this — "

He smiled and waved his hand to abruptly cut off Maggi's recitation. It was the smile and gesture of a Malay in the marketplace who knows when someone is trying to con him. "A scholarly and poetic answer, but I will cut out a thousand years," he said.

"I was born in a small fishing *kampong* near the mouth of the Malacca River. My great-uncle could not read nor write, but he could recite our family history back to my father's fathers for thirty fathers."

Maggi nodded. The *tusut*, or family annals, committed to memory and passed on orally from generation to generation, was an honored practice in a culture where ancestors were revered.

"Do you know Malacca?"

"I've never been there, but I hear it's a beautiful city."

Tengku nodded. "Yes, it is a small city and not very important anymore. But it is very interesting. The Portuguese conquered it, and the Dutch conquered the Portuguese. Then the English came from India to trade with the Dutch, and they bartered the port of Bencoolen in Sumatra for Malacca, one city with all its people for another people, as my father would trade fish for jackfruit."

Tengku had spoken the last not in anger but with a heavy sadness that moistened his dark eyes. He was quiet a moment, then gave Maggi a small smile. "You see, at the university in Kuala Lumpur I studied history. It is good for a Malay to study history. It makes him proud to be who he is. And he understands his father and his father's father."

He looked at Maggi, his eyes measuring her. "If you really want to know of my people, you should talk to my cousin Ahmed. He learned the *tusut* from his father and, if God wills it, he will teach it to his son. He will tell it to you, and you may write it down. It will be of importance to your studies," Tengku said completely without conceit, as if he were an official setting up a key background briefing with one of his aides.

Maggi loathed Ahmed, the small, gaunt man who had escorted her from the bridge to her cabin that first horrible night. When she visited Tengku in the lounge, Ahmed sat at his right hand, as in a formally ordained position. But it was the mean, dark eyes in the narrow simian face that made Maggi nervous. They were watchful, flickering constantly from Maggi to Tengku, hanging on their every word with the suspicion of a jealous wife. "Yes," Maggi said tactfully, with forced enthusiasm, "it would be fascinating to record your family history." In truth, it was important for scholars to record the fast-disappearing remnants of the oral histories of Southeast Asia.

"What did your father do?"

"He had a boat. Sometimes he fished, but mostly he carried trade between the islands, Sumatra, and Malacca. When I was a child, I thought taking a boatload just from Tanjung Pinang to Malacca was like a game of hide-and-seek."

Maggi nodded. To the thousands of inter-island traders, smuggling and trading were synonymous. On both sides of the strait they spoke the same *pasar* — market language — and Muslim law guided their business dealings with one another. But governments, tariffs, boundaries, trade restrictions had all changed constantly. The Straits Settlements, the British, the Dutch, the Japanese, then the British and Dutch again, Malaysia, Indonesia, Singapore. The government patrols became another hazard to be avoided like freak tropical storms or shifting sandbars.

From her Peace Corps experience Maggi knew that sons always worked on their father's boat as soon as they could walk. She could easily envision Tengku as a boy living in a *kampong* built on stilts that held the houses just above the high tide. A gangling and slender youth with enormous brown eyes, laughing, splashing, playing, and living in the water as much as out of it. "You were born a man of the sea," she said.

It had been an offhand comment, but Tengku stared at her in an intense way as though reading another meaning into it. Then he smiled, a strange and mischievous grin. "Yes, I was born a man of the sea. My fathers have always been men of the sea."

A languid cooling breeze drifted down the river, stirring Maggi's hair, carrying the heavy, sweet musk of distant blossoms on the air. With the setting of the sun, the jungle about the ship began to stir and chatter, birds, monkeys, cicadas whistling, chirping, and crooning out to one another, searching for food or mates.

The majority of pirates were camped along the shore, where they were now gathered around small fires in groups of four and five cooking, eating, and smoking. Only a handful of guards remained on the ship along with Tengku and his hierarchy of lieutenants, who had taken over the lounge. The clove-scented smoke of *kretek* cigarettes spiced the air. In their leisure many of the pirates had donned batik sarongs and now bared their torsos in the humid, sultry evening air. A few wore thick brass arm bracelets and intricate tribal tattoos.

Maggi, the scholar, did not know what to make of this barbaric banding of outcasts of the islands — a renegade *haji*, Malaysian university dropouts, Indonesian pirates, tattooed Dayaks with blowguns. Normally they would have little to do with one another. What had brought them together?

"We are not *thugs*," Tengku said suddenly, as if almost reading her mind. He used the Indian word for robbers and murderers. She turned back to him. He had been following her gaze, and his eyes now studied the men gathered on the river bank. "We are a great people. But to survive, to be men and not coolies, we must be men of the sea."

Men of the sea. *Orang laut*. Maggi suddenly realized why Tengku had secretly smiled when she had commented, "You were born a man of the sea." The Malay term also meant "men *from* the sea," the marauders who suddenly materialized, as if out of the waves and spindrift itself, to attack and plunder any trading vessel or coastal village. It was a poetic language that, in its violent history, made no distinction between seamen and pirates. Tengku had been born a pirate.

"But come, you will advise me whom we will free tomorrow," he abruptly ordered.

179

"Did you take someone to Singapore today?"

"Yes, a Russian sailor. He was injured when we boarded the ship. He needed a doctor."

Maggi was startled. She was sure it must have been Vladimir Korsakov, the young officer whose face Tengku had slashed for his gallantry in protecting Maggi. But the reply had been so detached and impersonal that she was intimidated from asking anything further. It chillingly reminded her that Tengku, whatever his charm, was as sharply clawed and unpredictable as a jungle cat. And yet, in a confusion of emotions, she was grateful to him for having released Korsakov so that he could get immediate medical attention for his wound.

"We must go over the list of passengers. Tomorrow it will be an American." The dark, sultry eyes now questioned her, demanding her suggestion.

Alan Schneider. The pirates apparently did not yet realize that one of their hostages was the former American Secretary of State. He might be in terrible danger when they found out. Maggi nervously twisted the wedding ring Liz had given her. "I really don't know the passengers very well yet," she said truthfully, then added, "except for my cousins."

Tengku's eyes widened with interest. "Ah, your cousins," he nodded.

"What are you going to do with all of us?" she suddenly whispered.

Tengku stared at her, and for a long, breathless time there was no expression in the dark eyes, not a hint. Then he smiled, the canny, charming smile of the bazaar. "Don't you know? We are going to trade all of you," he said, as though it were the most obvious thing in the world. "Just as the English traded the Dutch the city of Bencoolen for Malacca."

14. The Suit from Singapore

FROM COMSEVENTHFLEET
TO USS DECATUR
SUBJECT: EMERGENCY CHANGE
OF ORDERS
1. UPON ARRIVAL ANCHORAGE
SINGAPORE IMMEDIATELY
DISPATCH EMBARKED HELO TO
AMERICAN EMBASSY HELIPAD.
HELO TO TRANSPORT CAPTAIN
JOHN CAMPBELL (US NAVAL
ATTACHE SINGAPORE) AND MR.

HAROLD BLOCKER (AMERICAN
EMBASSY SINGAPORE STAFF) TO
DECATUR.
2. ALL LIBERTY IN SINGAPORE IS
HEREBY CANCELED. NO
DECATUR PERSONNEL TO
DISEMBARK. CAPTAIN CAMPBELL
AND MR. BLOCKER WILL BRIEF
YOU CONCERNING ORDERS
FORTHCOMING FROM THIS
COMMAND.

The Man of War Anchorage, as the historic site was officially labeled on the navigational charts of Singapore harbor, lay just east of the downtown marina. The *Decatur* moored there, and from the flight deck on the fantail Stewart had a breathtaking view of the city's skyline. White concrete and glass blocks, trapezoids, towers, and cylinders, some layered and frosted like wedding cakes, reflected back the setting sun against a rose-hued tropical sky. It was a surreal, futuristic skyline that announced not Asia but the twenty-first century.

"What *the* hell is this all about?" the executive officer asked for the third time.

"You read the dispatch. You know as much as I do." Stewart heard the edge in his own voice and immediately regretted it. Directly in Stewart's line of sight was a gleaming cylinder of lights, the seventy-three-story Westin Stamford, the tallest hotel in the world. He pointed at it. "If we ever get ashore, I'll buy you a drink at the top," Stewart volunteered. "And a Singapore Sling at the bottom. That's where the old Raffles Hotel is, probably the most famous landmark in Singapore. I always go there to pay homage."

Robinson seemed startled by the invitation; Stewart had extended it as an apology for his surly temper. "Pay homage to what?" the XO asked.

"The Singapore Sling. That's where it was invented. Without it my sex life would probably have been delayed for years."

Robinson's laugh was rich and reverberating. "Amazing. We have that in common. My wife, she still collects those little umbrellas when we go out."

Stewart fell silent again. He stared toward the marina entrance, the direction from which the helicopter should be returning from the American embassy. Directly in his line of sight, deeper inside the city, was another tower, a giant pagoda about half as tall as the Westin Stamford. The four flat, angled sides facing the harbor suggested that the building was actually a hexagon, crowned by a startling, green-tiled pagoda roof with

183

a round red ball at its apex.

"The crew's pissed," the XO said. "This was supposed to be their first real liberty in months."

Once again it was as if Stewart did not hear him. He shook his head and made a sweeping gesture that embraced the skyline. "None of this existed in '69."

"You were here in '69?"

Stewart nodded. "Flew down here on R and R for a week." He fell silent again. He could remember every beer, the face and silken feel of each girl, the pungent taste of each stick of *satay*.

"Good times?"

"We thought it was going to be the last good time we'd ever have. For most it was. Our outfit had 70 percent casualties."

"Jesus!"

Stewart checked his watch again and peered through his binoculars, trying to pick up the returning Seahawk chopper. The *Decatur* was the only military vessel in the anchorage. All about the frigate were supertankers and giant container ships waiting their turn to move into the terminals, where great pumps and motorized cranes would suck out their cargoes in an automated assembly line. But Stewart's interest was in the rusty, scummy tramps, their overloaded decks almost awash, that plowed with ragtag crews between Singapore and Borneo, Surabaya, Palembang, and Makassar, hauling cargoes of lumber, rice, papayas, durians, and diesel generators that would not fill a container. He watched intently as a crane swung out and lowered its teeming cargo net into a flat-bottomed barge alongside the tramp.

Suddenly Stewart's binoculars focused on a Chinese junk, its two sails of woven straw close hauled to trap the east wind, beating across the harbor. The brightly painted red and green prow, made fierce by yellow and black dragon's eyes, cut under the looming bow of a container vessel riding at anchor. He smiled at the anachronism until he discerned the crowd in tropical shirts with drinks in hand on the raised poop deck. It was a twilight cocktail cruise for tourists.

Behind the junk, moving in fast, was the returning Seahawk. "Here come our mysterious messengers," Stewart said and handed the binoculars to Robinson.

The helicopter banked to circle the frigate once and then swooped down toward the stern, dropping to the deck in a slow, hovering descent. The first man out of the bird was a civilian, who jumped awkwardly to the deck and peered all about with great curiosity. He was immediately followed by the familiar figure of a short, stocky officer in short-sleeved khakis. The bulky survival belt that he wore only emphasized "Plug" Campbell's chunky build.

Both men immediately unhooked and shed their heavy life vests laden with breathing apparatus, flashlights, and flares and handed them to the helicopter's crewman. Then the civilian meticulously unfolded and donned a seersucker suit coat and adjusted his tie. He was a big man, as tall as Stewart but barrel-chested as a pro tackle.

"The suit is a spook," Stewart shouted into Robinson's ear over the deafening whine of the Seahawk's twin turbines, then immediately strode out to greet his visitors. "Welcome aboard, Captain. Mr. Blocker."

Plug Campbell returned Stewart's salute smartly and grinned back at him, but behind the smile his eyes searched Stewart's face. Then he seized the outstretched hand and gripped it fiercely. "It's goddamn good to see you, Henry."

Robinson escorted the civilian through the centerline passageway between the two hangars and up to the captain's cabin. Stewart and Campbell had stopped to talk in the passageway. The executive officer glanced back. The short senior officer had his hand on Stewart's shoulder, an odd, confidential, almost comforting gesture, which appeared all the more awkward because of the Mutt and Jeff disparity in their heights.

Stewart had not mentioned to Robinson beforehand that he and Campbell were old friends. He must have recognized the name on the dispatch. Damn it all, the man always kept things from him. And what had Stewart meant by his remark that the suit was CIA? The XO turned to the big man striding along next to him. "What do you do at the embassy, Mr. Blocker?" he asked in a hearty, guileless voice.

"Political affairs officer."

That sounded spooky enough. "Been aboard this class of guided-missile frigate before?"

"No, I haven't."

"This is the state of the art. I'll be happy to take you on a tour, if there's time afterward."

"I'm afraid there won't be."

No apologies, no rain check, no conversation — just no time. So much for the pleasantries. Robinson kept quiet until he ushered the big man into Stewart's cabin. Endicott, a clean-cut kid who had mess duty in the wardroom, was standing by in a starched white jacket.

Robinson watched the spook curiously survey the cabin, as if he were taking a reading of Stewart from the artifacts there. He would find few clues. There were the wood-framed lithographs of eighteenth- and early-nineteenth-century sailing frigates and men-of-war that decorated the wardroom, as if the commanding officer were deliberately trying to instill the guided-missile frigate with a more ancient tradition. But there were no pictures of Stewart's wife or a family.

Stewart and Campbell came in after a minute, and the captain gestured everyone to take seats at the round table in the center of the stateroom.

As soon as he was seated, Campbell cast a baleful eye at Robinson. *"Charlie Robinson,"* he pronounced, as though naming the accused. "I lost a year's sea pay on the '77 Army-Navy game."

The executive officer shook his head in sympathy. "Yes, sir, I figure the navy could finance another frigate with the money lost when that fourth-down pass was batted down in the end zone. We all just hope by the time our class comes up for selection to commander that inflation will make the losses look *a lot* smaller."

Everyone around the table laughed. They were making conversation while the mess man poured out tall glasses of iced tea, garnished with green sprigs.

"There's hot coffee on the chest there, if anyone prefers," Stewart offered. "But that's as strong a drink as we're allowed to have aboard without a doctor's prescription."

The last comment was for the benefit of Blocker, who was sniffing the sprig. "Fresh mint," he identified with a note of pleasure in his voice.

"The supply officer picked up a few bunches in Songkhla," Stewart explained. The mint was another of his Southern gentleman mannerisms that set Robinson's teeth on edge.

"What were you doing *there?*" Blocker asked.

"A joint exercise with the Thais." Stewart turned to the mess man. "That'll be all, thank you, Endicott." He followed the mess man to the door, locked it behind him, turned back, and stared directly at Blocker, who spoke first.

"We have a hostage situation, and your ship is the only American ship in the area, actually our only military asset. Others are being scrambled, but . . ." Blocker shrugged his shoulders indecisively.

"There are a few problems — clearances with the local governments, security — that have to be cleared up," Campbell explained with an edge of frustration in his voice. "Subic Bay is our closest base in the area."

There was a moment of silence during which Robinson glanced in confusion at Stewart, who nodded as if he understood exactly what the hell was going on.

"What's the situation precisely?" Stewart asked.

"We believe a passenger liner with 135 American citizens aboard . . . 134 now . . . has been captured by terrorists. But it's a faction we've never heard of before. The picture is still muddled."

"Where's the ship now?"

Blocker shook his head. "We don't know. It left Singapore the night before last, and no one has heard a word from it since — as far as we know."

"What flag is the liner?"

"That's one of the complications, Henry," Campbell said. "It's Russian. To be frank, there's a lot of information we don't have yet. We just got hit with it this morning, and new intel is coming in every minute. The shit has really hit the fan in Washington, and we're still going back and forth on what to do."

"Do you think the Russians are working with the terrorists?"

Blocker shook his head. "That scenario

190

doesn't make any sense."

"Are you in communication with the ship or the terrorists at all?"

"No, but they've communicated with us . . . *very persuasively,*" Blocker said in a low, ominous tone. "They dropped off the head of one of the American passengers at a luxury hotel in the heart of Singapore last night."

"The head!" Robinson was genuinely shocked.

"Hacked off, bloody stump and all," Blocker exclaimed. "They did everything but stick it up on a spike. They left it right on a table at the hotel's sidewalk cafe. But they left the guy's passport in a neat little plastic bag so we'd be sure to know who it was, his nationality, and have a photograph to verify his identity, along with his ship boarding pass."

"Jesus!" Robinson looked at Stewart. The CO stared at Blocker, but his eyes seemed vague, as if he were looking through the man at some scene in the distance. "What ship was it?" Robinson asked.

"The *Black Sea,*" Stewart answered.

Both Blocker and the naval attaché were startled. "How the hell did you know that?" Blocker demanded.

"We received an Emergency Notice to

Mariners that the ship was missing."

Robinson had forgotten about the dispatch. "You get it this morning?"

"No, yesterday."

Blocker was out of his seat. "But the head was found last night. We only got the terrorists' demands in the embassy's morning's mail."

Stewart rose, went to his desk, and flipped through his message board. "What do they want?"

Blocker exchanged a look with Campbell. "For the moment I'm afraid that's classified."

"But you've received definite demands from them?"

"A long shopping list." Blocker's voice again assumed a gruff, ominous tone. "Along with a read-out of the ship's passenger list with the name of the head crossed out."

Stewart found the Notice to Mariners, unhooked it, and handed it to Blocker. "This probably went out when the ship didn't make a scheduled position report." He said the last as much to the naval attaché, as if looking for confirmation. "Each line has its own procedures. You might check with the Port of Singapore Authority why they sent this out."

Campbell nodded. "Look, Henry, we have no other resources on the scene yet, and no senior operational commander has been designated. You're *it*."

Stewart nodded. "How much can I tell the crew?"

"Why do you have to tell them anything?" Blocker challenged.

"Because we've been at sea for seven months, and they're straining at the bit to get home. I've got two men who haven't seen their babies that were born during the deployment, six young married men who are worried sick their wives are screwing around on them, and another dozen who haven't received any mail at all. And now the crew's one real liberty in all that time has just been canceled. An explanation is required, because unless I'm reading the signal flags all wrong, our scheduled arrival in the continental United States has just been indefinitely postponed." It was as long and impassioned a speech as Robinson had ever heard Stewart make.

The naval attaché held up both hands as if pleading a case. "Henry, *we* don't even know what's going down yet, let alone how to classify it. Use your best judgment on a need-to-know basis. Until you hear differently, report directly to ComSeventhFleet."

Robinson was totally in the dark. "Report what, Captain? What are our orders?"

Campbell stared at the executive officer

as if he were an idiot, then said in a soft voice, "Find the *Black Sea* and stop those crazies, whoever the hell they are, from lopping off any more heads."

15. *The Fanatic*

The dark bumboat, one of the thousands that peddled provisions and taxied passengers among the vessels at anchor in Singapore harbor, slid to a landing on the south side of Clifford Pier. A half dozen cracked and bald automobile tires hanging along the side silenced its bumping. A young Malay sprang off the boat and scrambled up the short ladder. A stuffed shopping bag hung from his shoulder by a cord handle, freeing his hands for the climb.

A few berths away a platoon of tourists — Americans, Japanese, and Australians — disembarked from a Chinese junk after their dinner cruise. The Malay stared with fearful eyes at the foreigners noisily trooping down the gangway, then he scurried off the pier and plunged into the evening crowd strolling along Collyer Quay Road.

The side-by-side white towers of the Bank

of East Asia Building, Singapore Rubber House, Shell Tower, Asia Insurance, Straits Trading, Far East Finance, and Bank of China which walled in the marina were dark, but the street-level shops, the arcades, the money changers of Change Alley, and the Old Market were gaudy with lights. The Malay in his short-sleeved batik shirt, cheap cotton slacks, and running shoes appeared, at first glance, to be just another shopper with a parcel. He glanced about nervously, peering into the crowd, his head swiveling right and left, and then he whirled on his heels to look behind.

Back by the crosswalk onto Clifford Pier he spotted a blue uniform with the distinctive white cross-chest belting of the Singapore police. But the policeman was busy directing the flow of pedestrians. The Malay hitched the heavy bag onto his shoulder to ease the weight and moved deeper into the stream of late-evening strollers along the quay.

It was cooler here at night — the air stirred with the China Sea breezes — than in the sweltering concrete blocks of government-financed apartments in which 80 percent of Singapore now lived. Despite the relative cool, the Malay sweated noticeably, his taut brown face gleaming in the electric street-lights. He impatiently bobbed along in the crowd toward Merlion Park, the point where the tepid, narrow Singapore River flowed into the bay. Along the marina and the river were several of the city's popular outdoor food centers, sprawling gastronomic bazaars where hawkers hustled the specialties of a hundred cramped, steaming stalls, and the odors spiced the air.

Food was the furthest thing from the Malay's mind. A dank, dark stain now soaked the bottom of the sack, thumping against his hip, and flies flitted about it. The flies terrified the Malay, who was certain everyone around him heard their ominous buzzing. The rank carrion stench, which had grown stronger during the prolonged hot boat ride, assailed his nostrils, making him gag, and he now elbowed his way through the jam of people, desperately trying to flee the flies and the terrible smell.

The road jogged to the left, spanning the Singapore River across Anderson Bridge. To the right a lion's head on a fish's body spouted water into the spot where the river poured into the harbor, as if the fantastic creature were the source of both waters. Brilliant spotlights gave the long, scaly body, the great maned head, and the jet of water an iridescent golden hue.

The Malay's orders were to leave the package here at the Merlion monument. But if there were police or too many people about, he was simply to keep walking over Anderson Bridge. This was the historic heart of the city. Just on the other side of the bridge was the bronze statue of Sir Stamford Raffles, on the spot where he had first stepped ashore in 1819 to found an East India Company trading post. A few meters beyond that were Parliament House, the Supreme Court, and the City Hall. The Malay might leave his package at any one of these sites.

But he was eager to be rid of it as quickly as possible. It was a rotting abomination, and as a fastidiously clean and devout man, the Malay was sickened by the garbage stink of it that he feared might never wash off. The stench was an evil spirit, a ghost that hovered about him wailing, unheard in this crowd but screaming nevertheless, if anyone listened closely. He was more terrified of it than of the police.

Merlion Park was a small point of land jutting into the bay. There were only a handful of people — Chinese and Malay couples, lovers, and a few big-nosed tourists — gazing out at the lights of the ships at anchor. No one was looking at him or the Merlion stone chimera. Above his head the great curled fish body rose up out of carved rock waves.

The Malay feverishly unshouldered his package and, holding it by the rope strap, heaved it up onto the high granite base of the monument. It smacked against the stone with the sickening sound of meat and bone being crushed. The Malay whirled to flee.

"Stop! Halt right there. This is the police."

He spun toward the voice. A young Chinese man in civilian clothes emerged from the crowd on the quay and trotted toward him. As he came he reached into the pocket of his shirt and brought out a whistle.

The Malay was paralyzed. The one thing he had been warned not to let happen was happening. His feet were mired fast by his overwhelming shame. He had failed abjectly in his mission. The piercing blast of the policeman's whistle sounded like the scream of demons in his head.

"What's in the bag?" The plainclothes policeman was now next to him.

The Malay reached under his batik shirt, grasped the bone handle of the dirk in his belt, and in one quick sweep, like the swipe of a cat's paw, jabbed the blade into the policeman's stomach.

The second whistle blast was cut off in an agonized gasp.

The Malay bolted. Now the people on the quay all stopped and stared at him, then fell back and flailed their arms to get out of his way. He ran blindly into the crowd. The people parted right and left, creating a path for him through frightened, astonished faces. But behind, like the scream of pursuing demons, a whistle sputtered, then shrieked out in full cry after him.

A man suddenly stepped out in front of him. For an instant the streetlight gleamed on the yellow bamboo baton, then it blurred into a flashing bolt that exploded across the Malay's eyes.

> *What is a good man*
> *but a bad man's teacher?*
> *What is a bad man*
> *but a good man's job?*
> *If you don't understand this,*
> *you will get lost,*
> *however intelligent you are.*
> *It is the great secret.*

Yee contemplated this verse from the *Tao Te Ching* as he studied the Malay. The doctor finished strapping the bandage across the smashed brown face, then handed the man two pills and a cup of water. "Swallow these," he ordered in a soft voice.

The Malay did as he was told.

"How do you feel?"

"I thought I was going to wake up in Paradise." There was a grieved, woeful expression in the Malay's voice and in his eyes, as though he were about to break down into tears of disappointment.

"He has to take two of these pills every three hours," the doctor said to Yee.

"I'm not concerned about his headache."

"He has a concussion. The pills will keep down the swelling and prevent a blood clot." The doctor's voice was mechanical, as if he realized that a concussion, broken nose, and blackened eyes were to be the least of his patient's injuries before the night was over.

The Malay sat stark naked on a low, backless wooden stool. His hands were cuffed behind him. To one side of him stood a light-skinned Sikh, a strongly built man whose dark turban, hawk's beak of a nose, and orthodox uncut black beard gave him a fierce appearance. He held a thick rattan baton, which he impatiently beat against his meaty left palm. It bothered Yee that the Malay was not frightened by Sergeant Govind.

Yee escorted the doctor, a young Chinese in his first post after medical school, to the cell door. "Please stay in your office. We will need you." Yee made no effort to lower his voice.

The young man glared at him. "I'm a

doctor. I save lives, not destroy them."

"So do I save lives," Yee snapped. "Yours, your pretty wife's, your new baby's. If you had to choose between *their* lives and *his,* doctor, would you hesitate to cut out this cancer, shrivel him with chemicals, burn him with radiation to save your family?"

The young doctor's eyes went wide. "What's this all about?" he whispered.

"Please be in your office so that I can reach you quickly." He shut the cell door in the young doctor's astonished face.

Yee walked back to the Malay and flipped on the compact Japanese cassette recorder on the table. "What is your name?"

The Malay stared back at him, silent. There was no fear in his eyes, just a dull despair. To one side, within his arm's reach, Sergeant Govind stood rhythmically beating his truncheon against his hand like a metronome ticking off the time the Malay had to answer.

Yee felt the chill and incipient nausea in his own stomach. It was going to be a very difficult interrogation. "We need to know your name," Yee said in a not unfriendly voice. "You may die here. If you do, we will notify your mother and father, your family. That much I give you my word we will do, if you tell us your name and where you are from."

The Malay grunted, lowered his head, and was silent a moment. "I am Abdullah bin Taib. My father is Taib bin Munir."

"Where are you from?"

The Malay was again silent.

"Are you from Singapore? We will not punish your family for your crimes. I promise you will pay enough for your own crimes."

Abdullah Taib did not raise his head. "My father lives in Kuala Selatan. He is a fisherman."

Kuala Selatan was a fishing *kampong* on the coast of Malaysia, north of Singapore. The man was a Malaysian national. That would create diplomatic problems, but Yee would deal with those later.

He walked around behind the Malay. "Are you a fisherman, too?"

"I have worked on my father's boat."

Yee knelt and seized the manacled hands. He carefully examined the palms and fingers, lightly running his own smooth fingertips over them. The hands were strong and calloused, but the callouses were all healed, soft, not the cracked, dry, horn-hard flesh of a fisherman who hauled saltwater-soaked nets and lines from the sea every day of his life. "It has been a very long time, years, since you worked on your father's boat," Yee said. "What are you doing now?"

There was silence, punctuated by the menacing tattoo of Govind's baton.

Yee walked around to face the young Malay. He looked to be in his early twenties. "Are you a student?"

The Malay kept his eyes down and said nothing.

Yee nodded to the Sikh.

The rattan cane whooshed as it whipped down and cut into the bare brown back and pinioned arms. The Malay screamed and pitched forward on his face onto the concrete floor, unable to break the fall with his hands tied behind him.

Yee felt his stomach heave and the acid surge to his throat. He clamped his teeth hard and motioned brusquely to Sergeant Govind.

The Sikh grabbed the fallen man's arms and painfully jerked him back onto the stool, almost dislocating his shoulders. The Malay screamed again and sat hunched over, his head almost in his lap.

"What are you doing now?" Yee repeated the question.

Slowly the Malay raised his head. The mouth was now bloodied and smashed from hurling into the floor, and blood stained the bandage holding the already broken nose in place. The brown eyes were blackened and swollen into slits, but gleamed oddly at Yee. "God's work," the Malay croaked.

"And what is God's work?"

Abdullah Taib was silent, his body braced for the next blow. He had no intention of answering further.

Yee glanced at Sergeant Govind. The big Sikh did not move. The expected blow did not come. A second passed. Two. Three. Yee saw the Malay's shoulders relax. At that instant the rattan cane whipped, the prisoner screamed and crashed face first into the floor.

Sergeant Govind was not a sadist, but he was a hardened, experienced jailer. Once again he savagely yanked the Malay back onto the stool by his bound arms, causing him to cry out.

This time the Malay's head came up. The bloody, swollen mouth was set, and the dark, nearly shut eyes shone at Yee, strangely triumphant, as if Abdullah Taib were winning whatever terrible contest was going on.

Yee was confused. He looked at the Sikh, who shook his head. They might beat him to death, but the Malay would not break this way.

Yee motioned the burly jailer to the door to talk to him outside the cell, leaving the Malay perched stark naked and bleeding on the wooden stool. As Yee opened the door,

Abdullah Taib muttered something.

"What did you say?" Yee moved closer.

The Malay moved his bloody lips, painfully forming the words, "Which way is west?"

Yee was astonished at the question. "West? Which way is west?" he repeated. And then it hit him with the clarity of a lightning flash, suddenly illuminating what was right before his eyes.

"There is no west here," he said fiercely, his voice shaking. "There is no east, no sunrise, no noon, no sunset. There is no way to Mecca from here. You are deep in *hell*. And we are going to bury you deeper, so deep God cannot hear you. He cannot see you. But we will *not* kill you. We will *not* let you die. We will keep you alive. We will let you rot here in hell for ten years, twenty years, forty years. And by then our doctors will find a way to keep you alive another *hundred* years. You will never, never see Paradise."

For the first time since the man's capture Yee saw fear in his eyes, a deep, primordial fear that pierced beyond the mere clinging to life and cut into the man's soul. The recognition of it sickened Yee, more than the brutal beating had.

He left the cell. Outside he spoke to Sergeant Govind. "He *wants* us to beat him to death. Each blow makes him a martyr. We are sending him to Paradise."

The Sikh nodded thoughtfully. "Ah, yes, he is a fanatic. Cutting off heads. But what is this all about I am wondering, sir?"

"God's work, he says."

Sergeant Govind grunted, a harsh, emphatic sound. "This is sometimes a very terrible thing, God's work. I am knowing it very fully, sir. Muslims doing God's work on Hindus with fire and sword. And Hindus doing God's work back on Muslims. Then both Muslims and Hindus making same devotions to Sikhs. This is truly a very terrible thing when fanatics do God's work."

"We have to find out *what* this is all about."

"What do you want to do with him, sir?"

"Put him immediately in the padded cell for violent prisoners so that he can't hurt himself."

"Ah, yes, number seven."

"Keep a light on. Don't let him know whether it's day or night or what the time of day is. Feed him at odd hours. Never, never let him know what the hour of prayer is."

The Sikh let out a soft, lowing sound of exclamation. "Oooh, this fellow will go crazy, being a fanatic."

"And don't give him water to wash. Or

toilet paper. I want him to feel *unclean*."

"Oh, yes, indeed, this plan being crueler than my baton."

At that hour the lavatory of the Central Police Station was empty. Yee washed his face and then let the cold water run across his wrists, cooling his blood, restoring his *yang*, bringing him into harmony. He had to be in balance when he briefed the minister.

Beatings were always hot-blooded, emotional affairs — pain, fear, anger. The dark side. The *yin*. The Singapore penal code prescribed not less than six strokes of the cane for robbery committed during daylight, but not less than twelve strokes for robbery committed after 7 P.M. and before 7 A.M., and fifteen strokes for trafficking in opium in a quantity of not more than 1,200 grams. In any one case no more than twenty-four strokes might be awarded by the judge or magistrate, and the rattan used for caning should not be more than 1.27 centimeters in diameter. The punishment for trafficking in more than 1,200 grams of opium or for murder was death. A man sentenced to death could not, by law, be caned. Thus order and balance were maintained in the very modern, prosperous city-state of Singapore.

Singapore was not a police state, but it

was a very well policed state. A visiting official from Los Angeles had once told Yee that there was no crime in Singapore. It was statistically insignificant, compared to crime figures for American cities.

But the interrogations were another matter. The Internal Security Act allowed the government to jail indefinitely, without trial, anyone it suspected of being a threat to Singapore's peace. This was the area of chaos beyond the law, the violent shadow world beyond the balancing of *yin* and *yang*, where the wise man had to tread very carefully or else chaos would overwhelm him.

Yee turned off the tap and carefully dried his hands and face. He was ready to coolly brief the minister on what he now knew. He did not yet dare tell him what he feared.

Part V
The Parameswara Jihad

16. Who Will Be Released Next?

Maggi did not know Mrs. Clarence Murdock of Houston, Texas, but apparently Mrs. Murdock knew who she was and was waiting for her at the foot of the stairs leading to the dining room, as Maggi headed for breakfast.

"Maggi, dear, may I have a word with you?" She was a heavy woman in her fifties, beefy in the way a once voluptuous young woman, now self-indulgent in middle age, thickens in the breast and hips.

"I'm a widow, dear, traveling alone, and I'm not really up to all this," she launched in immediately after an introduction that assumed Maggi *should* know who she was. "I'm afraid I have a rather serious heart condition." She touched her left breast with a delicacy of which Maggi would have thought the chunky hand incapable. "The doctor, of course, told me to lose all this weight, but then food and travel are the few pleasures I have left since Clarence died."

There was a respectful pause for Clarence's memory. Maggi jumped into it. "What can I do for you, Mrs. Murdock?"

Mrs. Murdock smiled. "Mr. Murdock and I were very good friends of the President . . . well, I guess I still am. Clarence was a very substantial fund raiser for his campaign." She held her smile, as if it were exuding some power of the presidency over Maggi.

"Yes?"

"I understand y'all are in charge of releasing the passengers."

"No, I'm not. Where did you hear that? I'm a hostage, just like you. And I don't know why."

"Why, we're being held until their people are released from jail for being terrorists somewhere or other."

Maggi was astonished. "Where did you hear that?"

"That's what everyone is saying. That's what they always do."

"Who's *they?* Where are you getting this information?"

"The terrorists, isn't that what they're doing?"

"I don't know."

"Well, y'all are friendly with them."

"I'm not *friendly* with them, as you put it. I speak their language, Bahasa, and I'm just trying to help prevent any problems. When you have desperate men with guns pointing at you, a simple misunderstanding might turn into a disaster. We saw that on the deck the other day."

"It looks like y'all are very cozy with them."

The word *cozy* took on an obscene innuendo in Mrs. Murdock's East Texas drawl.

"What *exactly* do you want, Mrs. Murdock?"

"I want to get off this damn ship!"

"We all want off this ship right now."

"But I'm not well, and y'all are releasing sick people. That's true, I know it." Mrs. Murdock looked strong enough to bust broncos.

"I don't have anything to say about it."

"But y'all have *influence* with that head terrorist. I can see that, a nice-looking young girl like you."

Maggi was furious. She whirled to leave, but Mrs. Murdock seized her arm. She had a grip like a cattle wrangler.

"You know, honey, we're going to be rescued, and then, mark my words, y'all are going to need all the friends you can get. Being a collaborator with these terrorists."

"Take your goddamn hand off me."

Mrs. Murdock pulled back at the anger in her voice. Maggi burst through the doors into the dining room. As soon as she entered, a current seemed to pass through the breakfast eaters. A few looked up, whispered to the people at their table, and in a moment all eyes in the dining room were fixed on her. From their expressions — a tentative smile here and there from people she had not met, a frown of suspicion, a measuring glance of curiosity — she suddenly realized that the other passengers on board all shared Mrs. Murdock's view of her position. The fury she had felt at the woman suddenly abated, and now Maggi felt an acute embarrassment. Keeping her eyes averted, she made her way to the table where the Schneiders were having breakfast.

She sat down and whispered fiercely to Schneider, "My God, they all think I'm some sort of collaborator who can get them released."

"In fact we're counting on it," Liz Schneider whispered back.

"What?" Maggi stared at her and then at Schneider, who looked levelly at her and said nothing. "I can't do anything like that."

"It's his heart," Liz Schneider confided in a low, persuasive voice. "The brave dear, you wouldn't think it to look at him, but his robust appearance is a fragile facade. This is his last fling before triple bypass surgery, as soon as we return home."

Maggi regarded Liz Schneider with amazement.

Schneider smiled and patted his wife's hand. "I think we'd better get some of the more obviously sick and frail off the ship first, or else we'll raise their suspicions immediately and put Maggi here in danger." He turned back to her. "I've discussed this with Captain Khromykh and the ship's doctor. We have to agree to some sort of procedure among ourselves, so that we can exercise more control . . . through you, of course." He made a bow of his head toward Maggi, acknowledging her link in the chain of command. Schneider, as a former Secretary of State, appeared to have automatically assumed the mantle of leadership for the American passengers.

"Do you have someone specific in mind?"

Schneider nodded. "A Mr. Garrity, a retired executive. He indeed has had a double bypass operation this year. He is stable now, but the doctor would be happier if he were off the ship." Schneider made a discreet nod. "He is the rather fat man two tables away, facing us."

Mr. Garrity was an overweight, florid-faced Irishman with a shock of white hair; he was attacking his ham and eggs with a gusto that denied his mortality and cholesterol

215

count. Next to him a thin, weary-looking woman watched him eat with apprehension, then suddenly glanced up and stared directly at Maggi. Maggi turned back to Schneider.

"In any event the captain wants to speak to you as soon as you've had your breakfast. He's in the doctor's office."

"Captain Khromykh?"

"In a situation like this the captain of the ship is the final authority," Schneider said, reading the question in her voice. "The terrorists are outlaws. It's important for our survival to maintain our normal chains of authority, at least as long as we can." He indicated with a nod the dining room, where the waitresses in white ruffled peasant blouses and scarlet doublets were serving breakfast as though it were a routine meal. The only extraordinary presences in the room were the two pirates who lounged by the door, smoking sweet-scented *kreteks,* one cradling an M16 and the other a Russian AK-47 assault rifle in his arm. Maggi noted that all the diners were still in their seats, intently watching their table, especially Mrs. Clarence Murdock. Even the guards were eyeing them with a lazy suspicion, but they were focused on Maggi.

She practically bolted from the table. The doctor's office was on the same deck as the dining room, but there was no direct access, so Maggi first had to climb up to the promenade deck, walk forward, and then descend back down to the main deck. She worked up a head of steam en route. She had been thrust into an impossible situation. Let someone else be their translator, their go-between, whatever the hell it was she was supposed to be doing.

"There *is* no one else, Professor Chancellor," Captain Khromykh's heavily accented voice rumbled across the doctor's littered desk. "It is extraordinary, no? I have very well trained crew, who travels around the world more times than I can count. Speak dozen languages. And very distinguished passengers, much educated, much traveled. We are on cruise through beautiful tropical islands with strange customs, strange language. How many peoples speak this language?" he suddenly interrogated Maggi.

Maggi was surprised by the question. "I don't know. Between Indonesia, Malaysia, and Singapore over two hundred million."

"Aaach," Captain Khromykh nodded emphatically. "But you, professor, are only one aboard who speaks this strange language, knows customs of peoples. Why? That is *your* position on *Black Sea,* your *responsibility.* Yes, that I think is correct word in English, is it not? My *responsibility* is safety of all peoples aboard this ship, passengers and crew. Dr. Yakovlev," the captain nodded to the other officer with him, in a white uniform with shoulder boards, "his responsibility is *health* of all peoples aboard. Our responsibilities do not end, professor, because ship is commandeered by terrorists. No, no, they are more heavy, very more heavy. That is the way, the *law* of civilized peoples. And you do your responsibility also."

Captain Khromykh's English was thick-tongued, but the grave authority with which he spoke made his meaning, if not always the individual words, absolutely clear. Maggi was taken aback by his speech. She felt she had become the liaison with their captors merely by the chance of circumstance, but now the Russian officer was insisting that it was not only her professional obligation but her legal duty by some law of the sea she did not quite fathom.

"I understand the leader, Tengku, has asked for your suggestions on which prisoners to release next," Dr. Yakovlev addressed her. His English was excellent, flavored with a Slavic purr that, along with his peppery-gray Vandyke, gave him an immediate air of Old Worldliness.

"So far he's released a sick old man, a

Mr. Benjamin, and, I believe, a Russian crew-man who was wounded by the pirates," Maggi said.

Dr. Yakovlev nodded. "Then this Tengku shouldn't be suspicious of any recommendations you make on the grounds of health."

Captain Khromykh nodded his head vigorously. "Yes, yes, but I have much . . . fear for safety of Mr. Secretary Schneider. If terrorists know he is . . ." Khromykh shrugged his shoulders, implying unimaginable horrors by his uncompleted thought.

"There seems to be a lot of heart trouble going around suddenly," Maggi suggested.

Only the doctor laughed. "I had a long queue at my office yesterday and early this morning. They all want a letter from the doctor to the terrorists stating they are very sick and should be released immediately."

Khromykh asked him something in Russian. The doctor shook his head and responded at some length, then turned back to Maggi. "None of the passengers are seriously ill. Several, of course, are older and have conditions that require medication. They cannot stand too much stress. Perhaps they should be released first."

"What about the alternating Russian crew members?" Maggi asked.

"Captain Khromykh and I have discussed

this," Yakovlev answered. "We have no health problems. We will make choices on other humanitarian grounds. Those with families, children, who are not essential to running the ship and caring for the passengers."

"If the pirates agree to it," Maggi said.

"That, of course, is your . . . responsibility." Dr. Yakovlev's mouth twisted in an ironic smile. "You have their trust, and you must cultivate them all you can."

"Have you talked to Tengku?" Maggi asked Khromykh.

The Russian gave her a strange, sardonic smile and nodded. "He hold sword *here*," he jabbed a finger into his own throat, "and say take ship here, do this, do that, feed passengers. My English, bad; his English, very bad. I don't understand him, and I think he cut my throat many times." He made a slicing motion with his hand.

Maggi realized that it was the terrorized captain who had had to navigate the ship up the river. "Where are we now?"

"In an uncharted river on an island off Sumatra," a vaguely familiar voice behind her answered.

Surprised, Maggi turned to find Vladimir Korsakov, the young blond officer from the bridge, a thick bandage across his slashed cheek, standing behind her.

17. At the White House

The admiral had served a tour in the Persian Gulf, and he knew a minefield when he saw one. The White House Situation Room was definitely a minefield with unstable, politically planted high explosives lurking beneath the choppy surface waiting to blow him out of the water. Several of the flannel-suited men about the long mahogany table, such as the national security adviser and the Secretary of Defense, were anchored mines; the admiral had their positions on the seabed charted. Others, like the President's contentious chief of staff and the head of the Central Intelligence Agency, drifted about just below the surface, and they might pop up at any time and blow a hole in his bow unless he kept a very sharp lookout.

It was the Secretary of State, who was mysteriously absent at the moment, that he had to keep checking on sonar. He was anchored for now, but if the weather got very rough, he might break loose from his moorings and suddenly turn into a hard-to-spot drifter that would sink him.

The door swung open and the lanky figure of the President, his forehead deeply furrowed and the flesh of his face haggard, the symptoms of sleepless nights, suddenly strode into the room, holding a black leather attaché case. At his right hand was the Secretary of State, undoubtedly no less exhausted, but the brushed silver hair and patrician features gave his shadow-eyed fatigue a distinguished look.

The nine men around the long table suddenly jumped up, breaking off the heated arguments that had been volleying back and forth and up and down the table.

The President placed the attaché case on the table and motioned with both hands. "Gentlemen, please be seated. I apologize for keeping you all waiting." He wearily eased into the chair at the head of the table, as though his bones ached, although the admiral had seen him loping about a tennis court the previous Sunday.

A beat later the Secretary of State took the empty seat at the President's right. It was State from whom the others took their lead. He had been the President's confidant, hunting companion, and campaign manager for over thirty years, through humiliations and triumphs. In Washington, where opportunism was revered, the Secretary of State was regarded with awe.

"The Secretary of State and I have just

been meeting with the Russian ambassador, trying to sort out this thing," the President began immediately. "As you know, yesterday we informed the Soviet General Secretary that we held *their* government totally responsible for the lives and safety of our citizens aboard that ship of theirs. Well, the first thing this morning — what time is it now? — their ambassador requested an immediate audience with myself and the Secretary here. He's conveyed to us information — I guess it's top secret or something, because our embassy and agents in Singapore sure didn't tell us about it," he noted in a querulous voice and looked directly at the CIA director. The glance was not an admonition but a signal to take notice.

"Three nights ago . . ." The President waved both hands in small circles, as if groping. "I haven't worked out the exact chronology here, because of the International Date Line, but about that time, the remains — oh, heck, I might as well say it — the *head* of one of the Russian officers aboard the *Black Sea* was found in Singapore. It's horrible, just horrible, no doubt about it. The next morning the Russian ambassador there received, in the mail mind you, a list of demands, uh, just like we did."

He clicked open the attaché case and with-

223

drew several sheets of paper. "It's in English. We've looked it over briefly. We're not arms experts, of course, but it looks like it's essentially a similar shopping list to the one we got, except that here they want the Russian models." He handed the papers to the man at his left, the chairman of the National Security Council.

The President continued to stare at the sheaf of papers as if they held a peculiar horror, then looked up, shook his head, and grimaced. "Last night, and again I'm not sure of the time differential here, another . . . it's just horrible . . . another head of one of the Russian crewmen was dropped off in Singapore. I guess it's to underline that these guys, whoever the hell they are, mean business."

"Jesus Christ!" someone at the far end of the table exclaimed.

The President nodded. "I don't mean to be facetious, but — ah, I was just telling the Secretary of State — it appears that we and the Russians are in the same boat."

"How do we know they're telling us the truth?"

"The President and I kicked around that possibility walking over here," the Secretary of State responded. "Can anyone come up with a scenario to their advantage? It's their ship, their embarrassment."

"And our people being held hostage and murdered."

"And theirs, too."

The director of the CIA leaned forward. "I'll have my people check about the Russian . . . victims. The Singapore authorities didn't tell us about them," he added with an angry, betrayed note in his voice.

"And we didn't tell Singapore there was a ransom demand," the Secretary of State noted.

"I'd like to tell you we have all the facts, but . . ." The President looked sharply at the director of the CIA. "Do we even know whom we're dealing with here yet? — I mean, your briefing paper was pretty thin here — who these terrorists, or whatever, are?"

The director of the CIA shook his head. "We've got a lot of lines out there. But all we have at the moment is the name on the ransom letter, the Parameswara Jihad. We've drawn a total blank on that. There's not a byte in the computers on them. We're checking right now with other intelligence agencies and with scholars on the area." He took off his horn-rim glasses and toyed nervously with them. "The word *jihad,* of course, means a Muslim holy war, and our sense is that we're dealing with a Muslim fundamentalist group bent on some sort of sustained terrorism. Their demands would certainly tend to support that hypothesis."

"Yes, yes. What does this *Parameswara* mean? Is that how you say it?"

"Close enough, sir." The director of the CIA shook his head. "We don't know yet. It's an East Indian or Indonesian name, as far as we can tell, but we haven't deciphered its meaning in this case."

"Well, what do you think? Should we let the government of little Singapore in on it?"

The admiral watched the director's eyes defer to the national security adviser, a former three-star general whose entire career was an anomaly — a succession of staff and political jobs in Washington, academic assignments, and diplomatic posts, but never the command of armed forces. "I'd like to hold that card for the time being, sir, until we have more information on what or whom we're dealing with here," he said. "The surrounding countries — Malaysia and Indonesia — are officially Muslim, and Singapore has a significant population." He chose his words carefully, a phrase at a time leaving the thin, pursed lips. "It's a very volatile area, sir. The Muslim fundamentalist movement is always a threat. We just don't know what can of worms we might be opening." A self-effacing, slightly built man — the shortest at the table — in a gray suit with a balding gray head, the national security adviser had been described in *Newsweek* as the "classic bureaucratic beetle," a glib cruelty that ignored that his now closeted uniform bore a fighter pilot's wings.

"Okay, I'd like to take that under advisement, but there's the question of, ah, Congress." The President looked down the table at the Secretary of Defense, an imposing ex-Congressman who, with his high-domed brow, rampantly receding brown hair, and rimless glasses, looked the epitome of the chief executive officer of a financial corporation rather than a canny politician.

"Of course, we've already informed the key congressional leadership, but beyond that . . ." Defense cocked his head and made a questioning motion with his left hand. "Ongoing military operations ought to be left to the Executive." He glanced at the admiral. "There isn't any way members of Congress can contribute in that regard." The tone was low-key, amiable, even with a hint of humor.

"Not to mention the leaks to the press," the White House chief of staff added.

"Absolutely. We don't want this *event* degenerating into the seventeen-day carnival of TWA 847 in Beirut."

Behind Defense's amiability, the quiet humor, the admiral knew that his boss was a pretty cold-blooded man. Part of it was, perhaps, confidence. The national security adviser, the Secretary of State, and he were close friends, who all went trout fishing in the Rockies together. They were comrades from past wars, campaigns, and administrations who — according to Capitol Hill scuttlebutt — first reached a consensus among themselves on policy.

The President smiled and nodded. "That's fine. There are always limits in matters of this nature, and, ah, we have to consider these things."

"In my view it's a question of the Russians."

"Oh, they'll keep it quiet," the security adviser insisted. "The last thing the Russians want or need is to publicize or encourage any *jihad*. They've already had enough trouble with Islamic fundamentalists in Azerbaijan and Turkmenistan. One of their primary reasons for getting out of Afghanistan was that they were fighting against a self-proclaimed Muslim holy war. The Soviets' own Muslim troops were fragging their ethnic Russian and Slavic officers." The national security adviser had a Ph.D. from Columbia in Russian studies.

"Okay," the President nodded. "What's next? For the moment let's put aside the Russian thing and take a sharp look at what options we have here. It seems to me — we kicked this around just now walking over — the situation boils down to two questions." With his left forefinger the President tapped the fingers of his right hand. "*One,* do we pay the ransom? And, *two,* if we don't, what are the consequences? And *three* — I guess there are three questions here — what other alternatives do we have?"

There was a general reluctance to speak, as if each man at the table was waiting for the President to answer his own questions.

"Hey, I'm throwing it open for discussion," the President prompted. He nodded at the Secretary of State.

State pursed his lips, as if he had bit into something distasteful, then reached across the table for the sheaf of papers detailing the ransom and shook it. "This is political suicide. To quote the President during the — "

"Darn it, I know what I said. I wrote the antiterrorist report for this government, and it's the best antiterrorist report written. But right now my priority is to save 134 American lives."

"Paying the ransom will eventually cost

even more lives."

"That's a worst-case scenario."

"Are we sure the Russians won't pay it? What did the ambassador say?"

The President shook his head. "Too hypothetical to answer. I think we're going to have to act unilaterally here. Work out our own plan of action, whatever the Russians do." He nodded to the national security adviser. "I mean, they've got their own serious internal problems with their 45 million Muslims — I think that's a heck of a briefing paper you all ought to read, if you haven't already — that have a priority here."

"Our satellite reconnaissance shows that the carrier *Minsk* and a small battle group have sortied Cam Ranh Bay and are steaming toward Singapore," the general volunteered.

"If we can see the Russians, why can't we see this goddamn ship?" the chief of staff challenged, hunching his shoulders forward over the desk.

"We don't know. The radar on the La Crosse satellite can pick up anything ten feet or longer under a cloud cover. And we've identified thousands of fishing boats the size of Fords on the regular satellite photos. But we haven't found this three-hundred-foot luxury liner." The frustration was evident in the national security adviser's tone, but he was not kowtowing to the chief of staff.

"Well, now, is it possible — I don't like to think about this, but I guess we have to consider it, you know — that these guys, whoever they are, have already sunk this ship and are holding all the passengers somewhere else? Or, they have killed them, except maybe for a couple they're still holding as hostages, bargaining chips for later?" The President did not address the question to anyone in particular but rambled on as if thinking aloud.

State peered down the table and with a nod indicated that a younger man sitting across from the admiral should field it. "Yes, sir, it's possible," the assistant secretary for terrorism answered. "At this point any scenario is possible, but it hasn't been the pattern over the past two decades. Whether it's a ship like the *Achille Lauro* or a TWA airliner, the pattern has always been to keep the passengers and crew aboard, under guard, because they're easier to control that way. Assuming they've got any kind of organization at all. Also, if they kill their hostages up front, they've dangerously narrowed their options and lost all credibility for future operations."

"Well, maybe they haven't read the official

terrorist manual," the director of the CIA drawled.

The admiral saw the assistant secretary for terrorism glance down the table at his own boss. One of State's objectives was to keep the CIA out of foreign affairs. "Oh, we think they have," the assistant challenged. "Judging from that shopping list they've sent us."

The President held up his hand. "Look, before we get into all this, I want to get the consensus of this room on paying the ransom." His voice cracked with fatigue, and the troubled eyes looked about the table, questioning a face here and there. "Anyone?" he asked, a pleading note in the call.

"I don't think the size of the swap makes it any less *morally* objectionable," the national security adviser said. "Pragmatically it's pouring gasoline, make that dynamite, on a raging fire we're fighting like hell to put out." He addressed the President. "Of course, there may be political considerations that are overriding. That's out of my purview." He nodded across the table to State. "Or diplomatic ones."

"There's something else in the pot to tally."

All heads turned toward the director of the CIA.

"This is not just a boatload of tourists. It's a special charter cruise of the National

Oceanographic Society. Most of their board of trustees is aboard. It's a blue ribbon panel. In addition to Alan Schneider, there are university presidents, several CEOs of *Fortune* 500 companies, a prominent ecologist or two like Ralph Levine. The passenger list is, well, formidable."

"What the hell are they all doing on the same ship?"

"Schneider's now teaching at Stanford, and he was aboard to brief them on the strategic importance of the lower Pacific Rim. This type of specialized luxury charter is not uncommon. With a distinguished guest lecturer. It's a thriving business."

"Is there any compromise of security with what these people know?"

"We're working on that right now with the FBI. But our preliminary estimate is that there is no significant breach here. Schneider's information is dated. The dark secrets of a past administration. It's the stuff of memoirs. And so far as we've been able to uncover, the university presidents and CEOs aren't involved in any classified work."

There was a prolonged silence. Then the national security adviser placed both palms flat down on the mahogany table. "Okay, I'll say it. It's my shop that screwed up in the past. This room, the White House itself,

233

is still haunted by the ghosts of Iran-Contra Past, rattling their chains."

"Amen to that."

"The bottom line is — we . . . are . . . opposed . . . to . . . trading . . . arms . . . for . . . hostages." He bit off each word.

"But there are 135 American hostages, all civilians."

"Two hundred and seventy died on Pan Am flight 103."

The admiral could not see who made the remark.

"Jesus, is that the acceptable loss now?"

"I didn't say it was *acceptable,* but, God help us, it's what we've learned to live with."

On the bridge of the USS *Decatur* Stewart stared at the navigation charts. The sea south of Singapore was a forbidding maze of islands, a labyrinth of *pulaus, kepulauans,* and *selats,* the native names for islands, archipelagoes, and straits. And there were countless razor-tooth *karangs,* or reefs, menacing *batus,* or rocks, and treacherously shifting *betings,* or shoals.

"A great place to hide a ship," Stewart said grimly.

"Or run one aground," Robinson added.

Stewart glared at him. "That's a hell of

a note." Then he nodded reluctantly. "But you're right. We'd better go by the book." There were so many goddamn little islands, half of them did not have names; only the clusters were identified — Kepulauan Riau, Kepulauan Lingga, Kepulauan Rukan. "We'll follow the *Black Sea*'s projected course to Jakarta and work the helos on a standard ladder-pattern area search." He looked up questioningly. "That is, unless anybody has another idea. Eddie?"

Lieutenant Commander Eddie DiLorenzo, the officer in charge of the *Decatur*'s helicopter detachment, shook his head. "We don't have anything else to go on."

Stewart traced the sea lane between Singapore and Jakarta. The southern narrow of the China Sea between Sumatra and Borneo broke into two straits — Selat Karimata and Selat Gelasa — both leading into the Java Sea. The more direct passage to Jakarta, the Gelasa Strait, then forked into three separate channels — the Macclesfield, Clement, and Stolze straits — and several unnavigable traps. "We have to assume that the ship was hijacked somewhere in this area. But it's been almost two and a half days. They may be halfway to Shanghai or Bombay, if they went east or west."

DiLorenzo, bouncing on the balls of his

feet, looked over Stewart's hunched shoulder. "We'll alternate the helos in the air right through the night," the pilot outlined. "When we pick up a contact on radar, we can visually identify it with our night-vision goggles at twenty-five miles. They won't see us or hear us. Maybe we'll get lucky."

"We'll need more than luck."

"Well, as you said, Captain, it's a great place to hide a ship," DiLorenzo said.

"Or destroy one."

The red radio telephone on the ship's console buzzed. An officer dove for it. "This is the *Decatur*. The officer of the deck, Lieutenant j.g. Gerling speaking, sir." He listened a moment, then nervously covered the mouthpiece with his palm. "ComSeventhFleet in Japan is up on the satellite, Captain." He passed the phone to Stewart.

In the White House Situation Room the President cocked a bushy eyebrow and squinted down the long table; suddenly the presidential eyes had focused on the admiral. "So let's take a hard look at our other options. This is a naval thing. Admiral, will you please brief us on the operational situation?"

"Yes, sir." He rose and strode to the situation map of Southeast Asia already in place on the wall at the President's right. "Of course, first we've got to find the damn ship. A detachment of P-3 Orion search planes is now en route from Subic Bay to Singapore. The government of Singapore has given us permission to use their civilian airfield at Changi. A second detachment from elements in Japan, Guam, and Hawaii is being deployed to back them up." He looked at State. "The State Department is working on getting permission from both Malaysia and Indonesia to conduct a search in their territorial waters."

"We don't anticipate any trouble on that," State nodded. "They don't have the resources to mount something of this breadth, but it's going to cost us something in foreign and military aid down the road. Maybe an obsolete destroyer or two."

The admiral tapped the island of Singapore on the map. "Along with the squadron support crew we've sent a SEAL assault team. They're part of the new Delta Force with special training in hostage and terrorist situations."

"Has Singapore given us permission for *that?*"

The admiral glanced at State. "Ideally we'll locate the ship and move in before *anyone* is aware of their presence."

"We've had a dozen people held hostage

for years in Lebanon, and we're still looking for them."

"This time we're working with a three-hundred-foot cruise ship with 225 people aboard."

"We hope to God we're still working with a ship with that many people aboard."

"What about the Russians?"

The admiral looked directly at the President, as if to defer the question to him.

"The General Secretary and I have agreed to keep each other informed, and both task-group commanders, when they arrive on the scene, are ordered to do the same. But we're not going to place our ships and planes under their command, nor are they going to work under ours. That's a given. But frankly, I'm very concerned if they attempt a rescue . . ." The President shook his head and didn't finish the thought.

"Their naval Spetsnaz have no special training in hostage situations," the security adviser commented.

"Their naval *what?*"

"Spetsnaz. It's short for Spetsial'naya Naznacheniya," he enunciated. He spoke both Russian and Serbo-Croatian. "Their special forces. Each of the four Soviet fleets has a Spetsnaz amphibious brigade that operates with it."

"Are they any good?"

The national security adviser shrugged. "They're tough and well trained, but it's all behind-the-lines reconnaissance, sabotage, and assassination, not hostage situations. The Soviets have no experience in that sort of thing."

"It will be a bloodbath."

"What about the SEALs?"

"They've had Israeli trainers for these situations," the admiral answered.

"Where are the Russians now?"

"They've already got search planes working the area out of Cam Ranh Bay, and we expect that they'll move them to Saigon — excuse me, Ho Chi Minh City — which is a little closer. It's still a 1,300-mile round trip, but their Bear reconnaissance aircraft have a five-thousand-mile combat radius. In addition to the *Minsk* carrier group, they have another half dozen ships in the South China Sea they can move into the search. Our nearest carrier group at the moment is the *Midway*. It's three thousand miles away in the Arabian Sea, but it's steaming for Singapore."

"Jesus Christ, do we have *anything* there yet?"

The admiral shrugged. "Just one frigate, sir. It was returning home from the Persian

Gulf." The admiral jabbed at the Karimata Strait flowing between Borneo and Sumatra. "It's out there now searching for the *Black Sea*."

Off the *Decatur*'s port bow a breathtaking sailing ship out of the nineteenth century beat toward Java, its huge black trapezoidal sails puffed with the wind. While Robinson watched, a half-naked crewman shimmied with his bare feet along the bowsprit out over the sea and unfurled three black flying jibs which immediately caught the wind. The schooner leaped forward.

Robinson ached that he did not have his camera, and for a moment he considered dashing to his stateroom for it. But he didn't dare; the search was serious business. He glanced at Stewart, and to his surprise saw that the commanding officer was also staring at the sailing ship, but with an expression of rapture illuminating his face.

Stewart caught Robinson's eye and smiled, as if embarrassed to be caught in a secret vice. "I'm on the wrong ship," the CO said with a sigh.

"It's a beauty," Robinson nodded.

"It's a *prahu*, a native Indonesian schooner. Beauty is the word for it." He pointed at the sailboat. "Double-masted, gaff-rigged. It doesn't even have a rudder. It's steered with that lashed-up tiller. The hold is like a truck's, an open frame to carry freight between islands. But if you put a motor on it, the vibrations will shake the boat apart. It's a pure sailing ship."

Something in Stewart's speech became more Southern, a throwback to the Tidewater of Virginia. The captain's mercurial shifts in mood kept the executive officer on edge. One moment Stewart was at war with *something* out there, and the next he was waxing poetic about the local rice and lumber haulers.

On leaving Singapore Stewart had briefed the crew that a cruise ship with 135 Americans aboard had been hijacked by terrorists whose cause was as yet unknown; the lives of everyone aboard were threatened. He did not mention the heads that had been found in Singapore.

With his helo pilots, combat systems officer, and radar air controllers Stewart had methodically worked out a detailed search plan for the liner, and the helos had immediately launched area searches. Once again the CO ordered the .50-caliber machine guns reinstalled on the ship's decks, unmanned but with ammunition stowed nearby. The pintle door mounts were attached on the two Seahawk helicopters and rearmed with side-firing 7.62-mm.'s. The M14 assault rifles, M60 light machine guns, grenade launchers, and shotguns were taken out of the armory and made ready, and the boarding party and small-craft action teams were assembled. Robinson felt that the dangers were more imagined than real, but he noted that the preparations had an effect on the crew. Rather than their pissing and moaning about the trip home being put off, a current of excitement galvanized the ship. And Robinson now wondered if that had not been Stewart's unstated purpose in his preparations for guerrilla warfare. The man was tricky, no doubt about it.

A sudden burst of prolonged thunder made both men look up. A white plume of contrail and its silver arrowhead jetted across the blue-white vault of the tropical sky at 37,000 feet. Robinson did not know what flight it was, but from the south-by-southwest course that paralleled the *Decatur*'s own, he reckoned it was a commercial shuttle from Singapore to Jakarta.

"An hour from takeoff to touchdown," Stewart snapped. "Australian tourists, shoppers, Japanese businessmen in black suits. The stewardesses have to hustle to serve the Australians their beer before landing. But the *Black Sea* left Singapore at night, was scheduled to spend a day at sea cruising, and dock in Jakarta the next morning."

Robinson didn't say anything. The sudden change in tone in Stewart's voice told him they were back at war.

"We're going on the assumption that that's what the ship did. That it followed its intended course, and that somewhere along that course the ship was hijacked."

"Washington is going by the book." Robinson believed in going by the book. He always executed the play the way it was in the book. If he executed it well, he made yardage, and if the team ground out enough yardage, they would win the game. That was how Robinson had always played.

"That book was written by jet setters in a think tank." Stewart pointed at the contrail of the disappearing plane. "Their case studies were airliner hijackings. The only ship has been the *Achille Lauro,* and in that case the Palestinian terrorists panicked when a steward popped into their stateroom while they were sitting on their beds cleaning their AK-47's. Then they sailed around the Med trying to figure out what to do next while the Sixth Fleet tracked them. That's the book."

"The suit from the CIA thinks they got aboard the same way, with phony passports. It's logical."

"The essence of logic is Occam's razor."

"Occam's *what?*" Robinson exclaimed.

"Occam's razor. It's a tool of logic formulated by William of Occam, an English philosopher in the fourteenth century. It states that assumptions introduced to explain a situation should not be multiplied beyond necessity. In short, the simplest explanation to a given set of facts is most likely to be right, rather than a complicated one."

"What about the heads? That's neither logical nor by the book."

"A very good question," Stewart mused. "That's a distinctively *native* touch."

The strange way in which Stewart said it made Robinson turn to him, but the CO had his binoculars up and was again studying the *prahu*. "At first glance it looks like a classic schooner, but the foresail is twice as large as the one aft, the opposite arrangement of a Western schooner. And the big sail is loose-footed, not lashed to a lower boom."

"Is that important?" Robinson heard the impatient edge of his own voice.

"Totally changes the way the ship handles, especially in a big wind." Stewart lowered his glasses and turned to Robinson with a strange smile. "Know what the old sailors called the Java Sea?"

Robinson shook his head.

"The sea of wandering rocks and islands."

"Let's pray it's just superstition."

"No, let's pray our fathometer doesn't break down. It's not the rocks and islands that really wander, it's the underwater sandbars. They shift with the currents. You can't plot them, and a course that's safe on one voyage may be a disaster on the next. But that schooner out there navigates several seas and literally thousands of islands with no radio, no sextant, no navigational aids whatever, except an old compass, which the Chinese invented, and maybe some out-of-date charts which don't mark half its ports of call — generally fishing villages, upriver lumber camps hacked out of the jungle, and one-Chinaman trading posts."

The CO had a way of communicating with him that infuriated Robinson. Half the time Stewart didn't say anything at all but was sunk in dark, brooding silence. Then he started lecturing, thinking aloud really, as though compelled to educate this thick, black ex-Navy jock with whom he had been stuck as his executive officer.

"The only thing they've got in that shack on the stern," Stewart rambled on, "is the rice the crew eats, tea, and a handful of spices. They catch their dinner from the sea or go hungry." He was talking with a mounting intensity that disturbed Robinson. Stewart suddenly turned to the chart table and for perhaps the thirtieth time that day hunched over it, as though it would reveal the answer to the mystery if he just studied it long enough. "The suits, the think-tank Ph.D.'s, the carrier admirals, they don't have a clue as to what the hell's going on." He rapped the chart with his knuckles. "That ship's nowhere near Jakarta."

The executive officer was bewildered. "Captain, our orders were to search along the *Black Sea*'s intended course," Robinson insisted.

Stewart stared at him, and there was a strange half-smile on his lips. "Our orders were to find the damned ship. And we're looking in the wrong place."

Aboard the *prahu* a brown-skinned seaman squatted in the raised stern, his hand on the tiller, and watched in awe as the silver helicopter, its blades invisibly whirling the air, hovered like a monstrous dragonfly and then settled onto the fantail of the American warship. The mate was a Bugis, a race of seafarers and traders from the Celebes Islands of Indonesia, notorious throughout the South Asian seas for piracy as much as for their sailing skill.

The aluminum mast of the American warship visibly leaned to starboard, and the wake traced a white arc on the cobalt sea, as the frigate suddenly changed course to the west. The sailor pointed and shouted, "Pak!" to catch the attention of the captain working up forward by the windjammer's mainmast.

The captain, a middle-aged Bugis with thick, unbarbered hair and a thin mustache and goatee, waved back, rather than shout over the hiss of the sea and boisterous creaking of the spars and mast. He moved aft, picking his way along the teak planking and tangle of lines on bare feet, but never taking his eyes off the American warship until it was hull down on the horizon. Then he banged open the door to the ramshackle cabin on the stern.

The ceiling was so low that even the short Bugis had to crouch to enter. He squatted down and pulled off the rubberized cloth covering the marine radio and the automobile battery. The only light in the cabin came through the open door, creating a twilight gloom, and Pak had to squint to check the frequency. He flipped the switch, listened for the speaker's responding hum, and then he called Tengku Haji Azhar.

18. Shashlik, Shish Kabob, or Satay?

Yuri Yevshenko genuinely liked his American counterpart. The big man was gregarious and hearty in his appetites, almost Russian. The French always insisted that the Americans and the Russians were by nature so much alike that they would be great friends if they had not been enemies for decades. Of course, the French had such an exalted opinion of their own sophistication that they probably had not meant it as a compliment to either nationality, but it was nonetheless true.

The CIA station chief Harold Blocker sat across the table conferring with the hawker, a constantly grinning Chinese boy of about sixteen.

"Who's got the best chili crabs?"

The boy whirled and pointed across the outdoor tables set up on the esplanade along the river to the cluster of food stalls. "Yee Ming number one chili crab!" the boy exclaimed.

The hawker stalls were encamped under a long candy-striped awning, and their festival of lanterns and strings of lights danced on the dark water. Each cramped stall cooked a specialty, ranging from *murthabak,* the Muslim Indian stuffed pancakes, to *Hokkien mee,* the noodles and squid of Hokkien, China. A babel of aromas of spices and pungent meats saturated the tropical night air.

"These are the best chili crabs in Singapore?" Blocker teased the boy.

The boy hesitated, then answered, "Not Singapore. Number one *here.* Best chili crab in Singapore in Bedok. I give you the name of restaurant."

"Yuri, I think we got a real gourmet here we can trust," Blocker said.

The boy nodded and his smile broadened, now that he was assured of a healthy tip. "You want rice or *roti?*"

"Roti," the local name for the French bread used to sop up the garlicky red pepper sauce.

"And who has the best *satay?*" Yevshenko asked.

"You like chicken, lamb, or beef?"

"Lamb."

"You like peanut sauce spicy or sweet?"

"A little spicy."

"I bring you number one lamb *satay,* okay," the boy said, with a confident gesture that indicated the Russian was to leave it to his judgment.

"And two big bottles of Anker beer." The

hawker ran off, and Blocker turned to Yevshenko with a sly smile. "Ah, you can take the Russian boy away from his *shashlik,* but not the *shashlik* away from the boy."

The Russian shook his head. "*Shashlik* and *satay* are two very different ways to roast skewered lamb. And in savoring these differences — how the Indonesians and Malays spice and prepare the same dish — we learn something of their national character. You, in turn, overwhelm and inflame your senses with hot, exotic dishes and create chaos in your mind, not subtle understanding."

Blocker laughed. "Yuri, old buddy, you've been in the Seventh Department too long." The KGB's Seventh Department embraced Singapore, the surrounding East Asian countries, and Japan. "You're beginning to talk like a Confucian."

The Russian fell silent and gazed down at the Singapore River, a dark, narrow stream flowing sluggishly below the high stone embankment. The reeking bumboats, *tongkangs,* and *sampans* with their watchful painted eyes were now gone, and the working lighters had been hauled to the Pasir Panjang wharfs. The dank, firetrap godowns and warehouses had been razed for the futuristic skyscrapers of the financial district on the west bank. And the army of wiry *swalos* in sweat-stained singlets and shorts who had shouldered coarse, backbreaking sacks from the lighters to this very boat quay had been left unemployed by the great railed cranes that now lifted boxcar-sized containers from the holds of giant cargo ships.

When Yevshenko had first been posted to the Orient as a young man, the palm-roofed fishing *kampongs*, raised on stilts above the tidal shallows, had been the romantic landmarks of this tropical island. *Where had they all gone?* Three-fourths of the world's computer hard disks — for one item — were now made locally by delicate-fingered Asian women perched over microscopes, patiently threading tiny wires through pinholes. But what had happened to all the natives dispossessed by Singapore's acceleration into the twenty-first century? Even Yevshenko, as a Soviet, felt impoverished here, demoralized by the city's new wealth, its sparkling modernity. Socialism had never erected such towering crystal and alabaster paeans to its progress.

Blocker suddenly intruded into his brooding. "So, what does your subtly educated palate tell you?" Blocker asked. "Are we dealing with *satay* or *shish kabob* eaters here?"

"An interesting way of putting the question." Yevshenko shook his head. "To Moscow, it looks and smells like *shish kabob*."

"This is out of their territory."

"The *Achille Lauro* was out of Genoa. It is now obvious to *Middle* Eastern terrorists that a cruise ship has certain advantages over a jetliner. For one, it carries enough fuel and food to sustain itself for weeks. For another, it doesn't sit baking on a hot runway surrounded by snipers itching to pick off your brains."

"But why a Russian ship?"

Yevshenko pursed out his lower lip, like a clown simulating sadness. "They don't love us anymore. With *glasnost,* the friend of their enemy now becomes their enemy. To the Iranians and Iraqis we've become one with the Great Satan, which is your country, of course," he told Blocker. He might have added — as in the communiqué from Moscow — we've cut off their supply of guns. We were the enemy in a holy war in Afghanistan. With the Muslim Azerbaijanis fighting the Christian Armenians, the southern Caucasus had become a second Lebanon.

The teenage Chinese hawker materialized out of the crowd and banged down a battered metal tray on their table. "Number one chili crab and lamb *satay* with spicy sauce," the boy announced.

The food center was crowded and noisy

at that time of night, with all the tables on the boat quay close to the river occupied. Yevshenko and Blocker were no more conspicuous than the other tourists and Western businessmen amid the loudly chattering Chinese and scattered Malays and Indians.

Yevshenko nibbled at a stick of *satay*, while Blocker paid off the kid, who acknowledged the generous tip with a cheek-splitting smile. "You want something else, just hold up your hand. I see you," the boy instructed.

When the hawker left, Blocker tipped his glass of beer. *"Perestroika,"* he toasted.

Yevshenko reached into his breast pocket and withdrew several sheets of paper folded into a small packet. He handed them to Blocker with a small smile, lifted his own glass, and said, *"Perestroika."*

Blocker handed Yevshenko a similar packet. "It's a modest shopping list, all things considered. A couple of crates of our new M16's with the revised flash hiders, the thirty-round clips, and grenade launchers, with both armor-piercing and high-explosive grenades," Blocker enumerated. "Modest but damned sophisticated."

Yevshenko studied the list item by item. In addition to the automatic rifles, there were specified a half dozen M14's adapted for sniping with telescopic sights and flash suppressors; the Belgian Minimi light machine guns, not the older American M60's, which had had problems with jamming in the Vietnamese jungle; the British 81-millimeter mortar, and the Swedish AT-4 antitank rocket. Yes, it was damn sophisticated. The Americans were in the midst of converting to all the itemized NATO arms. "Stingers," Yevshenko hissed aloud. The *mujahedeen* had shot down over a hundred Russian helicopters and aircraft with the American missile in Afghanistan.

Blocker quickly scanned the printout sheets Yevshenko had handed him. "What's on your list I should know?"

"It appears to be the Russian analogs of the weapons demanded here," Yevshenko noted. "However, they specify our AKS-74 rifles and RPKS light machine guns with the tubular folding butts, the ones used by our Spetsnaz."

Blocker grunted. "Whoever these bad guys are, they want to travel fast and light. Nothing that can't be hand-carried by one man. No vehicles, artillery, heavy mortars, or even machine guns and rockets."

"Yes," Yevshenko agreed, "but they can resupply ammunition and spare parts from any NATO, ex-Warsaw Pact, or a host of Third World stockpiles now on the market."

Blocker picked a chunk of *roti* from the basket, dipped the bread into the fiery chili sauce, and smacked his lips. "So, what does it all add up to?" he asked, savoring the morsel. "Two battalions of guerrillas, both very well equipped, one with American weapons, the other Russian, able to carry out a variety of special ops, and at least temporarily hold off tanks, aircraft, or superior forces. Still, at the worst, it's just a regiment of troops."

Yevshenko shook his head and emitted a rueful laugh. "That is a military assessment that comes straight from the Pentagon. It could come from the Russian General Staff. They too think that only an armored division is threatening. They have already forgotten that the Vietnamese People's Liberation Army was founded by a history professor with thirty-four men armed with a hodge-podge of French, Japanese, American, and British small arms."

Blocker was silent, then said, "There's something else about this shopping list that bothers us very much. The method of delivery."

"Ours specifies that we are to put an ad in the *Business Times* when we are ready to deliver everything."

"We've gotten the same instructions. But

255

nothing here's bigger than a crate of rifles, and even that can be broken down into a couple of M16's per hostage." Blocker glanced at the Russian list. "Say two 7.62-millimeter Dragunov snipers for the ship's chef. What's the swap for an ex-Secretary of State? Three Stingers, maybe?" Blocker wagged his head. "It's horrendous."

Yevshenko nodded. "Parameswara Jihad," he read aloud. "Who are they?"

"We were hoping you could tell us. We've never heard of them before."

Yevshenko shook his head.

Blocker picked up a crab leg dripping with sauce and prodded the flesh from the shell with his fingers. But it was a distracted act, one absent of any appetite. The hot chili made his scalp sweat, and Yevshenko noticed tiny bubbles of perspiration on his brow. "You're welcome to try the crabs, but I don't want to confuse your delicate intelligence assessment here," Blocker drawled. "You told me what Dzerzhinsky Square thinks. But what does their man in Singapore compute?"

The Russian reached across the table and picked up a crab leg. "This is a *nonya* dish," he said. "Do you know what *nonya* means?"

"A mixture of Malay and Chinese," the American answered, as if not quite sure.

"It is the Malay word for 'woman' or 'wife.' When the Chinese first came here — and some families go back to the sixteenth century — there were no Chinese women. The Chinese men who stayed took Malay wives. And over the years their descendants took on a Malay identity in their language, dress, even their food. The local spices — chili, *blacan,* coconut cream — were used to flavor Chinese sauces, vegetables, pork. Malays are Muslim, and they would never eat pork."

Blocker studied the Russian, waiting.

Yevshenko picked up a stick of *satay,* stirred the end piece of roasted lamb in the bowl of spiced peanut sauce, and then held it up before his face, not to eat but as an object of contemplation. "The Arabs and the Persians have been trading here for over a thousand years. They also took Malay wives."

Blocker silently sipped his beer.

"I think this is just *shish kabob* cooked by an Arab trader's Malay wife centuries ago." Yevshenko nibbled the stick of *satay.* "Now it is the national dish of Malaysia and Indonesia."

The Russian was not talking about food. He was talking about trading a boatload of hostages for a regiment of arms.

In the darkened interior of the van Yee

sat sipping a bowl of *cheng tng*. The hot herbal broth was *yin;* it cooled the digestion. He regarded the small pile of dishes with their now congealed red and black sauces, the sucked-out crab shells with distaste. Why did men on stakeout always eat immoderately? Was it to ease the tension of the forced confinement and concealment? But it was not just the hot chilies and tamarind-sour *laksa* that had his stomach inflamed. It was the terrible knowledge he had just acquired.

There was a polite knock on the door of the van. The technician started, glanced sharply at Yee, then guardedly opened the door and looked out. He turned back to Yee. "Your nephew."

Yee stepped out of the van into the glaring lights that illuminated the food stalls along the boat quay. The van was white with red-lettered Chinese and English advertising "Golden Phoenix Noodles," indistinguishable from the others servicing the stalls except, perhaps, for the darkened windows. The boy grinned up at Yee and handed him the basket of bread chunks.

"Did the American give you a good tip?"

"Yes, uncle."

"I hear that you know of a restaurant in Bedok that makes better chili crab than your father." The boy's grin evaporated and his

258

eyes widened in surprise. "If you give me the name and address, it will be our secret."

The boy nodded, and there was a deferential bow in the nod of his head, but then the easy adolescent grin asserted itself again. Yee watched his nephew saunter away. The lad had a jaunty spring and swing to his movement that neither his uncle nor his father had ever had as a youth. Yee reached into the basket, pushed aside the chunks of crusty *roti*, and unwove the strands of rattan. From between the weave of the two bottom layers he withdrew a miniaturized transmitter the size and thinness of a coin.

He reentered the van and handed both the bug and the breadbasket to the technician. Abdullah and Wang were now tailing the American and the Russian, and he had to wait until they checked in by radio. He sat down at the console and rewound the tape to the section he had electronically marked.

"So, what does it all add up to? Two battalions of guerrillas, both very well equipped, one with American weapons, the other Russian, able to carry out a variety of special ops, and at least temporarily hold off tanks, aircraft, or superior forces. Still, at the worst, it's just a regiment of troops."

Yee pushed the stop button. He sat back and sipped his *cheng tng* to soothe his burning stomach. The herb brew was cold now, cooled by the van's air conditioning. But the chill that coursed through Yee, making his delicate frame shudder, had nothing to do with the air conditioning. Piece by piece his bloodiest nightmare was coming true.

The telephone buzzed. The technician picked it up, listened for a moment, then handed it to Yee. "Yes?"

"Mr. Yee, this is Teh Tang." There was an audible intake of breath. "The police have found another head. At the foot of Raffles' statue."

Part VI
The Fourth Day of Captivity

19. The Market Value of a Hostage

After breakfast Maggi dressed for her audience with Tengku as deliberately as she would for a faculty meeting. She donned a long-sleeved batik blouse and cotton sarong she had bought in Jakarta on a previous trip. They were clinging, floridly colorful materials, but they modestly covered her arms and legs in the Malay fashion. She had dressed in this manner each time she had met with Tengku, a courtesy she had learned in the Peace Corps in Kuala Besut. Bare arms and legs offended Muslim sensibilities. She briefly considered putting on some sort of headdress —older Malay women often wore loose scarfs, and the uniform for girls at the schools attached to mosques included a nunlike wimple drawn in folds about the chin — but she rejected this idea. Such an unprecedented display of modesty might only arouse Tengku's, and especially Ahmed's, suspicions. Young Malay women seldom covered their luxuriant ebony hair, and for that matter the demureness of their clothing was a seductive deception, the long, color-splashed, limb-hugging blouses and sarongs conveying a voluptuousness beyond nudity.

At the door to the salon Maggi removed her shoes, the Oriental custom that was now observed in the sections of the ship the Malays had commandeered.

Tengku smiled, and the grossly lashed dark eyes appeared to gleam with a secret pleasure at her entrance, an erotic gaze that unsettled her as much as Ahmed's mean-eyed suspicion.

"I do not like this Russian idea," Ahmed complained as soon as she was seated. Even in Bahasa his voice had a belligerent quality. The small dark eyes flitted from Maggi to Tengku and back to focus warily on Maggi again.

"We thought that releasing the Russian men and women with the largest families would be a humanitarian gesture," she appealed to Tengku. "It would show that you were a great man, a compassionate man of God, strong but merciful."

Tengku nodded thoughtfully. He reclined back into the coral plush of the armchair, contemplating this image of himself. It seemed to Maggi that at each meeting the pirate chieftain became more the Oriental potentate, the cruise ship's lounge with its ivory fluted columns more transformed into a sultan's court, as though Tengku were playing out some unspoken fantasy. A cache of expensive Oriental rugs looted from the *Black Sea*'s hold were scattered about the room as prayer rugs. His original court of Mahmud and Yusof was now deployed elsewhere, and only Ahmed remained constantly at his right hand as chamberlain. A pirate armed with an assault rifle guarded the port and starboard doors to the verandah, and one of the ship's waiters in black and white livery stood by the bar to attend to Tengku's constant whims for cold drinks, coffee, and snacks.

"The Russians with the biggest families would be the oldest, most important, richest men in the crew," Ahmed said. "If you are trading fish, you do not first give away your fattest fish." He did not argue but stated his point as an unassailable fact of the marketplace.

The pirate chieftain laughed, slapped the table, and wagged his head, his eyes twinkling. "My cousin is always the sharper trader. When we were children, I would give away the whole boatload, and the boat also, to the Chinaman for a shiny sword, if Ahmed did not trade for me. I must leave the trading of the fish to him."

Ahmed turned to Maggi, the black beads of his eyes shining with triumph. "Are any of the Russians sick?"

"Not that I know."

Tengku leaned forward. "The gallant officer with the yellow hair who protected you on the bridge," he inquired. "The wound on his face heals?" There was a teasing, playful quality in Tengku's voice and expression.

"Yes, the doctor sewed it. He said it was a clean wound that will heal with a small scar. But he doesn't know yet if any nerves were cut."

"A sharp sword makes a clean wound," Tengku pronounced, as though it were a proverb with some universal truth. As always, his *parang* leaned against the right arm of his chair.

"If no Russian is sick, then we should release the lowest servants first." Ahmed proffered it as advice, not as a declaration. "The bartenders. The bar is locked and shut, and there is no honest work for them to do."

Tengku nodded.

The elaborate teak and chrome-trimmed bar stood in a recess in the forward area of the lounge. A locked grillwork protecting the bottles had not been disturbed. Alcohol was anathema to devout Muslims, and a bartender was a pariah.

Hundreds of lives, including her own, depended on Maggi's tact. She did not challenge

Ahmed. Instead, she ventured, "What about the women?"

Both men were silent, their faces blank of expression. Finally Ahmed said, "It is not yet time to release women."

"Why? It is the humanitarian, righteous thing for men of God to do." Immediately Maggi sensed a tense undercurrent in the room, but she had not the slightest clue why.

Ahmed strangely nodded in agreement. "It is an uncomfortable, dangerous journey to Singapore from here."

But not too uncomfortable or dangerous for a man recovering from double bypass surgery, Maggi thought. Suddenly she was frightened. Why were the pirates holding the women?

"I don't want to discuss releasing the prisoners," Tengku said abruptly with an imperious gesture of his right hand. "Ahmed will make these decisions for me." The dark, sensual eyes focused on Maggi. "Your family is well?" he inquired with a gentle smile.

"My family?" For a moment Maggi was confused.

"Your cousins you are traveling with."

"Oh, yes, they are well." Maggi hesitated, then frowned. Captain Khromykh had ordered Maggi to get Schneider off the ship

267

as quickly as possible.

"Yes, there is some problem?"

Maggi gave a reluctant shrug, as though loath to bring up the matter. "My cousin, her husband, he is an old man with heart disease." She wondered how Schneider would react to being described as an old man.

"The professor?"

"Yes. Being in the jungle. The confinement. All the fear and tension. We are very worried about him." Maggi was careful not to ask a favor, at least not this time.

Tengku nodded and glanced at Ahmed. Among the Malay nepotism was considered not a vice but a virtue, an obligation in the natural order of things.

"Your husband, he does not mind your traveling alone?" he suddenly asked.

"I'm not alone. I'm with my cousins."

Tengku studied her with the hint of a smile, his eyes appraising her. "Your husband, what does he do?"

"He is also a professor at the University of California. In fact, I work with him."

"What about your children?"

"I don't have any children." Maggi was disturbed by this sudden veer in the conversation.

Tengku nodded, first at Maggi, then at Ahmed, as if confirming something that was obvious. "You are a professor. Your husband is a professor. Your cousin a professor. Too many scholars in one family makes the blood thin. Even the Chinese know that. Only one child is a scholar. The rest must go into business."

The white *haji* cap framed Tengku's sooty lashes and eyes, making them more prominent and arresting. "A pretty woman like you should have married a man of the sea and had many children," he said. Maggi wanted to laugh, but not because the thought was ludicrous; at a deep, primal level she was shaken.

He was sitting very close to her, face to face, and he gave off an elusive scent, not just his body odor but his *world*. Yes, that was it — an earthy yet clean smell, like river water, and a tantalizing, exotic whiff of chilies and curries eaten so commonly that the spice permeated the flesh. It was not unpleasant, not at all, but Maggi was unsettled by it.

Then the half-smile broadened, and Tengku laughed, a low, teasing chuckle. He turned to Ahmed. "You will tell the *mem-professor* our family chronicle that she will record how princes become men of the sea, and men of the sea become princes." He again used the Malay term *orang laut,* meaning both seamen and pirates.

He suddenly rose, a figure slim and broad-shouldered as a Brahmin prince who now towered over Maggi. "But first you and the Russians must choose another man to be released, as Ahmed says."

Maggi found Vladimir Korsakov in the teak-paneled reception foyer on the promenade deck, conferring with a chunky, dark-haired woman in a blue skirt and white blouse that looked like a uniform despite the blouse's ruffles. Vladimir introduced her as Svetlana Fedorova, the assistant purser. Maggi had met her the night the *Black Sea* had sailed from Singapore, when the absence of the ship's senior purser had completely over-whelmed the woman.

"The pirates won't release the crew members with the largest families," Maggi told the young Russian officer. Since Captain Khromykh's English was so marginal, Korsakov had been designated as Maggi's liaison with the Russian crew to minimize language problems. "They insist the lowest-ranking crew members go first." Maggi hesitated. "They used the word that meant household servants, but they meant people like waiters and maids. The bartenders first, because to a Muslim they're practically untouchables."

Maggi shook her head. "Either Tengku or Ahmed has already thought this out. It has a twisted logic to it."

"Why?" Vladimir was obviously upset.

"They're negotiating for something. I don't know what. But they think that the men with the largest families are probably the older, more senior people with the most important positions. They'd be letting loose their most valuable hostages."

"They think like peasants in the market, but they're right."

"What do they want?" Svetlana asked in an insistent tone.

"They're very vague. We're being traded for something. Usually in hijackings like this the terrorists have other members of their organization in prison and are negotiating for their release."

"We do not have the American experience in these things," Svetlana said, and despite the heavy accent Maggi heard the harsh, accusatory note in her voice. "This terrorism would not happen to us if there were only Europeans, no Americans or your Zionists aboard."

Vladimir looked sharply at the Russian woman, then touched Maggi's arm, as though to steer her away from a confrontation. "We must talk to the captain," he said.

Svetlana had sloe eyes, almost Oriental, which regarded Maggi with an unveiled feminine distrust. There was something strikingly familiar about her expression, although Maggi had met this woman only once, upon boarding, and then briefly. Maggi was out the door with Vladimir at her elbow when she suddenly recognized where she had seen that look before. Ahmed had watched her with the same suspicion and jealousy.

At the foot of the ladder leading up to the captain's bridge, Maggi stopped and questioned Vladimir. "Do the rest of the crew think it's the Americans' fault that they've been hijacked?"

The Russian officer did not bother to deny it politely. His pale blue eyes studied Maggi a moment, then looked away to inspect a pair of guards loitering under the trees along the river bank, hefting M16's and AK-47's. "They don't understand what's happening. It has never happened to a Russian ship or aircraft before, or if it has, we have never been told of it. It's very frightening to them. We are told of these things happening to Americans, but it is always because they have been taken prisoner in a people's war of liberation."

"And what do you believe, Vladimir?"

He turned back to her. "I believe that

we also have now been taken prisoner in somebody's war. And they are releasing one American, then one Russian each day, so that somehow the socialist workers aboard and the rich capitalists must be equally important prisoners to them. And they will release first only the oldest and most sick capitalists and the injured or lowest-grade workers. And that is interesting, because it is a value they have put on each person, according to their worth. Why I do not know."

Vladimir was silent a moment, then shrugged in an angry gesture of frustration. "But I do not need to know. It does not change my duty as an officer. And that is to protect both the passengers and crew. And I cannot do that." There was an almost painful earnestness in his eyes underlined by the thick slash of bandage from temple to jaw.

"I've never thanked you," Maggi said.

"For what?"

"For stepping in to protect me that first night on the bridge. If it hadn't been for me, you would never have been hurt."

Vladimir smiled, but there was a look in his eyes, essentially sad and tragic, that remained unchanged. "I don't think so. I think this terrorist had to draw blood that night, make a cruel gesture, to assert his authority. Perhaps it was good that he cut me. Otherwise he might have killed a crewman or passenger."

Maggi did not really believe that of Tengku. She had not seen any other evidence of cruelty since that first night. Tengku had described Vladimir as "gallant," and the young officer was possibly now trying to spare Maggi feelings of guilt. He would carry the scar for life. Perhaps he felt it comforting to enlarge the significance of his sacrifice.

"I'm grateful to you," Maggi said. "When I heard they had released one of the Russians who was injured, I was sure it was you. I was so surprised to see you again yesterday."

"It was a sailor who was wounded during the boarding."

Maggi was about to ask what had happened, when Vladimir again grasped her elbow to escort her up the ladder. "We must tell the captain and select another," he said. "It must be a barman, yes?"

"Yes." She started up the steps, then recoiled when she spied Ahmed on the deck directly above staring down at her and Vladimir, watching them with a pinched, distrustful face.

20. Think Like a Terrorist

The blast of the .50 caliber machine gun from the frigate's port side jolted Robinson, and the acrid smell of cordite permeated the sweltering air. The *Kapow!* of a 12-gauge shotgun exploded from the starboard side and then the crackling of M14 assault rifles and M60 light machine guns.

The executive officer wandered from side to side on the 02 level, atop the *Decatur*'s boxy superstructure, as a roving safety officer, watching the men on the narrow main deck directly below bang away at sacks of garbage, cardboard boxes, target balloons — anything aboard the gunner's mates could find that would float for a few seconds until it was blitzed out of the water.

In a strange, almost jealous way, Robinson was impressed by the crew's proficiency. Chief Gunner's Mate Maggio flung a crate over the side, waited until the ship's bow wave had carried it off thirty yards, then barked an order. The target disintegrated almost immediately in an eruption of red tracers and white waterspouts.

One of the threats to American frigates and destroyers on patrol in the Persian Gulf was small, high-speed motorboats armed with portable rocket launchers. The crews deployed there were now trained in small arms like a company of infantry grunts.

Since Annapolis, Robinson had been assiduously schooled in fighting with the *Decatur*'s Harpoon antiship missiles and the surface-to-air SM-1's, with their digital computers and monopulse radar. He had studied tech manuals until his eyes burned to learn to knock out missiles with the automatically controlled Vulcan/Phalanx weapons system, hunt submarines with the SQS-56 sonar and the SQR-19 towed array, then kill them with the MK-46 homing torpedoes. The *Decatur* extended its radar eyes and sonar ears out hundreds of miles with the ship's two Seahawk helicopters, and the aircraft transmitted their electronic displays back to the *Decatur*'s combat information center via real-time datalinks. Robinson had hustled, cajoled assignment officers in the Bureau of Naval Personnel, and uprooted his family three thousand miles to be the first in his class to become the executive officer of a state-of-the-art guided-missile frigate. It was painful, professionally repugnant to him to watch the crew of the *Decatur* popping garbage crates with shotguns and assault rifles like a bunch of ghetto gang bangers.

Up forward he caught a glimpse of Stewart on the bridge wing, watching the small-arms practice. There was a look of satisfaction, almost glee in the commanding officer's eyes. The executive officer had read Stewart's service jacket. The man was a Vietnam warrior, a former jungle river rat who was more at ease with an M14 than a guided missile. That's why he had been so hot to hunt down a junk of scurvy, cutthroat Thai fishermen. The commanding officer was a glitch, the anachronism in *Decatur*'s high-tech weapons systems.

There was a sudden break in the firing, and in the lull Robinson heard the distant high-pitched roar of a turboprop. He peered into the glaring haze. A swept-wing, four-engined reconnaissance plane paralleled the *Decatur*'s course at five thousand feet. The plane was Russian. Robinson dashed forward to the bridge.

Stewart was on the starboard wing studying the aircraft through his binoculars. Eddie DiLorenzo, the helicopter detachment's senior officer, was next to him. "He's probably out of Cam Ranh Bay."

"One of the most beautiful beaches in the world," Stewart muttered. "Sand is pure white, and the officers' club sits right at the edge of the surf. Spectacular view. Crystal-clear blue water and swaying palms. And now it's *their* club." Stewart never lowered his binoculars, nor did his eyes leave the Bear.

"Don't shoot him down. Maybe they'll invite us to fly over for a drink." DiLorenzo greeted Robinson. "The Russian Bears are prowling."

"He's being very, very careful not to do anything that might be construed as a hostile maneuver," Stewart said.

"They're supposed to be on our side in this operation."

"Yeah, famous last words of the captain of the *Stark*."

An electric motor whined, and Robinson glanced down onto the ship's bow. There was a surface-to-air missile on the launcher, and it was hunting for the Bear. He looked aft. The 20-mm. Gatling gun was unsheathed and automatically tracking. No one had been called away, nor had Robinson been notified.

The overhead speaker crackled, and Stewart jumped inside the bridge. "Captain of *Decatur,* ve send you happy greetings of peace. Ve search for lost Russian ship *Black Sea.* Also ve vant to take your peecture." The accent was thick as borscht.

Stewart laughed. "Well, I asked them their intentions." He raised his mike. "Russian

278

aircraft, the captain of the *Decatur* returns your happy greetings of peace. Good luck in your search. Call us if we can assist you. And I compliment you on your command of English. Over."

"Yes, thank you very much, captain of *Decatur*. Out." The Tu-95 banked east, the long, graceful swallow wings and tail and the silver fountain-pen body silhouetted against the milky-blue morning sky.

"Officer of the deck, tell combat to stand down the missile and the C-WIZ." It was the acronym for the Gatling gun, the Close-in Weapons System against missiles.

"Aye, aye, sir. Standing down the missile and C-WIZ."

The *Decatur* was sailing northwest, now paralleling the coast of Sumatra off the mountainous island of Bangka. Stewart bent over the chart table. "Eddie, look at these charts."

DiLorenzo was a short, wiry man who bounced on the balls of his feet when he walked. The helo pilot took off his blue cap, which bore his squadron insignia rather than the name and silver silhouette of the USS *Decatur,* and rubbed a freckled pink scalp from which the thin blond hair had already fast receded for his thirty-three years.

"Okay, we did it by the book," Stewart said to him. "Now let's think like terrorists.

Don't think like a gung ho Airedale. Where would you hide this goddamn ship we're looking for?"

"I was studying the charts of this area when we secured from flight ops last night, Captain. This maze of little islands here just south of the Singapore Strait. There are hundreds, maybe a thousand little rocky, jungly islands out there. Peaks that go up to a thousand feet and drop-offs down to . . . nine, ten fathoms." He pointed to the chart. "Look at this narrow, snaky channel here. It's just about wide and deep enough for a ship that size." He traced the channel between Pulau Parit and Pulau Papan with his fingertip. "Twenty-nine to fifty-two feet deep," he read off the chart.

"There are a hundred places like that. Our radar can pick up a Coke can at forty miles on the open sea, but *in there* the ship would be lost in the land return. What about your ship's radar?"

Stewart shook his head. "The SPS-55 and fire-control radars would have the same problem."

The helicopter pilot's pink head bobbed in acknowledgment. "Yeah. And I doubt a plane or satellite would spot it unless they flew directly over it, even if it weren't camouflaged."

"What about your MAD gear?" The Magnetic Anomaly Detector picked up changes in the earth's magnetic field created by the presence of the ferrous body of a submarine or ship.

"Max range is a thousand feet, and that's if we have a clear shot. I'm not sure what our infrared sensors would pick up. If they were running their auxiliaries or generators, the scope could detect the heat a half mile out, provided we were looking right at them. Heavy vegetation or any land mass would absorb the radiations. The satellite sensors would have the same problem."

DiLorenzo nervously drummed his fingertips through the islands of the Riau archipelago. "Yes, sir, with my terrorist cap on that's where I'd stick the ship."

Robinson felt mortified that Stewart was apparently ignoring him in this conference. "Would a bunch of wild-eyed terrorists know that much about our technology?" he asked.

"You don't need a Ph.D. in physics to be a successful smuggler. We learned that in Vietnam. Any fisherman in this area instinctively knows the basics. The bottom line is that no one has seen this ship for four days now." He turned back to DiLorenzo. "What about the mangrove swamps here along the coast of Sumatra?"

"What does the *Black Sea* draw?"

Stewart shook his head. "That's a good question. I haven't seen anything on it. It's 333 feet long with a forty-eight-foot beam." Robinson was surprised that Stewart had the figures memorized.

"It's a hundred feet shorter than *Decatur* but three feet wider," Robinson volunteered. "We draw twenty-five and a half feet. But that's with the sonar dome."

"We only draw fifteen feet at the keel." Stewart shot a look across the bridge. "But all the officers of the deck forget that figure. As far as you're concerned, there's always fifty feet of water under this ship, and if it ever gets a foot less you're in trouble."

"Aye, aye, sir," the two junior officers chorused.

"The swamps don't make any sense to me," DiLorenzo continued. "For one thing they're too shallow. A cruise ship would probably run aground on a sand bar before it got in close. The mangroves wouldn't cover it from the air, and it would stand out pretty good."

Stewart put his hand on DiLorenzo's shoulder. The pilot had been living for the past two days in his flight suit. "You've got your work cut out for you, until the fleet gets here. We have to check out every one of those islands."

"That'll teach me to venture an expert opinion. You think I'm right, huh?"

"I'll bet on it. They're not out there on the open sea. They're hiding somewhere in here." His outstretched palm on the chart only partially covered the jumble of islands from the Singapore Strait to Sumatra.

"How do you know?" Robinson asked.

Stewart rubbed his side, as if he had a stitch. "I don't, but I have an old wound that's beginning to ache and itch like hell," he said.

"A horrible thing, just horrible, awful," the President exclaimed. "This poor fellow Garrity, does he have a family?"

"Yes, sir," the CIA director responded. He had come to the Oval Office to brief the President personally. "According to our information, his wife was on the ship with him."

"It's an atrocity, no other word for it, an atrocity. Why are they doing this thing, do you suppose?"

The CIA director looked in confusion at the President, then at the White House chief of staff. The latter merely blinked back behind his gilt-framed glasses, his jowls pressed to his chest with the gravity of the situation, but said nothing. "Which thing is that, sir?"

"This head thing. It's just horrible."

"Yes, sir, it is. I suppose it's handier."

"Handier!" The President looked revolted.

"I mean it would take several men to lug a whole body around, trying to dump it in a prominent spot. They'd be bound to be caught. This way it just takes one person, even a kid, to deliver the goods."

"A kid?"

"Why not? That's what other terrorist groups use."

"No word has leaked out?"

"Not so far. The Russians have certainly agreed to it. Although we don't have the total picture, the government of Singapore is enforcing a news blackout for reasons of their own. A local newspaper reporter there who got wind of one of the heads is now in police custody."

"Hey, can we do that?" the chief of staff asked.

"No kidding, I want a plumbers job on this as long as we can, you know. Must keep our options open, have to stay flexible. If there are any negotiations, the TV cameras, we don't want them around. The same goes for any rescue operation."

"But what about the families of the hostages?" the chief of staff asked. He was a short, hefty, energetic man, hovering at the side of the seated President, yet he managed to convey that at any moment he would stride out of the room to exercise great power.

"Yes, they should certainly be notified," the President said, his brow furrowed with uncertainty.

"Yes, sir, if you think so. But the *Black Sea* was on a two-week cruise to some pretty remote and exotic spots. Jakarta was the only real city, and their phone and mail service is worse than Rome's. No one really expects to hear from these people for two weeks."

"Two weeks, huh?"

"Yes, sir."

"Well, that's an option, then, isn't it?" The President hunched his shoulders, deep in thought. "Do we even have a clue as to where this ship is? Might be?"

There was a long, reluctant silence, then the CIA director confessed, "No, sir. And neither do the Russians, and at the moment they have considerably more assets searching the area than we do."

"Where's our fleet now?"

"The *Midway* battle group is in the Indian Ocean, still two, three days away."

The President absorbed this and sat brooding for several moments. "They really don't want all that much, do they, when you add it all up. I mean, it's really this principle thing, arms for hostages, isn't it." He looked sharply at the CIA director. "Would you deal?"

"It's not my place to recommend policy, sir."

"What if it were your kids or father and mother or wife on that ship?"

"They could probably have whatever they wanted. What does that say about me?"

The chief of staff touched him on the shoulder, smiled, and said, "You're a good family man, like the rest of us." They both looked back at the President.

21. An Experiment with Pork

Captain John Campbell, the naval attaché of the United States embassy in Singapore, jabbed at a wall chart of the South China Sea. "A submerged submarine creates a turbulence, conical in shape, as it slides through the water. In due course this turbulence rises to the surface, well astern of the sub, and it begets minute deviations in the wave patterns. We now have over-the-horizon, back-

286

scatter radars in the Aleutians, Guam, and Okinawa that can read these patterns at great distances and track the submarine. Our satellite and aircraft sensors can analyze the temperature differentials in a ship's wake, hours after it passes, and read its size, speed, and type. Our space tracking stations can pinpoint a target with an accuracy of twenty-five nanorads; that's an error of not more than one foot in 7,500 miles — "

Blocker finished the thought for him. "But we can't find a gleaming white three-hundred-foot luxury liner with 135 well-heeled American tourists, probably 90 percent of them solid Republicans."

Campbell pointed to the Lingga archipelago south of Singapore. "The *Decatur* reports the Russians have their long-range search planes working the area."

Blocker sipped his coffee, savored it, and threw out his next comment as if it were a chance remark rather than something he had been pondering for two days. "Your friend Stewart is an interesting man."

"Why do you say that?"

"His reactions when we briefed him. He didn't bat an eye when we told him about the head. His executive officer was somewhat shaken, but Stewart acted as if he's been there before."

"Maybe he has. He was in the 'brown-water' navy in Vietnam. Your CIA guys would bail out locals who were in jail for murder, rape, something particularly nasty, under the condition that they would work in reconnaissance units. They'd give them a bounty to assassinate a particular individual, say a Viet Cong tax collector, or kidnap a village chief for interrogation. Fight terror with terror, that was the program. They'd move in at night on navy boats with a SEAL backup to a village or a stronghold. If they were to assassinate a certain individual, they would have to bring back evidence that the person had been killed. Ears . . . whatever."

"And Stewart stayed in the navy after 'Nam?" Blocker questioned.

Campbell shrugged. "He had the right credentials. A regular commission from the University of Virginia NROTC. Then a first tour salting down his stripes on a destroyer off Vietnam. But he was one of those Southern boys with a wild macho streak. He told me that he felt he was missing the war. So he volunteered for the Swift boats. At first they just interdicted the supplies the North smuggled down the coast to the Viet Cong by trawler and junks, boarded fishing boats. Then the navy moved into the Mekong Delta, that whole maze of inland canals and rivers."

"You knew him then?" Blocker was surprised.

"I was the ops officer aboard an LST that was mother ship for the patrol craft. The Swift boat officers were ensigns or lieutenant j.g.'s, little more than a year out of school and anxious to have their career tickets punched with a quick combat tour. They would check in with me and ask, 'What's the tactical doctrine?'

"And when I said there wasn't any, most of the career men didn't know what to do, except sit tight and protect their asses. Stewart just grinned and said, 'Terrific, you mean I can make this up as I go along.' "

"What kind of guy is he?" Blocker asked casually.

Campbell gave him a wary look, but then his face unexpectedly split into a sly smile, as if he were remembering a favorite story. "We had a running battle with the CIA and navy intelligence in the Delta. Your guys had a book that said that infiltration into the South was through an extension of the Ho Chi Minh Trail. We *knew* the enemy was coming by *sampans* down the smaller canals and creeks from Cambodia. Hotshots like Stewart, operating on their own, ignored the intelligence, and, frankly, 90 percent of the time they were right. In violation of direct orders, Stewart — and he wasn't the only boat who did this, mind you — went upriver into Cambodia, where he knew the VC and North Vietnamese were infiltrating. At dusk he pulls into a canal so narrow his boat is scraping the banks and so shallow his screws are churning mud. They're under the overhanging jungle growth, but his crew cuts down more branches with machetes and drapes them over the boat for camouflage. Then they wait for hours in the pitch black.

"About midnight they hear a convoy of *sampans* coming downriver, but they can't see anything. Stewart's crew is really wired — remember there are only five of them — and they wait until the *sampans* are within twenty-five feet before they open up. All hell breaks loose; Stewart's .50-calibers pour literally thousands of rounds into the *sampans*. Blow away everyone on board. Then he unloads the *sampans*, strips whatever intelligence he finds on the bodies, and hightails it back downriver before it gets light. It's so pitch black they can only see the river banks on radar.

"That morning he dumps AK-47's, mortars, all kinds of weapons, medical supplies from Sweden at the intelligence officer's feet, and drawls in that laid-back Virginian accent of his, 'My compliments to the CIA and navy intelligence, sir. These are merely a token of the weapons and supplies that you gentlemen and scholars maintain are not being shipped down the canals from Cambodia.' "

Blocker laughed. "This guy's a man after my own heart. But I'm amazed he made it to commander."

"Hell, the Pentagon considered the Delta some kind of backwater banana navy. The real navy was out on the carriers in the Gulf of Tonkin. Everybody knew that. But the commander of the in-country navy was Elmo Zumwalt, and when he was made chief of naval operations, all of his brown-water task force commanders became admirals. Crowe, who ran the riverboat operation, made it to chairman of the Joint Chiefs of Staff. Stewart's been on the fast track ever since."

"And you've been buddies all this time?"

Campbell shrugged. "Not really. But I visited him in the naval hospital in San Diego when I was passing through."

"He was wounded?"

Campbell nodded. "He was lucky. He healed without any disability." But the dour way in which he said it gave Blocker the impression that there was a great deal the naval attaché was not telling him about the wounding of Henry Stewart.

"The hospital was where I met Charlotte, his sweetheart from Virginia," Campbell volunteered, as if changing the subject. "I was stationed in Norfolk, so I was invited to the wedding. You know how it is. The wives exchange Christmas cards. We ran into each other occasionally, when paths crossed or ships passed. And the wives passed on all the horror stories." There was a lowering note in Campbell's voice, a mournful dirge of past tense that said they did not live happily ever after.

"What happened?"

"She . . . died." For several moments Campbell did not elaborate, then said simply, "Raped. Murdered."

"Jesus. What happened?"

"No one really knows. It happened on his last job. Stewart was assigned to the Pentagon. Executive assistant to the navy's chief of legislative affairs. He and Charlotte bought an old house in Alexandria, just a subway stop from work but right on the edge of where the better-class white folks are supposed to live. You know how it is — Alexandria, Georgetown, Philadelphia. You have the black slums, houses falling apart, but a transition area where the homes are *historic*. You get all sorts of tax breaks if you restore them. Then they're worth a small fortune.

That's what Charlotte was doing while Stewart was putting in sixteen-hour days at the Pentagon."

"They ever catch who did it?"

Campbell shook his head. "A neighbor said she saw some black guy. But there were workmen coming and going all the time, so she didn't pay that much attention. Stewart discovered the body when he came home. It's not something he ever talks about."

There was a long silence, and Blocker sat contemplating the tragedy — and the question that came immediately to his mind. There was no delicate way to word it. "So what, in your professional opinion, have we got out there? The right man in the right spot, or a loose cannon primed to explode?"

Campbell shot him an angry look. "That's a lousy question." There was outrage in his voice, but then doubt, as if he were asking himself the same question.

The telephone on the naval attaché's desk buzzed. "Yes?" Campbell listened for a moment, acknowledged with a formal "Yes, sir," hung up, and looked at Blocker curiously. "The ambassador wants to see you in his office *immediately*. You kill someone?"

"Just the usual suspects."

The ambassador sat behind his desk in

stone-faced silence as Blocker entered. There was a small Chinese man with him.

"Mr. Blocker, this is Mr. Yee Baiyu with the Office of the Prime Minister," the ambassador said with a grave formality. It was not an introduction, and neither Yee nor the ambassador rose.

Yee made only the slightest movement of his head to study Blocker but otherwise did not acknowledge him. Blocker had seen this man before at various foreign embassy functions. Blocker's first impression was of a delicacy, almost a physical fragility, about the man, and his second was of the disciplined intelligence in the thin ivory face and black eyes that examined him and the erect authority that frail frame mustered.

"Mr. Yee has informed me that the Republic of Singapore has declared you, Mr. Blocker, persona non grata. You have twenty-four hours to wrap up your affairs and leave Singapore by the first available flight." The ambassador shifted his gaze from Yee to Blocker, as if the move required great effort. "And I am requested to contact Washington for further instruction concerning the *Black Sea* affair and, if necessary, return to Washington for those instructions."

After his encounter at the American embassy, Yee immediately returned to his office and briefed the minister by phone. He was about to leave for lunch when he received a sudden urgent call from Ballinger.

"I have several rather curious things to show you," the pathologist said.

When Yee arrived at the forensic science institute, the stooped old Englishman showed him into his cluttered office. Yee was grateful that they were not going into the autopsy laboratory. "I will examine the two . . . remains later," he volunteered.

"It's not really necessary. That's my job, you know." He seemed more amused than annoyed by Yee's insistence on examining the heads.

"I learned a great deal from the first one."

"Oh, did you?" Ballinger questioned with undisguised cynicism.

"Yes. What is it you wanted me to see?"

"This." He picked up a small plastic envelope in which Yee could see what looked like a black splinter of wood an inch long. "I almost missed it, a slight puncture wound in the neck. Not the sort of thing you readily notice in a head that's been lopped off at the neck, as it were. But there it was. I probed it with a tweezer, and that's what I plucked out."

"What is it?"

"The tip of a bamboo dart, I expect. That black stuff is probably the sap of the piva tree. It's rather toxic by itself, but it's often mixed with cobra venom, and that gives it quite a deadly kick. Almost instantaneous. So don't prick yourself with it."

Yee held the envelope gingerly by its corner and peered at it incredulously. "A poison dart?"

"A good shot can down a boar or deer, knock a two-hundred-pound orangutan out of a very high tree. The Dayaks in East Malaysia are quite expert. It doesn't poison the meat if you bake it over a fire, but if you boil or fry it, the poison may kill you."

"Why?"

"I don't really know why. Possibly the higher heat of baking destroys the toxin."

"I meant *why* did they kill him with a poison dart?"

"Oh. Well, it's quite silent, of course. *Poof!*" Ballinger blew out air forcefully. "That doesn't raise an alarm. And it's considerably less chancy than sneaking up on a man and trying to cut his throat with a knife. I would venture that this shot was rather close, considering the depth of the penetration. It hit with some force."

Yee nodded but said nothing. The ancient Englishman's military and medical career spanned the Japanese invasion, internment as a prisoner of war, the campaigns against the communist guerrillas on the Malay peninsula, the violent early years of independence. He was a font of bizarre and terrible knowledge. Yee made a mental note to have a young Chinese or Indian doctor assigned as his personal assistant so that it would not all be lost.

"You're certain he died of the poison?"

"Yes. We ran a sample through the GCMS, the gas chromatography mass spectrometer, to analyze it. The tests are reasonably conclusive, even though he was quite ripe."

"Ripe?"

"Yes, that's the other curious thing. This is from the head of the Russian seaman delivered the night before last. It was then two, three days old. The others have all been relatively fresh."

"Why is this one older?" Yee wondered aloud.

"An interesting question. The heads are rolling rather ritualistically, aren't they? One day a Russian, the next an American. My guess is that this second Russian was killed the first night and held for two days. Last night it was another American. Tonight I expect a third Russian head will turn up."

Yee was appalled that Ballinger had so

flippantly voiced this speculation, but the same thought had occurred to him. "You are reasonably certain of the time of each death now?"

Ballinger nodded and twisted the tip of his nicotine-stained mustache. It was an oddly self-conscious, almost prideful gesture. "I've been running a rather interesting scientific control, you see. Since these things have begun showing up with a certain punctuality, I thought it might be useful to have an accurate, day-by-day measure of the rate of putrefaction of flesh in our climate."

Yee felt queasy, but he leaned forward with excitement. "You can do this?"

"It has a native ingenuity, actually. Each morning on my way to work I stop in China-town and pick up a bit of freshly butchered pork at the Kreta Ayer market. One must elbow through the *amahs* at that hour. You Chinese are quite keen on meat being freshly butchered, much more so than we British, who have a taste for a bit of gaminess in our meat."

"Pork?" Yee's stomach heaved. The old man constantly astonished him.

"Yes. I've been told by unfortunate fellows who've had occasion to eat it in order to survive that human flesh has very much the same texture, *and taste,* as pork. Indeed, one might speculate that this is the origin of the Hebraic and Muslim prohibitions — "

"Last night, the American?" Yee's stomach surged alarmingly, but he had to know.

"A critical case of arteriosclerosis. Judging from the fatty deposits in his neck arteries, this poor chap Garrity didn't have all that long to live. But without going into the gamy technical details, as it were, I can state with reasonable certainty that he was killed twelve to eighteen hours before we found the head."

"And tonight . . . ?" The appalling question had to be asked.

"I can give you an estimate rather quickly now." Ballinger limped to a sliding glass door opening onto an outside balcony wide enough only for tropical flower boxes. He threw it open. Yee heard the savage buzzing of flies and smelled the gruesome stench a moment before he discerned the meticulously labeled piles of decomposing, bloody offal.

"I keep a variety of comparable pig head meats — ears, brains, jowls . . ."

Yee's stomach exploded, and he dove for a waste paper basket.

It took a while for Yee to clean up. He was completely mortified and kept apologizing, "My stomach is too delicate — " but the Englishman waved off his apology with an imperious hand and motioned Yee to take a seat. Yee in his red-faced embarrassment was painfully eager to leave, but the grimness of the pathologist's expression arrested him.

"What is it?"

"Something quite horrible is happening, an escalation, as it were."

That anything could horrify the old Englishman was unthinkable. "What is it?"

"Remember my telling you that we can deduce certain things from the bloodiness of the neck stump?"

Yee's mind reeled, but he said, "Yes."

"Well, this last head, the American — it was lopped off while he was still alive, and presumably kicking."

22. The Sons of Sultan Iskandar Shah

Without a single fence or barred window, the luxury liner *Black Sea* had become a prison ship. The river itself was a fast-flowing, steep-walled moat beyond which a handful of armed guards loitered in desultory patrols, assault rifles slung haphazardly over their shoulders, as much a threat to their own lives and limbs as to their hostages'.

Aside from Tengku's immediate lieutenants, the counsellors of his court, the pirates camped ashore along the shady river bank. Tengku appeared to rotate them haphazardly on board four or five at a time as a personal bodyguard or randomly spot them about the ship to intimidate the passengers. But the chaotic shooting and terror of the first day had not reoccurred.

The passengers and crew members emerged from their air-conditioned staterooms and quarters to suffer the hot, fetid air and stare off into the dark green shadows of the tropical rain forest beyond. Large orange-striped leeches dangled from the low leaves of bushes ashore, waving their slimy, snakelike bodies, sensing the blood feast just a few feet away. The steady sibilance of the cicadas beat through the forest like a sustained wail, broken only by the ghastly cries and hoots of other unknown insects, birds, and primates, and the occasional roar of a prowling great cat.

The prisoners shuddered at the sounds that resounded through the woods as though they were the tortured cries of those who had dared venture into the jungle. The giant trees along the bank loomed as more than the outer walls of their prison, for beyond them there was not freedom but punishment for escape.

Those with portholes had glimpsed a trackless, steaming swamp downriver as the ship had sailed through. From the descriptions, Maggi reasoned it was a tidal mangrove swamp, but her knowledge of the local natural history afforded her no immunity from the quicksandlike muck, the clouds of blood-draining mosquitoes, the poisonous kraits, or the monstrous crocodiles that inhabited this morass.

With no more obstacles Devil's Island had imprisoned tougher, more desperate men than the crew and middle-aged and elderly passengers of the *Black Sea*. They remained aboard, affording their captors no cause to abuse them, made prisoners more by their air conditioning, soap and showers, toilets, three gourmet meals a day, movies, books, and card games, and the hope of an orderly release made tangible each day by the visible departure of one of their number, than by the guns of their captors.

Normally passengers and crew embarked on a long sea voyage equipped themselves by design for long periods of idleness, but now boredom loomed as the most immediate menace. The American passengers sensibly comforted one another with phrases like, "It could be a lot worse, believe me." And when someone complained, the sardonic catch-word was, "Look, don't rock the boat."

The Russians found little solace in Captain Khromykh's assurance that they would still be paid. Only a third of the ninety crew members were actually the officers, seamen, and engineers who operated the ship. Their work and routine was actually easier ashore than at sea, but for the majority — the cooks, waiters and waitresses, maids and stewards — the demands made upon them by the confined, frightened American guests increased daily. At first the Russian staff grumbled about it privately, then openly. But Captain Khromykh and his officers prowled the ship, maintaining discipline and grand-hotel service, as if there were a special Siberia awaiting those who let down the shipping line's standards.

Still, the constant threat of violence crackled in the heavy, summery air like static electricity. That afternoon — the fourth day of captivity — it erupted.

Eight or nine passengers had crowded into the narrow starboard passageway outside the doctor's office. Each silently waited for his or her interview with Dr. Yakovlev to convince the physician that this patient's high blood pressure, diabetes, or prostate trouble had become life threatening and required immediate medical evacuation. The jammed corridor's only ventilation was the stairwell leading to the promenade deck above. The stifling heat and the hostility among the sweltering passengers quickly rose to critical mass.

"So what's wrong with you?" the emeritus professor of biology Arthur Strauss interrogated the banker Whitney Elliott III, who stood ahead of him in line. The suspicion in Strauss's tone was as heavy as the humidity.

"It's my heart. I should never have come on this trip. My doctor warned me."

"You would desert your wife?" Strauss asked, genuinely shocked.

"She's safer here with all the passengers, I assure you, than making the trip to Singapore alone with these savages."

"You're a coward and a liar!" Strauss exploded. "At least my wife's not here."

"You're both liars," yelled the vice president of a telephone company. "You're no sicker than I am."

A sweating, red-faced, and enraged Strauss punched the executive in the face.

The Society's attorney, Williard Howell, Jr., and a retired government economist simultaneously grappled to restrain Strauss, but in the melee they shoved others aside, and a free-for-all exploded. Two Russian crewmen on the promenade deck above jumped down the ladder to stop the fight, and they were immediately attacked.

The sudden explosion of a Kalashnikov detonated in the corridor. There were screams, and everybody dropped to the ground, the bodies falling in writhing heaps atop one another, clawing to get closer to the ground. A pirate in a red batik headcloth stood on the ladder and fired another burst up the ladder into the air. There was a shout. The pirate shouted back, and a second pirate poked his assault rifle down the ladder. He stared at the squirming, whimpering passengers piled on the floor, then laughed uproariously. The two guards poked and kicked the rioters to their feet. None had been shot. The passageway was too cramped for anyone to throw a damaging punch, but several of the men were bleeding, and Williard Howell, Jr.'s, nose had somehow been broken.

Maggi rushed to Dr. Yakovlev's office as soon as she heard the shots, but by that time the guards had herded the brawling passengers back up the ladder. Like chastised children they were sent to their rooms. The doctor was at his desk leafing through a large stack of passenger forms. The assistant purser Svetlana Fedorova was with him. Both looked up at once and glared at Maggi with disdain, as though she were personally responsible for the behavior of the American passengers.

Yakovlev held up one of the papers and waved it at Maggi. "Each of our distinguished guests has completed the required declaration that they are fit and well and able to undertake this cruise. None notified the shipping line of a physical disability or illness, as required when reservations were made. Any particular dietary requirements noted were minor, certainly not threatening in any way. There are no cases of life and death. Aside from Captain Khromykh's desire to get your Mr. Schneider off the ship as soon as possible to prevent an international incident, there are no obvious medical choices."

"What about Garrity, the man who went yesterday?"

Yakovlev shrugged. "He is a fat sausage about to burst."

Svetlana smiled, but there was a dark, mean-spirited humor in the twist of her mouth.

"Well, who are you recommending to be released next?"

Yakovlev shuffled through the papers on his desk, but from the perfunctory way in which he did it, Maggi had the impression he already knew the name. "Ah, yes, Mrs.

Clarence Murdock."

Maggi was appalled. "That woman's healthy as a horse."

"She has a heart condition aggravated by her weight." Yakovlev averted his eyes.

"Did you examine her, or did she tell you that? Did she also tell you that she and the President were good friends?"

The doctor looked directly at her with an ironic smile. "She said she had access to great funds which she generously makes available to those who act in her interests. That is the American way, is it not?"

The Russian was beyond pretense. Mrs. Murdock had bribed him, and he was now suggesting that Maggi get her own piece of the action. She wondered if the fat sausage Garrity had also greased his way to freedom.

A handsome Oriental carpet, a blood-red geometric weave, hung on the wall behind Yakovlev, apparently an objet d'art he was loath to have his patients trample.

"Tengku won't release women," Maggi said. "He insists the journey is too dangerous."

"Then you must convince him that he should," Yakovlev snapped in a biting voice. "Even most American men will not leave the ship unless their wives are safe first."

After the debacle in the passageway outside, Maggi could not protest the insult. She turned on her heel and left the office.

To her surprise Svetlana immediately followed her out. "Ah, Mrs. Chancellor, congratulations." She seized Maggi's left hand with a fierce strength that astonished her and held it up to inspect Liz's wedding ring. "I see you have remarried so quickly. Your husband's face should be cut with sword for you, not Vladimir Korsakov." The Russian woman glared at Maggi with a hatred and jealousy that seared. Then, as abruptly as she had seized the hand, she dropped it and bolted up the ladder to the next deck, leaving Maggi stunned.

What was the relationship between Vladimir and this woman? Maggi understood her infatuation, if that was all it was, with Vladimir — the sensitive, handsome face set off by the straw-colored hair and the pale blue eyes, exotic, Slavic, and soulful in a way that was peculiarly Russian. To see that face mutilated, scarred for life because of another woman, however blameless, had evidently enraged her. Maggi had no logic, no argument against that naked rage.

None of the Malays was in the lounge. Through the windows she spotted Tengku outside on the forward deck with Ahmed, three armed guards, and a stocky pirate with long, lank, hippie-length black hair whom she had heard called Mohammed. They were all peering up into the jungle canopy. At this point the great trees of the rain forest on either bank spanned the river, totally covering it.

Mohammed raised his arms as though he were holding an imaginary rifle and fired, pantomimed a kickback, made a soaring motion with his left hand and a loud *whooshing* sound, wiggling his fingers as he raised his arm higher to indicate a missile in flight, then swept both in a wide, expanding explosion, *"Barrrooom!"* The pirates all laughed but continued to stare up into the trees.

Through the open windows Maggi now heard the sound, the distant high-pitched roar of an airplane overheard. It was muffled by the trees and very high. She stepped back into the shadows of the lounge, where she could still see and hear the pirates but they could not readily see her.

"Is it American or Russian?" Tengku asked.

Mohammed shrugged. "American or Russian, my little hornet will sting him to death five kilometers away."

Tengku smiled broadly and patted him on the back. "But not five kilometers from *here*. When you fish for sharks, you do not pour blood into the water near your village and fish traps. You sail a day to the south."

"A 'diversionary attack.' " Mohammed used the English phrase.

"We have a 'professional soldier.' " Tengku also used the English phrase and gripped Mohammed affectionately by both shoulders. "We are blessed." He turned to Ahmed. "This is our general in the field," he pronounced.

Mohammed grinned broadly.

"The fast American warship with the helicopters?" Tengku asked him.

"The fishing boats say it is a day to the south. The Kepulauan Lingga."

"That is a day's sail for a *prahu,* not for the American warship. We must lure it away. The Americans and Russians are like fish. Pour a little blood in the water, and they all swarm here from everywhere and rush back and forth crazy, looking for the meat. So now we must throw some blood in the water, and they will all rush to that spot."

"Yes, Abang."

"God go with you, Dik." The conversation had an easy Malay intimacy in which everyone was addressed by family terms. Tengku was *abang,* "big brother," and Mohammed was *dik,* "little brother." Whatever pretensions Tengku paraded before his hostages, Maggi noted that he was always Abang to the other pirates, and he warmly embraced them as Dik, as if the band was interwoven with fraternal ties of blood.

Dik Mohammed disappeared down the ladder to the promenade deck.

Tengku made a gesture toward the airplane, which by now had flown out of earshot. *"Superpowers!"* he roared. *"Superfish!"* The pirates all laughed with him. "Did I tell you this *jihad* was blessed?" he asked in a quieter, enticing tone. "You will be rewarded like *tunkus* in this world and in Paradise." Each state of Malaysia had a hereditary sultan, and the *tunkus* were the members of the royal families, born to power and wealth. The three armed brigands now encircled Tengku. "The winds of Paradise are blowing," he intoned, as though the phrase were an incantation.

"Ah, yes, Abang." The pirates grinned and nodded as happily as children who had been promised a fabulous excursion.

"This is his destiny," Ahmed pronounced in an oddly wheedling voice.

Tengku twisted about and stared at Ahmed with shining eyes. "Yes, my destiny," he repeated, hypnotized by the word. Both used the Arabic term *kismet*.

He moved forward to reenter the lounge, and Maggi scurried back and hurled herself into the chair in which she usually sat during her audiences with the pirate chieftain. She posed with her hands folded demurely in her lap, as if she were patiently waiting for his return. At the sound of his footstep on the inlaid-wood floor of the lounge, she turned and smiled at him.

He strode into the room with his retinue of Ahmed and the three guards. The danger, and the power, he radiated at that moment seemed almost an aura, and it startled Maggi. He smiled at the sight of her, a surprisingly broad smile of even white teeth. "Ah, Mrs. Chancellor, some of your countrymen do you no honor. A fistfight to decide who is the most sick and should be released. Tsk, tsk, tsk." He clicked his tongue in disapproval.

Through some grapevine of his own Tengku already knew the reason for the riot outside the doctor's office. Rather than showing anger, he regarded it with glee, like some great cosmic joke. "See," he said, wagging his finger at Ahmed, "God now chooses for us the biggest liars and cowards among the passengers. That is how He shows mercy."

Maggi was taken aback. At first she had believed that the pirates were releasing the sick and wounded for humanitarian reasons. But she had been wrong. Like a slave trader Tengku was placing a value on each of his captives. The ill and disabled were worthless; that's why they had been let go. Then he had decided that the lowest-ranking members of the crew would be set free. A bartender was deemed lower than a waiter or steward. But even that had been a practical, not a moral, judgment. As devout Muslims, the terrorists had outlawed all liquor, but food still had to be served and the ship's compartments cleaned. In Tengku's scale of values, he would rank the lowest able-bodied seaman above the black-tied and tuxedoed maitre d', whom he considered little more than a liveried house servant.

But now the judgment was *moral;* there was no other word for it. Those who feigned sickness would be released — Maggi did not dare broach the subject that they might have bribed the doctor — because they were cowards and liars.

"You're going to release them?" she was astonished.

Tengku nodded. "In their time. The Faithful do not keep pigs or harbor dogs."

Maggi was at a total loss. But perhaps this was the same self-righteous code that dictated Tengku not abuse his hostages and allow them to exist as comfortably as they had. Maggi chose her next words with great deliberation. Dealing with the pirate chieftain was not unlike coddling her ex-husband's vanities. Only the language was different. "Your way is righteous, I know, and I want to understand the Law. The women passengers are also of little worth. Why would you not release them first?"

Ahmed shifted uneasily in his chair, and he stared at Maggi with even more wariness than usual. But Tengku smiled, and the extraordinary long, dark lashes batted at her. "But you are of great value to me. Your learning, your intelligence, your beauty. You are like a *tunku*." A Malay princess. His voice was deep, persuasive, almost a purr.

"It is a pity you are married," Tengku said matter-of-factly. "It would be stimulating to have a wife who is so educated and spirited."

"You already have a wife." He wore a wedding ring.

"Ah, yes, but I am allowed four by the Koran," he said with a teasing smile. The dark, heavy-lidded eyes took measure of her in some unaccountably sexual way.

Maggi was stirred, then acutely uneasy, not because she felt threatened but because Tengku somehow drew her in, a magnet that pulled at fine wires deep within her. She felt herself blush. It took a moment for her to speak. "I am deeply flattered and

314

honored by what you say of me." She did not dare look into his eyes, and not merely out of a pretended modesty. She took a deliberate breath. "I do not speak for myself."

"For someone else then?" he asked with concern.

Maggi took the plunge. "My cousin, who is like a sister to me. Her husband is not a coward. He will not leave the ship without her, and he will die here. His heart. He should have had an operation, but he took this cruise to please her, and now all that has happened will kill him." Maggi fell silent but kept her eyes down. She had given it her best shot. Schneider could not have asked for a better pleading.

There was a long silence, then Ahmed broke it. "It is not proper for a woman to make such a trip. Only one may go at a time. She would be alone with other men. There are no toilets, no separations. She must sleep with them." He shook his head vehemently. "No, it is not proper."

"We will pray for your cousin's husband. He is in God's hands, and He will be merciful," Tengku stated. The matter was closed.

He turned to Ahmed. "This is a good time. You will now tell *mem-professor* the family annals, so that she may write down who I am. This *orang laut* who challenges the great powers of the world." To Maggi he said, "You have been chosen to record this." Tengku stressed the word *chosen* as he had said "my destiny" just a few minutes before, not with conceit but with a sense of awe at being the instrument of fate.

Margaret Chancellor, Ph.D. in political science, University of California, Berkeley, had prepared for this opportunity. From her purse she pulled out her note pad, pen, and a small Sony tape recorder. "May I please record this?" she asked Ahmed with careful politeness. "It is important that it be exactly as you say it." Maggi had seen Sony cassette players in the grass shacks of Malay aborigines, so she knew it should not be alien to the pirates.

Ahmed, in fact, appeared to regard it as a compliment. *"Mari,"* he said, inviting Maggi to go ahead.

"I will begin in the time of our ancestor Prince Parameswara in the country we now call Sumatra," he pronounced. To her surprise Ahmed visibly relaxed. The probing suspicion with which he had always regarded Maggi now evaporated, as he eased into what was apparently a familiar role as storyteller.

"Parameswara was a prince of the Srivijaya, a great people who commanded the sea between China and India for five hundred years.

But wars with the kings of Java and Thailand bled and weakened the kingdom of the Srivijaya, and Parameswara had to flee. He sailed first to Singapura, but the chief there was a lackey of the Thais. So Parameswara killed him and ruled there and the neighboring islands for five years. The Thais attacked with a great army, and our ancestors fled once more. They sailed up the Malay coast for a day, until they saw the mouth of a great river, and there they built a new city, which became Malacca. That was in the Christian year 1402."

Maggi listened intently. She knew the dates were debatable and the stories as much legend as history, but somewhere in this *tusut* were clues to where they were now and what exactly Tengku and his men were after.

"It was in his city of Malacca that Prince Parameswara heard the Word of God and converted to Islam. He took the title Sultan Iskandar Shah. And in their submission to God, our ancestors once again became a great people. Malacca became the center of Islam and the center of trade. Arab, Persian, and Indian traders sailed on the southwest monsoons, and under the protection of Malacca they met with the great Chinese junks who came on the northeast monsoons. It was said that more than a hundred languages were spoken in the marketplace. The city over-flowed with gold, silver, tin, precious woods from these jungles, silk and porcelain from China, cloth from India, but especially the spices from these islands."

Tengku interrupted, "The spices were so valuable that a full cargo paid for the ship and the cost of the voyage *ten times* over." His voice lowered with awe at the profit margin. "Europe could not live without our spices." Tengku smiled broadly to share a great joke with Maggi, and he waved his hand in an elegant gesture. "It was these Spice Islands that your Columbus was seeking when he found America instead."

Maggi laughed, because it was true. These were the fabled Indies toward which the great explorer had sailed.

Ahmed's tone suddenly grew solemn. "Malacca was the richest seaport in the whole world, with the greatest number of merchants and abundance of shipping that could be found. Iskandar Shah, now Sultan of Malacca, was succeeded by Muzaffar Shah, then Mansur Shah, Ala'ud-din, and Mahmud Shah. The empire of Malacca embraced the whole of the Malay peninsula, Sumatra, and ranged from India through the Spice Islands of Indonesia to the Philippines, but always spreading Islam throughout."

Maggi glanced at Tengku. He listened with a rapt expression, like a child who has heard a bedtime story a hundred times before but each night renews his fascination.

"Then in 1511 the Portuguese came, not to trade, but with their cannons and their crosses. They attacked the city like a pack of ravenous dogs for seventeen days and seventeen nights. They blew down our mosques and murdered our people, and then they burned the Faithful at the stake, shoving the crosses in their face while they screamed their lives out. The air was so thick with greasy smoke that the sun could not be seen. The Portuguese said they saved our souls for Christ, but they stole our rich bazaars, our laden ships, our bountiful warehouses, and sold our people into slavery." Ahmed's voice was soft, but it quavered with the practiced sorrow and rage of an adept storyteller.

The son of the last Sultan of Malacca fled to Johor, but the Portuguese followed and sacked that city. For the Portuguese Catholics, the conquest of Malacca and the Spice Islands had become a fanatical holy war of appalling brutality against the Muslim traders. Ahmed spared no horrifying detail as an ancestor writhed in the flames of the auto-da-fé.

The surviving sons of Parameswara fled for their lives to the sea as their ancestors had. At this point Ahmed's narrative picked up with one of Mahmud Shah's nephews and chronicled a succession of begats in *kampongs* up and down the Malacca Strait.

"Then the Dutch, who worshipped Christ in a different way, drove out the Portuguese. And the English followed from their trading bases in India to trade with the Dutch. They traded their port of Bencoolen in Sumatra for Malacca, as you might trade fish for jackfruit. And the English took Malaysia and Singapore. The Dutch took what we now call Indonesia, and the Spanish the Philippines. We were no longer one great people in Islam but a hundred million slaves with many cruel masters."

Every scion in Ahmed's tree was heir to an ancient grievance — an ancestor butchered by the Portuguese, enslaved by the Dutch, cheated out of his fishing boat by Chinese or Indian merchants, an *orang laut* sunk, jailed, or hanged as a pirate by the British — as exact an accounting as any kept by the Chinese on their abacuses.

Maggi was lulled by the succession of "sons of," waves endlessly breaking upon the Malay coast, then dissolving back into the sea, until suddenly, in a small *kampong* north of Malacca, Tengku Azhar material-ized, the son of Tengku Rahman, a trader and fisherman.

With this pronouncement Ahmed fell strangely silent. Despite all the clues, Maggi had somehow lost track of where it was all leading. Now it struck her with the force of a revelation. This fisherman's son Tengku Azhar, was tracing his direct descent back to the Sultan of Malacca, the propagator of the Faith, proclaiming himself heir to the ancient throne.

It was all hearsay and myth, totally un-provable. Historically, the sultans had been weak and corrupt. But Ahmed stared at her, a small smile playing on his lips, as though daring her to challenge it. She recognized instantly in that mean, cunning face why he had created such a glorious *tusut*. In estab-lishing this heritage for Tengku, his tall, handsome, charismatic cousin, that ugly gnome Ahmed had also claimed it for him-self. But why?

"It is important that you know this his-tory," Tengku said in a soft voice. "That we are not a gang of terrorists running amok in the name of Islam."

"What do you want?" Maggi exclaimed.

"To be what we are. To again be a great people in Islam. The colonialists are now

321

gone, but we are left divided and poor. Malaysia and Indonesia are brothers quarreling in the same language. Singapore greedily hoards all its wealth and trade for itself, and Brunei is obscenely wealthy with its oil. While all around them our brothers starve. In the southern islands of the Philippines, the Muslims bleed to death, fighting to be free of a corrupt Catholic government in Manila. Five countries but one people. The sons of the soil are paupers in their own lands, while the Europeans and Chinese and Indians grow rich." Tengku's voice was impassioned not with anger but with pain.

Maggi saw only the gleaming dark eyes framed by the white *haji* cap. They burned into her with a feverish intensity. This pirate really believed his birthright was to reign over the largest Muslim population in the world, and she and everybody else aboard the *Black Sea* were hostages to that delusion.

23. Memories of Mangrove Swamps

Stewart sat back in the swivel-mounted, black leather captain's chair on the starboard side of the bridge and read the dispatch aloud. "The *Black Sea*'s scheduled ports of call were Jakarta and Semarang on Java, Komodo Island, Bau Bau on Butung Island, Pare Pare on Sulawesi, and Bali. On Bali the passengers were scheduled to transfer to the airport for a flight to Hong Kong and then to San Francisco."

"That's some exotic cruise." The executive officer Robinson shook his head. "The only ports you mentioned that I've even heard of are Jakarta and Bali. But if ComSeventhFleet gives us a choice of where to look for this ship, my vote's for Bali."

Stewart continued to study the dispatch silently, then suddenly exclaimed, "Hey, listen up to this. 'The *Black Sea* is described by her agents as luxurious. A one-class ship, whose level of comfort, service, and cuisine are in keeping with the finest European tradition, while providing the ambience and relaxed atmosphere of a private yacht. Yet she is small enough to perform unusual itineraries and to dock at *remote ports* and *untouched islands* which are *inaccessible* to larger vessels.' "

"Hell, they told me the same thing about the *Decatur* back in Washington."

Several on the bridge laughed at the XO's joke. But Stewart brooded over the dispatch, divining another meaning in the lines of black type. "Wherever she's hiding, we probably can't get in there."

"What do we do now?"

"What we've been doing. Use the helos to search, only more."

"They're already working from sunrise to sunset now. They're starting to have maintenance problems."

"In Vietnam we . . ." Stewart didn't finish the thought. He turned to Lieutenant junior grade Nguyen, who was officer of the deck. "Have the air boss report to the bridge."

"Mr. DiLorenzo's in the air right now, sir. Should I call him on the radio?"

Stewart shook his head in frustration. "Never mind. I'll talk to him when he gets down."

The bridge telephone squawked. The officer of the deck picked it up, listened for a moment, and gestured to Stewart. "Captain, Lieutenant Mitchell."

Mitchell was the engineer officer. The

Decatur had been operating continually for almost a year without a yard break for repairs, and the heat, humidity, and windblown sand of the Persian Gulf had accelerated breakdowns; the engineer inevitably had only bad news to report. Stewart punched in the speaker by his chair. "Yes, Marty, I'm sitting here in my bridge chair watching a gorgeous tropical sunset, and you're going to ruin the day for me, aren't you?"

"Yes, sir, I'm glad you're sitting down, sir."

"What is it?"

"The number three air-conditioning plant. We had to shut down the compressor. The bearing finally seized. That was the one making noises. It was about to throw a shaft right through the casing."

"Christ, what do we have left?"

"Just one plant, sir. We'll have to manually cut out the loops to the living and working spaces in order to save the chill water for the radar and electronics."

All the air conditioning aboard the ship, except the tubes that cooled the vital heat-sensitive electronic equipment, had to be shut down, the crew sacrificed to save the radar, sonar, computers, and communications.

"It's going to get very hot," Robinson commented.

"Hot? This isn't hot," Stewart drawled. "Hot is 110 degrees during the day, and humid, so humid you splash in your own sweat every time you take a step."

"That sounds like Vietnam."

Stewart nodded. "But actually we didn't mind the heat, because we constantly had dysentery. We were nauseous and had diarrhea so much of the time that when we felt normal, we worried that our plumbing had stopped working. We became so dehydrated we had to have intravenous fluids." He pointed to the shoreline. "A mangrove swamp like that is a many-splendored hell. Not a breath of air, just the jungle dripping slime on you. When we went on patrol, we'd splash on insect repellent like it was aftershave lotion. But the mosquitoes still swarmed all over us like bees to honey. If we docked near a village or an old ferry landing, rats as big as pit bulls, and just as vicious, would swarm right onto the boat and crawl all over us. This, gentlemen, is a pleasant South Seas Islands cruise." Even to his own ear, Stewart sounded like a crotchety old veteran telling war stories.

His eyes gazed about the bridge — the deck officers Nguyen and Ensign Fine, the helmsman Johnson and his apprentice Whittaker, the boatswain Wisniewski and the quartermaster Saldana. They were men who had enlisted straight out of high school or junior officers fresh from college, serving their first tour. Most would not stay in the navy — they would find the life too restrictive — but still they had all volunteered at a time when there was no draft. Why?

Stewart knew the reason, the one that was never articulated or spoken of. All these young men, just past adolescence, of scattered bygone tribes, sought a primordial rite of passage into manhood in a modern society that no longer held such initiations.

Stewart had almost not survived his own initiation. There were friends who hadn't and others who had been so deeply disturbed by the fear and horror that they were maimed more deeply than if both their legs had been blown off. Now they lived on the edge of their own society.

Lying in Balboa Naval Hospital in San Diego, his wounds healing, Stewart had fathomed that it was their blood and insanity that sanctified the rite, made it holy. Without that sacrifice they were all merely civil service workers, bureaucrats, technicians — and, frankly, most of the navy were only that. But the combat-blooded officers and cadre of petty officers were the priesthood. Lying in his hospital bed, Stewart had received his calling.

Through his binoculars Stewart now scanned the nipah-palm- and mangrove-shrouded shoreline, the red-brown effluence of a jungle river pouring into the sea. The hairs on the back of his neck prickled, and perspiration flowed down his brows into his eyes. He swiped at his eyes with the back of his hand. He couldn't shake the feeling of being watched, that all hell was going to break loose at any moment. It was irrational, he knew, a twenty-year-old instinct triggered by the offshore stagnant-ooze stench of the mangrove swamp, the solid, concealing wall of nipahs within sniper range. He worked his neck and massaged his trapezius muscle with his fingertips to ease the knots of tension.

Stewart suddenly sprang up and stepped to the chart table, where Lieutenant Balletto, the Ship Control Officer, and Chief Quartermaster Fields hunched, shoulder to shoulder, plotting their course. "The charts of the coastline are almost worthless in this area," Stewart told them. "The mangrove swamps are like a reclamation project. They grow out into the sea over a hundred feet a year." The U.S. Defense Mapping Agency chart of the Selat Gelasa was from Netherlands surveys between 1864 and 1934. The chart of the Kepulauan Riau was from Indonesian and British charts to 1958. "Some of the towns marked on the coast are now probably a mile inland."

Balletto groaned. "We'd better keep a special sea detail on round-the-clock."

Stewart nodded. "That's why we're paid the big bucks. Because we don't need sleep like real human beings."

Balletto gave him a weary, sardonic smile and shook his head.

Stewart examined the plot, then pointed at the shoreline to port. "We're coming up on a wide river mouth, and it isn't on the chart."

The officer of the deck, Nguyen, studied the river estuary through his binoculars, turned to Stewart, then hesitated.

"Yes, Tram?"

The young officer shook his head politely, his inherent Oriental reserve making it difficult for him to volunteer an opinion.

"You looked like you were about to say something."

"The *sungais,* sir, most of them aren't on any charts."

"*Sungais?* What the hell are they?"

"Streams or rivers."

"Are they streams or rivers? The bottom line is, can you get a ship up them?"

Nguyen shrugged. "In the dry season you can't get a canoe up them. But they have steep banks, over thirty feet high in places, and during the rainy season they overflow."

"Jesus," Stewart moaned.

"Bridge, Combat," the intercom called out.

"Go ahead, Combat."

"Sir, we're on the radio with that air contact at three-three-zero. It's an Orion operating out of Singapore. They send their respects and want to know if you have any further information or instructions for them."

"The rest of the navy is finally starting to arrive," Robinson said.

"Combat, ask them how far inland they are cleared to fly."

"How far inland, sir?"

"Right."

Robinson gave him a quizzical look, and they waited in silence while the question and answer radioed back and forth.

"Bridge, Combat. The Orion says that they are only cleared to search the coastal waters."

"That figures," Stewart acknowledged. "Combat, tell the Orion that we have no special instructions or information at this time. Proceed on their assigned search and wish them good hunting."

Stewart and Robinson went out on the starboard bridge wing. It was several minutes before the four-engine turboprop patrol plane materialized between the towering columns of pink and magenta rain clouds to the north. It flew directly over the *Decatur,* then banked southeast, as if in salute.

They watched the Orion until it dissolved into the darkening sky to the east. The Lockheed P-3C had advanced radar, magnetic anomaly detectors, directional and ranging sonobuoys, all integrated by digital computers, to detect and track high-performance submarines and warships. "They'll search the entire Karimata Strait and the Java Sea from Singapore to Jakarta," Stewart said. "Then they'll expand the search north into the South China Sea and west up the Strait of Malacca, and they won't find a goddamn thing."

"Why don't you tell them that?" Robinson asked.

"Who?" Stewart indicated the red radio telephone hanging from the bridge overhead. "The suits in the CIA? ComSeventhFleet in Japan? How do you tell a three-star admiral that you have a Purple Heart that itches?" He rubbed his side again.

"We've got no intelligence or charts we can rely on. We're not even familiar with this area. Yet we can come up with a dozen ways to hide this ship so that our planes and satellites can't find it."

"What alternatives do we have?" the XO asked.

Stewart shook his head. "For the moment, all we can do is keep boring in and force something to break."

Robinson was silent, then asked, "Captain, may I speak to you privately?" He glanced at the starboard lookout who stood a few feet away with a sound-powered phone and a pair of binoculars about his neck.

Stewart moved down the narrow catwalk to where the deck opened up behind the wheelhouse. "Something bothering you, Robbie?" The black man was five foot eleven, half a head shorter than Stewart, but the ex-Navy fullback was so broad in the chest and shoulders, a disquieting power now tense with frustration, that Stewart had the uneasy feeling that the man could rip him apart.

The XO visibly took a deep breath. "Yes, sir. I've been aboard almost a month now, and I feel I'm being bypassed, ignored."

"In what way?"

"I'm the executive officer. All the business aboard should be channeling through me. But you and DiLorenzo personally work out where and how to search, Lieutenant Balletto the ship's course. If there are engineering casualties, the engineer's on the horn right to you. I'm just a spectator. That is, if I'm around to catch it. This morning, when the Russian plane was prowling around, the ship went quietly to GQ, a SAM on the launcher, the C-WIZ armed, and I wasn't even notified."

"Is that it?"

Robinson nodded tensely.

"Look, XO, no one is ignoring you. But I've had this ship almost two years. Each of my department heads — Balletto, Mitchell, Nielson — qualified for command aboard this ship before we deployed. I've worked with DiLorenzo for a year. The last couple of months we've all been in heavy operations in the Gulf. Something like that Russian plane, maybe more threatening, might happen several times a day there. My lookouts, bridge, and combat watches are trained to automatically respond. We don't hit the panic button and call General Quarters."

The way Stewart had said "my" and "we" implied Robinson was not yet part of the crew. "When we get back to the States, I'll be getting my orders elsewhere. And you can start taking over. You'll be the old hand and break in the new CO of the *Decatur*."

"Yes, sir." The way Robinson pursed his lips indicated that he wasn't satisfied. But there was nothing more Stewart had to say to him. Robinson was probably a reasonably competent officer: Annapolis, a former star athlete, and a black man clearly on the fast

333

track to promotion. But they now were in tricky shoal waters, and Stewart was not going to trust his ship to this man he did not yet know. The hairs on the back of his neck bristled again.

Stewart raised his binoculars and peered at the mangroves, once more feeling himself transported to a Mekong River estuary — the fear and rush of adrenalin priming him, the inescapable sixth sense that the cross hairs of a weapon were tracking him.

Stewart never heard the shot. The lookout a few feet away suddenly cried out, grabbed at his chest as though the breast plate of his telephone had stabbed him, and pitched on his back to the deck. Blood spurted from the wound in his chest.

24. Of Rats and Trade

Sergeant Govind led Yee through the dank jail corridor. He moved silently to the cell door with a soft, catlike step of which Yee would have thought the hulking Sikh jailer incapable, and peeked through the Judas hole. He motioned Yee to look.

The Malay sat curled on the floor in a

corner, his head on his chest, not moving. He might have been asleep or catatonic, but a slight, troubled nodding of the head indicated he was not dead.

Govind motioned Yee away from the cell doors so that they would not be overheard by any of the prisoners. "I thank you for coming so quickly, sir." Under the dark blue orthodox turban and fierce brows Govind's brown eyes were strangely melancholy.

"How long has he been this way?"

Govind shrugged. "At first this fanatic praying on his knees all the time. Not knowing which way is Mecca, he is spinning and spinning like a top, first a prayer to the south, then north, east, west, bowing to all points of the compass. His knee will wear down to the bone, I am fearing. But then he stops, and this is the way I am finding him now, sir." The Sikh looked concerned.

"What is it?"

"Malays run amok, and then they are curling up and dying if we leave them in solitary too long. This is the truth, sir. I am knowing this very fully. Malays are needing fellowship like food and water, more than Indians and Chinese prisoners."

Yee studied Sergeant Govind. It sounded like an old grandmother's story, but he knew the jailer had great experience in these matters. "Tell me your thoughts."

"There is a Malay detective Mr. Yee is trusting fully?"

"Sergeant Salleh."

"Oh, yes, very good man, sir. For what I am thinking, this is a very good man. Sergeant Salleh will bring the prisoner all his meals, but he is dressing like lowest kitchen worker. All the time Sergeant Salleh complaining about the hard, dirty work, and Indians and Chinese having all the good, easy jobs. The prisoner, being truly a fanatic, will talk to him and try to convert him, I think, and Salleh will learn what this terrible business being all about."

Yee stared at the jailer a moment, then smiled and patted him on the arm. "You are a fearsome man. You have the body of a Sikh warrior, but you think like a Hokkien Chinese."

Sergeant Govind smiled back. "I thank you, sir, this being a compliment. But my father is not thinking so."

Both men laughed.

By nature Sergeant Salleh bin Ali was a handsome, athletically built Malay. He disguised the ranginess by slouching, and the high, broad forehead, the prominent cheekbones, and well-shaped chin were camouflaged by long black hair and a drooping Fu Manchu mustache. The effect was strikingly menacing, almost too theatrical for undercover assignments, Yee thought, but Salleh somehow made it work. Depending on the circumstances he was a pimp, a drug dealer, a smuggler, or a thief to reckon with.

Salleh often worked across the strait in Indonesia, infiltrating easily where a Chinese would be immediately under suspicion and harassed. But, more important, Yee trusted him. And now he told Salleh everything he had learned to date, even the crucial intelligence developed in the maggoty pork festering on Ballinger's verandah.

Salleh listened with his dark eyes hooded, and Yee had the distinct impression that he was hearing very little for the first time. "So that's why the crazy old Englishman stinks up the place, *lah*."

"You knew of it?"

Salleh shrugged. "The rotting pork is an offense to the religious Muslims." Although they made up less than one-fifth of the population of Singapore, Malay Muslims like Salleh were heavily represented in the salaried government jobs, such as the police.

"Tell me how much of this business you already know," Yee asked.

"It's easier to tell you what I didn't know.

You or the minister can pick up the phone and see the *Straits Times* or *Nanyang Siang Pau* does not report foreigners having their heads chopped off and dropped at Raffles, on Orchard Road, Merlion Park, and at the feet of Sir Stamford Raffles." He tallied each of the four heads on his fingers. "But you can't stop the cops from talking, *lah*. I know, of course, you caught this Malay at Merlion, and you have men out asking official questions, but not these interesting things you have now found out. And I didn't know for sure this Malay was a fanatic, but I guessed. But this ransom of guns in the name of *jihad*, this is all news to me, terrible news. This is a fanatic group I have not heard of. But they're not Middle East, Palestinian, or Iranians. That's all American and Russian bullshit, *lah*."

The language of the Singapore streets was not formal English but "Singlish," a varying mix of English and the speaker's mother tongue. But whatever the Asian language, the Malay suffix -*lah* was used by all races to emphasize a point, or merely punctuate a sentence, *lah*.

"You think they are local?"

"Yes, of course. For the same reason you do. The durians, *lah*. I don't know if they are from Singapore, Indonesia, or Malaysia, but who else would put those stinking fruits with a head at a busy sidewalk cafe to make sure no tourist picked it up, but no Indonesian bus boy could resist it?"

Yee nodded. "Yes, yes."

"Of course, if these durians were the big, spiky ones covered with elephant shit — the ones the elephants swallow whole but can't digest — then I would know that these fanatics were gourmets from the north, perhaps Kelantan." Salleh smiled broadly, displaying gleaming, even white teeth.

Yee felt nauseated. But Salleh was not entirely joking. Yee's own father, who had a passion for durians, had craved these elephant-processed fruits as other men coveted Ming dynasty porcelain. "These were not shit by elephants."

"Then I must go undercover to find out where this terrible fruit comes from," Salleh said solemnly.

"This is not a case for British justice. This is a matter of national security."

Salleh nodded.

"You will work the prisoner, gain his trust, *lah?*" It was a question, not an order.

"No problem." But the Malay hesitated a moment before he continued. "But I thank you for asking. For you, Singapore is your religion, I think. I am a Muslim, then perhaps a Singaporean, and a Malay. That is the order of importance to me. I do not think about it often, but God must come first." The teasing twinkle faded from the dark eyes, clouded by anguish. "This terrorism of fanatics, this *jihad*, this is not Islam. This is not obedience to God. God does not ask men to murder. This is a madness when men go amok. They think they hear God, but it is only devils." He rose to leave and checked his watch. "The prisoner should be very hungry by now and very happy to see me." At the door he turned back and grinned. "Sergeant Govind is a very good man. A big, strong Sikh who thinks like a Malay."

"Yes, you must compliment him on that."

The telephone suddenly rang. "Yes." Yee listened a moment and emitted a long, satisfied "Aaah!" then ordered, "No, not my office, interrogation room three." He hung up.

Salleh was still standing at the door.

"The CIA station is here."

Salleh made a gesture as if gathering in a fish net. "The mountain comes to Mohammed, *lah*."

Harold Blocker did indeed seem an intimidating mountain of a man to the diminutive, fragile Yee. At a big-boned six foot three, the CIA agent had the build of a former NFL pro and the disconcerting arrogance of his size.

"This isn't a very friendly room," Blocker said, surveying the bleak interrogation chamber.

Yee dismissed the uniformed policeman at the door with a flutter of his hand. "You are persona non grata in the Republic of Singapore. You have withheld information in the brutal murder of four people. Of more concern to my office is that this information directly imperils the security of this country."

"Just what is your office, Mr. Yee?"

Yee ignored the question. "If it were not for your diplomatic immunity, you would be in an even more unfriendly cell." American and Russian intelligence agents were almost always attached to their embassies. It made them easy to identify, but it gave them the advantage of diplomatic immunity when they were caught doing something illegal. Other nations, particularly the French, scorned this practice, and their agents used the cover of legitimate businessmen or journalists. They were more difficult to uncloak, but when they were, they could then be arrested and interrogated at length. Either way it was a trade-off.

Blocker held up both meaty hands, as if conceding the point. "Your government will receive a formal apology within the next day or two. It is being drafted now — "

"Now that you no longer have the option of trading arms for hostages in Singapore without the knowledge of the Singapore government."

"We still hold that card. Singapore as a venue may be irrelevant." Blocker said it in a matter-of-fact way, with neither malice nor threat.

"Something else has happened?"

Blocker nodded. "One of our navy ships, a frigate searching for the *Black Sea,* was fired on. A sniper. A single shot from shore, but it killed the lookout. The captain was standing next to him. He immediately sent in a helicopter, but they didn't spot anyone. It was at sunset; they put a boat in the water with an armed party, but it was already dark. It wasn't an accidental shot."

"Where did this happen?"

"A mangrove swamp off Sumatra, near the Bangka Strait. About two hundred and fifty miles south."

Yee sat a moment absorbing this new information. "It has nothing to do with this matter," he stated peremptorily. "We have intelligence that the hostages are not in that area."

To Yee's surprise, Blocker grunted and

nodded. "The captain of this ship, the *Decatur*, agrees with you. He thinks it was a diversion, just a shot to keep their heads down and keep our attention away from where the *Black Sea* really is."

"The captain of this *Decatur* told you *that?*"

"The naval attaché talked to him by radio."

"And who fired the shot?"

"We don't know."

Yee stood and walked to the door. "I wish you a pleasant flight home. Since you have not yet troubled yourself to make a reservation, we have taken the liberty of securing you a seat aboard Singapore Airlines flight 2 at eight tomorrow night. Your Russian counterpart is leaving for Ho Chi Minh City about the same time. Perhaps you can have a farewell dinner together. I understand that chili crabs are a favorite of yours, and the best in Singapore are right on your way to the airport, in Bedok on the East Coast Road. Mr. Yevshenko might enjoy the frog legs from Indonesia. Compare our spice of ginger and spring onions to the French, or even the Vietnamese way of preparing that particular dish, and then philosophize what that tells about us as a people."

The American agent sat in silent humiliation, his stony eyes fixed on Yee, then the thick lips twisted in a sardonic smile. "Just professional curiosity. Where was the bug?"

"You have such a healthy appetite, Mr. Blocker, my technicians were very fearful that you were going to swallow it at any moment."

Blocker sighed, visibly deflated. "A man's gotta know when to hold and when to fold," he breathed.

"Who are they?" Yee demanded.

"We don't know," Blocker insisted.

"You have the largest intelligence operation in the history of the world. You must know something."

"Only background."

"What background?"

Blocker made a vague motion with his hands. "The whole Muslim fundamentalist revolutionary . . . thing."

"We lock up these extremists without trial and make no apologies," Yee snapped.

"Then you've got no problem here, right? In Malaysia a bunch of Iranian-trained revolutionaries have taken over the local Islamic party. In Indonesia, there've been antigovernment fires, bombings, and attacks by fundamentalists. But no problems here in Singapore. You don't need our help."

Yee did not answer. Blocker was cocky, confident, not at all intimidated by the prospect of being deported, which could have a chilling effect on his career. Was he just being stupid, a naturally arrogant American, or did he have a card in his hand that Yee had not counted?

"What do your analysts say?"

Blocker shrugged. "They love international conspiracy theories. The American economy is practically based on them."

It suddenly seemed to Yee that Blocker was enjoying this debriefing. He had not folded, but was apparently still holding a card to play. Yee backed off. He nodded and smiled at the CIA agent. "And what is your *private* assessment, Mr. Blocker?"

Blocker eyed him cannily. "Well, now, I punch all this into my personal computer, and what it crunches down to is a *local* revolutionary group — Islamic fundamentalists with their own agenda. They're acting independently, outside the control of Tehran, Baghdad, or anyplace else. This isn't the only place it's happening. Only this group is more sophisticated than any we've dealt with before."

Yee was offended. "Sophisticated?"

Blocker nodded. "Oh, yeah. At least they're not the Islamic Jihad, dynamiting a four-story, reinforced-concrete building down on three hundred sleeping marine peacekeepers. Just a sick old widower and a retired Amer-

345

ican manufacturer on alternate days and a low-grade Russian seaman in between. But they've riveted our attention waiting for each drop. And they're doing it in a sophisticated modern city, one with instant communications to Washington and Moscow, but one with a controlled press so that we can all negotiate discreetly, free from public hysteria. As a professional I have to admire the operation. It's elegant."

"And are you negotiating discreetly?"

Blocker shook his head. "But if the American hostages are just the pawns in a local situation, then it's not really *our* problem, is it? You ship my big ass back to Washington as persona non grata, and I'm going to recommend that we make the swap to save 135 — no, that's 133 now — American lives. It's morally objectionable, but what the hell. Two battalions of armed guerrillas will be *your* problem, and we'll live with it. When those hostages land home, weeping and God-blessing America, fall on their knees to kiss the runway of Los Angeles airport on TV, and then pose with the President on the White House lawn, do you think any politician or pundit is going to voice the caveat that the ransom price has been a nasty guerrilla holy war in a place most of our college graduates can't find on the map?"

The thought of killing the CIA man occurred to Yee. "What is it you want, Mr. Blocker?" he asked.

"Everything you've got." Yee was surprised by the change in the tone of his voice. Then Blocker smiled like a snake. "Your tape recorder first, please."

Yee took out the tape recorder inside his jacket and handed it to Blocker. The big man clicked it off, then got up and walked about the stark, windowless room. "I don't want to be shipped home, Mr. Yee. That would be depressing as hell. I love Singapore. Best damned duty I ever had." He peered into every corner and cranny, pressed his fingers against discolorations in the paint on the wall. "The food is a wonderment. There isn't a day goes by I don't discover an exotic new dish to tickle this country boy's palate." He tapped the air-conditioning grille and then put his ear to it. "And the Singapore women, the most beautiful in the world, no doubt about it." He bent over and searched under the table. "And everyone speaks English, at least 'most everyone. About as much as Los Angeles nowadays, only this city is ten times safer. And cleaner. Meticulously clean. I mean a $500 fine for littering. Damned if it isn't the first country successfully run by anal compulsives."

Yee was fascinated by the professionalism of Blocker's search for bugs.

The big American ran his fingers delicately over the inside edges of the table, then suddenly rose and winked at Yee. "We must learn to trust one another, Mr. Yee."

"We have the strongest foundations for trust," Yee said. "Vital mutual interests."

"Amen to that. It's definitely in both our vital mutual interests to find that ship and neutralize the bad guys."

"Yes, and we have no objection to your Special Forces' making the final assault. The SEAL teams that are disguised as air crews for your search planes at Changi airport." Yee enjoyed Blocker's embarrassment. "It is dangerous to have men who are not trained pretending to work on aircraft. My government objects to your not consulting with us on their presence in Singapore. Our own Special Forces are well trained and entirely capable, but as a practical matter they should not make the assault when the ship is located."

Blocker regained his composure. "Why is that?"

"For one thing many of the Americans will be killed, no matter what precautions are made."

Blocker grunted and nodded.

"The second consideration is that it will be politically awkward. The ship is in Indonesia."

Blocker pursed his lips. "Indonesia is one hell of a sprawling place. Some thirteen thousand islands. Can you be a little more specific?"

"Yes, but we can't pinpoint it. We can scientifically narrow the area."

"Scientifically, huh?" There was a note of condescension in Blocker's voice.

"Yes, our pathologist ran tests on each of the heads as soon as we discovered them. The rate of putrefaction is very rapid in our warm, moist climate. Incidentally, that's the reason we use such strong spices in our native cuisines that you enjoy so much. In any event, the state of decay of the flesh defines a radius within which the decapitations took place."

The arrogance faded from the big American's face, and Yee savored the other man's unwilling expression of queasiness. Blocker swallowed hard. "And that is . . . ?" he asked.

Yee smiled. Now he held the face cards. "The government of Singapore would like certain guarantees."

Blocker nodded. "Your bid."

"Whatever terrorists are captured, wherever they are captured, we want them turned over to our authorities, not the Indonesians."

"That's a little tricky."

"Not if you must move swiftly to save American lives. You already have permission to conduct a search in their waters. We suspect many of them, if not all, are actually Malaysian citizens. However, they are pirates by international law. It is the right and obligation of all nations to apprehend them. It is certainly our legal right. The act of piracy and the first murder were committed in Singapore."

"How do you know that?" The CIA man leaned forward eagerly and gripped his knees with big-boned knuckles.

"It was the purser of the ship. He missed the sailing, but his head was dropped just a few hours later at the Raffles Hotel by a trishaw driver."

"Sounds legal to me," Blocker agreed emphatically. "But that's the State Department's play. I'll strongly recommend it. We don't want another miscarriage like the *Achille Lauro,* where the Italians turned Abul Abbas loose forty-eight hours after the SEALs had turned him over to the *carabinieri.* What other cards you holding?"

"The purser's head — an interesting head, not at all Russian. I particularly remember the nose, large and sharp like a hawk's, with wide nostrils. The straight black hair, the thick black eyebrows. The eyes were very dark. His death was apparently so violent that they remained open, and no one bothered to close them. But I don't blame them for not wanting to touch his eyes."

Yee had forced himself to record these images in memory, not as some willful test of courage or manliness, as the pathologist Ballinger had accused him, but because he had suspected the dead man's unusual features might be a clue. He had stared at them with a fascinated revulsion, until his own stomach had revolted in horror.

Blocker, quiet and pale, studied him across the table.

"This Russian purser," Yee continued, "according to his papers was from the port of Baku in Azerbaijan."

Blocker's head came up sharply. "*Bingo!* The Iranian connection. Azerbaijan is one of the Soviet powder kegs. The population is Muslim and right on Iran's border. Half of the Azerbaijanis live in Russia, the other half in Iran."

Yee nodded. "It is more than a coincidence, but less than an international conspiracy. You Americans see international conspiracies where there is only trade. You always overreact. It will be your undoing. Politics and religion are like rats. They often crawl off the ship with the trade goods and stay in port and breed."

To Yee's surprise Blocker laughed good-naturedly. "Goddamn, you got a real talent for writing fortune cookies. But why don't you think the Azerbaijani was one of the bad guys?"

"The obvious. They killed him. He was more valuable to them as the first grisly demonstration of their will than as their spy in the crew. After they had obtained from him whatever information they needed about the ship, its crew, and passengers, they couldn't let him go. I suspect if we had the rest of his body, we'd find it . . . abused."

"That computes," Blocker agreed. "The purser knows more about the passengers than the captain. But how did they get their hooks into him?"

"It was, as I said, just a little trade, not a revolutionary conspiracy. When I realized he was an Azerbaijani, I had our investigators make discreet inquiries on Arab Street and in the Pakistani shops along Serangoon Road. The Russian purser was well known to the rug merchants. He had quite an expert eye for Oriental rugs."

"It was in his blood."

"Yes, indeed, and over the years the purser has visited Singapore quite frequently on various Russian ships. And each time he made several purchases, excellent Persian and Afghan rugs, costing thousands of dollars."

"That's a little rich for a Soviet merchant officer." Blocker sat musing a moment. "But he was probably making more in the rug business than he was on his salary. Hell, even in the States a good Oriental bought in Singapore has a terrific markup. In Russia, among the elite, they'd be worth their weight in rubles. And this is a major market for them."

Blocker nodded vigorously. "Yeah, you're right. At first it was trade, not conspiracy. The rug merchants probably cultivated the hell out of the purser. He was not only a steady buyer for an expanding market, but he could steer whole boatloads of rich European and American tourists to their shops. Then one day, over thick black coffee and *baklava*, he told a particularly friendly rug dealer about a luxury liner with a special charter of wealthy and prominent Americans. He probably even negotiated his commission on all the business he'd steer to him. Only this dealer was one of your rats who'd scampered ashore with a shipment of rugs from the Middle East."

"So it no longer sounds like a fortune cookie to you."

"Do you know who this particular rat is?"

"Yes. An Iranian, as you suspected. He told our investigator that he did not know the Russian. Did not remember him at all. Which was very suspicious, because he was the only big rug dealer who did *not* know the Russian purser."

Blocker sighed deeply. "Greed is such a deadly sin. Are you going to bring in the Iranian?"

Yee shook his head. "Oh, no. But we watch him very closely to see who contacts him. *They* are the danger, not the Iranian."

"Does he know where the *Black Sea* is?"

"We strongly doubt it. There is a Malay in the cells under our feet. We caught him with his hands red with the head of one of the Russians, and now he prays five times a day to die. Not even that Malay knows where the ship is."

"What's your next play?"

"We wait, Mr. Blocker." Yee checked his watch. "For the next head to be . . . *dropped* was the word I believe you used. A Russian this time, I think."

Blocker stood, glanced at his watch, and moaned, "The perfect way to top off a really bad day."

Yee studied the CIA agent's pale face, its normally ebullient color now drained. Like the pathologist Ballinger and the homicide detectives, Blocker was given to black, baleful humor, as though the resilient spirit must make jokes of horror to cope with it on a regular basis. His dark jokes perhaps said more about Blocker's experience than any top secret dossier.

Part VII
A Scholar and an Assassin

25. The Nature of Rape

Morning mists still veiled the river, and spooky tendrils of vapor floated among the golden mengaris trees along the bank like ghosts fleeing the rising sun, although its rays never actually penetrated the overhead jungle canopy. Morning was a shifting twilight that persisted through noon and afternoon, until it faded into the moist, sooty blackness of the jungle night. Morning was the stirring and crowing of red forest cocks, the hooting and eerie *whoop-whoops* of the great gibbons at breakfast in the wild tangkol fig trees, the clatter of the cicadas before the mounting heat stifled them.

Liz Schneider sprang onto the Lido deck determined to promenade aerobically about the ship for twenty minutes. She had already worked out in the deserted closet-sized gym on the deck below — sit-ups, stretches, leg lifts, bust-firming flies with light dumbbells — and worked up a sweat that caused her sleeveless jersey to cling and her bared legs to glisten. This was the fifth day of captivity, and she had not exercised since flying from San Francisco to Singapore over a week before.

Liz was regular but not fanatical about her exercise. Her mother's genes and tennis had gotten her through two children, the first thirty-five years, and into her second marriage, but now a more scientific program was required to keep her figure. Imperceptibly the full bust had begun to sag, the voluptuous hips inflate, the long, slender neck, arms, and legs either wither with dieting or curdle with suet. It was inexorable, but she was determined to postpone it as long as possible with diet, exercise, and, nature eventually failing, cosmetic surgery.

But this morning her need for exercise was more than cosmetic. The nerve-racking confinement, she and Alan cooped up in their cabin, the fear were all taking their toll. She needed to get out, just by herself, and perhaps dissipate some of the tension. She had politely invited her husband to join her, and to her relief he had demurred.

She swung briskly into her walk, the rubber soles of her Reeboks slapping on the wood planking of the promenade, still wet with the heavy morning dew. She checked her watch and wondered how many turns about the ship might make a mile, a dizzying amount probably, as the Lido deck was not all that long. She strode by the glassed-in windbreak that enclosed the swimming pool area, abandoned since the pirates' boarding. Aft of the pool was the section of more expensive Type AA cabins with portholes onto the promenade. Feeling self-conscious in her brief exercise shorts, Liz quickly climbed the port ladder onto the after sun deck that formed the roof of the AA cabins, circled the brief upper deck, and came down the starboard ladder, thereby both avoiding the unnerving stares and adding a buns-tightening ladder climb to her workout.

As she scampered down the port ladder, she was startled to see two of the armed pirates, sprawled on the poolside chaise longues, cigarettes dangling from their grinning mouths, eyeing her. She could think of nothing else to do except to keep walking. There was really no reason not to. The passengers had not been prohibited from using the promenades. As she circled the forward section of the ship, Liz made a conscious decision to suppress her fear, not let the presence of the guards intimidate her into quitting. She would ignore the swarthy louts, as she would the construction boors at home who howled and whistled at her when she jogged by. She strode again down the starboard side, not looking at the pirates, and dashed up the ladder, but as she circled the sun deck, her courage evaporated. Liz hesitated descending the ladder and coming within arm's reach of them. The image of their rapt, lecherous faces suddenly seemed more threatening. She stopped and looked around. There was no way down from the sun deck other than the two ladders to the pool patio.

She backtracked to the far ladder, opposite the one the guards would now be expecting her to come down. One of the pirates was halfway up it, his assault rifle slung over his shoulder, and he grinned up at her, yellow, tobacco-stained teeth in a pockmarked face. Liz whirled toward the other ladder. The second guard stepped off onto the sun deck and smiled obscenely at Liz. He said something she did not understand, then gripped his crotch and fondled it suggestively.

It was Maggi who heard Liz's cries for help. She had been on her way to talk with Tengku in the lounge, as the Malay was generally up and having coffee long before the passengers gathered for breakfast. She dashed down the promenade toward the cries and up the ladder.

Liz was sprawled on the sun deck. One of the pirates was wrestling with her, struggling to pin her shoulders, but she was as big as he was, and rage had given her almost equal strength. The second pirate had already ripped off her shorts and, with his own hanging down about his ankles, was between her naked legs attempting to mount her. But when he released his hold on her squirming legs, she bucked violently and kicked him in the chest.

"What the hell are you doing?" Maggi screamed.

The pirate attempting to rape Liz grabbed the assault rifle lying on the ground beside him and staggered to his feet, tripping on the tangle of his own downed shorts. His erection, a knarly brown root at his crotch, stuck out paralleling the barrel of his rifle, pointed directly at Maggi. Maggi was more outraged and flabbergasted by the spectacle than frightened. She pointed back at the pirate. "Tengku Haji Azhar will cut your *cock* off," she shouted in her most authoritative Malay, using the colloquial expression her schoolgirls in Kuala Besut had told her in giggles. "You are an offense to God."

"That's Abang's woman," the other pirate warned the gunman. Maggi was again dressed in Malay fashion in a long-sleeved blouse and ankle-length sarong for her audience with Tengku.

The interrupted rapist glared at her, the expression in his flushed, scowling face transforming itself from rage to fear, and for two heartbeats Maggi thought he was going to shoot her, but then he dropped his rifle and yanked up his shorts, fumbling to cover his still distended penis. The other pirate let go of Liz, and both now backed away toward the far ladder, never taking their eyes off Maggi, as if she held some concealed weapon that she might spring at any moment. At the ladder they bolted down.

Maggi ran to Liz. She retrieved her ripped shorts and helped Liz struggle into them. "Are you hurt badly?"

Liz's lip was cracked and bleeding, her face swollen and discolored, but she grasped her right shoulder as though in pain. "The son of a bitch hit me and knocked me down with his rifle," she wailed angrily, but then the anger suddenly went out of her like an exhaled breath, and she clutched Maggi and sobbed pitifully, burying her battered face in Maggi's shoulder.

Dr. Yakovlev gingerly placed ice packs on the purpling bruises on Liz's face and on her shoulder, where she had been beaten with a rifle butt, and gave her a sedative. Alan Schneider sat stroking his wife's hand, his face bloodless, haggard, and grieved. He looked as though he had suddenly aged ten years and was indeed the sickly heart attack victim Maggi had portrayed to the pirates.

Yakovlev placed a hand on Schneider's shoulder. "She is not injured, but let me know when she wakes up."

Schneider nodded, "Yes, thank you, doctor," then looked up at Maggi. "If you hadn't been there . . ."

"Liz might have beat up those two guys," Maggi smiled faintly.

Dr. Yakovlev indicated with a curt nod that Maggi was to follow him out of the stateroom. He silently led her down to his cramped office on the main deck, where he sank down in the chair behind his desk before he finally snarled, "Mrs. Schneider is an incredibly stupid woman." His baleful glare and the anger in his voice somehow seemed to include Maggi. "And in her stupidity she has now endangered everyone aboard this ship."

Maggi was outraged. "What are you saying? This wasn't Liz's fault. She was attacked."

The Russian stared at her, as if she were an absolute fool. "She was attacked," he repeated. "How very extraordinary. She paraded half naked in front of her armed captors, and she was attacked." His voice was now calm, rational, its very composure mocking Maggi.

"She was exercising," Maggi protested; she felt her face flush with anger.

"Ah, yes, exercise. Perhaps you should show the pirates a video of one of your scantily clad American actresses bouncing around to rock and roll and explain exercising to them."

Maggi was infuriated at Yakovlev's attitude. "This was a crime of violence."

To her amazement the doctor smiled and tugged at his salt-and-pepper goatee. "Yes, yes. Rape is a crime of violence, not a sexual act. That is what you American feminists always tell one another. And your media, which is financed by advertising which sells to women, repeats it. It is an axiom of your faith. Unfortunately in Russia we have not always been able to protect our women so that they could develop such romantic notions. When I was a boy the Germans invaded and raped the Russian women, and when the Red Army eventually retaliated, they drove into Germany and raped every German woman who could walk. There you have rape as an act of conquest, subjugation, perhaps even patriotism." Maggi was incited to turn her back on Yakovlev and stamp out of his office. But if they were all to survive, she needed his cooperation.

"Yes, rape is violent and dangerous, especially when the rapist is facing a prison term if the victim can identify him. But it's definitely sexual." There was, strangely, no longer any irony in the doctor's voice, only a resignation, as though he were delivering a mandatory lecture. "It requires an erection on the man's part. A quite strong erection, since the woman is not encouraging him and is, in fact, not physically receptive to him. Men don't get erections because they are angry or violent. They must be sexually aroused." Despite Yakovlev's clinical tone, Maggi felt somehow violated just listening to this rationalization.

"Some rapists undoubtedly are aroused by terrified women, but that doesn't make the act less sexual, any more than the fact there are men who prefer strong, dominating women who beat *them*. In my particular case I find myself stirred by slim young women in red silky dresses." He gave a slight, creepy smile. "I make this point not to expose my fetishes but to illustrate how important your dress is. In Pakistan, gangs of Muslim fundamentalists have stripped and raped Pakistani women who appear on the street in revealing Western clothes."

Maggi must have looked startled, because the doctor nodded significantly. "Yes, rape as an act of religious zeal. One of the attractions of the Crusades was the license to rape exotic, non-Christian women beyond the protection of the Church. The popularity of pogroms in my own country was undoubtedly related to the rape of Jewish women. When the Azerbaijanis rioted in southern Russia recently, there were numerous rapes of Armenian women. And *all* these motivations were released this morning aboard the *Black Sea* by the indiscreet Mrs. Schneider."

Maggi remained silent. Yakovlev was, in some perverse way, trying to goad her.

The doctor studied Maggi for several moments, then commented in a mocking voice, "But I notice you yourself dress with your arms and legs covered."

"I do it out of respect for Tengku Haji Azhar's beliefs."

"It is a pity that you didn't convey your respect to Mrs. Schneider or the other women aboard. As Captain Khromykh explained to you, these matters are your responsibility. But that no doubt would have made you appear unfashionable, not a feminist."

Maggi said nothing, but she felt her cheeks become hot and flushed again.

"And now your terrorist chieftain is in a dangerous position."

"Why?"

"Because if he does nothing, then the other pirates — lonely, desperate men separated from their own women — will regard that as approval to sexually use the women aboard at gunpoint, whenever the desire strikes them. If he punishes the two pirates, then he must balance the punishment with a harsher example on the passengers in order to maintain his authority with his own men."

Yakovlev held up his hand to thwart Maggi from speaking. "Please, madame professor, do not offer me your enlightened arguments. This is the real world, the jungle, not a seminar, and this clever terrorist will instinctively do whatever he must without ever rationalizing it."

"If you're trying to frighten me, you're doing a very good job," Maggi said.

"Good," the doctor nodded. "There's an old Russian proverb: A gram of terror is worth a kilogram of cure."

"What do you suggest we do?"

Yakovlev shrugged. "There is very little we can do. For one thing you will belatedly educate the women passengers in the proper manner of dressing while they are being held captive by Muslim fundamentalists." The doctor's voice shifted from resigned to sardonic to an authoritative tone. "As of this moment any woman appearing with exposed arms or legs outside of her cabin will be immediately escorted back to her cabin. Do you have any objection to this?"

Maggi shook her head.

"Good. You must try again to get Mr. and Mrs. Schneider off the ship. This incident will focus attention on him and place him in even greater danger."

"Tengku has been reluctant to release any women, let alone husband-and-wife hostages."

Again the doctor tugged thoughtfully at his beard. "Yes, but perhaps this incident may change his mind. Getting Mrs. Schneider off the ship may be a way of his saving face."

Maggi nodded. "I'll try again."

Despite her outrage at the attack on Liz Schneider, Maggi was loath to confront Tengku and Ahmed. If a worldly European like Dr. Yakovlev believed, however wrongly, that Liz herself had been responsible for provoking the guards, then how would the devout Muslims view the incident?

She went back to her stateroom and again changed her clothes, dressing almost like a Malay bride in a white lace blouse and a long off-white skirt, and, as a final wily suggestion of modesty, coiled a batik shawl about her neck and shoulders, as though it might be raised as a veil.

But Tengku's face was a dark scowl as she made her entrance into the salon. "Who is this woman?" he demanded. The guards had apparently reported the incident, or their version of it, to Tengku. Ahmed watched her with gleaming black eyes, deriving some perverse satisfaction from what he regarded as Maggi's embarrassment.

It was Ahmed's attitude that signaled to Maggi that any sign of weakness on her part would be misinterpreted. "It was my cousin that the two animals attacked," Maggi snapped angrily.

Her outrage confused both Tengku and Ahmed, and they exchanged a dismayed look. "This was your cousin? This woman who comes naked to the guards where they sleep."

"What? The guards are lying. My cousin was not naked, and she went to the upper deck to exercise. She was wearing shorts and a T-shirt, and they ripped her clothes off. I was there. I saw it. They beat her with their rifles, but she kicked and fought them. They would have attacked me, too, and I was dressed like this for my meeting with you."

"The two men said the woman was like a monkey in heat," Ahmed said. "Parading in front of them with no clothes on, all sweaty, wiggling her behind, climbing up the ladder to show off her behind."

Maggi almost laughed at this perception of Liz, the shady lady of Georgetown, performing her Jane Fonda power walk. But a glance at both Tengku's and Ahmed's faces stopped her. The whole situation was not a vicious rape but a grotesque farce, a ludicrous culture clash that was comical in its misunderstandings. Malays were normally easygoing and good-humored, but this now involved not only their Oriental saving of face but also their Muslim sense of righteousness. Maggi could be no less righteous. She plunged into her handbag and pulled out the ship's *Daily Program,* the only one that had been printed for that first aborted day at sea: "7:00 A.M. — UP & AT'EM EXERCISE CLASS . . . . . SUN DECK."

The *Daily Program,* with its black and white photograph of the cruise ship and Captain Khromykh, seized their attention. Maggi was not at all sure how well either Tengku or Ahmed read English, but she pointed to the item and translated, as best she could, the concept of an aerobic exercise class to the sons of Malay fishermen. Tengku claimed to have studied, however briefly, at the university in Kuala Lumpur. The idea of working out and jogging should not be utterly foreign to him.

Ahmed frowned. "There has been no such exercise class."

"My cousin does it by herself in the morning."

"Why?" he asked with great suspicion.

Cottage-cheese thighs, saddle-bag ass, low-density lipoprotein cholesterol. How did Maggi explain the plagues of middle-aged America to Third World revolutionaries? "She is a champion tennis player," she embroidered. Liz had mentioned to her that she and Schneider played mixed doubles socially.

To her relief Tengku nodded, "Ah, tennis." He swung his arm with a mock forehand motion, but Maggi was chillingly reminded of the sword stroke with which he had sliced Vladimir Korsakov's face. He appeared to relax visibly, as if the association of tennis, a white woman in revealing shorts, morning exercise all made some sort of sense.

But Ahmed remained as wary as ever. "The *mem-professor* told the men that Tengku Haji Azhar would . . ." he paused and regarded Maggi with bright, mocking eyes, "punish them severely."

"Tengku Haji Azhar will cut your *cock* off," she remembered shouting in her most authoritative colloquial Malay. She glared back into Ahmed's contemptuous eyes. "I had to stop them from raping my cousin. If their guns, which they had dropped, had been one meter closer, I would have shot both of them."

The pirate's expression did not change, but Maggi had the disquieting feeling that her outburst pleased him. She turned back to Tengku. "What these men did was wrong."

Both men were now silent, ruminating, troubled, Tengku's dark brows fiercely knitted. The foxy Russian doctor Yakovlev had foreseen this dilemma. Tengku could not admit to his men's wrongdoing without punishing them and then inflicting a greater retribution on the passengers to save face.

Maggi had to offer another solution. "Perhaps Tengku Haji Azhar would consider releasing my cousin." Both men looked at her with narrowed eyes but, for the first time, not rejecting the thought. "This is a selfish request. As I have told you before, my cousin's husband is very ill, but he will not leave without his wife, as is honorable. In your great compassion you have insisted that the trip is much too hazardous and immodest for a woman. However, since this unfortunate misunderstanding the presence of my cousin aboard this ship may be more difficult."

Maggi looked down and took a deep breath. "If you would protect her honor, then we think it would be better if she were sent away to Singapore despite the discomfort of the trip."

Maggi knew she was breaching a very delicate line. Tengku had released only those hostages he considered worthless because of either their ill health or their lowly position on board. Liz Schneider's release would be viewed as a condemnation, and yet it would remove a source of further trouble.

There was a long silence, and when Maggi finally raised her eyes to Tengku, he nodded solemnly. "The *mem-professor* has made this request three times now. This trouble this morning is a sign that it is God's will. You have my word that her honor will not be violated." He turned to Ahmed. "It is God's will that we take this path," he repeated.

Maggi could read no thought in his counsellor's face.

26. The Ambush

At first light Stewart launched the motor whale boat with a seven-man landing party armed with M14's, 9-mm. pistols, and shotguns to search the mangrove swamp. One of the helicopters, rigged with a door-mounted machine gun, was airborne and searching the shore. The other squatted on the fantail, armed, fueled, its crew ready to launch in a moment.

Robinson watched the twenty-six-foot fiberglass whale boat, fragile and exposed on the glaring sea, churn toward the shadowy green bog. It was low tide, and through his binoculars the XO could make out the air-breathing mangrove spears sticking straight up out of the shallows like spikes set to deliberately impale the boat. "Think they'll run into trouble?" he asked Stewart.

He shook his head. "I don't think they'll find a damn thing."

Robinson was surprised. Stewart had spent hours the previous night in the wardroom — now as sweltering and airless as the steaming swamp with the ship's air conditioning broken down — personally briefing the landing party on what to look for, what to watch out for, trying to transfer all his terrible, pain-wrought knowledge of jungle and river ambushes before morning, until the two young officers and five enlisted men, sweat-drenched and exhausted, could absorb nothing more in their fatigue. For Robinson the briefing had been a revelation, not of tactics he was certain they would never use but of the man under whom he now served and the nightmares that still haunted Stewart.

"What about the possibility that it was just a lucky shot by some crazy native?"

"The nearest cover is a half mile away, and he hit a moving man in the chest. I suppose it's a possibility," Stewart drawled.

"But Occam's razor says that the assumptions introduced to explain a situation should not be multiplied beyond necessity. And if we're searching for terrorists, a trained sniper with a 7.62 Dragunov with a telescopic sight is the more logical explanation."

Stewart had mapped out a search area, an arc of swamp within the range of a sniper, but after a tense hour both the whale boat and the chopper came up empty-handed. Stewart recalled the boat and radioed Di-Lorenzo, piloting the Seahawk. "Extend the search pattern to the south and cover any back channels you can spot through the mangroves. He'll have to be moving by small boat."

"Yes, sir, but this swamp is too shallow for anything that draws more than a canoe. I can see the shoals and mangrove roots from up here, Captain. My gambling money's still on that ship being stashed further north among those islands."

"I agree. But these guys, whoever they are, are tricky. So they'll probably head south first, wait until we're out of the area, then double back toward home."

"Captain, you think like a Sicilian."

"I take that as a compliment, Mr. Di-Lorenzo."

"Compliment intended, sir."

Stewart turned to the officer of the deck. "Mr. Balletto, as soon as the whale boat's aboard, we'll get under way and continue working this track close along the coast."

"Aye, aye, sir."

Stewart's long, lanky limbs stretched out of the black leather captain's chair. "I'll be in my cabin, Mr. Balletto."

"Captain's departed the bridge," the boatswain's mate of the watch bellowed out.

Robinson followed Stewart to the ladder in the middle of the bridge that led down to the captain's cabin directly beneath. "You look like something's bothering you, Robbie," Stewart said, as soon as he closed the door.

"It's really a question, Captain. I don't have your combat experience to draw on, but we've already been hit once. And we suspect, with good reason, it was a trained sniper. The next time the shot could just as easily be an RPG rocket into the bridge."

Stewart said nothing, merely nodding, inviting Robinson to go on.

The XO took a deep breath. "I think that our present course will carry this ship into harm's way."

"And what's your recommendation?"

"That we don't continue to thread our way through these islands, sir. As you yourself noted, the charts are out of date, practically worthless. The shoreline and depths are constantly changing. I think we should operate well offshore in safe waters, out of the range of any fire, and use the helicopters to search. That's what the LAMPS system is designed for, to be an extension of the ship's sensors."

"Okay, Robbie, your objections and your recommendation are noted, and I'll pass them on to the ship control officer. Your ass is covered."

Robinson felt his cheeks grow hot. "It wasn't my intention to cover my ass. My first concern was for the safety of this ship and crew."

Stewart stared hard at his executive officer, and then, to Robinson's astonishment, the narrow, handsome face broke into an easy grin, "Damned if you're not going to be an admiral, Robbie, maybe the first black chief of naval operations. You've got the knack that I've never mastered: how to follow orders conscientiously and cover your ass at the same time."

Robinson started to object, but Stewart cut him off.

"There are satellites, Russian reconnaissance planes, and our Orions searching for this *Black Sea*, and they haven't a clue yet. We can put one helo with limited range, flying low and slow, into the air at a time. And from my *combat experience*, as you phrased it, I expect they're not going to see a damn thing either unless we provoke the bad guys. We're down at their eye level with a ship just about the same size as the *Black Sea*. And this crew just coming back from the Persian Gulf is as well trained and experienced as a navy crew gets nowadays. Your point is well taken, XO. These *are* unsafe waters. That's what that shot was all about. They — whoever the hell they are — want us offshore and out of range. So this old brown-water sailor is going to take a few calculated risks, threading through these islands, sticking our nose up an uncharted river or a monsoon-flooded *sungai*. And if we get lucky, there are going to be more shots. And, God help us, more casualties."

At his desk Robinson brooded over his conversation with Stewart. It had been the commanding officer's first reference to his race. But being told he might be the first black CNO was hardly a racial slur. It was Stewart's comment that he, Robinson, was concerned about covering his own ass that disturbed him, not because it was unwarranted but because Stewart had touched a nerve. As a black man with a wife and three kids in a white man's navy, he always had to cover his ass. There were too many people out there eager to take a bite out of it if he left it sticking out.

Robinson's job was complicated by the fact that he was the only black officer aboard. As always, a majority of the wardroom went out of their way to be friendly and helpful, but a certain percentage was silently resentful, and the rest — after the initial novelty wore off — just did their jobs.

But it took only one superior son of a bitch to fuck it up for him. There was always that danger in the navy. Or if the guy above you screwed up, you'd be left with the short end of the stick. Every passed-over commander or lieutenant commander in every wardroom had a horror story like that. Most were just self-serving excuses for their own lack of competence, but there was an element of truth to them. Now Robinson had the CO he had always feared, an arrogant, duck-hunting, aristocratic Virginia son of a bitch who had won medals in 'Nam and thought he was John Fucking Wayne. It wasn't that Stewart didn't go by the book, or even that he thought he knew more than Com-SeventhFleet or Washington. The guy was really crazed. Back in Thailand, Stewart had wanted to personally kill those pirates. Robinson had seen it in his eyes.

And now that loose cannon was going to run the ship aground or get it shot up. And Robinson, as executive officer and second in command, would hang along with the CO. But he didn't have Stewart's twenty-year pension to fall back on.

Above the executive officer's littered desk hung a framed sign: "When I'm right, no one remembers. When I'm wrong, no one forgets." Robinson had inherited it from the previous XO, who in turn had gotten it from his predecessor. The sign had never seemed more ominous.

A sharp rap on the door startled Robinson

out of his brooding. Marty Mitchell, the engineer officer, slouched in the open doorway as if he had been waiting there for the XO to notice him for some time. He carried himself with the harassed, weary air of a man who never got an uninterrupted night's sleep, and behind the horn-rim glasses his brown eyes looked particularly doleful.

"Okay, Marty, first give me some good news, anything." To Robinson's surprise he heard himself picking up Stewart's teasing manner of dealing with the engineer.

Mitchell gnawed on his lower lip. "I'm afraid I don't have any, sir."

"And the bad news is . . ."

"The evaporators, sir. It's the same problem we sometimes had in the Gulf. This water we're sailing in is too hot. It gets up into the nineties. The evaporators just can't condense at that temperature. We're using up water twice as fast as we make it."

"We have to go on water hours?"

Mitchell shook his head. "We're already nearly down to 50 percent."

"What's your recommendation?"

"We're just going to have to cut out showers, shaving, laundry, and dishes, even brushing our teeth, until we hit cooler water. Everything but drinking water and water to the vital machinery."

"Christ, everybody's already beginning to smell like a moldy armpit with the air conditioning down."

"Yes, sir, I know." His nose twitched, making his glasses bob. "But if we don't do it, the tanks will be bone dry in less than a day."

"This happened before in the Persian Gulf?"

"Yes, sir. Around Bahrain and Kuwait, close to shore the water gets real hot."

"So the crew knows the drill?"

"Yes, sir, here's a list of the things we have to do." He handed Robinson a printed readout, as though to double-check that the XO knew the drill.

Robinson read it over and sighed. "Okay, have the boatswain pass the word to the crew. And I'll notify the supply officer that it's paper plates and cups until further notice."

"Yes, sir." Mitchell lingered uncomfortably by the desk waiting to be dismissed.

Robinson attempted a smile. "I understand that you qualified for command before the ship deployed."

"Yes, sir, all the department heads did. The captain said he wouldn't sail with us if we didn't."

"Was he kidding?"

Mitchell gave a faint smile and shook his head. "None of us wanted to find out."

The XO barked a short laugh and waved a dismissal. But the brief exchange made Robinson feel totally alone. It was not that he was the only black face in the wardroom of sixteen officers. He'd handled that situation before without any sweat. With the exception of the scrawny, nervous Ensign Fine, who was just out of the surface warfare officers' school in Coronado and had reported with Robinson, the officers had all been aboard with Stewart over a year, most of them two years. They had just spent seven months patrolling the Persian Gulf, riding shotgun on tankers, dodging mines, waiting to be bushwhacked by Silkworm missiles, vengeance-mad Iraqis in French Mirage jets with Exocets, or Revolutionary Guard crazies in Boghammer motorboats. And nothing about Stewart's behavior now seemed off the wall to them.

DiLorenzo, the only other officer aboard of Robinson's rank and experience, was responsible only for his five pilots, his fifteen-man air group, and his helicopters, not the ship.

Stewart was The Captain — a tall, lanky, handsome Southerner with well-bred manners, and a rap of Vietnam War stories always couched as lessons in tactics or discipline. In their weeks at sea in the tropics Robinson had never seen Stewart in his dress uniform, but he must have cut an impressive figure with a chestful of ribbons, a battle star for every story.

That was the problem. Stewart had become a warrior in a peacetime navy again, but he was still seething with some unexploded anger from Vietnam, like a live mine buried in the jungle muck for twenty years waiting to be tripped.

Neither Washington nor ComSeventhFleet knew the jagged shoals through which the frigate *Decatur* was now sailing. The search had gone beyond aggressive tactics, the rational deployment of this ship. Robinson saw the barely suppressed rage, the dark, faraway fixation in Stewart's eyes, and it frightened him.

"I said it to Sikorsky, and I'll say it to you," DiLorenzo said to his co-pilot Lieutenant junior grade Stan Stone. "This bird ain't natural. If God meant it to fly, He would have put real wings on it." With that he smoothly eased up the collective pitch lever by the left side of his seat, increasing the angle at which the helicopter's whirling rotor blades bit into the air, and simultaneously twisted the throttle handle to full power.

The Seahawk gently rose from the deck of the *Decatur,* banked slightly to port to fly out of the turbulence churned up by the ship's boxy superstructure, and accelerated ahead, quickly gaining speed and altitude, the downwash from its rotors lashing the tropical sea into a froth, until the chopper rose up out of its own ground effect.

"Lucked out again," Stone responded.

It was an incantation and response that pilot and copilot repeated on each liftoff. DiLorenzo had learned it from his first helicopter instructor in navy flight school in Pensacola. It summed up that the helicopter was the most elaborately inefficient, unnatural machine the mechanical ingenuity of man had ever contrived. It hovered, climbed, or descended, flew ahead, back, right, or left by literally beating at the air with brute force, and that force created equal and opposite reactions that had to be countered by other machinery. As a young pilot DiLorenzo had taken great pride in mastering the control of those forces with a precise touch. But now, middling in age, he took his three children to play on the beach in Coronado, marveled at the hovering gulls, and wondered.

DiLorenzo circled south to pick up the

search pattern for the *Black Sea* where it had ended the previous afternoon when the sniper hit. They had found no sign of the shooter that morning, but he was still out there hidden under the mangrove boughs where the two pilots could not visually spot him and the sensor operator at his console behind them could not detect the small boat on radar. That knowledge gave the search an edge, a shot of adrenalin that triggered neither fear nor nervousness but an excitement that was not unpleasant.

Flying over a shining tropical shore was — barring a mechanical failure or a sudden squall — a pleasurable but boring occupation. The Seahawk was an electronic powerhouse of long-range radar, sonar, and infrared sensors designed to discover and track ships, submarines, and aircraft and transmit computerized information and images back to the ship. The helo's main contractor, in fact, was not the aircraft manufacturer but IBM, which built the avionics systems. The paradox was that the most important instruments aboard had now become the pilots' eyes, and they ignored the glowing radar scope on the console between them. That was the province of the aviation antisubmarine warfare operator second class, twenty-four-year-old Dennis Quigley, in the compartment behind them.

The *Decatur* sailed northwest into the Berhala Strait which separated the mountainous islands of Kepulauan Lingga from the mangrove swamps of the east coast of Sumatra. The helicopters flew a ladder pattern that bracketed the ship's path. The underbelly of the Seahawk was a circular radome for the APS-124 search radar. Every ship contact in its eighty-mile sweep had to be visually checked out, along with each river mouth, *kuala,* bay, or island in whose radar shadow the *Black Sea* might be concealed.

"At least the ship's now heading in the right direction," Stone said.

"Where's that?"

"Toward Singapore girls. That's the only way to fly."

DiLorenzo sighed audibly. "Wait till you get married and have kids."

"Why, does that cancel your yen for sexy, silky Oriental women?"

"No, it just leaves you so little money you can't even afford to think about it. Especially at today's exchange rates."

The tops of the range of mountains to the west were shrouded by a squall line of purple cumulus clouds. Jagged lightning flashed in the towering thunderheads. DiLorenzo could make out the bloated rivers looping down through the lowland jungles, the mud-colored streams swelling monstrously like gorging snakes as they twisted toward their gaping mouths in the misty coastal swamps directly below.

"Hey, we shouldn't complain. This is now the only spot on the ship that's air conditioned. Tomorrow we're both going to really appreciate this environmental control system."

"Why tomorrow?"

"Didn't you hear the word? No water again. No showers, no washing, laundry, or dishes. We'll all be just one smelly crotch." As if in anticipation DiLorenzo scratched with his free hand.

"The XO will go bonkers." Stone, as the most junior officer in the air detachment, by tradition had drawn the upper bunk in the executive officer's stateroom when the crowded ship deployed.

"Why?"

"He's the most fastidious man I ever roomed with. Showers twice a day. Gets up a half hour before reveille to shower, and again in the evening. He apologized to me. Says it's because he sweats heavily, because he's so beefy."

"*Beefy?* He looks like he can walk through the hatches without opening them."

"He played football at Annapolis."

"He *was* the Annapolis team. You're too young to remember. He was drafted by the pros but decided to stay in the navy. It made the news at the time."

"The navy must have loved that."

"Oh, yeah, that's why he's on the fast track. First in his class to make XO of a — "

"Sir, I've got a small contact," Quigley, the sensor operator, broke in over the intercom, "bearing one-seven-three, forty-seven miles. Looks like a small boat in a bay. Probably a fisherman."

DiLorenzo banked, and both pilots stared off to starboard, but the afternoon haze that hung on the sea surface like a shining veil obscured the visibility. Stone peered through the binoculars. It was a while before he reported, "I got it . . . Doesn't look much like a fishing boat. More like a fast outboard motor, the kind you water-ski with."

"Oh, that's interesting." DiLorenzo eased into a bank and glanced up over his shoulder. "Let's get the sun behind us here before we drop down to look this sporty boat over." Then, almost as if it were an afterthought, he ordered, "Quigley, man the machine gun."

The yellow-and-black-banded snake coiled in a fork of a young mangrove stared at

Mohammed with relentless, unblinking eyes. Mohammed could not discern if it was a harmless mangrove snake or a deadly poisonous krait, which had almost identical markings. He groped about at his feet for one of the spikelike nipah seeds and threw it at the snake. It slithered down the branches into a low bush and disappeared.

Mohammed swiped at the cloud of mosquitoes that swarmed in to envelop him and sprayed them with the can of repellent he gripped in his left hand like a grenade. He shook the can. It was almost empty. Then the mosquitoes would swarm in and eat him alive.

Mohammed crouched on a hummock of dank peat amid the nipah palms and mangroves at the high-tide mark. From this point he could watch the sea and sky to the east and south and the shallow bay in which the boat rode its anchor a mile away, like bait trolling at the end of a fishing line. The dark green firing tube of a Stinger missile launcher lay across the buttressing roots of the mangrove tree next to him.

Mohammed had chosen his ambush and the boat's position with the dark green mountains and banks of rain clouds beyond it only after sighting in from three other points. The Bugis fanatic who ran the boat had become impatient and angry. But how could Mohammed explain to an illiterate pirate that infrared rays his eye could not see were obscured by the blinding glare of the sun off the water?

"Aaaaaayaa!" he screamed and slapped at his leg, smashing a large rusty-red ant. The fierce weaver ants had already bitten him half a dozen times. Their nest, a sloppy basket of woven leaves, hung above his head in the next tree. At any moment he expected an angry army of red ants, even larger than the cloud of mosquitoes plaguing him, to rush out of the nest, swarm over him, sting him to death, and carry him off to their nest as food, as he had seen them haul off a still wiggling beetle. He dared not sit on the wet, oozing ground.

The mangrove swamp was an evil place, a fetid tangle of dark, looping roots that curled away all about him, now above and now below the gray-green slime. Even the steaming air was poisonous, a stinking, rotten, stagnant vapor that made him gag if he breathed too deeply. But above all else he feared the crocodiles, the monstrous twenty-five-foot-long estuarine reptiles. This swamp was their wallow as devils inhabit hell. He had seen them when Ahmed had thrown a body into the black water, as though the scurrying, snorting monsters had been sent by Satan as a confirmation of the hostages' damnation.

Mohammed checked his watch. He had lost track of how long he had crouched here in the mangroves, tormented by the mosquitoes and ants. The tide had come in, flooding the mud flats and the spiky mangrove roots. The dark water now lapped at the thicket of trees at the high-water mark. The scattered mangroves rooted in the tidal ooze were completely surrounded by water, and on the top branch of one a white-crested Brahminy hawk perched, staring at Mohammed with merciless eyes, just as the snake had done. God was surely testing His soldier Mohammed.

A sudden flare of sunlight blinded him. He looked across the bay to the boat. There was a second flash. The Bugis was signaling him with the mirror. There was a pause, then two more quick flashes. Mohammed quickly reached for the Stinger missile launcher and detached the protective cap that covered the electronics and infrared seeker at the front of the tube. He unfolded the foot-long optical sight into position and heaved the thirty-five-pound weapon onto his shoulder. The slender five-foot-long missile was already loaded in the tube. He braced his foot against the buttress roots of the mangrove and listened, his ears straining to pick up the sound.

It was several minutes before he heard the slap of the approaching rotors and the Doppler effect as it passed almost overhead. The densely layered mantle of mangroves muffled the sound, but the Bugis on lookout had seen the helicopter, a glint of sunshine on the curved cockpit canopy, when it was still a dot on the horizon. Now the thick canopy of shiny green leaves rustled in the downwash. "The winds of Paradise are blowing," Mohammed spoke aloud, as if in prayer.

The helicopter broke out into the open sky just beyond the trees. Mohammed panicked. The aircraft was already within the missile's three-mile range, and in a few moments it would be gone. He hurriedly plugged in the battery and rushed to acquire the helicopter in his sight before it soared out of range or dove below the altitude for which the computer was programmed, where the missile could not track the target. He aimed the launcher like a rifle, his right hand on the pistol grip, his left on the stock, a metal box that housed the computerized controls. The launch tube of the "rifle" extended three feet over his right shoulder to keep the flames of the backblast behind the shooter. With a practiced movement, his right thumb twitched for the button that activated the missile's infrared seeker.

The helicopter filled his sight, and a steady, high-pitched tone sounded. Mohammed slowly squeezed the trigger, then froze. There was a sudden flare in the sight, as sunlight reflected off the water. The missile would not engage if he fired into the glare. The helicopter flew on, rising up and circling around the boat, as if it were about to swoop down. Mohammed lost the target, and his heart lurched in dread. The battery was good for only thirty seconds, then it would go dead, leaving the Stinger useless.

The helicopter abruptly hovered in the air like a giant dragonfly, silhouetted against the distant rain clouds. Mohammed realized that the pilot was keeping the sun behind him in a direct line with the boat. He did not suspect an attack from shore.

Mohammed trained the Stinger's sight at the broadside the helicopter now presented to him. The small infrared-sensitive eye of the missile immediately picked up the heat spewing from twin 1,690-horsepower turbines, and a microchip the size of a coin locked on the image. The quavering electronic sound changed in frequency. Mohammed's heart faltered for several beats. In the weeks of his training, the years since, the days of dry runs, he had never actually fired a missile. "In the name of God the compassionate and merciful," he whispered.

He felt the flash of heat but did not see the flames of the backblast behind him. He kept his eye pressed to the sight, and he never saw the missile.

As soon as the Stinger shot out of the launch tube, four small cruciform canards in the nose and similar wings in the tail popped out. Beyond the mangroves, out over the bay, when the missile was safely clear of the shooter, the rocket engine ignited, spewing a white smoke trail that was almost imperceptible against the milky tropical sky. The infrared-seeing cyclops eye in the Stinger's nose fixed on the hot exhaust plume of the Seahawk's turbojets; the nickel-sized microchip transmitted minute corrections in course to the fins. A moment before the missile reached the helicopter, it angled down, and a proximity fuse detonated the high-explosive warhead into the aircraft's mid-section right below the turbines.

"I only make out one guy aboard," Stone said.

"It only takes one — "

Something slammed into the aircraft with the impact of a high-speed collision, throwing the helicopter onto its left side. The pilot was stunned by the explosion and momentarily blinded by the flash across his canopy. He instinctively moved the cyclic pitch lever in his right hand to roll the helicopter level and pushed on the right pedal. In that instant DiLorenzo realized that he had no control over the main rotor, but the tail rotor controlled by the pedals apparently still worked, and the unbalanced maneuver caused the aircraft's nose to yaw upward to the right, spilling whatever lift the powerless main rotors still generated.

The Seahawk lurched and dropped sideways, now plunging with no more flight characteristics than an elongated stone. "We're crashing!" the pilot screamed into the intercom. The helicopter had no ejection seats, which would only catapult the crewmen into the rotor blades overhead. DiLorenzo's hands darted about the hurtling cockpit. He jettisoned the side windows, locked his harness, pushed the collective lever down to pull off power to the engines, armed the flotation bags, flipped the IFF to its Emergency mode, the radio to the Guard channel, screamed, "Mayday! Mayday! Mayday!" then realized that he had no time left to send out a position report.

As the Seahawk gathered speed in its free fall, the heavy weight of its electronics and turbines caused the aircraft to nose down and roll over. In the few moments before the crash DiLorenzo hung in his shoulder straps, upside down, staring straight down into the dark water. As in a dream he had a fleeting image of his wife, Gloria.

The helicopter's canopy struck first, taking the full impact of the crash. There was a searing blood-red flash, then blackness, as DiLorenzo's neck and spine were crushed.

27. The Soothers of Care

The sun was just now rising behind ominous thunderheads to the east, and mist still shrouded the hillside cemetery, veiling the pale tombstones and the dark trees surrounding Yee like attending ghosts. The mist concealed the Gothic white stone entrance gate only a hundred paces down the path. There was a dank chill in the air, strange for Singapore but not, perhaps, for Forbidden Hill.

Yee stared at the fifth head and, for the first time, did not feel nausea, only a deep primal fear. The blue eyes, now lifeless and glassy as marbles, stared out, fixed on a distant horror. The Russian crewman had been a young man with long reddish-blond hair and a thick, virile mustache.

"That's the way the attendant found it this morning," the detective said. "It wasn't covered, just sitting right in front of the tomb, the little plastic bag with the sea book and identification next to it."

"It's fortunate a tourist didn't find it first." Keramat Iskandar Shah was Singapore's oldest landmark, the site of the ancient palace and fortress of the Malay kings of Singapura, the sacred burial place of Iskandar Shah, the last Sultan. "It must have been placed here late last night," Yee speculated.

The detective nodded. "They're not afraid of ghosts, *lah.*" The summit of Forbidden Hill was haunted, officially designated a *keramat,* a holy place. Even the weathered tombstones of the first European settlers kept to the Old Christian Cemetery on the lower slope.

Yee turned and stared at the detective. "Perhaps they are true believers," he said thoughtfully. "Perhaps this is an offering to the old kings."

Yee drove through the still vaporous corridors of the city onto the Ayer Rajah Expressway. He had called ahead to the National University, and Haji Ishak bin Hanafiah was waiting for him when he arrived. The old Malay's hazel, almost green eyes behind the heavy-framed glasses examined Yee with concern.

"I have not seen you since the death of your father."

"It has been too long," Yee agreed.

"But it is not necessary for you to visit me. You always know what I'm doing, *lah?*"

"We don't spy on you. We honor you."

"Ah, someday you'll honor me by exiling me across the Johor Straits."

"You are free to come and go as you like. But you are a father of Singapore. You are needed here."

The *haji* smiled at this. "Yes, you do need me. But do you indeed watch me, Baiyu?"

"No more than we do a Chinese communist."

Haji Ishak bin Hanafiah laughed richly. "Good, good. That is fair," he nodded. "Quite cricket, as your father used to say."

"Yes, my father believed cricket was the symbol of all that was straight, fair, and honest about the British system of government."

"The British, of course, were terrible

snobs. But then they were snobs to their own people as well, their *other ranks*. Why should they not be snobs to Chinamen and wogs? It did not matter if we were educated at Oxford, as your father and I were. We still could not dance at Raffles. Your wife, she is well?"

"Yes, very well, thank you. And your wife?"

"She is old and querulous." Ishak studied Yee thoughtfully for a moment, and his eyes gleamed with mischief under his white *haji* cap. "You have the two children, I recall, as recommended by the government?"

"Yes, two children."

"What a well-ordered society you Chinese have created here in Singapore. But you are fair, so very cricket. You ask no more of the Malays and Indians than you do of yourselves. You insist that we all study and preserve our own language and heritage. You still sing the national anthem in Bahasa, *lah*." Ishak frequently punctuated his speech with the "Singlish" of the streets, which contrasted with his Oxford English. "And in your prosperity you have endowed this chair for me to teach and preserve our Malay history and traditions."

For a moment Yee thought that Ishak was mocking him, but then the green eyes dark-

402

ened with seriousness. "But this overdue visit is not a politeness."

"I need my uncle's counsel and wisdom."

The Malay smiled at the familial term.

"This is a matter of the gravest national security and secrecy."

The old man nodded, and the nod was Haji Ishak bin Hanafiah's oath.

Yee told him of the first head that had been delivered to Raffles.

The *haji* was dumbfounded. "This is an atrocity. I have read nothing about this in the newspapers, or on the news."

"We have kept it out of the newspapers."

"Of course, like my articles." His eyes narrowed. "But you have other atrocities to tell me."

Yee briefly described the disappearance of the *Black Sea,* the discovery of the other heads, including that morning's horror on Forbidden Hill. Ishak listened, his face pale, his eyes widened and blinking behind his heavy glasses, silent except for an occasional exclamation.

When Yee had finished, the old man said nothing at first. Then, "This is unthinkable. Parameswara Jihad." He seized on the phrase and repeated it.

"What is Parameswara?"

"An ancient prince of the Srivijaya in Sumatra. Their empire had declined by the end of the fourteenth century, exhausted by wars with the Majapahit on Java. Parameswara first fled here. It was at the site of his palace where you found that atrocity this morning." The *haji* leaned forward and shook his forefinger at Yee. "The legend is that Parameswara founded Malacca, but that is nonsense. The town was a port for Arab and Indian traders for centuries before he landed, this time escaping from a Thai army. But this fugitive prince converted to Islam there and established the Malacca Sultanate. Now this is where the story perhaps becomes relevant. Malacca became the center of Islam for Asia. Its strategic control of the strait allowed the city to dominate all the east- and westbound trade between China and India and the Arabs, and the Spice Islands. Its missionaries spread Islam throughout what are now Indonesia and the Philippines. For the Malay it was the Golden Age of trade, politics, literature, and religion. But then the Portuguese sacked Malacca. And that began the Dark Age of three and a half centuries of European conquests."

"And the end of the Malacca Sultanate."

"Not quite so. Several of modern Malaysia's royal families claim links with the original Malacca Sultanate. But more important, despite the Catholic Inquisition, the Dutch Reform, and Anglican missionaries, we are still devout Muslims." He touched his white cap.

"But this Parameswara is all ancient history," Yee complained.

"But these things are very much alive in the little village mosques. Ancient glory is a great solace to people whom the twentieth century has impoverished, *lah*. Throughout all the islands of the Malay archipelago, our history, our folk tales and proverbs were passed orally from generation to generation by a class of itinerant singers and storytellers, who sailed from island to island, *kampong* to *kampong*. These keepers of tradition were called the 'soothers of care.' " He motioned to the shelves of books behind him. "That is how we know all this."

"Ancient history," Yee repeated, as though the idea offended him.

"The Prophet died in 632," Ishak said matter-of-factly, "and still blood is shed in his name every day."

"*Jihad.*"

Ishak shook his head angrily at the word. "This is not holy war. This is not Islam. This is atrocity. Islam condemns violence. *Jihad* is to protect justice, human dignity, and the Koranic law with a formal declaration of war against those who would destroy them.

But this is terrorism against innocent people. It is madness under the pretext of *jihad*. No Islamic scholar would condone these crimes."

"They are not committed by Islamic scholars."

"Have you caught any?"

"Yes, one. A fisherman's son."

"Of course he's a fisherman's son. Any fool could have told you these are fishermen's sons," Ishak snapped. He removed his glasses and rubbed his eyes as though they troubled him. When he spoke again, his voice was solemn, his words softened so as not to offend the younger man. "Singapore has high-rises that are the twenty-first century. My students are experts in computers and fly in jets. But out there in the straits, it is still the nineteenth and eighteenth centuries. Asia is not a melting pot. We are what sociologists term a 'shatter belt.' The Malay, the Chinese, the Indians all keep to themselves, practice their own religions and customs.

"Oh, what a little bastard of a country you Chinese have become heir to!" Ishak exclaimed. "*Singapura*. An Indian name. A Malay national anthem. English laws, language, and public buildings. So we conduct our business in English and get rich, *lah*. And we have dedicated men like you to keep the peace. But all around Singapore is a very old and unstable powder keg. More ancient history. In 1740 over ten thousand Chinese were killed in riots on Java. But how many were butchered in Indonesia in '65? How many Chinese massacred, mutilated, castrated, beheaded? Three hundred thousand? A million? Nobody knows for sure. They called it a coup to prevent a communist takeover."

Yee nodded in acknowledgment. "Why do you tell me my own people's history?"

"Because you hide from it, and you come here and repeat this shit the CIA has fed you. The CIA thinks it is the *dalang* manipulating his shadow puppets behind the screen in Southeast Asia. They still believe they engineered an anticommunist coup in Jakarta. They don't understand in Washington what really happened. They still play the *dalang* in Manila."

"I know all this," Yee snapped impatiently.

"Do you indeed?", Ishak asked, and his eyes fiercely probed Yee's face. "Your father didn't. He was an idealist. He once told me all the cities in Malaysia, even Singapore, would lose their predominantly Chinese character. A true Malaysian identity would arise. My son will be a Malaysian, he said. Are you a Malaysian?"

"I am a Singaporean."

"And what is that? You don't remember the bloody rioting in the streets between the Chinese and Malay in 1964."

"I am old enough to remember."

"How long have the Chinese been here? Back in the jungles and caves of head-hunters in East Malaysia we've uncovered T'ang dynasty pottery 1,300 years old." Ishak sighed. "And still we are two very different people, *lah*."

"And still the Malays can't make pottery."

Ishak laughed until his eyes teared. He wiped his eyes with a large handkerchief, then reached forward and patted Yee on the arm. "I miss your father," he sighed. "That is his wit."

Yee's own smile quickly faded. "And Malays still treat Chinese who have lived here for generations, and fought and died for independence, like pottery traders who will take the next boat back to China."

Ishak sighed again. "To many you are always the overseas Chinese, the nationals of another country. But when a poor Chinese boy — whose father does not have a business — cannot find a job or get into the university in Malaysia because the seat is reserved for a *bumiputra*, what does this Chinese boy do? He joins other unhappy young Chinese as a communist." *Bumiputra*, "son of the soil," was the official government term used to differentiate native Malays from Chinese and Indians. There was an edge to Ishak's voice that offended Yee.

"And a young 'son of the soil' who is too lazy to study and work hard to make a place in the modern world, what does *he* do?" Yee snapped angrily. "He becomes a Muslim fanatic to bring back the past."

Both men were shocked into a shamed silence by the exchange. Although a Malay or Chinese might think these things, it was inconceivable that they would say them to one another, and so rudely. They had said too much in heat, and now in their acute mutual embarrassment they avoided each other's gaze.

The old man removed his glasses and once again rubbed his eyes. When he replaced them, he looked back at Yee reluctantly, with a heavy sadness. "There are over a hundred million 'sons of the soil' out there," he said with a weary sweep of his hand, "living in wretched poverty with no hope other than Paradise after a martyr's death. And if they rise up in this Parameswara Jihad with the guns the Americans or the Russians give them, whom will they kill? The *tunkus* in Kuala Lumpur or the bureaucrats of the Berkeley mafia in Jakarta?

A few, perhaps, but most of those rascals will fall on their knees, kiss the Koran, throw shawls over the coiffures of their chic, shopping-crazy wives, and loudly renounce their evil Western ways. The sword will fall on the Chinese — the infidels, the communists, those the fanatics say bleed the land of the sons of the soil. And this blood, of course, will have the immediate earthly reward of canceling debts and mortgages and looting the richest shops. But perhaps the Chinese in their wealthy, independent city-state of Singapore will be safe."

He suddenly stood and, distracted, limped to the window and gazed out.

It pained Yee to see that old Ishak walked with difficulty. He must have been ill or had an operation, and Yee had not known about it.

Outside the mists had thickened, and there were black storm clouds blowing across the city. "No, this perversion of Islam must not be allowed." Ishak turned back from the window and stared at Yee. "I don't know anything, but my students talk to me of things they hear. There is a small fishing *kampong* a little south of Malacca. Kuala Selatan. The *imam* tells stories from the *Sejarah Melayu*, the ancient *Malay Annals*, and preaches of a prince like Parameswara who would restore the Malays to their ancient glory in Islam. Why do you smile?"

"The fisherman's son is from Kuala Selatan."

Outside the clouds suddenly burst, and the storm that had been menacing all morning exploded in a wind-lashed deluge that pounded at the window, threatening to shatter the glass and inundate the cramped, booklined study.

28. The Release of Liz Schneider

"Take care of my darling, till we meet again. And remember me — oh, what was it that Myrna Loy said? — remember me as sexy and witty and soignée." Liz Schneider touched her hair nervously. "Although I don't feel very soignée at the moment." Liz was almost giddy with fear, but she was keeping up a glib front for her husband, who stood with her and Maggi at the top of the gangway. On the river below a longboat waited with a pirate squatting in the stern by the coughing outboard engine.

Maggi removed her scarf and draped it

over Liz's head. "Here, this is more soignée than your straw hat, and it won't blow off if there's any wind on the river."

Liz fingered the silver-bordered Kelantan silk. "Oh, it's lovely. I couldn't take it."

Maggi insisted. "It has a charm to protect you woven into it. A woman who wove it on her backyard loom gave it to me."

"In that case I'll borrow it, temporarily. I'll take all the protection I can get right now. And I'll return it to you in Singapore." She hugged Maggi fiercely and kissed her on the cheek with passion. Maggi could feel her trembling badly under the long-sleeved blouse and long skirt Liz had worn for the trip on Maggi's advice.

Maggi moved off a few feet to give her and Alan a moment of privacy. From her vantage it appeared to Maggi that it was Liz who was reassuring Schneider, visibly sweating heavily in the afternoon heat on the river.

Tengku suddenly strode down the ladder onto the narrow promenade. Behind him his bodyguard, bare-chested, an AK-47 slung over his brown-skinned shoulder, carried Tengku's sword, as though it were the pirate chieftain's mace of office. He glanced at the Schneiders. "You have my oath before God that your cousin's honor will not be stained,"

Tengku said solemnly.

"Will she be safe on the boat ride?" Maggi whispered.

Tengku shrugged, *"Inshallah."* It's in God's hands. "She will travel aboard another boat now waiting at the mouth of the river. It is arranged, and I will personally put her into the hands of a brother whom I trust with my own life."

"I gratefully thank you," Maggi said. The *haji*'s oath before God was to be respected. She wondered what he had done to the two pirates who had attacked Liz. They had immediately disappeared from the ship. Perhaps the foxy Yakovlev was wrong that Tengku had to balance their punishment with an even greater one inflicted on the passengers to keep control of his men.

"We must go now," he ordered, "while there is still light to navigate."

They rode downstream, on a river roofed over by huge jungle trees creating a tunnel of foliage. It reminded Liz of her grandparents' old neighborhood, where the branches of the columns of ancient elms on both sides of the street met overhead, completely shading the road. The canopy gave Liz a childhood sense of security; nothing bad could happen to her, as long as the trees sheltered her.

She sat in the middle of the long, narrow *perahu*, a dugout canoe fashioned from a single giant tree trunk and wide enough for only one person. Ahead of her was the shining brown back of one of the pirates, who squatted cross-legged in the bow peering at the river ahead. Just behind her sat the white-capped chieftain, Tengku Haji Azhar. He had not said a word to her since they had left the ship, but Maggi had forewarned her that he was shy about speaking in English.

The giant trees of the rain forest drew back from the bank, and the sudden glare of the sun bursting on the dark water seared Liz's eyes. She groped in her bag for her sunglasses. A sulphurous stench now swept up the river, borne on the light breeze that blew in from the sea. The river widened into a region of nipah swamp, the walls of palms on both banks seemingly impenetrable, and even to Liz's eye the water became noticeably sluggish.

The pirate riding shotgun in the bow, hunched over his rifle, suddenly sat straight up and quickly brought up the gun, pointing it toward shore. *"Buaya,"* he snarled.

At first Liz didn't see the crocodiles in the glaring sunlight. The dark gray-brown armored scales against the mud were an effective camouflage. Then one beast gaped, the huge pointed jaw opening wide, exposing the yellow inside flesh of the mouth and the rows of spiky, carnivorous teeth.

"Oh, my God!" The biggest of the crocodiles looked to be twenty feet long. They were onshore, apparently basking on the shallow mud bank, their clawed forepaws and feet splayed out.

"Please sit very still, Mrs. Schneider. Keep hands in boat," Tengku whispered behind her in perfectly clear English.

One croc scuttled down the glistening mud into the water and disappeared. The biggest one rose up on its forepaws and stared at the boat with evil reptilian eyes. They were only a few body lengths away, and they might be upon the boat in two strokes of their thick, square, muscular tails.

The outboard engine revved up and moved past the crocodiles at a heightened speed. The boat did not slow down again to cruising speed until they were a safe distance beyond.

"My God, they're monsters." Liz let out her breath. She was more awed than frightened. "Could they attack the boat?" Unnerving as the crocs were, they were a seen danger, and now the incident had broken the terrifying spell of silence.

"Yes. They will jump into boat and pull

man into water," Tengku said behind her. "Now time of day they lie in sun. Night they hunt. Night we not go on river."

"Why don't you shoot them?"

"They protect us. Fishermen and farmers fear this place."

"Are they man-eaters?"

"*Man-eaters?*" Tengku savored the phrase. "Oh, yes, they eat men. Not like shark or tiger. They are . . . ," he hunted for a word, "*gourmets* of men. They hold under-water until man drown, then shove under log, roots of tree, two, three days. Meat ripe like fruit. *Then* crocodile man-eater."

In the full blazing heat of the sun, Liz shuddered. She did not stop shuddering for several minutes.

The river forked, or rather three large islands, overgrown with nipahs, divided the waters into three narrower channels. The *perahu* swung to the left. Ahead Liz could make out a region of low trees that appeared to grow right across the tortuous channel. The water exhaled the stench of rotting, like the bad breath of a sick old man.

The *perahu* rounded a bend, and Liz was suddenly startled to see several boats — two very fast-looking speedboats with powerful outboard motors and a Malay fishing craft — hauled up on a mud bank with a large group of natives assembled, apparently waiting for them.

The *perahu* abruptly veered toward the landing without slackening speed, as if it were going to plow right into the mud bank. At the last moment the half-naked pirate in the bow sprang into the water, heaved up on the prow, and beached almost half the length of the canoe.

He grinned at Liz and held out his hand in a chivalrous way that took her completely by surprise. She was able to step ashore without getting her feet in the water, but the convenience was only momentary as her sandals sank into the oozy black tidal mud. A dank odor rose up from the squishy mud like a poisonous vapor, and it loudly sucked at each foot, like some shapeless, malevolent creature of slime that wanted to swallow her. Liz fled to the top of the bank, where wiry grass firmed the footing, creating a small clearing amid the nipah palms.

A touch at her elbow startled her. "Please wait here, Mrs. Schneider," Tengku said in a soft voice.

Ashore the heat was heavy, wet, breathless. Mosquitoes swarmed about her with a relentless hum, as though they were another primal element of the air like the heat, the humidity, the stink. Tengku stood off to one side conferring with the pirates, but their voices were so absorbed by the thick walls of palm that they seemed a mile away, like voices overheard in sleep.

Liz was badly frightened. The danger that Tengku radiated was as hypnotic as his rajah looks. Liz kept reminding herself, as Maggi had done earlier, that before the incident that morning none of the passengers had been harmed. She did not know what was about to happen, although it had been explained to her earlier that she would be taken to Singapore aboard another larger boat, not the *perahu*. She wondered vaguely if it would be one of the speedboats or the fishing boat, but the oppressive wet heat and stench made even that thought an effort.

A group of the pirates loitered about, totally silent, keeping their distance but staring at her with a bright-eyed, expectant leer. Liz felt faint. For the thirtieth time she reminded herself that Tengku had taken an oath before God that her "honor would not be stained."

She willed herself to note her surroundings, as Alan had suggested, so that once in Singapore she might give the authorities a clue as to where they were being held captive. There was a beached and overturned *perahu* beyond the speedboats. Liz made out two men stretched face down across the boat bottom. She squinted at them through the glaring sunlight off the river. Her puzzlement was transformed to horror; even at twenty paces she could see the blood on their backs.

"Please come." Tengku was again at her side, and with a relentless grasp on her arm forced her to move forward to the two apparently lifeless bodies. Both men were stripped to the waist and barefoot, their backs a butchery of bloody welts and torn flesh, as though they had been flogged with a cat-o'-nine-tails. Liz was sickened by the carnage. She noted that both men's chests heaved with the strain of breathing in their keel-hauled positions.

Tengku bent and picked up a slender bamboo cane leaning against the hull. He pointed at the two men with it, and the fresh blood on the cane glistened in the sunlight with a metallic sheen. "This is two men who rape you. This punishment, it is enough?"

Liz was astonished. He was asking her if the beatings should continue. Behind the *haji* she spotted his bare-chested bodyguard holding a sheathed sword at the ready to hand to him. "Oh, my God, yes. Yes, it's enough punishment," Liz exclaimed.

Tengku nodded, the gleaming white *haji* cap bobbing, and gave her an oddly satisfied smile, as though they had completed a painful negotiation. "Good. God is compassionate, and justice is made." He said something in Malay, and several of the other men helped raise up the two pirates from the overturned *perahu* that had been their rack. They could not stand and collapsed onto the sand in sitting positions, their hands still bound in front of them. They peered from Liz to the *haji* and back again, their sorrowful eyes glazed with pain but still fearful.

As horrified as she was, Liz was oddly reassured. Tengku, true to his code of honor, had punished the two men who had attacked her.

The other pirates, perhaps a dozen in all, now pressed about them. Tengku spoke to them, and although Liz could not understand a word of his Malay, she sensed the formality of his address and a strange undercurrent of excitement in their responding mutters.

Then he turned to her. "It is time departure for Singapore," he announced. He held up a black cloth. "Blindfold," he smiled, and added in a gently apologetic voice, "You not tell where we are."

Liz nodded obediently. So much for Alan's instructions to note carefully the landscape and any navigational markers. She turned, lowered the silver-trimmed shawl Maggi had given her, and bent her head to accept the blindfold. She felt Tengku's warm fingertips linger a moment on her neck, a perversely exciting sensation, then touch the silk of the shawl, as if carefully rearranging it.

There was a rustling behind her. Suddenly her arms were violently seized, and the cloth or a rope was wound tightly about her wrists, biting painfully, fastening her arms behind her.

Liz cried out, "What — why are you tying me?" But her voice was choked with terror. She was roughly shoved forward onto the overturned *perahu*, her stomach and chest slamming the keel with a stunning blow, driving all the air from her.

She was on her knees, her hands pinioned behind her, totally helpless. Someone grabbed at her hair and yanked her head, stretching her neck painfully. She gasped but could not lift her chest off the hard, wooden hull to catch her breath.

Tengku intoned something in Malay in a reverent voice, but Liz made out only the word *Allah*. In a reddened blur of pain and paralyzing fear she thought that Tengku was now going to cane her viciously, as he had the two pirates who had attacked her.

There was a moment or two of silence, hushed and expectant, and Liz strained to hear what she could not see. For a fraction of a second she heard a whistling hum in the air as though some great insect were winging toward her, then felt a terrible blow at her neck and in the next instant all consciousness ended in a searing white flash.

29. Recovering Bodies

"United States Navy warship *Decatur*, this is Soviet Navy aircraft, 158 kilometers east of your position. We have no hostile intent. Over."

Stewart grabbed the phone next to his chair. "Soviet aircraft, this is *Decatur*. Over."

"*Decatur*, we hear Mayday from Eagle Claw 39 and mark emergency IFF on radar. But no more radio report, and now IFF is also gone. We hold your position on radar. IFF bearing 158 degrees, 109 kilometers from your position."

"Eagle Claw" was the radio call sign of the ship's helicopters. Stewart repeated the range and bearing. "We have a helicopter on a search mission in that area. Please repeat your present position. Over." The Russian's accent was barely comprehensible, and Stewart carefully enunciated each word.

"We are 158 kilometers east of *Decatur*. We have no permission to overfly territorial waters of Republic of Indonesia."

Stewart bent over the intercom. "Combat, Bridge. Are you in contact with Eagle Claw 39?"

"Negative, Captain. He dropped below the horizon to check out a contact. We're not holding him on either radar, radio, or data link. We copied the Russian, and where he picked up that Emergency is just about where Eagle Claw 39 would be. We're switching and trying to contact him on HF now."

"Roger. Let me know the instant you do. Any of our search aircraft in the area?"

"Negative, Captain. Should I try to raise them and tell them the situation?"

"That's affirmative." Stewart leaped to the chart table.

"We're here. The Russian is there. And the Emergency is there." Chief Quartermaster Fields jabbed at three *X*'s on the chart. "It's in a bay. Teluk Ikan Hiu."

Stewart grabbed the radio mike again. "Soviet Navy aircraft, this is United States Ship *Decatur*, over."

"This is Soviet Navy aircraft."

"This is Captain Henry Stewart, the commanding officer. We believe the Emergency IFF you reported is a United States Navy helicopter from our ship. It is in a bay in the territorial waters of the Republic of Indonesia. I officially request your assistance. Repeat. The commanding officer of *Decatur* officially requests your assistance. Over."

"Captain of the *Decatur,* this is Commander Dmitry Szedlov of Soviet Naval Air Forces. We happy assist. Overfly Emergency IFF maybe fifteen minutes."

"Thank you, Commander Szedlov."

"Can you do that?"

Stewart turned and stared at his executive officer, as if Robinson's question astonished him. "I'll worry about the diplomatic niceties after I have my helicopter crew safe on board." He immediately looked away, dismissing the XO, and peered right and left. "Christ, we're damned to starboard and damned to port. Mr. Gerling, I have the conn."

"Aye, aye, sir. The captain has the conn," the officer of the deck sang out.

"Left full rudder."

"Left full rudder, aye, sir," the helmsman responded.

"Mr. Gerling, please sing out the fathometer reading every fifteen seconds."

"Aye, aye, sir. Eight fathoms and dropping."

"What's the chart indicate we have under our keel?"

"Twelve, Captain," the chief quartermaster responded.

Jesus, Robinson thought.

"XO."

"Sir."

"I want the second chopper briefed, in the air, and on its way by the time we've reversed course."

"Aye, aye, sir." The executive officer was down the ladder in two strides, grateful to be off the bridge with orders elsewhere. The loose cannon was rolling around the gun deck again.

"Seven fathoms and dropping, sir," he heard behind him.

The four-engined Russian Tupolev-95 swept over Teluk Ikan Hiu at five thousand feet, and — not suspecting any ambushing Stingers or spotting the American helicopter — Commander Dmitry Szedlov banked into a shallow descent.

Below, where the mangroves encroached into the sea, the water was coffee colored with silt, almost indistinguishable from the mud flats. But the dark water on the northwest shore of the bay ended abruptly in a blue-white curving band, a long coral barrier reef that held back the mud spilling out of hidden streams.

Beyond the reef the water was a crystalline emerald, and the Russian pilot might never have spotted the small blue-gray smear near the center of the bay. It was the flash of yellow that caught his eye, and he focused his binoculars on it.

"No apparent survivors," Stewart radioed Eagle Claw 37. "And no other contacts in the area. No signs of whatever it was DiLorenzo had dropped down to check out. The Russian will circle overhead until you get there. You can contact him on Guard channel."

"Roger, Blue Knight. It'll take us about thirty minutes to get there." "Blue Knight" was the *Decatur*'s radio call sign.

Stewart turned to Lieutenant junior grade Henshaw, one of the two pilots now on board with two in the air and two in the water. "According to the charts, that bay's only twelve to eighteen feet deep. They should have been able to get out even if it sank immediately, unless they were hurt in the crash."

Henshaw nodded. "They're probably on the beach waiting for us to show up. DiLorenzo's the best. Even with a complete engine failure, he could make a relatively soft water landing."

"How long will it float?"

"Not very. We call those big yellow flotation bags DRIs, Diving Rate Inhibitors. They won't hold up ten tons of metal, but there's still plenty of time to get out."

"What if the window jams?"

"He'd have popped them before he Maydayed."

Stewart nodded, encouraged by this information. "What if the Russian is right and the chopper's upside down?"

"It probably is." Henshaw held the palm of his hand out flat and slowly twisted it upside down. "They roll when they sink. The engines and shafts are on top, and they're top-heavy. But there's still lots of time to get out and get organized before they start to go."

Stewart studied the soundings around Teluk Ikan Hiu marked on his chart and envisioned the Seahawk with its great top cap of rotor blades rolling over and sinking. "What if it hit upside down?" he speculated.

The young pilot shook his head vigorously. "Captain, I don't even want to think about that possibility."

At flank speed it took the *Decatur* over two hours to reach the crash area. Stewart anchored offshore, five miles outside the shallow bay, and launched the motor whale boat.

The boat surged through a glittering azure sea toward a coconut palm-fringed beach south of the mangrove swamp making up the northwest shore. Ensign Leonard Fine eyed the three body bags stacked in the bottom of the boat and immediately regretted volunteering to dive. It had been an act of romantic bravado inspired by that distant palmy beach. "Think there's a chance they made it ashore?"

Lieutenant Tom Callahan shook his head. "We can hope, but we searched for over an hour, and we didn't see anything. They all three have signal flares. Someone's should have worked." Callahan was the helicopter pilot who had spotted the wreck, and he was in charge of the six-man boat crew.

Fine nodded grimly. He had shared a late breakfast with DiLorenzo and Stone just that morning at the side table in the wardroom, when they were coming off a patrol flight and he off the morning bridge watch. He had liked both pilots, their easy, humorous camaraderie, the way Lieutenant Commander DiLorenzo had treated the young co-pilot, not as the junior officer but more like a kid brother.

Suddenly to seaward a huge, flat black manta ray rose up out of the water, flapped for a moment like a great bat, then hit the water with a loud slap and disappeared. Fine was alarmed by the sight, an ominous portent of what lurked beneath the surface. "Do you think there'll be sharks?" he interrogated Hull Technician Second Class Sonny Giles.

"There's a good chance, sir." Giles looked as frightened as Fine. The petty officer was about the same age as the ensign. Giles was a qualified diver and had a spare regulator and tank. Captain Stewart had asked for another volunteer who knew how to scuba dive. To satisfy a physical education requirement at UCLA, Fine had taken a course in scuba diving one semester and tennis the next. He had had a future vacation at Club Med in mind, not the recovery of mutilated bodies, the salvage of classified electronics, and underwater demolition. They had not been covered in the coed class at UCLA.

"I'm really glad you're along, sir," Giles said. He seemed very sincere. "To be honest, I've never done anything like this before. Just some wreck diving and spearfishing in the liberty ports we hit."

"Hell, my biggest dive has been for abalones off Catalina."

"Well, if you run into sharks, bop them on the nose. That's supposed to drive them off," the coxswain said knowingly. "I seen it on TV."

"That's just lore," Fine snapped. "Maybe it's not true. Maybe it worked for one or two shy sharks, and now everyone says it does. Maybe it really excites or maddens them, the 95 percent who are man-eaters. And all those people who tried it never lived to tell us it really pisses them off." Fine heard the note of hysteria in his own voice. The coxswain and Giles stared at him strangely.

Fine turned to Callahan. The pilot peered ahead, his brow creased with a troubled expression, and did not offer anything more assuring by way of experience. The boat engineer, coxswain, and gunner's mate all wore dungarees, having no intention of jumping into the water. They carried M14's, Fine and Callahan 9-mm. pistols.

Fine felt queasy. He wondered if it was the bobbing of the boat on the gentle northeast swells or fear.

"Coxswain, it's there about two o'clock." Callahan pointed off to the right. "That's the tail wheel sticking up out of the water. Jesus, it hit totally upside down."

Fine could now make out the two main landing wheels thrusting up like the curled black claws of a stricken bird on its back.

"Hey, it can't be too deep," Giles said, as if encouraged by the sight.

"The tail is seventeen feet high," Callahan

said, as if taking a measure.

The coxswain fixed a line to the exposed tail-wheel strut.

The water was wonderfully clear, and Fine could make out the details of the sunken helicopter — the circular radome, the landing-gear struts, and the brightly painted red and yellow MAD "bird" like some exotic tropical fish. The aircraft had come down on the edge of a coral reef, a solid bottom of blue-white splashed with splotches of yellow, red, and black coral growths and waving anemones. Here and there schools of brilliantly colored fish darted about like clouds of confetti caught in a swirling wind. The clarity of the tropical water was inviting, and Fine felt his fear abate somewhat. He started strapping on his air tank.

"*Decatur,* this is *Decatur One,* over," Callahan reported in on the walkie-talkie.

"Go ahead, One."

"Captain, we're over the chopper now. It's in about sixteen to seventeen feet of water. It doesn't look good. It must have crashed upside down. The divers are suiting up now to go down."

"Roger, we're standing by. Out."

Giles trailed his hand in the water, relishing its warmth. "It's really beautiful — *Aaaaaaaaa!*"

A helicopter crewman, his eyes wide open, staring at death, his mutilated, swollen face ghastly and totally leached of blood, rose straight up out of the water like an avenging ghoul.

In its frenzy the big shark feeding at the gaping wound in the crewman's back drove the corpse right up out of the water, propelling it to the end of the wire cable which harnessed the door gunner to the airframe. Then the body jerked away from the shark like bait on the end of a trolling line. A second shark seized the corpse's arm in its jaws and shook it and shook it and shook it.

"Sharks!" everybody screamed at once.

The gunner's mate Armbruster was the first to grab an M14 and fire. The gunfire galvanized the others.

A third fin surfaced and ran straight as a torpedo into the thrashing body. Now all five guns were firing, and the water erupted in spouts of bullets.

"Aim for their fucking heads!" Armbruster shouted. "These fuckers are too dumb to know they've been shot up."

Fine grabbed at the corpse — writhing in the water face up, an agonized expression as though even in death it could not bear the horror consuming it — and tried to haul it into the boat, then realized that it was

432

still tied to the sunken helo. "Help me get him aboard," he shouted to Giles.

He lay down his pistol and reached down into the water to feel for the cable attachment. A shark's gaping mouth broke water a foot away from his head.

Giles jammed the muzzle of his M14 into the shark's face and fired a half dozen rounds. The shark thrashed and snapped, then, convulsing, mouth still gaping, sank as suddenly as it had surfaced.

Fine and Giles, working together, managed to roll the corpse over and unhook the cable.

"Stop firing! Stop firing!" Armbruster shouted. "We'll need our ammo."

Fine looked up. The sharks' bullet-riddled death throes had now carried them thirty yards beyond the whale boat and ignited a cannibalistic frenzy. "Give us a hand here."

By yanking and hauling at it, they manhandled the sodden, bloated body over the gunwales into the boat. The right arm was ripped off at the elbow, hunks of flesh had been torn from both thighs and calves, and there was a huge wound at the back, but the tattered flight suit still clung to the body. The shredded flesh and tendons were pink, not at all bloody, as though all the blood had been drained from the body. The face, with its open, transfixed eyes and the flesh of its left cheek ripped off to the skull bone, was the horror. Callahan stared at it, visibly trembling.

"Who is it?"

"Quigley. The sensor operator." Callahan's voice was a whisper.

"We better get him into one of the bags."

"Are DiLorenzo and Stone still down there?" Fine asked.

Callahan shook his head. "I don't know. Probably."

Fine peered over the side. He was amazed at the clarity of the water. He could make out the patterns of the lettuce and brain corals directly below. "I don't see any sharks."

"They're all over there," Giles pointed. Thirty yards away sinister fins and blue-black bodies exploded from the churning water.

Fine studied the shark frenzy and then looked at the young diver. Ensign Fine feared being a coward in front of the others as much as he did the sharks. "I think we can do it, if we keep the helo between them and us. Cover us with the guns," he said to Armbruster.

"No, I won't be responsible. They're already dead. If you get hurt, it's my ass," Callahan protested.

"No," Fine said excitedly. "I'm not leaving

them down there for those . . . *things*. They're my shipmates too. They're Americans. They're navy officers. It's a desecration." He was surprised by his own vehemence.

"You're crazy!" Callahan shouted.

"I'm fucking certifiable to even be out here!" Fine yelled back. "Let's try it," he gestured to Giles. "Keep the helo as protection between them and us."

He pulled on the line to maneuver the whale boat on the other side of the aircraft. "Ease into the water. Don't splash," he said as much to himself as Giles.

"I hear ya," Giles responded.

Using the strength of his arms, Fine squirmed over the gunwale into the water. "You see anything?" he whispered, his head nervously swiveling all about.

"No, it's all clear so far."

Fine let go of the boat and allowed himself to sink to the bottom without kicking. The helicopter was completely upside down, resting on the main-rotor hub, the four blades fanned out supporting it like a pedestal, the tailfin atop a flat coral reef. The balmy warmth of the water and the brilliant sunlight made the danger seem unreal, an illusion. But then the burbling sound of his own exhaled breath, the burst of bubbles, and the loud, rasping suck on the regulator startled Fine. He wondered if the sound would attract the sharks and peered about. For the moment the only fish around him were bright-colored tropicals — blue parrotfish and yellow butterfly fish — that shyly kept their distance. Giles drifted down beside him, and Fine signaled him with a thumbs-up.

Giles repeated the gesture, indicating he was all right, but his eyes, magnified by the glass face mask, seemed unnaturally large and anxious.

Fine waved "follow me" and pulled himself very slowly toward the cockpit of the wreck, being careful not to kick too strongly. Somewhere in his memory was the caution that sharks are attracted to thrashing, awkward movements like those an injured creature might make, and his safety now depended on moving gracefully, confidently.

He noticed a good-sized hole just aft of the rotor hub. Forward of it the side window had been jettisoned, and the cockpit was open. Both pilots dangled lifelessly in their seats, held in by their seat belts and harnesses. Their faces were still masked in helmets and sun visors, their bodies protected by flight suits and gloves, and they appeared not to have been molested yet by the sharks. A few curious small fish swam about, then scattered as Fine moved in.

Any squeamishness about touching the corpses had ended with the horror in the whale boat. He groped around in the dead man's lap for the release, found it, then gently yanked him by the arm. Weightless in the water, the body moved easily, then the head suddenly jerked back. Fine's heart lurched. Then he spotted the radio cord still attached to the helmet, detached it out, and the body drifted free.

He and Giles could handle the body easily in the water. The sailor pointed to the toggle on the dead pilot's jacket and motioned that Fine should pull it. With a popping noise the vest inflated, and the body immediately rose to the surface, lifting both Fine and Giles with it.

"Give a hand. Don't splash," Fine gasped, spitting out the mouthpiece. "Where are the sharks?"

"They're still busy chowing down on each other over there. We got him."

"Who is it?"

"I don't know. I don't think the sharks got to him yet." Somehow that thought gave Fine a surge of confidence. "We'll get the other now. Cover us."

"We can cover you on the surface," Armbruster said. "But the bullets don't reach down there. You're on your own."

Fine submerged and dropped down again to the reef, this time with infinitely more assurance, after having recovered one of the bodies without great difficulty. There were still no sharks to be seen on this side of the wreck, but a brightly banded sea snake undulated away, fleeing the bubbling intruders.

He pointed out the hole in the helicopter's fuselage to Giles. The hull technician ran his fingers around the edges and peered into it, as though he were contemplating how to repair it. Then they moved together to the cockpit.

After one try it was apparent that they could not wiggle into the cramped cockpit through the left window and extricate the pilot in the right-hand seat. They had to move around the aircraft and work from the other side. Fine swam around the shattered branches of a staghorn coral, broken by the crashing blunt nose, and froze.

The reef sharks, frenzied and ravenous, ripped, slashed, and snapped at one another. They were dangerously closer underwater than on top, no more than a few lengths away, a bloody, murky swirl of a half-dozen blue-gray torpedo shapes. The largest one convulsed, its long body twisting and bowing, as the others darted in to nip and tear at it. Several of the attackers swam erratically, biting at one another in their confusion. Several smaller sharks maneuvered just outside the pack, switching back and forth excitedly but not plunging into the melee. A dense cloud of smaller silver fish nervously darted hither and thither, schooling tightly for defense yet always close by, excited by the blood in the water.

Fine dropped below the nose of the overturned cockpit and motioned Giles to follow him. By hugging the aircraft they might be ignored by the crazed sharks. The cockpit was slightly crushed on the right side, the canopy shattered, and the pilot wedged against the instrument panel. When Fine released his seat belt, he did not float free but hung upside down, his head and torso outside the cockpit but his legs still caught inside. They appeared to be pinned underneath a control lever. The stick was jammed, and, suspended underwater, Fine could not get the leverage to force it.

Giles dropped underneath the nose, wiggled halfway through the shattered front panel, and yanked the booted legs free. Fine got a grip under the dead man's arms and, standing on the reef itself, pulled the body out the side window. He was suddenly bumped forcefully in the back.

He turned just as the tail of a seven-foot shark whipped by him, then turned sharply. Fine glanced frantically at Giles, who was still pushing himself out of the cockpit, his exposed legs kicking ineffectually, not yet aware of the attack.

The shark circled around, stalking Fine in a leisurely, gradually decreasing spiral, the circles ever tighter, the dark scythe of its tail switching back and forth, the gleaming marble eyes always fixed on him. A powerful thrust of the tail suddenly drove the grinning saw-toothed mouth directly at Fine.

He instinctively shoved the body at the shark, using it as a shield. The crash helmet struck the creature in the nose and mouth. Whether the shark deliberately tasted it Fine never knew, but the shark instantly recoiled from the blow of rock-hard plastic, twisted about, and swiftly swam away. Fine was amazed at its speed. It retreated a good distance, then turned back and hesitated, apparently confused by the aggressive move. Fine forcefully thrust the body toward it, as if launching it after the shark. The animal fled.

Something seized Fine's arm. He whirled around. Giles, his eyes enormous behind his face plate, hung there. Fine gave the sailor an emphatic thumbs-up.

He checked the water all around them. There were no other sharks prowling about, and the whale boat was directly over them. Fine studied its bottom a moment, then decided not to surface right there. Their three pairs of legs, dangling and kicking in sight of the sharks, was inviting another attack. He motioned to Giles, and they each grabbed an arm of the corpse and towed it around to the other side of the helicopter.

"When I saw that shark come at you, I almost shit in my pants!" Armbruster bellowed as he hauled them aboard.

"I did shit in my pants!" Fine yelled back. He felt giddy with relief at their escape.

He unstrapped the dead pilot's helmet and removed it from the bald head of what had been Lieutenant Commander Eddie Di-Lorenzo. "Let's take both helmets down with us," he said to Giles. "If a shark gets too close, bop it with this." He unzipped the second body bag.

"You're going back down?" Armbruster asked, astonished.

"We're supposed to salvage the black boxes. Those are our orders."

"Jesus! You got balls the size of cannon-balls, I'll tell you that." The gunner's mate looked at Lieutenant Callahan, who just stared down at the now exposed faces of the two dead pilots, his own no less drained of blood, and said nothing.

"Maybe we better check with the ship," Armbruster suggested.

"What's Captain Stewart going to say? It's our call. We've been down there. I think we'll be all right, if we keep close to the helo. But if any of those bastards come near the surface, put bullets in them. Keep them busy tearing each other apart."

"Yes, sir!" Armbruster picked up an M14 and sighted at the darting black fins and writhing shadows thirty yards away. He fired several rounds. "Son of a bitch."

Fine hooked his arm through the chin strap of DiLorenzo's helmet, as if it were a shield. "Ready?"

Giles nodded. "Let's do it."

The black boxes were the helicopter's classified avionics — the APS-124 radar's digital-scan converter, the MAD "bird," the electronic-surveillance analyzer, its secure SRQ-4 data link with the ship. Both Giles and Fine had made dry runs on board the *Decatur* locating and withdrawing the equipment on the other helicopter. The electronic boxes were designed to be readily removable for servicing and quick replacement, but working underwater on an upside-down helicopter at first completely disoriented Fine. He stood guard while Giles wrestled the data link from the nose nacelle.

A gray reef shark, perhaps a foot smaller than the one that had bumped him, circled curiously to within ten feet. Fine watched the stalking maneuver as the shark spiraled closer, not yet facing him directly, but cautiously sliding by, eyeing him as it passed. When it closed to a few feet, Fine lashed out, wielding the helmet like a club, and struck the shark on the side of its head. It fled instantly, a gray blur in the water. Again, Fine was awed by the shark's explosion of speed. If one, two, or more ever came at him that fast, there would be nothing he could do.

He looked back at Giles. The technician was crouched under the helicopter watching him, holding a black box. Fine gave him a thumbs-up, and Giles repeated the signal. He pointed at the cockpit, and they sculled about to the left side, where the wreck formed a barrier against the ferocity and blood in the water. In the sun-dazzled calm of the reef, Fine peered about; for a moment he was absolutely amazed at where he was and what he was doing.

In the cockpit Giles worked relatively quickly salvaging the electronics, while Fine stood guard ready to defend the technician from sharks. The black boxes, weightless and lubricated by the sea water, slid out easily. But inside the cabin, at what had been the sensor operator's station, the console was smashed, a hopeless tangle of metal. Both Giles and Fine almost simultaneously ran out of air before they were able to salvage anything more, and they groped back to the surface.

Fine reported to Stewart on the walkie-talkie. "It looked like some sort of explosion."

"What kind of explosion?" the captain demanded. "The engine blow up?"

"No, sir, more like it was hit by a missile or something."

"What do you mean a missile?" Not even the small radio speaker muted the excitement in Stewart's voice.

"There was what looked like an entry hole just below the engine cowling on the . . . I don't know, everything's turned upside down . . . on the left, the port side. But the inside was blown to shit and looked like it was scorched. It pretty well obliterated the console, whatever did it. I'm sorry I can't be any more specific than that, sir. We ran out of air just then. Maybe Giles saw more."

"Put him on."

But the hull technician only repeated what Fine had reported.

"Okay, bring it in," Stewart ordered. "It'll be at least a week before the navy can get any sort of salvage boat to it. If the Russians don't get to it first."

In the wardroom Stewart questioned the boat crew as if he were conducting a board of inquiry. "I didn't dive down there to inspect it, no, sir. But the water was very clear, and I did look down at it, after the two divers mentioned the explosion. Examined it best as I could." Callahan talked as if he were short of breath. "It was partially hidden by the flotation bags, but as far as I could see, it's as . . . the divers described it." He couldn't remember Fine's, Giles's, and Armbruster's names, even though he had spent half the day in hell with them.

"Damn it, Mr. Callahan, was it a missile entry or not? A Stinger? What do you think?"

"I've never seen a Stinger hit, sir. Or any other kind of missile for that matter. It could be. I mean it was in the right location, if it were homing in on the engine heat, behind the main rotor shaft. Something blew them out of the air."

"How do you know that?" Robinson asked.

"It didn't *land* in the water. It *crashed,*

upside down. They didn't have a chance." Again the pilot seemed to be having trouble with his breathing.

"Couldn't it have just rolled over after it landed? I understand they do that."

Callahan shook his head agitatedly. "The water wasn't that deep. The main rotor blades are twenty-six feet long, and they would have propped it right side up. The crewman Quigley never even had a chance to strap himself in. Otherwise he might have survived. The way that bird's built, sometimes the crewman survives a crash when both pilots are killed. But he's got to be strapped in his seat."

"Why wasn't he?"

Callahan just silently shook his head.

Armbruster spoke up. "He was still attached to the wire when we found him, sir, bobbing up and down like bait for the sharks. That's what was driving them crazy. At least until we shot them up."

"Jesus!" Robinson exclaimed.

There was a polite knock on the wardroom door, and Doc Blowitz came in. "I found something you might be interested in, sir." He held out several small, jagged pieces of metal.

"Shrapnel?" Stewart asked.

"I found them sticking right in the

crewman's back. Some blew all the way through to the chest. He was torn up by something else besides sharks. They came later."

Stewart delicately ran his fingers over the sharp edges of the shards of stainless steel.

"Are you sure it's shrapnel?" Robinson asked.

"I know what shrapnel from a man's belly looks like," Stewart snapped. He immediately realized from everyone's reaction that there had been no need for that particular revelation. "What about the pilots?"

"Not a mark on them, sir. They must have been killed by the crash. Or knocked unconscious, then drowned."

Callahan visibly shuddered.

"I understood the armored seats were designed to absorb the shock of a crash," Robinson asked him, "through steel hydraulic tubes."

"They don't work upside down."

Stewart turned back to his chief medical corpsman. "What type of wound did Quigley originally have?"

"It's too much of a mess now. I don't think anybody could tell."

"You think it was a small antiaircraft missile or rocket explosion?"

"I'd be guessing, Captain. It might be.

But that would be consistent with the shrapnel."

Stewart studied the pieces of metal in his hand with loathing. "Doc, I know it's asking a lot, but please get as much of the shrapnel out as you can. Without taking apart the body. And let me see it."

"What am I looking for, sir?"

"Whatever hit him."

Stewart looked over at Callahan. The pilot was deathly pale. Both hands had a noticeable tremor and were pressed flat on the table, as though for support.

"Why was the crewman Quigley on the line and not strapped in his seat?" Stewart asked him in a quiet voice.

"He was probably manning the door gun."

Stewart made a humming, ruminative sound. "So Eddie suspected something, and they got him first with a missile."

"Who's *they?* And what the hell is going on?" Robinson snapped.

As the others filed out of the wardroom, Callahan hung back. "Captain, may I speak to you privately?" The voice was strained, tight in his throat, and the pilot's hands were trembling.

"Why don't we go to my cabin?"

"Yes, sir, thank you."

Neither spoke on the walk forward through

448

the main deck passageway and up the ladder to Stewart's cabin until he shut the door. "Have a seat. Would you like a cup of coffee?"

"No, sir, I'm still too wired as it is." Callahan didn't smile at his own remark and remained standing. Stewart noted the fluttering of his trouser legs, but the trembling, he knew, was caused by an overdose of adrenalin which had not burned off yet.

"Captain, I'm now officer in charge of the helicopter detachment."

Stewart waited.

"I'm responsible for the safety of the remaining crews and the helicopter."

Stewart remained silent.

"Captain, it is not safe to fly."

"No, Mr. Callahan, it isn't, and it seldom is. And we must assume that they — whoever the hell they are — have Stingers. Eddie didn't, but we will. When we get back on track tomorrow morning, we'll resume the search for the *Black Sea*. You'll outfit the helo with flares, the IR jammer, and whatever else you need. And you'll fly whatever altitudes and use whatever tactics are necessary to reduce the Stinger threat, but you will have the helicopter airborne tomorrow morning."

"Captain, with all due respect, I'm the

officer in charge, and I deem it unsafe." Callahan's voice was thick and charged with anger.

"Mr. Callahan, this is not a training exercise where safety is the primary consideration." Stewart spoke quietly, without menace or anger, but in a voice as unyielding as stone. "One of my crewmen was shot dead next to me on the bridge yesterday. Today we both lost a good friend, two other shipmates, and a helicopter in our charge. And each day we don't find the *Black Sea* another hostage is murdered. I am the officer in operational command, and I am ordering the remaining helicopter back up on search tomorrow. You had a very bad shock out there today. I understand that. You can stay down tomorrow and send up another pilot. But the order stands."

Callahan's face was ashen despite its scorching that day by the tropical sun, his lips tight and bloodless, his "Yes, sir" a constricted whisper.

Stewart stood alone on the bridge wing in the pause of night. The long, ghostly, phosphorescent arrowhead of the bow wave curled away beneath him. And in the black sea the present flowed seamlessly back into the past. *"I know what shrapnel from a man's belly looks like."*

It had been a little crazy out there in riverboats in the Mekong Delta. The rest of the world just did not exist. Not even the navy really. It was just you and whatever it was that was out there. And you were going to hunt it down, because that had become the whole meaning of life.

They had had helicopter gun ships aboard the LST. Seawolves. The pilots and the more aggressive Swift boat commanders like Stewart, all in their early twenties, invented their own tactics. A boat would *deliberately* go out as bait and cruise a suspected VC area. Then, *Bam!* As soon as they drew fire, the Seawolf gun ships would dive in blasting away with rockets, M60's. But their casualty rate was the highest in the navy.

"Lay low," Jack Campbell, the operations officer, had advised him. "You've beaten the odds." Stewart was now the senior boat commander. It was three days before he and his crew were scheduled to fly out to Saigon and rotate home. But he took his two-boat element on a last foray up a seldom-patrolled tidal river. They were bushwhacked in a cross-fire; small arms and rockets hit them all at once.

His crewman Whiting screamed. He was hunched over the .50-caliber, but not firing.

451

"Are you hit?" Stewart yelled.

Whiting looked down but said nothing. The young sailor's belly was sliced open. Bloody pink intestines and entrails hung down to the Swift boat's deck. Stewart grabbed Whiting by the shoulders and shoved him down, then carefully piled the wet guts and bowels in a heap onto Whiting's ripped stomach. A large piece of still smoking shrapnel from an exploded rocket was sticking out of Whiting's back. Stewart frantically tried to cover the whole mess with a large battle dressing, then noticed that blood from a wound in his own side was dripping onto the gunner's guts. He wondered vaguely if that was good or not.

By the time the Seawolves finally arrived, everybody aboard both PCFs was either badly wounded or dead. The other boat was crippled. Under fire, and wounded a second time, Stewart managed to secure a tow to it. But he brought both boats and every *body* back.

On the bridge wing of the *Decatur* Stewart could feel the feverish heat of Whiting's bowels searing the palms and fingers of his hands. Despite his father's urging that he go on to law school, Stewart had stayed in the navy after Vietnam. There was simply nowhere else he was comfortable with his pain. After his wife's death the pain had become unbearable. But he had borne it by trusting that one day there would be a purpose for it all.

Overhead, the equatorial sky burned with constellations beyond count. And in this pause of night Stewart sensed that there was a moral order that had now brought the violence and chaos of his life to the *Black Sea.*

30. *The Mullah of Kuala Selatan*

Sergeant Salleh Bin Ali, astride a red Honda motorcycle, his long, glossy hair streaming behind like a black battle pennant, roared away from the Central Police Station and down Eu Tong Sen Street. He wove through a maze of side streets, skirting Singapore's Chinatown.

The teeming old shophouses — where the Chinese had lived twelve to a room above musty stores, half a hundred people sometimes using a single bucket latrine — had now been razed, but to the Malay the streets seemed no less congested. In Salleh's youth the Chinatown tenants had leased out already occupied space to other immigrants, with people sleeping on stair landings, sometimes in shifts.

"What is a Chinaman with his own room?" Salleh's father and his Malay friends had joked.

"A family man."

"What is a Chinaman with two rooms?"

"An innkeeper."

Salleh had then lived in an airy *kampong* on the coast, an unregimented collection of little plank-walled thatched houses garlanded with bright, disorderly blossoms. As a child he had run splashing through the knee-high tide that washed beneath the houses raised on stilts.

Salleh now headed the motorcycle west out Tiong Bahru Road, past the twenty-story white concrete apartment blocks of Queenstown, arranged in rows, one after another, like so many bleached-out dominoes set on end. Queenstown had been the first of the government projects that now housed 80 percent of Singapore's millions. To the Chinese — resettled from the disease and squalor of the crumbling, overcrowded shophouses which had been demolished to build the new commercial towers — the low-cost apartments were a deliverance.

But Salleh's family had also been uprooted, their *kampong* on a palm-fringed estuary on the south coast filled in for the Jurong container docks and industrial park. The government's new towns — Bedok, Ang Mo Kio, Clementi — pierced the skyline at an astonishing rate, a new two-room flat built every seventeen minutes. But the Malays of Singapore, increasingly displaced from their traditional *kampongs* to the regimented blocks inland, reeking with the fumes of frying Chinese pork, frequently regarded the government housing as a curse. The Malay men now worked for other men — invariably Chinese — as clerks, hotel workers, and stevedores. Salleh's father, a taxi driver, read the Koran and reminisced incessantly about a youth of bananas and coconuts free for the plucking, fish that leaped into his *perahu*.

On sweltering evenings nowadays Salleh himself stood on the tiny balcony of his own fifteenth-story apartment, amid the tens of thousands of other units, stirred by dreamlike images of the lovely, sarong-wrapped women of the *kampong*, and like his father pined for a paradise lost where he made love to a wife as the flooding tide lapped beneath their bed.

Salleh now fled the city, gunning the Honda down Bukit Timah Road past the flower marts and into the nature reserve, the last 185-acre stand of the primordial jungle that had once covered the island. The motorcycle gleamed with four coats of wax. But by the time Sergeant Salleh arrived at the fishing *kampong* of Kuala Selatan on the west coast of Malaysia, both he and the Honda would be road grimy, windblown, and sunburned enough to disguise this spy from Singapore and his mission. It was not his appearance that the Malay feared might betray him, but the treachery of his own heart.

It took Salleh less than a half hour to cross the fourteen-mile-wide island-nation to the brief causeway across the Johor Straits that linked Singapore to the mainland of the Malay peninsula. It was a fragile separation, more political than physical. After the Second World War the English had given their Asian colonies their independence. *Merdeka.* The hereditary sultans held a tenuous political control. In the British Crown Colony of Malaya, the Malays barely outnumbered the Chinese, but if it were united with the Crown Colony of Singapore, the Chinese had the edge. The canny British politicians threw in northern Borneo just across the South China Sea. In 1963 the Federation of Malaysia united Malaya, Singapore, and the Borneo states of Sabah and Sarawak, adding up to a thin majority of Malays. The *tunkus* instituted a policy that the Malay "sons of the soil" would have preference for jobs and education and would own a declared percentage of Malaysian businesses. Within two years Singapore, with its protesting Chinese majority, was summarily handed its own *merdeka*.

It took seconds to motorcycle across the causeway from Singapore to Malaysia. On the north shore of the Johor Straits, Salleh stopped and stared back across at the misty towers leagues away and wondered, as he had often lately, which side he was on.

The road from Johor Bahru to the west coast wound through groves of oil palms, sunless and birdless rubber plantations, and flooded *padis*. In the interior a few Chinese families worked scattered farms, unmistakably identified as Chinese by their small ponds, green with water hyacinth, which was harvested as fodder for pigs.

Just south of Malacca, at the directions of a hawker of soybean milk at a roadside food stall, Salleh turned down a dusty dirt road all but hidden by banana trees. Kuala Selatan was a *kampong ayer*, a water village raised above the tidal flood on a forest of stilts. It had probably stood at the mouth of this tidal creek for a thousand years, constantly renewing itself yet remaining the same, the creaking poles, thatched roofs, and splintered planking replaced one by one over the centuries.

But here and there the thatch had been replaced by hot tin roofs, the poles by more permanent concrete pilings. Gasoline generators hummed among the shanties, each machine supplying electricity to three or four cabins, and television aerials poked the sky like leafless branches, drawing signals from Singapore and Kuala Lumpur.

Salleh parked his motorcycle and started down a puddled lane between the banana trees. In a small clearing a handful of teenage boys were practicing *sepak takraw,* kicking around a heavy rattan ball. They stopped when Salleh rode up, and now they watched as he approached, their happy, curious eyes darting between Salleh and the now dusty red Honda. Salleh grinned and motioned to the boy holding the rattan ball.

The boy dropped it, caught it on his foot, then easily kicked it. Salleh leaped straight up into the air, took the ball on the sole of his foot about chest high, and popped it back to the boy. The boy was so startled by the leap he just grabbed the ball. Then he grinned and kicked it back to Salleh.

Salleh leaped a little higher this time and returned the rattan ball to a second boy. The children immediately caught on to the drill, and with shouts they spread out an arm's length apart. The game was not to let the ball hit the ground but to keep it in the air, not touching it with the hands but only with the feet and head. Now with each ball Salleh leaped a little higher, and the younger boys tried to emulate his technique. The object was not the high-kicking acrobatics but the accuracy of the return. The older man scissor-kicked the sixth ball high over his head, twisted in midair, and dropped catlike to his fingertips and feet. He caught the returned ball with his hands and laughed. "I am too old for this game," he said in Bahasa. "My legs feel like *mee* noodles."

"You're a champion," the tallest boy said.

"Tonight this old champion will not be able to walk."

The boys laughed and crowded about him.

He handed the rattan ball to the tall boy. "I am Salleh," he said. "I am here to visit Taib bin Munir, the father of my friend Abdullah."

The boy handed off the ball to one of the younger ones. "I am Majid. I will take you there," he announced proudly.

On the sand above the high-tide mark amid the coconut palms stood the *surau*, the village mosque, a whitewashed wood-plank building with a peaked corrugated tin roof. On its veranda a half dozen men sat conversing after evening prayers, but they stopped to silently watch the stranger pass. Salleh noted that three of them were covered with black velvet *songkoks,* but the others wore the white skullcap of the *haji.*

"You're not working," Salleh commented to his guide, who was older than the other boys.

"It's hard for a Malay boy to find a good job."

The older man grunted in acknowledgment. "Pretty soon the Chinese will own *everything,*" his sweeping gesture embraced the fishing boats and the coconut trees, "including the government in Kuala Lumpur, just like they do in Singapore." There was scorn in his voice.

"You speak like my brother. And like Abdullah."

"Then may God be with your brother."

Majid was suddenly alarmed. "What has happened to my brother? To Abdullah."

"I don't know who your brother is."

"He is Mahmud bin Haji Ibrahim."

"Ah, Mahmud." Salleh nodded and studied the boy, as if searching for a family resemblance in his face.

"You know my brother?"

"Your brother is a soldier of God, like Abdullah."

The boy nodded eagerly. "Yes, he is also with Tengku Haji Azhar." He pronounced the name with a boy's awe.

Salleh's smile embraced Majid as a brother. "Then, Dik, you know where he is and that he is in God's hands."

The boy shook his head solemnly. "No one knows where they are." The people of the *kampong* knew one another's lives, as if they shared a common nervous system, but the young boys, ubiquitous, curious, splashing underneath the houses, climbing into every secret cranny and nook, knew the most.

"Good." Salleh patted Majid's shoulder, as if they shared the same secret. "I must talk to Abdullah's father."

A narrow boardwalk was the only access to the *kampong*. Salleh stepped gingerly across the swaying planks to the cluster of palm-thatched huts, crossing beyond the realm of the overseas Chinese into the world of the coastal Malay.

A kitten-faced young girl, small-boned but already voluptuous in her sarong, smiled up at him, then bent back to tending the jasmine, hibiscus, and bougainvillea that grew in earth-filled tin cans on a tiny porch garden. A baby swung in a suspended cradle, and its

461

mother, wrapped in an orange sarong, stooped over a charcoal fire. The smell of broiling fish and curry gave Salleh a pang that was as much sweet nostalgia as hunger.

There was a rooster, a fighting cock, tethered beside the door of almost every house. An old man, his eyes clouded by cataracts, dozed over a fishing pole on his back porch. Below, waterborne on the rising tide, a lone hawker still peddled produce to the housewives from his *perahu,* now supported more by tradition than necessity. In another *perahu* three children paddled aimlessly about him. Scattered lamps reflected on the flotsam-strewn water. The tides sloshing beneath the houses were a twice-daily automatic street-cleaning and sewage-disposal system.

The boy led him to the seaward side of the *kampong.* A dozen fishing boats, several little bigger than canoes and larger ones with bright red and yellow cabins, bobbed in the rising tide. Outboard of them were moored a half dozen lateen-rigged interisland traders, their triangular sails now lashed to their sloping masts. They carried goods — as often as not smuggled — across the strait between Malaysia and Indonesia. "Ah!" Salleh smiled with pleasure at the sight of the native sailing boats with their gracefully rising poop decks, but he carefully noted their size, number, and as many of the names as he could spot.

The boy knocked at an already open door. A middle-aged man in a black cap and sarong came to the door and smiled with genuine friendliness at the stranger on his threshold. "This is a friend of your son Abdullah," the boy introduced Salleh. "He also serves Tengku Haji Azhar."

"The boy tells you more than I have told him," Salleh said. Indeed the boy had given him two more names, and these names would be bait fish to catch other, larger fish.

"Selamat datang." Welcome, or, literally, "may your coming be blessed." Taib bin Munir's smile remained constant, but an unguarded charge of fear widened his eyes.

Salleh removed his shoes, but he felt a flush of shame that he was entering this Malay house, accepting this open-handed hospitality, only to betray it.

It was several hours later that Salleh left the home of Taib bin Munir. The tide had risen, and unseen waves sloshed just beneath his feet and splashed against the pilings. In the darkness he had to grope his way over wet, narrow planks between the closely crammed shanties. He was grateful for the occasional light through an open window.

His motorcycle would be safe on the beach,

but it had undoubtedly been meticulously inspected by the boys and, perhaps, the more suspicious eyes of the men from the mosque. Salleh had been careful to leave nothing in his bag except a well-fingered copy of the holy Koran, one that had belonged to his father.

As he reached the single plank bridging the *kampong* and the beach, Majid stepped out into the light of a bare electric bulb. The boy's pants were soaked to the waist, a gleaming puddle at his bare feet. He had apparently stood in the flooding tide under the house of Taib bin Munir, listening to everything that was said. Salleh made out other men in the shadows behind Majid, on the beach by the small, white-washed mosque, and heard footfalls creaking on the planks behind him.

"The *imam* will speak with you," the boy said.

Salleh was led to an anteroom off the mosque's prayer hall, a small porch open to the stars and waxing moon over the shimmering black bay. The *imam* was frail and old, very old, and a white shawl of rough silk draped over his shoulders added to his air of fragility. His hair was so white and thin that the strands that grew underneath the white lace *haji* cap appeared to be the frayed threads of the lace, and the eyes that blinked at Salleh behind rimless glasses were watery with seemingly perpetual tears.

"Where are you from?" the *imam* asked.

"I am from Singapore." The license plate on his motorcycle was from Singapore.

"Ah, yes, you look like a city boy, not a fisherman. But are you from Tengku Haji Azhar?"

Salleh smiled softly, and he glanced slyly to the right and left, so that only the *imam*, seated directly in front of him, might see his eyes. "I am from Singapore," Salleh said.

The *imam* nodded vaguely, apparently accepting that he would not speak in front of strangers. "Are you a pirate, then?" he asked suddenly.

The *imam's* question surprised him, and there was no hiding his reaction from the old man's fixed gaze.

"Or are you another assassin from Iran?"

Again Salleh was not quick enough to mask his confusion completely.

"You say you are a soldier of God, but I do not see God in your eyes and heart. There is blasphemy on your breath and treachery in your heart."

The night sky, the stars, and the crescent of the waxing new moon hovered just behind the *imam,* and the pale, liquid eyes, magnified by his glasses, framed by the white purity of his cap, transcended the space between them and probed Salleh's soul. He felt lost, and he simply stared back into the old man's eyes, powerless to stop the *imam* from reading whatever was written there.

The *imam* suddenly broke off and wagged his head vehemently. "There is blasphemy and treachery in all of this," he pronounced in a shaking voice. "And where does it all start? Or end? A handsome, quick-witted boy sat at my feet and listened with big eyes to my parables from the *Sejarah Melayu,* of when the Word of God came to the Prince of Malacca on the ships riding the west wind." The *imam* was no longer addressing Salleh but the men gathered behind him.

"But the boy looks about and says, 'Why is it that I am such a poor boy in a rich land, where the faithful are poor and the infidels rich?' He studies hard, wins prizes in the Koran, and goes to the university. But he is an unhappy poor boy among the sons of *tunkus* and rich Chinese and Indian merchants. 'How is this?' he asks. And so he makes the pilgrimage to Mecca to seek an answer. And this is good." The *imam* gestured sharply with his hand for emphasis and looked about the small room.

Salleh slowly let out his breath, relieved that the *imam* had apparently launched into a sermon.

"But one must go to Mecca with the right question in his heart. How may I serve God? The question in your heart must not be, How may God serve me? For that is the heart of treachery."

He glanced back at the stranger, for no more than a heartbeat or two, but it seemed to Salleh that he again peered right into his soul and saw the treachery there.

"For such a heart will listen avidly to false prophets. Our brother did not end his pilgrimage on the Plain of Arafat on the tenth day of the month of Dhu al-Hijjah. Instead he went on to Tehran. And when finally he returned here to Kuala Selatan as Tengku Haji Azhar, now an elder to respect, he came with other young men, men inflamed with God who were going to change the world. They wanted to build a new society based on equality and ruled by the *Sharia,* the sacred law that is the path to God. The laws now are based on English laws, they said. We are not English, we are Malay. So why should we govern ourselves with foreign laws? They talked of a great Islamic revolution of the Malay people, a return to our old traditions. They rejected the imported

467

Western and Chinese ways that impoverish our bodies and, more important, our souls.

"Our brother Tengku spoke of the old days of glory, when Prince Parameswara heard the Word of God and became the Sultan Iskandar Shah, a light to all of Asia. It was good to hear young men talk of glory, when so many are heavy with despair and have no hopes and dreams. So I counseled them, and more gathered here. But soon I came to see that these young men had not embraced a revolution of the heart, but a revolution of guns. It was the creed of the Assassins, a false creed from when Iran was called Persia.

"Every great light — and the Word of God is the brightest of lights, so that even a blind man may see it — casts a shadow. And Assassins are the darkest of these shadows. And when I saw it was this darkness that had cloaked their hearts, I ordered them to leave. They obeyed and left, and some of your brothers and sons went with them. They went across the strait to the islands where the men of the sea are pirates."

The *imam* shook his head and emitted a sharp bark of a laugh. "Assassins and pirates. This is their unholy brotherhood in the name of God. And from this they would make an Islamic revolution. I said no good can come of it! And *now* we have a messenger from this gathering of darkness." He looked sharply at Salleh. "And it is the worst message a father could ever hear. He will never see his son again. And there will be no grandchildren to carry his name into the future. And whatever the son's crime is, this messenger knows it but cannot speak of it. And, mark me, he will not be the last."

The pale eyes again focused on Salleh, somehow in their very gentleness flowing into him. "I know you are not a soldier of God bearing light, but only a messenger from the darkness," he said in a voice so soft that perhaps only Salleh heard it. He fluttered the fingers of his right hand, dismissing Salleh in an almost contemptuous gesture.

Salleh rose, but at the doorway the *imam's* voice stopped him. "Messenger."

Salleh turned.

"You may return when you are ready to bear the light."

Part VIII
The Winds of Paradise

31. The Release of a Dead Sailor

The bar steward was a dark-haired man in his thirties with a proud black mustache that would have looked splendid on a Cossack officer. He settled himself in the front of the longboat, then smiled broadly up at the ship and waved.

Vladimir waved back. "I envy him. He should be in Singapore tonight."

An armed pirate squatted down in the *perahu* right behind the Russian barman. Maggi looked around the bridge for Tengku, but he was nowhere about. She had not seen him at all that morning.

"Perhaps he will finally bring our rescuers here."

The wistful way in which Vladimir spoke made Maggi turn and stare at the ship's officer. "*Here?* Do you know where we are? Does *he* know?"

Vladimir looked about to see if he might be overheard, then nodded. "We have a very good estimate, I think. The captain, the helmsman must take the ship here with the pirates' knives at their throats. They have no charts, but the pirates know precisely where they are going. Turn here, turn at that rock. Go between those two islands. It is deep enough there."

Maggi recalled Captain Khromykh's account of his harrowing passage a few days earlier. She had a sudden realization. "You've been instructing your own hostages, only the Russians, so that they could bring help. So your Russians would rescue us, not Americans," she whispered, her voice taut with anger.

Vladimir made a shrug of apology. "Who could we tell? The fat, wheezing old man or Mrs. Schneider? Could they memorize a navigation chart? Our own men — " he gestured with frustration at the departing *perahu* " — are bartenders. We show them, we drill them over and over, beat their brains, but they cannot read a chart. They remember a few places, maybe, but these are Indonesian names, so they make no sense to them."

"Show me," Maggi insisted.

"It would be better if you did not know. Perhaps you say something to the pirate."

"You damned fool!" Maggi was furious that the Russians, in their paranoia, had kept this from her. "Did it occur to you that I know more than you do? These aren't foreign names and places to me."

Vladimir flushed, the pale, fair cheeks reddening. He studied her, still suspicious, then abruptly made a decision. "Come with me, Professor Chancellor. I will show you where we are, and you will tell me these things we do not know."

He led Maggi up two decks to a small, cramped cabin behind the bridge. Tiny as her own stateroom was, the Russian officer's was even more confined and Spartan. "You're up here?" she said, somewhat surprised.

"Yes, the captain is on the other side, so that we can be on the bridge immediately in an emergency."

Maggi had imagined that the Russian officers had more luxurious quarters. She understood now why Tengku, having inspected the entire ship, had commandeered the passenger lounge for his own quarters.

Vladimir locked the door. He ignored the built-in chest of drawers and desk, groped under the mattress of his bunk, and withdrew a folded chart cached there. He spread it out on the bed and pointed to a large island almost due south of Singapore. "We estimate that we must be here. The whole area is marked as a swamp, and as you can see, there is not a river on the chart. But I think this is the mountain we see up the river." He shrugged. "During most of the year this river is perhaps very small and not big enough to put on a chart."

This particular island was in the midst of an archipelago of islands that ranged in size from little more than huge rocks to others two to three times the size of Singapore itself, and largely uninhabited. Maggi saw immediately why it would be almost impossible for a layman to glean very much useful information from the chart that he might carry from the ship. "But the sailor who was released the second day," Maggi asked, "couldn't he read the chart?"

Vladimir shook his head regretfully. "We never spoke to him. He was the lookout on the stern. The terrorists said he was injured when they came aboard."

"The lookout on the stern," Maggi repeated, and she felt a piercing chill go through her. "He wasn't injured," she whispered. "He was killed. I saw him." In the terror and confusion of the first days, hadn't she told the Russians this? She distinctly remembered telling Alan Schneider. And Schneider had told Captain Khromykh, but with his mangled English perhaps he had not understood Schneider. In the relay of messages through their infuriating "chain of command," Maggi had not understood that the first Russian "released" had been the dead lookout.

"He was dead!" she insisted. "They killed

him . . . with a poison dart."

Vladimir Korsakov stared at her as though she were insane.

"A poison dart, yes. I know it sounds wild. The local natives use them to hunt deer, wild pigs, apes. I've seen a Dayak shoot a monkey out of a hundred-foot-high tree . . . with a blowgun, I mean. But this was . . . hideous. He went into convulsions . . . and then died. I was standing on the promenade, getting some air. It was just before I ran up to the bridge . . . to warn you." Maggi faltered. Vladimir's face was still swathed in bandages.

"I . . . I saw the lookout fall, and I ran to help him."

"Maybe he fainted."

"No," Maggi persisted. "I felt for the pulse, in his throat. He had none, and his eyes were frozen open . . . horrible. That's when I saw the poison dart in his throat."

"A poison dart." Korsakov mouthed the words, as if tasting an alien texture, totally unfamiliar, and debating whether to swallow it or not.

"He was dead. Believe me," Maggi demanded.

"But they said he was only injured, and they were sending him to Singapore for medical help."

"Then why didn't they let you talk to him? There was time."

He shook his head, as if trying to shake off his fears. "This was the first Russian released. We didn't make any demands. We were just grateful they were being humanitarian. What about the others? What has happened to *them?*"

"I don't know!" Maggi's voice was shrill, almost hysterical with her fear for Liz Schneider. "I've only seen the others leave the ship. Except for Benjamin, the first one. The sick old man. I never saw him. Tengku just told me he had been taken to Singapore for his health."

Korsakov did not want to believe that anything was wrong, but he kept fingering the bandage on his cheek, as though his wound pained him, reminding him that the pirates were capable of cruel whims. "But why would they lie to us?"

"I don't know. Maybe to keep us in line. To keep us pacified and cooperating with them. There are, what, 225 of us all told, and your crew are able-bodied seamen. There are maybe two dozen of them, and they seem to come and go, never more than half a dozen at one time on the ship, except for that first day. These are not professional soldiers. They're a gang of pirates."

Maggi suddenly had a terrible vision, a film clip from a TV news report — a body tumbling out of a Boeing 727 jetliner parked at the end of a runway in Beirut. "It's what terrorists do!" she exclaimed wildly. "They shoot their hostages one at a time and drop our bodies out of the plane, until their demands are met."

"What are you talking about? Bodies out of a plane. Demands. What plane? What demands?" He looked warily at Maggi as if she were crazed.

"I don't know what demands. I don't know what *exactly* they want. Tengku talks in pipe dreams of glory."

"Pipe dreams?"

"Of the old Islamic sultanate that once controlled Malaysia, Indonesia, and the Philippines. It was really a weak trading confederation, but in his mind it's become more powerful, more holy than it really was. His cousin Ahmed has him convinced he is the heir to all that, the one destined to become the all-powerful, all-holy modern Sultan of Malacca. The *mahdi* of Southeast Asia, the righteous spiritual and temporal ruler."

"I don't know what you are talking about."

"It may sound insane to us, but his men *believe*. And they're ready to kill for it."

"For *what?*"

"I don't know, but he's bargaining with us for *something*."

"For what?"

"I *don't know!*" Maggi shouted, her fury fueled partly by exasperation with Vladimir and partly by terror.

Vladimir's pale blue eyes studied her. His cheek and temple were covered with a dressing of thick cotton gauze held in place by adhesive strips, and the bandage across his face seemed to accent his eyes, the paleness of his skin, underlining the vulnerability. "Perhaps the terrorists get what they want," he said after a moment or two. "So they free one Russian, one American a day."

"My country — I mean this United States government — does not bargain for hostages," she stated in a flat voice. "They will ship a half million troops around the world and go to war first."

Vladimir shrugged. "I do not know what my government does. We do not have experience in such matters." He said this without sarcasm or rancor, but merely as a fact. "Then why would these terrorists release anyone at all?"

"First a sick old man, then a Russian corpse," — Maggi ticked them off on her fingers — "then the fat, wheezing American with heart disease. After the obviously sick and the dead, it was a bartender, who is an untouchable by Muslim standards. Then . . ." Maggi hesitated, "a woman Tengku thinks dresses lewdly and provoked his men to rape. Now another bartender. What does it add up to? Who is it going to be tomorrow?"

Maggi was badly frightened. She had the terrible feeling of dread that she had when she woke from a nightmare but still had not shaken it, and the images and horror still haunted her. "Something terrible is happening," she whispered.

Vladimir was silent, and his hand again gingerly fingered the bandage. The gesture gave Maggi a twinge of guilt, for she knew she was responsible for his disfigurement.

"I should try to escape," Vladimir said. "If I could reach help, I could lead them here. In the army they tell you if you are lost in the wilderness, you follow a stream or river. Soon you will find a village on it. But this river leads only to a terrible swamp worse than the jungle." He touched his face again, this time self-consciously. "And nothing more bad happens, so I wait until my face heals more. The wound would get infected very quickly in the jungle, and I would die in much agony from such an infection in the head, the doctor says." He looked at

Maggi, his voice, his eyes apologetic, asking to be excused for his lack of daring.

Maggi was surprised. It was the first she had heard that the Russians had been discussing escape. "You must trust me," she pleaded. "I can help you. I know the language, the customs."

Vladimir nodded. "I will tell the captain what you said about the seaman on lookout."

"You believe me, don't you?"

"Oh, yes." His lips twisted in irony. "He was the lookout on the special pirate watch."

"A pirate watch?"

"Yes. All ships going through the Singapore Strait at night post a pirate watch. So they knew to look for him. But to kill him with a blowgun and poison dart as they do a monkey . . . They are a very cruel people."

"I hope to God nothing has happened to Liz," she whispered. What could she possibly say to Alan Schneider? The revelation that the first Russian "released" had been the sailor Maggi herself had seen murdered now summoned forth her worst nightmares.

Vladimir walked to the door and opened it for her, a gesture that the ship's officer performed with a flair of practiced gallantry. It brought the wounded face close to hers. There was a faint blond stubble about the bandage where he could not shave.

"I'm so sorry," she said sorrowfully, her voice catching.

He looked at her, surprised by her grief, then smiled gently. "I will look very fine," he said. "Always I have too baby a face for a ship's officer. Now I will have a saber scar that will look quite dashing, Dr. Yakovlev says. And they will promote me to captain sooner," he said in a droll, almost cheerful way.

As Maggi left the cabin, she almost collided with the purser, Svetlana. "Ooh . . . excuse me." The stocky Russian woman, holding a large envelope and clipboard, was apparently heading toward Korsakov's cabin or the bridge on ship's business — or the pretext of business. But the dark, pretty Slavic face glared at Maggi with such venomous jealousy that the woman was choked speechless.

Maggi owed this possessive bitch no explanation as to why she was in Vladimir's cabin. She gave the purser an insinuating smile and stepped down the ladder without a word.

32. An Omen of Playful Dolphins

The admiral's voice broadcasting over the speaker on the *Decatur*'s bridge did not sound human — more like the speech of a computer than that of a man.

"Our Orions flew over every inch of that area. They didn't find a thing. Neither — or so they tell us — have our Russian associates."

"Yes, Admiral. I suspect it was a hit-and-run attack, meant to divert us from where the hostages really are."

"Why do you think it was a diversionary attack, Captain Stewart? By now that ship might be anywhere from Shanghai to Bombay." The admiral's voice had been digitized by a computer at Seventh Fleet headquarters in Yokosuka, Japan, the data scrambled, transmitted to an orbiting satellite, and bounced to the *Decatur,* where computers in Radio Central on the deck below the bridge decoded the signal and reconstructed the voice. To speed up the transmission, only a fraction of the information that makes up a human voice was encoded, and the voice on the speaker, like that of Stewart in Japan, was as devoid of any regional accent, emotion, or personality as the constant electronic background hum.

"Yes, sir, it might be. But they've hit me twice now. Once a trained sniper, and now what we strongly suspect was an antiaircraft missile." Stewart drew a deep breath and took the plunge. "From the dispatches I've received, these terrorists have kept to a schedule — if we can call it that — of delivering the . . . remains of a hostage to Singapore each night. To me, sir, that defines a radius of action, especially if they must use small boats to move in and out of Singapore and to hit us."

"Captain, that seems to me to be making a great leap in logic, making assumptions we really have no data to back up."

Stewart had already been sweating, but now freshets of perspiration drenched his shirt, coursed down his brow, stinging his eyes with salt. He was speaking on the radio to the commander of the Seventh Fleet, a vice admiral, and he was blowing it with half his wardroom as the audience on the crowded bridge. Robinson was standing at attention in the presence of the voice from ComSeventhFleet, as though the three-star were personally inspecting him.

"Yes, sir, I agree that we have very limited

information. But I'm within that radius of action right now, Admiral. It's the Riau archipelago and the east coast of Sumatra. There are hundreds of islands and swamps to hide a ship the size of the *Black Sea*. In the radar shadow of an island, up a dozen small rivers not even on the charts — but which are now swollen deep and wide enough with the monsoon rains. But it is a defined and limited area."

Stewart was talking in a rush now, trying to get it all in before higher rank and authority peremptorily cut him off. "It's a search quadrant south and southwest of Singapore to the Sumatran coast. With all due respect, Admiral, I would recommend we concentrate our resources in this area."

Stewart paused for a response. He took out his handkerchief and patted his neck to sop up the sweat, but the handkerchief was already limp and dank as a wet dishrag. From the way Robinson was eyeing him, Stewart could tell that the executive officer was aghast at his recommending a new search plan to Seventh Fleet. But there was still no response. Stewart wondered if they had lost communications with Japan. "I believe it's the *Decatur*'s presence here, sir, that's provoked them to haul out their heavy artillery."

Again the overhead speaker was silent, and Stewart was about to make a communication check when there was a hum on the radio. "Captain Stewart, we've been looking at the charts here, and the two incidents involving your ship and its helicopter took place well south of the area you're indicating." The *Decatur* was now 120 nautical miles to the north of Teluk Ikan Hiu, where the helicopter had crashed.

"Yes, sir, but we were clearly en route to this area."

"Captain, are you suggesting that they anticipated your search patterns?"

"Yes, sir."

"Captain Stewart, what you've speculated — and I have to use that word — would require a detailed knowledge that even we don't possess. I doubt that the Russian captain of the *Black Sea* does either. It is certainly beyond that of any terrorists with which we've had experience in the past. These guys are a bunch of political desperadoes who don't know where they are going half the time or where they want to go."

There was a break in the transmission. Stewart waited a moment and was about to speak when the voice of ComSeventhFleet resounded again. "In any event, Captain, our resources at the moment consist of a detachment of Orions, not even a squadron. But we're flying another detachment in to double our long-range air search. By tomorrow at this hour a carrier battle group will be deployed in the South China Sea." Another break. "However, looking at the charts in front of me, a carrier can't operate in the narrow waters you've defined."

"No, sir, you're absolutely correct in that. But they can concentrate their aircraft over this area."

"Well, Captain Stewart, we'll certainly take your recommendations under advisement."

Stewart could not tell from the digitized voice whether or not the admiral was irritated by his effrontery, as his own executive officer appeared to be.

"Admiral, do we know with whom we're dealing here yet?"

"No, sir, we do not. But I can tell you, Captain, that this situation has the President's full and personal attention."

The three-star hung up the red radio telephone and snapped, "Who the hell is this guy?"

"Well, he's been selected for the rank of captain. The promotion list just came out."

"Is he on the fast track or being promoted to retirement?"

The chief of staff shook his head. "His next assignment hasn't been made yet, sir. But he's got four-oh fitness reports."

"That's on the surface. What's the undercurrent?"

"A warrior. Somewhat reckless; doesn't watch his ass."

The admiral tapped the chart with his forefinger in an irritated tattoo. "One random shot. A helicopter down. Anything could have done it, and he jumps to the conclusion it's a Stinger. There's no evidence, except that a green-as-algae ensign and an E-5 *think* they saw an entry hole when they were underwater. No, I don't think we'll put all our eggs in Commander Stewart's basket. We'll continue the current extended search plan."

"Yes, sir."

"*Stingers.*" The admiral hissed the word. "Were there Stingers on that shopping list — the ransom demands, I mean?"

"Yes, sir."

"How about RPGs?"

"Yes, sir, they want RPGs too."

"Jesus. Well, for his ship's sake, I hope Stewart doesn't know something we don't." The Seventh Fleet commander continued to study the chart. "I wouldn't take a ship in there unless I was ordered to. And even then I'd voice a serious objection."

"No, sir, I wouldn't either."

"Well, Captain-select Stewart is on the fast track to a court-martial if he runs that ship aground."

"Should I order him out of the area?"

The admiral ran his finger down the Sugi Strait and the Tjombol Strait of the Kepulauan Riau. "No, he's on the scene. It's *his* decision. And it's *his ass*. He just may be the bait that's getting them to bite." The admiral shook his head. "God knows it's the only thing we've got at the moment." He looked up at his chief of staff and raised a quizzical eyebrow. "And what does that say about us?"

His chief of staff did not answer the question.

A trio of bottle-nosed dolphins cavorted right under the *Decatur*'s bow, beating their tails vertically to leap up out of the water, then riding down the shimmering bow wave like surfers. No matter how fast the frigate knifed through the clear green water, the dolphins kept up easily, gracefully darting six inches ahead of the bow. Dolphins were supposed to be a good omen, but the ship's executive officer, watching them from the bridge wing, took little comfort in it.

The *Decatur* needled into the Durian Strait,

its wake a white thread between Carnbee Reef and Richardson Reef. Beyond each reef was a mountainous island, the thousand-foot peak of Great Durian to the north and Sanglang-Besar to the south. And beyond each island was another chain of islands, all called *pulau* this or *pulau* that on the charts — Indonesian names, Robinson figured — or with no names at all, and no reef with Anglo-Saxon names indicated, because the chartmakers reasoned that no captain would be fool enough to take his ship through those islands. But Robinson knew the reefs were there, ready to rip the bottom out of the *Decatur* and his navy career.

A small native fishing boat, painted a bright red and yellow to ward off bad spirits and coax a good catch, drifted down the starboard side. The fisherman, in a filthy T-shirt and shorts, waved, but Robinson did not wave back. He was just too hot, sweaty, stinking, itching, and skin-crawling miserable to make the effort. With the ship's air conditioning broken down and the water cut off, he could not remember when he had last been cool or washed, shaved, or showered.

Suddenly Stewart was on the bridge wing beside him, staring back at the fishing boat now pitching erratically in the frigate's wake. "Why are the hackles on the back of my neck tingling?"

"You really think they're around here?"

Stewart didn't answer but continued to peer at the fishing boat.

Robinson glanced up forward where the dolphins played in the bow wave, but they were gone. That disturbed him somehow. He took out a huge, sopping rag of a handkerchief, gray with sweat and dirt, and wiped his face. "It's twenty degrees hotter here even than in the Persian Gulf."

"It's the humidity that makes it feel that way."

"I thought so, too, but I have this atlas with colored maps. They show the temperature, rainfall, natural vegetation, and population density for each area. And this time of year — where we are right now — is twenty degrees hotter than the Arab desert."

Stewart's head tilted sideways; he darted a look full of amazement at his XO. "You read an atlas for relaxation?"

"It's for my kids. I mark the spots where I've been and where I take pictures, so they can visualize it in their minds. They all get A's in geography. Hell, when I was their age I never even *heard* of Bahrain or Singapore, but *my kids* can tell you all about them." There was a gloating pride in his voice.

"Anything else in your colored maps that's not on the charts."

"Well, on the rainfall map we are in the deepest purple — over eighty inches a year — and on the vegetation map the deepest green. This whole area, in its natural state, is a tropical rain forest."

"Uh huh."

Robinson gestured vaguely somewhere off to starboard. "Over there, in Singapore and all the way up the west coast of Malaysia, the population density is as thick as Japan — the heaviest in the world. But these islands and the Sumatran coast opposite Singapore is the same pale yellow as the worst part of the Arab desert. Just about deserted."

"That's fascinating, Robbie. How wide is this area?"

"It starts around the equator — "

"About where DiLorenzo was shot down?"

"Yes, sir. And it runs up the coast about three hundred miles. Goes as deep as fifty miles inland with the swamps and jungle."

"Well, that doesn't cut our search area down any." Stewart leaned over the rail and peered ahead. Although they were sailing in radiant sunlight, there was a rain squall to starboard, a gray misty curtain that shrouded the passage between Great Durian and Little Durian islands. From beneath this veil another fishing boat suddenly materialized, its gaudy red and blue colors muted by the steamy rain. "There's another fishing boat to starboard," Stewart sang out to the officer of the deck.

"Yes, sir, we have it in sight."

"That's the second boat in the last few minutes. If this area is as deserted as your Rand McNally says it is, there shouldn't be that many small boats." He whirled around. "Officer of the deck, pass the word to the .50-caliber gunners that I want them trained on all small craft from the moment they are in sight."

"Aye, aye, sir."

An icicle chill seized Robinson's spine. Christ! All they needed was some nervous eighteen-year-old blasting away an overly friendly fisherman. He forced a smile. "I guess it pays to be paranoid when you aren't exactly sure what you're dealing with."

Stewart glared at him, then his eyes took on a canny look, and he nodded. "One of those boats is reporting to *someone* exactly where we are, where we're heading, and where our choppers are going."

"Yes, sir, but just for the sake of conjecture, isn't it also possible that the sniper was just an isolated crazy? Hell, it happens on the Los Angeles freeway all the time. And a bird got sucked into the chopper's engine. The turbine just blew and cut the tail-rotor connection, the hydraulics — one of those — and DiLorenzo had no control. That happened to a DC-10 over Sioux City a while back and killed 110 people. But it was a tragic accident, not terrorists tracking the plane."

Stewart was stone silent, and Robinson was afraid he had gone too far. Then Stewart spoke, and his voice was surprisingly soft, laconic, droll. "I have no doubt, Mr. Robinson, that the admirals in Washington have dismissed my report with the same thoughts. But there's still that pesky cruise ship that has disappeared somewhere around here with 225 people aboard. And there are those pesky heads that are delivered each night in Singapore."

"The point is taken, Captain."

"The point, XO, is that when you're patrolling in hostile Indian territory, and your lookout is shot by an arrow, and then you find one of your wagons burned, it's *possible* the first was a hunting accident. And it's *possible* somebody kicked over a kerosene lamp in the second case. But don't bet your ass on it."

"Occam's razor dictates that the simplest explanation for the circumstances is the most likely. And this is the area the razor cuts to." Robinson wagged his head and marveled, "You knew Washington and the CIA were off track four days ago."

"I didn't *know*. I suspected. But the *Achille Lauro* and the plane hijackings were the only scenarios we had to go on, so they made sense. When the body count went up in Singapore, and DiLorenzo went down chasing a contact, then I *knew*."

"But if they've stashed a ship around here where neither our planes nor satellites can spot it, and then they make that run into Singapore every night right through the harbor police, they must be home boys, not outside terrorists. But who? Why?"

"That's local politics. That's not our problem."

"Local politics in Lebanon blew to hell more marines than there are sailors on this ship."

The *Decatur* suddenly plunged into the tropical cloudburst, a warm deluge drenching the two men on the bridge wing. A stiff wind slanted the rain across the channel; drops splattered the windows of the wheelhouse. Robinson glanced about. Through the heavy rain and steamy mist he could not see the rocky summits of Great and Little Durian to starboard or that of Pulau Pandjang dead ahead. The brightly painted fishing boat had disappeared. For the first time Robinson was frightened. He whirled back to Stewart and shouted over the drumming of the rain on the aluminum deck, "Captain, I believe you are absolutely on the right track here. And I believe this ship is in the gravest harm's way."

Stewart's smile was tight and humorless. "You're right, Mr. Robinson," he shouted back. "Our difference is that I insist that's exactly where we ought to be."

In the American frigate's wake, the squall passed on, and the sun came out brilliantly and blazed on an aquamarine sea. The fishing *perahu* with the red and yellow cabin turned east, out of the main channel.

The fisherman waited stoically until the asthmatic diesel had chugged the small boat beyond Djora, the high, obstructing peak of Great Durian Island, out into the open waters of the east bank. Then the fisherman ducked into the small cabin and brought out the portable marine radio.

33. *Fitting the Pieces of the Puzzle*

"These are the pieces of an English jigsaw puzzle that you bring back to me," Yee complained.

"Yes, and the pieces make a picture with what we already know," Sergeant Salleh said. "Or at least with what you have told me, *lah*."

"I have told you everything we know. If you had been found out and tortured, all they would learn is how little we know." Yee had the definite impression that Salleh was holding something back. Yet the man was clearly exhausted. His head lolled with fatigue, and there were dark hollows under his eyes. "You rode all night?" Yee asked with concern.

"I did not think I would sleep well last night."

"Were you in danger?"

"I don't think so. The *imam* told me I could return, and I believe he was sincere. He wants to convert me."

"But you are already a Muslim."

"Yes, but I am a very bad Muslim. He wants me to end my evil associations."

Salleh's smile was an enigma, but it seemed to embrace Yee in its evil association.

"Is the *imam* part of this business?"

"No, he is a holy man." Salleh shook his head so emphatically that Yee knew he had touched a nerve.

"He allowed them to use the mosque to meet."

"Until he discovered they were assassins. Then he cast them out."

"Assassins?"

"Yes. He made an association with the old Persian cult."

"Persian?"

"Iran."

"Iran? This — " Yee glanced at the sheet of paper on which he had taken notes " — Tengku Haji Azhar has been to Iran?"

"The *imam* said so."

Yee felt as if he were conducting an interrogation rather than debriefing a trusted agent. Salleh was reluctant to give up any information, yet he had ridden a motorcycle all night at high speed down a winding country road from Malacca to Singapore.

"Is this Tengku their leader?"

"Whose leader? The outcasts or the *kampong?*"

"Who are we talking about?"

"I don't know."

Yee and Salleh now sat staring at each other in open mistrust. What had happened to the Malay in Kuala Selatan? Yee spoke quietly. "Who did you tell them you were?"

"I told them I drove a taxi. That I knew every road, alley, and dock in Singapore. These are a simple people, and this is a job they understand."

"They trusted you? They didn't question you more?"

"I spoke only to a boy, the brother of this Mahmud, and the prisoner's father, Taib bin Munir. But there are no secrets in a *kampong*."

Yee studied his agent with hooded eyes. There was something he wasn't telling Yee. "What did you tell the father?"

"I told him I was a friend of his son Abdullah. His son's thoughts were of his father, but he was in jail in Singapore. He would probably never see his son again, but he would die a martyr."

"You told him too much," Yee said angrily.

"It opened the father's heart to me." There was an anguish in Salleh's own voice that Yee had not heard before.

"You are too thoughtful. In China they execute a troublemaker with a single shot to the back of the head, and notify the family by sending them a bill for the bullet."

"Yes, the Chinese would do that."

Yee reacted sharply. He had not meant it as a Chinese practice but that of a Red dictator. But to the Malay it was the sending of the bill that was distinctly Chinese. What was Salleh holding back? To win the confidence of these Malays, he had aped their suspicion, perhaps hatred, of the Chinese. But to what extent were these Salleh's true feelings?

"Come with me," Yee abruptly ordered. "See what they sent us while you were in Malacca."

Liz Schneider's eyes were opened wide in a speechless astonishment that had never had the time to form a thought or word. The abundant glory of her blonde hair was still piled atop her head, held in place by a tortoiseshell comb, except for a few shining strands that had shaken loose.

"This . . . this was once a beautiful lady. The wife of a United States Secretary of State."

Salleh was pale, his brown skin yellowed by the draining of blood.

Yee was amazed by his own steadiness. Was he now so inured to these atrocities that they no longer sickened him and made his stomach revolt, or was it his anger at Salleh that girded his intestines? "Ah, yes, you have not seen this before." He turned to Ballinger. "Show him the others. The two young Russian sailors; the handsome old man with the beautiful long white hair; the fat man; the ship's officer from Baku, probably a Muslim, don't you think? They are just names to Sergeant Salleh."

"Why do you make me look at this horror?" Salleh shouted.

"Because you think this is Malay against Chinese, Muslims against nonbelievers!" Yee shouted back at him. "This is an abomination under heaven to all men."

"What do you want of me?" Tears streamed from the soft brown eyes, down Salleh's cheeks.

Yee was taken aback by this emotion. "Put the pieces of this jigsaw puzzle together for me."

Back in Yee's office Salleh wiped his eyes and said, "You were right to show me that. We must stop this."

"How? We don't know who they are. Where they are."

"The names I gave you — Tengku Haji Azhar bin Tengku Rahman and Mahmud bin Haji Ibrahim. Send them to Kuala Lumpur. They will probably have no information on Mahmud. Like Abdullah, he is probably just a *kampong* boy. But this Tengku went

502

to the university in K.L., and they have information on him. They should check the membership of the Muslim Brotherhood, the Islamic Tendency Movement, and any other fundamentalist groups at the university those years. Then they should cross-check the records of the Tabung Haji, the Pilgrim Management and Fund Board. He was a poor student. And the government packages are the cheapest way to go to Mecca."

"But there are millions of names — 25,000 Malaysians each year."

Salleh smiled that Yee knew the figure. "Yes. But Tengku went the last year he was at the university, and those 25,000 names can easily be matched on a computer with the rolls of the university groups. The match will give us the names of the people who went to Mecca with him, *lah,* and probably on to Tehran. It is no secret the Islamic Revolution in Iran actively recruited pilgrims in Mecca, until the Saudis ended it."

Yee nodded and mulled aloud. "K.L. has problems with Muslim fundamentalists who have been to Iran. The Prime Minister complains to the newspapers about it. Is that who is behind this, the Iranians?"

"No."

"The student troublemakers?"

"They could never hijack a passenger liner."

"Who then?" Yee was exasperated.

"Who boards and robs a hundred ships a year, then disappears into the night, and we never catch them?"

"The pirates?" An alarm bell sounded in Yee's memory. "But they are not terrorists. Why would they do this now? For the guns? For money?"

Salleh shrugged. "For guns. For money. Perhaps for *jihad*."

Yee rapped his skull with his knuckles. "The morning we found the first head, I went to the port operations center to call the ship. The supervisor was going this way and that. There had just been two pirate attacks."

"Where?"

"The bad trouble spots, I remember. One in the Phillip Channel," he waved his arm in frustration, "the other in sight of Singapore near Batam."

"Ah, yes, and the *Black Sea* sailed by the South Channel off Bintam."

Yee stared at Salleh with astonishment. "This was coordinated."

The Malay smiled. "Perhaps it is a coincidence, *lah*. One attack is to the west in the Malacca Strait, the other in the Main Strait, and the *Black Sea* sails to the east."

"But they are honest fishermen in Kuala

Selatan, not pirates, aren't they?"

Salleh shrugged. "This Taib is not exactly a fisherman. I noticed his boat was one of the larger interisland traders."

"And how did this unholy brotherhood of fanatics, pirates, and assassins — that is what your *imam* called it — happen?"

"In Singapore I could not see this, but in Kuala Selatan it was very clear to me." Salleh waved his hand in a sweeping gesture. "There are islands out there where piracy is still the traditional occupation. Their fathers and grandfathers were pirates before them. They don't know any other way of life."

"So you think these outcasts, this Tengku Haji Azhar and his followers, are related to the pirates?"

"By blood, by marriage, perhaps only by trade. Even pirates must trade what they have stolen at knifepoint. Why else would he go to the pirates when the *imam* threw him out?"

"Yes, these are pieces of the puzzle that fit," Yee nodded. "But would the pirates follow him?"

Salleh shrugged. "In these isolated *kampongs* they are very orthodox — fundamentalists. Some are fanatics." He rubbed his eyes, the whites bloodshot and reddened with exhaustion.

"You must rest."

Salleh nodded but remained seated. "This is a very old business. Riding back from the *kampong* in the night, I remembered my grandfather's stories about the old Bugis pirates. They would trade firearms to the warlords in the mountains in exchange for slaves and coffee. My grandfather was a very old man, but this trade went on when he was a young boy, until the English and Dutch ended it." Salleh smiled wearily. "Firearms for slaves and coffee. Nothing changes, *lah*. Your friend Professor Ishak did not tell you about the old Bugis trade?"

"No."

"Perhaps his grandfather did not tell him such stories. Ah, he was a *tunku,* and his father sent him to Oxford to become a proper English gentleman."

"Where would the pirates get missiles?" Yee asked suddenly.

"What?" Salleh's sardonic smile disappeared at the question.

"One of the American helicopters searching for the *Black Sea* crashed; the crew was killed. The Americans think it may have been shot down by an antiaircraft missile."

"Who has such missiles?"

"The Americans gave them to the Pakistanis, who shipped them to the Afghans,

506

who sold some of them to the Iranians."

Salleh pondered for a moment, then to Yee's astonishment broke out laughing. "These American missiles follow the old rug trade." He picked up an imaginary morsel between his thumb and forefinger and held it up for Yee's inspection. "This is the first piece in the puzzle. I think it is time now for me to speak to this Iranian rug merchant on Arab Street, the only one who said he did not know the purser."

In the parade of horrors Yee had forgotten the rug merchant. "Yes," he nodded, "it is time."

After Salleh left, Yee called the Marine Department and talked at length with an official, all the while jotting notes on his pad.

He hung up, then sat studying his scribblings. Between 1981 and 1984 there had been 179 pirate attacks on merchant ships in the straits, 51 in 1986, and since then the number of assaults had fluctuated wildly from only three a year to 61 in another six-month period, as if piracy were a virulent infection that broke out and receded spontaneously. No flag was safe. The *Sealift Arctic*, a U.S. Navy oiler with a largely civilian crew, had been boarded and ransacked right in the Singapore Strait.

The pirates possessed uncanny knowledge of their targets. A second U.S. military tanker, *Falcon Countess,* had already passed the "known pirate zone" in the Strait of Malacca, and the sleepy crew secured the standard pirate watch, when a half dozen men brandishing knives and bayonets slipped aboard about midnight. They terrorized the crew at knifepoint, rifled $19,500 from the ship's safe, and vanished back into the night.

In a later attack the giant container ship *President Madison* had posted an extra watch, with its deck lights blazing to illuminate boarders and high-pressure fire hoses laid out ready to repel pirates. As the ship traversed the channel between Singapore and the islands of the Riau archipelago, five men in green jungle fatigues armed with machetes slipped aboard. They burst into the chief engineer's cabin, bound and gagged the officer, looted the area, and disappeared over the side. It wasn't until the engineer wriggled loose from his ropes and screamed for help that the pirate watch even knew the ship had been attacked.

The paradox was that it was the most modern, thousand-foot-long supertankers and container ships that were the pirates' easiest and fattest prey. Automated and computer controlled, the vessels needed only a handful of men as crew.

Yee studied the reports, then rose and stood, his shoulders hunched with fatigue, staring out the window. A thousand pinpoints of lights flashed from the Strait of Malacca to Changi Point, the navigation lights of ships making the passage. Yee's own great-great-grandfather had arrived in the steerage of one of the wallowing junks from China — its hold crammed with starving indentured peasants and trade cargo — which had then been the pirates' primary prey. The swift, armed Indiamen and British warships had protected only vessels to and from the West.

Over the centuries the waterline and harbor of Singapore had changed completely. The docks had been reengineered, the Arab dhows, the high-stern, flat-bottomed Chinese junks, and eighteen-mast Indiamen replaced by steamships, and they, in turn, by turbine-propelled, computerized leviathans. But the ancient pirates of the Singapore Strait remained, and adapted — a desperate, isolated people bypassed by the modern world, yet still plundering it. Yee's fear transcended the statistics on his desk; it burned in his blood.

34. The Sword of the Law

Tengku Haji Azhar slid the scimitar from the leather crescent of its scabbard and gripped the horn handle with both hands. It was an executioner's sword of hand-wrought Damascus steel, the single edge of the curved blade honed to a razor's edge. A heavy, unwieldy sword with the weight of its multiple layers of folded, hand-hammered, and welded steel centered at the midpoint of the curved blade. The executioner's skill was to swing that point directly down on the right forearm of a thief, the left ankle of a robber, the neck of a heretic or murderer. Those were the punishments prescribed by the *Sharia,* the sacred law.

The blindfolded Russian crewman who knelt face down over the overturned hull of a *perahu,* his hands tied behind him, was neither a heretic nor a murderer, but this was *jihad.* The Russian did not know what was about to happen, yet he was terrified, trembling and dripping with sweat that gave off the sour fumes of his fear.

Tengku looked about at the half-circle of men on the river bank grouped about the *perahu.* They were at the base camp in the grove of nipah palms and spiny-leafed pandanus near the river's mouth. Several of the men looked away uneasily, averting their eyes. The execution of the woman the day before had offended them. But his cousin Ahmed leered back at him with the eager, shining eyes of a bridegroom.

Tengku lowered the sword. The Russian must wait. "Some of you are troubled by the killing of the woman," he said in a soft voice, his eyes still on the scimitar. He spoke in the Bahasa common to both the Malays and Indonesians of the Strait. "Your compassion and mercy does you honor as soldiers of God. For God is compassionate and merciful."

There were murmurs of assent from the men, and Tengku now looked up at them and met their eyes. "*You* did not bring the woman to this place of . . . retribution. And I did not bring her to this place — this place now made holy by her blood, and the blood of the others." He saw the puzzlement in their eyes. "Our course was set in this holy war, already sanctified by prayers and blood, and then it was *destiny* that brought the woman here." Several heads nodded. "In this holy war we must do God's bidding, and not tear out our hair about the results." There were more nods and murmurs of agreement.

"There are six pillars of Islam. Those who are lackeys and slaves of the West and the Chinese moneylenders will tell you there are only five. You must proclaim always, 'There is no god but God, and Mohammed is His prophet.' You must pray. You must fast. You must give alms." He counted off the five pillars on his fingers. "And you should make the pilgrimage to Mecca." He alone in the band wore the white cap of the *haji*. "But there is a sixth pillar of Islam that those who are weak in the Faith do not declare. And that pillar is *jihad,* the holy war." Tengku's voice had gradually increased in strength, so that now the word *jihad* cracked like a pistol shot. "The Koran tells us that those who believe in God should fight for Him. It is the obligation of the true believer. *Jihad* is the peak of worship. For this is the *only* act of worship that demands your life, and the only one that guarantees Paradise."

He had them now. He sensed it in their eyes, now fixed on him, and in their nods and moans. "We cannot form an Islamic nation except by fighting. Only in a righteous country can we respect God and respect ourselves. Others merely preach the call to Islam. But we undertake the armed struggle. The infidels and the tyrants will only vanish by the power of the sword." He lifted the scimitar now, hefting its weight with both hands. "This sword is not a symbol of our cruelty. It is a symbol of the ruthlessness of our devotion." The Russian, as though sensing something, squirmed at his feet.

"There are terrible things we must do, but this is a sacred terror we perform. We raise the righteous sword of our faith against the unbelievers in holy warfare, in *jihad*." On the cry *jihad* he heaved the heavy scimitar up in a powerful arc to his right, as a workman would swing a sledgehammer, poised a moment with the blade raised high above his head, flashing in the sun, then slammed it down.

The sword sliced cleanly through the vertebrae, muscles, tendons, and blood vessels and thumped into the heavy teak of the *perahu's* keel. The head simply tumbled off, but the muscular torso lurched back in a convulsion. Tengku jumped to avoid the two streams of blood that spurted from the neck stump. The decapitated body pitched off the boat into the mud, the still beating heart pumping blood from the thumb-thick severed carotid arteries into the black ooze.

The platoon of men were stunned into silence. Ahmed darted forward, seized the head by the thick, black mane of hair, and held it up at arm's length. *"Allah akbar!"* he shouted. God is great!

"God is great!" the men chanted back.

Ahmed waved the head and repeated the call. The men responded with frenzied chanting, "God is great! God is great! God is great!"

Tengku held up his hand, and the crowd was immediately silenced. "The winds of Paradise are blowing!" he cried out. "Are you ready for martyrdom?"

"Yes, yes!" they shouted back.

Tengku plunged into the gang of men, embracing one in a fierce hug, clasping another's shoulders, giving a word of encouragement to a third. He did not stop until he had touched or spoken to each one of them.

He trudged back to the headless corpse and nudged it with his toe. The arms and legs had stopped twitching. Several men stood gaping at it. "Drag this obscenity to the lagoon of nightmares," he ordered them. "Or else we'll have the flies and stink with dinner."

They threw a rope about each of the legs, not wanting to touch it, and dragged it off, plowing a red-lined furrow through the mud.

Ahmed wrapped the head in a tablecloth from the ship.

"Where will it be taken?" Tengku asked.

"I want to hang it on the gate of the Russian embassy," Ahmed leered, "but it is too well guarded."

"Where, then?"

"On Nassim Road. The Russian, Pakistani, Philippine, and Saudi Arabian embassies are all in one block. Also the Japanese. Somewhere in that area it will be found right away. There are several restaurants where the foreigners eat."

Tengku nodded. "And last night, the woman's head?"

"I have not heard yet. I told them you wanted it near the American embassy, but it is also well guarded. Across the street from the embassy there is the Chinese Chamber of Commerce. And next door is the famous old Armenian Church of Saint Gregory, the first Christian church in Singapore." Ahmed smiled. "Each head should be a message to our oppressors. But we cannot repeat a pattern, or they will be waiting for our messenger."

"Our brother Abdullah?"

Ahmed shook his head. "He is lost. But we can be sure they have the message."

"He did not know where we are?"

"The messengers never know where we are."

Tengku nodded. Each day he went over the drill with Ahmed, sometimes changing the pickup points, as they did when Abdullah did not return from Singapore. "Still we have heard *nothing* about the American or Russian guns." It was a pronouncement, spat out in frustration.

"Their governments will do nothing until they are so drenched in blood they must stop it at any cost." Ahmed spoke with the patience of a teacher repeating a lesson. "You see what happens in Lebanon. The Americans threaten, negotiate, talk, talk, talk. A year, two years, six years. But still they give nothing to our brothers. We would die of old age, and our hostages would still be alive. This way each day that they ignore our demands, they are punished by your righteous sword."

Tengku nodded impatiently. "Yes, yes, but still we hear nothing, not even stories on TV or the newspapers."

"The Singapore police don't want our people to know there is a revolution. But with each head more people know."

"The foreign press — "

"That is the first place the police watch," Ahmed said harshly. "If they did not hear

516

of the head at Raffles . . . We must not get reckless. We are safe here, as our fathers were safe here from the British warships and the Japanese, our fathers' fathers from the Dutch, and our fathers before that from the Portuguese. The Americans, the Russians, with their radar, jet airplanes, and spacecraft, cannot see us here — here where the eye of the day cannot see us between the great trees and the mountains — unless *we* lead them here."

"No one will betray us."

"We will betray ourselves if we get reckless."

Tengku became belligerent. His cousin was berating him, not for anything he had done but for what he might do. "I do God's bidding," he snapped angrily. He picked up the scimitar and carefully wiped the blade clean with a rough cloth, dismissing Ahmed with the gesture. His cousin strode away to deliver the Russian barman's head on the first leg of the relay to Singapore.

Only Ahmed knew that Tengku had hidden in the jungle and practiced on melons, coconuts, then dogs and squealing pigs, before his arms, nerves, and stomach had been strong enough to do his sword's bidding. The purser and the frail old man had had their throats cut first, the seaman died by poison dart. The fat, bloated, sweating American passenger — loud and offending in his complaints about the heat and the narrow canoe — had been the first executed by this sword. It had frightened and awed the men, but it had bound and strengthened their loyalty to him. Now with each stroke Tengku felt himself grow stronger, more determined, washed clean, and purged of his doubts by the blood he shed. There was no turning back from his destiny.

A speedboat, its powerful twin outboard motors idling, slid into the mud bank, and a stocky man, muscular for a Malay, with long, glossy hair and a pocked face, leaped off the bow and trotted up to Tengku.

"The American warship is now in the Selat Durian. Shooting down the helicopter did not stop it." Mohammed looked downcast, as though he had failed.

Tengku put his hand on the knotty shoulder. "If we do not stop it, it may soon be here. I don't know what special radar or technology it has to find the *Black Sea*. It can see in the darkest night. Perhaps it can see through trees when it gets close enough."

"I do not know how to stop a ship. What to shoot at. It is so large," Mohammed said in despair. "In the training camp in Tehran we were only taught where to shoot at airplanes and tanks."

Tengku laughed. "A ship is easier, because it is so large. I will tell you how, and you will know more than they teach in Tehran. When you return, you will be the master. The killer of ships."

Mohammed looked at him doubtfully.

"I have studied the *Black Sea*. It is a very modern ship, the same size and shape as this American warship, yes?"

"Yes, Abang."

Tengku nodded confidently. "All fish have their hearts and fins in the same place."

A few hours later Mohammed squatted in the stern of a small fishing boat, nervously smoking to calm his mind and hands. The Russian RPG-7, already loaded with an armor-piercing round, lay at his feet. The boat was tied to the channel buoy, so Mohammed did not have to bother steering it, and it swung on the line, heading into the powerful tidal current. In the narrow Sumatran straits, the tide surged up and down as much as nineteen feet.

He glanced apprehensively at the straining line and then back at the American ship now less than a kilometer away, heading directly toward him. He still could not make out the warship's smokestack. The main engines would be directly under the stack at the water line, Tengku had briefed him; an antitank missile exploding at that point would destroy the ship's power plant. Mohammed knew nothing about ships, and he followed Tengku's orders entirely on faith.

The shooter had covered the RPG with a fishnet in case the helicopter from the American ship flew over him, and he placed his bare foot on the tube of the rocket launcher, seeking reassurance from the hard, deadly metal. He scratched his head, his chest, then rubbed the skin vigorously, as if he could scrape away the dirt and stench with his fingers. He had put on the fisherman's filthy turban, jersey, and sarong as disguise, but the clothes — rancid with sweat, fish slime, and blood — made his skin crawl. Mohammed was a fastidious and devout man who washed before prayers five times a day. If he were to die a martyr, the thought of perishing in these unclean rags offended him.

Mohammed was very frightened. He had to lie in wait until the American warship was absolutely broadside, no more than a hundred meters away, before he could fire. The frigate surged toward him, the sword point of its bow thrusting through the water. The Malay knelt and nervously lifted the fishnet. Still on his knees, he hoisted the rocket launcher to his shoulder. It was only half the weight of the American Stinger with which he had shot down the helicopter, and an American sailor watching him from the *Decatur* might think the three-foot long, khaki-painted weapon was a bamboo tube, a piece of native fishing equipment.

The shooter now positioned himself carefully, looking over both shoulders to double-check that the end of the launcher was clear. If the boat cabin was behind him, the backblast might set it afire and the kickback drive him overboard. The rocket launcher's main drawback as a weapon of ambush was that it could not be fired from an enclosed space.

He sighted down the tube at the American warship. Tengku was right. It did look like the *Black Sea* — the sharply pointed prow, the long, flat forecastle, the abrupt rise of its bridge, followed by the elongated block of its superstructure. But where was the smokestack? Mohammed saw domes, towering masts, and the fans of radar antennas, but no funnel.

Mohammed's heart fluttered with panic, but then he remembered that Tengku had foreseen this. If he did not have a shot at the engine, he was to aim at the bridge. He lined up his sights on the row of windows.

Out of the corner of his right eye Mohammed suddenly spotted the short cone of the smokestack. It was only a fraction of the height of the towering white stack of the *Black Sea,* with its blazing red band and golden hammer and sickle, yet it was in the same spot.

Mohammed hesitated, his eyes flicking frantically back and forth indecisively from the narrow bridge to the broad, smooth flank of the ship, as it now swept by him.

He aimed, took a deep breath, let it out with a prayer to God, and squeezed the trigger.

35. Fire Down Below

The rocket hit a few feet above the water line directly below the *Decatur*'s exhaust stack. As Tengku had anticipated, that was where the ship's main engines were located. The armor-piercing warhead penetrated the half-inch steel plate covering the hull and blasted into the lubricating oil tank along the port side of the engine room. The steel skin of the tank and the oil did not stop the rocket, but they slowed it down and deflected it upward. The warhead broke out of the tank, shattered the heavy pipes transporting the JP-5 aviation gas, ricocheted through the engine housing, and exploded against the port turbine, shredding the fuel lines to the 25,000-horsepower engine.

Gas Turbine Technician second class Danny Novak was hunched over drawing a lube oil sample from the filter on the port side aft. He reared up at the first crash of the missile and was hit by the explosion of hot oil and steel and hurled down the narrow walkway like a giant dungaree ragdoll.

The explosion ignited the high-octane fuel pumping from the ruptured pipes. The flaming oil spewed down into the bilges, where the intense heat set off the less volatile lubricating oil, now pooling there from the spouting holes the missile had punched in the storage tank. The fuel still being pumped to the engines and the gushing oil fed the flames, which now splashed across the bilges beneath the main turbines, under the reduction gears and below the steel grating of the catwalk on which Danny Novak lay flat and bloody as raw hamburger on a grill.

"What the hell was that?" On the bridge, four decks above and 150 feet forward of the engine room, Stewart felt the hit of the missile and the explosion as a sharp bump. His first thought was that the ship had run aground. He ran swiftly to the port wing of the bridge and peered overboard with Ensign Fine right at his side. He could see nothing but the *Decatur*'s wake as the ship surged through the water. Off to port a small native fishing boat with a blue-painted wooden hull bobbed next to a buoy.

"Officer of the deck," the telephone talker yelled out excitedly. "The after lookout thinks a fishing boat fired at us with some sort of shoulder rocket."

Stewart instantly focused his glasses on the fishing boat. He saw a native kneeling in the stern, holding up a long brown tube.

"Telephone talker, this is the captain. The gunners are ordered to fire on that fishing boat. Kill the man in the stern."

"Yes, sir. The gunners are ordered to fire — " the talker began automatically to repeat the order back to Stewart.

"Give the order now, damn it!" He charged at the startled talker and yanked the microphone from his chest holder.

On the port .50-caliber mount eighteen-year-old Gunner's Mate Striker Martin Luther Rudolph heard the lookout's report over his headset and swung his gun around to where he could see the fishing boat. The man on the deck was too far away for Rudolph to make out what he was doing.

"Gunners, this is the captain. We've been fired on by that fishing boat on the port quarter. Shoot it out of the water. Kill the man on the stern. That is an order. This is the real thing. You have batteries released. Acknowledge. Over."

The gunner's mate was startled to hear the captain over his headphones, but he quickly acknowledged. "Yes, sir. This is the port gunner."

"Commence fire!" the voice in his head commanded.

The eighteen-year-old kid pointed the .50-caliber at the fishing boat and then froze. He had practiced firing the gun at whitecaps and boxes of garbage. He had never fired *at* anyone before in his life.

"This is the captain. You are ordered to fire," the voice commanded again.

Rudolph squeezed the trigger. The first burst of shells startled the gunner's mate. The red tracers streaked out over the water but fell short of the fishing boat.

The explosion of the shells and the acrid smell of cordite broke the young gunner's spell of disbelief at what was happening. He fiercely gripped the gun's handles and squeezed again. This time he pushed the fiery red-dotted line up to the stem of the fishing boat and held the burst there.

Mohammed stared down the barrel of the Russian rocket launcher in disbelief. It was inconceivable to him that he had missed the broadside of the American warship. It was four hundred feet long. But there had been no explosion — the eruption of fire and smoke that had blown the helicopter out of the sky — no gaping hole in the ship's hull. Either the rocket had misfired and dropped into the water with hardly a splash, or it had been a dud that had bounced off the side of the huge warship with less impact than a fly crashing into a water buffalo.

Mohammed had been well trained as a terrorist, but he had not actually fired the RPG-7 before. The fact that it was an antitank rocket meant to him that it would blow up a tank. That it did this by first penetrating twelve inches of armor plating was a concept he had not absorbed. From where he lay on the salt-bleached planked deck of the fishing boat, squinting over the gunwale, Mohammed could not discern the jagged five-inch hole the armor-piercing shell had punched in the ship's side two hundred yards away. The *Decatur* sailed on without the slightest flicker from its course indicating it had been hit.

But Tengku in his wisdom had foreseen this. "You will have a second shot," Abang had told him. "When it passes you, the American ship will show its ass to you. Fire your missile right up its asshole. In the middle of the stern, right at the water line, are the ship's rudder, its screw, and the shaft that drives it. But you do not have to be an engineer and remember all this machinery. Just remember the first missile must go right into its belly under the smokestack, and the second up its asshole. Either one will cripple the ship, if it strikes true." He had clasped Mohammed on the shoulder.

Mohammed was overwhelmed by his failure. He had to get off another shot quickly at the departing stern before the ship was out of range. As the ship moved away from him, presenting its stern to the shooter, there was little relative motion. Although the target became smaller, the accurate range of the shoulder-held rocket launcher increased to five hundred meters. But the Russian RPG-7 was not an easy weapon to reload. He had to screw the cylinder containing the rocket propellant into the warhead, load the assembled round into the muzzle of the three-foot-long barrel, then uncover the nose cap of the rocket and extract the safety pin. Mohammed had practiced the procedure blindfolded until he could do it quickly in the dark. He had not practiced it in the cramped stern of a small fishing craft, pitching violently in the wake of an American frigate. In his humiliation, Mohammed rushed to reload the RPG as quickly as possible and dropped it. The 40-mm. warhead was tossed out of its resting place in the pile of nets and crashed against the boat's thick wood gunwale. Mohammed dove after it and grabbed the rocket, half expecting it to explode in his face. For a frozen instant he waited to be delivered to Paradise, then breathed again.

It was then that he heard the staccato blast of the ship's machine gun. He turned in time to see the water thirty feet from the boat erupt in a line of white geysers that raced straight toward him and then fell short. Frantic now, he groped for the launcher unit, darting a fearful glance toward the American warship. This time he saw the silent, hurling flames that cut the water and disintegrated the planks under his feet into splinters an instant before his body was torn apart by bolts through his leg, groin, chest, and neck in a violence so swift and shocking that Mohammed never registered pain nor heard the gunfire that killed him.

Ensign Glover, the *Decatur*'s engineering officer of the watch, spotted the loss of fuel oil pressure on the control console an instant before the high-temperature alarm started screaming. According to the digital readouts and the wailing siren beating his ears, everything was leaking and burning up. He dove at the switches for the remote-controlled valves that shut off the fuel pumps and the main engine.

At that moment the klaxon blaring General Quarters reverberated through the compartment. What the hell was happening? "General Quarters. General Quarters. All hands man your battle stations. This is not a drill. The ship is under attack by small craft. Repeat, this is not a drill."

At the first beat of silence Glover rang the bridge to tell them he had shut down the main engine.

"This is the captain. What's the casualty?"

"Possible fire in the main engine room with a fuel and oil leak."

"Have you sent a man to check it?"

"Right now, sir."

"Do it!" Stewart clicked off.

The roving engineering watch Novak should have been in the engine room. Glover tried to call him there.

The mess decks were pandemonium as the crew members rushed in every direction to get to their battle stations. Engineman second class Gregory Washington collided with and bounced off his shipmates in his own charge toward the main engine room. He had been the first man into the control station, and Ensign Glover had ordered him back out to confirm visually the fire his computer readouts were indicating.

Washington dropped down the engine room ladder, sliding his hands along the steel railings, barely touching the rungs with his feet, and leaped the last four steps. At the bottom of the ladder was the spring-loaded fire door leading into the engine room. Washington peered through the glass porthole. Heavy black smoke billowed up from the bilges. There was sure as shit a fire in there. He started to turn to vault back up the ladder, but a pale yellow patch on the catwalk behind the gear housing caught his eye. He stared at it, struggling to see through the heavy smoke. It was blond hair . . . Novak.

Washington writhed in indecision. If he saw smoke in the engine room, he was supposed to jump back up the ladder. There was a bank of cylinders of fire suppressant

Halon on the next level. If he immediately released them, they might put out the fire. In the meantime Novak would fucking fry to death or be suffocated by the Halon. But if he banged through the fire door, the heat and smoke might overcome him and get both their asses fried. Washington didn't logically click off his alternatives. He just knew them in the tumult of his guts.

As Washington had run out the door of Central Control, Ensign Glover had thrown an emergency escape pack at him, as if this were another chicken-shit drill. At the sight of smoke, the engineman automatically ripped open the blue packet containing the hood. It was not fire-fighting apparatus; it was only a disposable breathing device that chemically generated oxygen just long enough for a sailor to get out of a smoke-choked compartment and onto an outside deck. Washington had the hood on in three seconds, and then he ran the wrong way — into the flaming engine room.

He immediately felt the blistering heat on his bare hands. Flames spewed out greasy black smoke beneath his feet. In a panicked dash he was over Novak. Jesus, his head and chest were covered with blood. The little mothah fuckah was dead. Washington didn't stop to examine him. He swooped down and grabbed under the white boy's arms and around his chest in a full nelson, heaved up, and backpedaled as fast as he could move, bumping and dragging Novak's limp ass over pipes and gratings. He backed in a crash right through the fire door, which was spring-loaded to open inward but then sprang shut, pinning Novak's legs. Washington yanked the door back, flung the limp legs into the escapeway, and fell against the door. The door now made a firm seal, but some smoke had swirled into the compartment.

Washington glanced down at the bloody and unmoving Novak and then up the ladder. There was no way he could carry his dead ass up the ladder. He ripped off his hood and yanked it over Novak's head, not even bothering to turn it around, so that the hairy back of the sailor's head showed through the plastic face plate. Then he clambered back up the ladder to the passageway on the mess-deck level.

The red containers activating the Halon fire-fighting system were right outside the hatch. How the hell did you turn those son-of-bitches on? Washington tore out the wire key and yanked the lever on the primary system. Nothing happened. No red light or alarm went off. *Shee-it!* There was a release for the reserve Halon alongside the primary discharge. Washington ripped at that wire and lever. And again nothing happened. He slammed the steel cylinder in frustration, winced with the pain, then noticed for the first time that his hand was burned. He must have grabbed a hot railing or something in the engine room.

Now he panicked. He felt that any moment the whole fucking ship was going to blow up right under him. He was supposed to report right back to Ensign Glover, but the mess deck was only a few feet away and he knew from all the chicken-shit drills that a fire-fighting party was suiting up there. Chief Knox would know what to do, and he could call Ensign Glover on their phones.

Washington bolted for the mess deck.

Stewart stalked about the bridge in a fury. His ship — a state-of-the-art United States Navy guided-missile frigate — had been ambushed and put out of action by a hand-held shot from a native fishing boat. He hadn't felt anything more than a slight bump, but now his main engine room was in flames, and the *Decatur* lay dead in the water.

"Bridge, Central Control." The intercom speaker boomed at Stewart.

He keyed the mike. "Go ahead, Central."

"Captain, the fire party reports the engine

room is now filled with white smoke. The Halon has taken effect. We've checked through the port and starboard doors, and the fire seems to be suppressed. But we're going to hold off entering the space for fifteen minutes to let it cool down."

"Roger. Let us know before you enter, or if there's a flareup."

"Central aye, sir."

Stewart turned to Robinson with a gesture of relief. "That was quick."

"We've still got a bilge full of hot fuel, and if it goes up again, there's no more Halon."

"What about the reserve?"

Robinson shook his head. "The sailor who discovered the fire released both the primary and backup."

"Jesus!" Stewart swore. The Halon in the engine room had smothered the fire by reacting chemically with the oxygen in the space so that it was not available to feed the fire. But once the oxygen was replenished through the hole in the side of the ship or an open door, the fire would flare up again. And this time they would have to fight it with men and hoses.

"Captain, the helicopter's off the deck."

"Very well. Do you hold any other contacts?"

"Only the same merchants that we've had

for the last hour."

"Double-check with Combat and have them sweep with their fire-control radar."

The captain's normal post in battle was in the combat information center one deck below — in the darkened, air-conditioned steel cave of radar scopes and sonar consoles that fired the ship's missiles and torpedoes. The bridge was the executive officer's post in battle. But computer-controlled missiles and torpedoes could not fight the enemy who had just bushwhacked his ship. Stewart had usurped the bridge.

"Put me up on the bird's channel," he ordered the officer of the deck, Balletto.

He grabbed the long-corded mike and moved out onto the port bridge wing. Ensign Chambers was studying the fishing boat through the mounted "Big Eyes" binoculars.

"Nothing's moving on the boat, sir."

The boat was scuttled and sinking, its gunwales almost at water level.

Stewart keyed his mike. "Eagle Claw, this is the captain. Move off to the east and keep your door gun boresighted on him. If they move, we've got them in a cross-fire. But keep a sharp eyeball lookout 360 degrees around. Another wooden hull could pop up from anywhere."

"Roger that."

"Captain, the boarding party's under way. I'm having them come up on the bird's channel."

"Good thinking."

Lieutenant j.g. Nguyen checked in on the motor whale boat's portable UHF radio.

"Okay, Tram, move out a couple of hundred yards and approach them on an angle so that you're not in the ship's or the chopper's line of fire if we start shooting. Your first priority is to stop them from firing again on the ship. Your second is to protect your boarding party. But if there's no resistance, we want prisoners. We need intelligence, anything. Over."

"Roger, out."

"Eagle Claw, did you copy that?"

"Roger. I've got a good eyeball on the boat now. There's one body laid out on the deck, but I don't see anyone else. Not unless there are one or two laying low in that tiny cabin. Over."

Stewart recognized the pilot's voice. It was Callahan.

The coxswain eased the motor whale boat behind the fishing *perahu*, and Nguyen could see the man flung across the fishing nets and over the gunwale. There were gouges of bloody red meat along his leg, crotch, chest, and neck; the blood from the neck wound dripped into the water, attracting a pack of fish that churned the sea in their frenzy.

"The guy in the boat looks very dead from here. Has big holes in him," Nguyen reported over the radio. The body was clothed in a faded orange batik sarong and a dirty yellow jersey. A purplish turban, also of faded batik, lay alongside the body, where it had been knocked off by the impact of the .50-calibers. "He looks like a fisherman."

"He's supposed to look like a fisherman, but he handles a rocket launcher like a pro. Somebody else probably got that boat out there and is still aboard," the captain coached over the radio. "Okay, that's a good position. Now move in slowly."

Nguyen checked the approach of the motor whale boat to make certain it was out of the line of fire from the ship and chopper. But once they were next to the fishing boat, they were on their own. "Spread out as much as you can in the boat," he ordered. "Johnson in the bow, Gumbs in the stern. All safeties off, guns cocked." There was the clatter of M14 bolts being drawn and released. Nguyen carried only a 9-mm. pistol. Next to him, Bellows held a 12-gauge shotgun pointed at the *perahu's* boxy deckhouse, incongruously painted a festive yellow and red.

"On the fishing boat, come out with your hands empty. We will not hurt you," Nguyen shouted. He repeated it once, then on an irrational impulse repeated it in Vietnamese.

"Do they speak Vietnamese?" Bellows whispered.

"No, Malay." Nguyen had a memory flash of a starving nine-year-old refugee boy on the Malaysian beach and shouted, "No shoot you. Fisherman, give you food, money, bananas, beer, water, melons." It was in broken Bahasa, and perhaps made no more sense than what he had said in Vietnamese, but at least anyone on the boat might understand it.

There was no response from the boat. The deckhouse was open toward the stern, but with the low afternoon sun glaring off the water, Nguyen could not see into its shadows. All the men in the whaler glanced at Nguyen and then back at the fishing boat, waiting for the next move.

He turned to the first-class gunner's mate. "Gumbs, I'm going aboard. Take charge here."

"I should go aboard, sir."

Nguyen shook his head and said in a strained voice, "If anyone's hiding, maybe

I can talk to them." He nodded at the coxswain, and the motor whale boat eased up to the *perahu*. Johnson caught the gunwale with a hook and brought the two boats together. Nguyen looked again at the mangled corpse. His bowels quaked, and he leaped.

His foot caught in the pile of nets on the stern. Nguyen tripped and banged down painfully on his knee. He immediately swung his 9-mm. into the cabin from that firing crouch, as if that was what he had intended. For a terrifying interval he peered into the darkened cabin, waiting for his eyes to adjust, expecting at any instant to be shot himself.

"There's no one there," he said finally, as much in relief as astonishment.

36. Secrets of the Persian Carpet Trade

The great golden onion dome of the Sultan Mosque and the towering gold-crowned minarets loomed over the two-story shophouses of the Arab Street district like a Byzantine fantasy castle. As a boy Salleh bin Ali had attended the midday Friday *Juma* prayers in the mosque with his father, and he had a dreamlike memory of the barefooted faithful flowing through the fourteen gates into the vast prayer hall, ethereally lit by a chandelier of gold and crystal, the men silently squatting cross-legged on the deep red carpets that covered the marble floors, the silver railings of the gallery above him emblazoned with the star and crescent, the inscriptions from the Koran in glistening gold and green mosaic tiles on the high walls behind the *imam* — the words in a mysterious and holy Arabic he could not read.

Now, stalking along Arab Street, Salleh wore the black velvet *songkok* cap, an immaculate *baju*, the loose-fitting Malay tunic, and a wraparound sarong of batik, the Friday best of a man who had just attended *Juma* prayers at the Masjid Sultan. This irreligious deception made Salleh uneasy. He had briefly considered wearing the white cap of a *haji*, but that would have been a sacrilege. True believer or not, Salleh felt it would be at best unlucky to have the sight of him offend God at the outset of a dangerous mission.

Arab Street denoted not just the five-block-long avenue that bordered the Sultan Mosque and the Muslim cemetery but also the maze of jammed streets and alleys surrounding the *masjid*. In the East India Company's original 1822 plan for Singapore, this site had been allotted to the trading post's dozen Arab traders. But as the immigrants from the East overflowed their assigned Chinatown on the other side of the Singapore River, Arab Street became the center of Muslim life for the influx of Iranians, Pakistanis, Bugis, Indonesians, and the original Malays, now a minority in their own city.

Salleh strolled by little shops, tucked tightly under the archways of the shuttered shophouses — a bazaar piled with Javanese batiks, lacy Indonesian scarfs, stacks of basketry, Indian cottons, brocades, silks and velvets, open gunny sacks of almonds and dried apricots, sticks of cinnamon, sandalwood, and incense. A merchant dumped a batch of spices into a rumbling grinder, and a fine dust of curry wafted into the street, tickling Salleh's nostrils and making him salivate. After prayers his father would take him to one of the traditional restaurants that served the savory *biryani* rice and curries of Muslim India, and he remembered Bussorah Street crammed with food stalls after sundown during the fast of Ramadan.

Racks of *jamu,* the pounded Indonesian herbs, promised youth, beauty, mustachioed virility, or a bigger bust — their specific benefits advertised by gaudy pictures on the packets. One crammed shop specialized in *barang haji,* the requisites for a pilgrimage to Mecca — prayer beads, scarfs, the seamless cloak of white cloth — and in a nook at the rear an old man sat sewing *haji* caps for the returned pilgrims. And *jamus* failing, Paradise beckoning, the Muslim undertaker on the next street displayed the traditional plain wooden coffins.

Salleh turned into Baghdad Street. Suliman's Carpets was tucked next to a goldsmith who fashioned intricate Malay-style jewelry. Suliman was a big, dark-bearded, turbaned Iranian who sat behind a desk at the rear overseeing the shop. He left the clerking to his nephew, a slender young man with a hooked blade of a nose and a jutting Adam's apple. Little paper signs on the carpets indicated the country of origin — thick pile rugs with cut patterns from China, a short-piled Turkoman *hatchli* from the hinterlands of Russia, geometrically patterned Baluchis from Afghanistan.

"*Selamat sore.* Can I help you?" the nephew asked.

Salleh ignored him for several moments, then without looking away from the rugs said in a voice just loud enough to be heard by Suliman, "I'm looking for a Persian for my office, perhaps a silk from Qum or Esfahan."

Out of the corner of his eye he saw the Iranian get up from his desk and approach. He waved his nephew away. "You have an expert eye for rugs," Suliman said with an ingratiating smile.

The Malay turned toward him. Suliman had the same scimitar blade of a nose as his nephew, a family trait apparently, but he was considerably fleshier. Salleh knew immediately why the Chinese detectives who had briefed him had several times described the Iranian as big. Perhaps Suliman had once been as slender as his nephew, but a life-time of unloading, hauling, and manhandling heavy carpets had developed the intimidating chest and arms of a Greco-Roman wrestler.

"No, I know very little, I'm afraid. But I've picked up some suggestions for an investment from business associates." Like an actor slipping into a role, Salleh affected the vaguely Oxonian accent of a Malay educated abroad.

"Yes, yes," the Iranian nodded eagerly, rubbing his hands together. "Truthfully, this is not just fine furniture but a fine Oriental painting whose value goes up and up. But because of the revolution in Iran — may the Almighty God be praised — and the wars in Afghanistan, Iran, Iraq, the market has been flooded. So there are great bargains to be had. The classic Persians are not the cheapest, but truthfully a few years from now, when all this terrible business finally ends — may peace be upon us — you will see your investment in the classic Persians increase tenfold."

"That's what my business associates inform me."

"And what business are you in, may I ask?"

Salleh reached under his *baju* for his wallet and withdrew a business card identifying him as a partner in a prominent Bugis trading company. Indeed, if the Iranian called to check, a secretary would confirm his association and take any message.

Apparently Suliman was impressed. He gestured toward the rear of the shop with an elegant, sweeping motion. "*Tuan,* the merchandise here are all very good carpets, but they are for the Australian, American, and Japanese tourists. The Americans like to walk barefooted on the thick pile of the Chinese carpets. Or they come with a color scheme from their decorators — desert pink, avocado green. So I show them the Pakistanis. The Pakistanis use chemical dyes, and they can give you any color that's fashionable."

"And the Australians and the Japanese?" Salleh asked.

"They'll buy any rug the Americans are buying."

Salleh laughed. "And according to the Prophet, he who makes money pleases God. Buying and selling and amassing wealth are acts of faith."

The rug merchant nodded solemnly and gestured with a thick forefinger. "But the Koran says, 'Woe to the defrauders, for when they take, they demand in full measure, but when they give, they measure less.' Truthfully, *Tuan,* the Pakistani carpet is first-rate, as well made now as the Persians. But the Persian is a better investment, although higher priced. It has a four-hundred-year tradition."

"And the vegetable dyes."

Suliman, ever the salesman, nodded eagerly. "Yes, yes, truthfully, they give the carpet a truer color." He looked at Salleh carefully, as if the next question were one of great delicacy. "Were you interested in silk or wool, did you say?"

Salleh raised an eyebrow. "Wool?"

"Yes, yes, silk, of course. It is the finest in color, and strongest — silk thread on a silk base. The Americans like wool. They say it is 'warmer.' "

"And the Australians and Japanese want what the Americans want."

545

Suliman laughed and nodded eagerly. "Yes, yes. *Tuan,* it is a pleasure to serve a man of the world. And a brother in Islam."

Salleh acknowledged the compliment with a lordly nod of the head.

There was a waist-high stack of carpets at the rear, and with a powerful flourish Suliman yanked off the top one and held it under his chin. "This is special, very beautiful, that I have just gotten in from the holy city of Qum. I have not even hung it yet."

The matrix of the carpet was gold, not a solid color but streaks and shadings of gold like a sunrise burning through a morning mist. Interwoven festoons of blossoms, fruits, and leaves, all outlined in black, formed a series of rectangular borders like the mats and fillets of a painting and framed the carpet's central image — a pointed Byzantine dome whose shape mirrored that of the Sultan Mosque outside, except that the dome was woven from the garlands of Paradise. There were only two colors — the blackness that gave the images their shape and the shadings of gold, shadowed, misty, here and there shimmering with a transcendent glory. Salleh stared at the carpet, transfixed by the weaver's vision.

"It is hand-woven, of course. Here, look at the workmanship." Suliman turned the carpet over, breaking the spell. "Each strand is hand-knotted, more than a thousand knots to the square inch. It took over a year to make." The merchant's voice was unctuous, wheedling, screwing the price up with each virtue.

"You said it just came from the holy city of Qum. How did you get it out of Iran?"

Suliman smiled. "That is a trade secret. They are smuggled from the port of Abadan across the gulf to Dubai." He shook his head in consternation. "The wars with Iraq, Kuwait, Afghanistan, the revolution — may the Almighty be praised — created a terrible inflation, from seven Iranian *rials* to the dollar to hundreds. These things keep the old smuggling routes open and flourishing." He shrugged. "People must trade, eat, make a living."

The Iranian was off guard. Salleh would never have a better opening. He nodded sympathetically and asked, "Is that how you smuggled the weapons, the Stingers that you supplied to my brother Tengku Haji Azhar?"

In the tactic of surprise there is a great difference in the reaction of someone who has been betrayed and one who is totally confused. The Iranian had been betrayed, but he quickly sought refuge in a blustering confusion. "What . . . what are you talking about? Weapons? Stingers? I don't know this fellow." He stared at Salleh. "Who are you?"

"I am who I say I am," Salleh said earnestly. "But I was in the Muslim Brotherhood with Tengku at the university in Kuala Lumpur. I was going to make the *haj* with him, but my father was ill. When Tengku returned from Iran, I was with him in Kuala Selatan, and together we planned this . . . *business*. When the *imam* made us leave, Tengku embraced me and said that he did not need an amateur pirate. I would be more valuable to the revolution here in Singapore. And perhaps that is true. I have learned that one of our brothers from Kuala Selatan has been arrested here in Singapore and is being tortured. The police have sent spies to Kuala Selatan." It was the best possible story Salleh could concoct, as it embraced everything he knew and, he hoped, several things the Iranian did not know but rang true.

Suliman still held up the carpet, as if hiding behind it like some sumptuous shield, peering at him over the border. He now laid the rug down on the pile, carefully smoothing it with the fleshy palms of his big hands, then stood and commanded, "Come. I have some beautiful carpets in the back room," as if nothing extraordinary had been said.

He led the way into a storeroom at the

rear. Rolls of carpets covered with heavy paper were stacked in a framework of two-by-fours raised off the floor. The Iranian suddenly whirled around; his powerful paws seized Salleh's shoulders and pinned him against the wall. "Are you crazy?" he snarled. "You come in here, a stranger, and talk about smuggling missiles. The penalty for this is death. You will get everyone killed!"

The explosive fury and strength of the Iranian startled and overwhelmed Salleh. "I have to contact my brother Tengku," he blurted.

"You don't know where he is because you are a fool who babbles to strangers. Ahmed does not deal with fools."

"Ahmed?" Salleh questioned, then caught himself. "I must talk to Ahmed," he insisted.

But he was not quick enough. The Iranian glared at him. "You do not know Ahmed. My God, you were never with them." In a fury he flung Salleh against the wall. "You are the police spy."

Salleh slammed into the wall and fell to his hands and feet, stunned by the ferocity of the assault. The big Iranian hovered over him, a gorilla about to tear his head off. Salleh was trapped in the narrow storeroom, his back against the wall. The Iranian charged forward, his hands thrust out to strangle the policeman.

Salleh sprang up on his fingertips and toes, leaped high, and scissor-kicked as he had practiced a thousand times in *sepak takraw*, only this time his foot did not drive into a hurling 170-gram rattan ball but into the Iranian's bearded face. Suliman bellowed, staggered, and crashed headlong into the heavy wooden rack of carpets. The framework collapsed, and a dozen carpet rolls the size of tree trunks crashed down on the Iranian, burying him.

Suliman lay still. Only his legs, disquietingly lifeless, stuck out from the disorderly log pile. There was a strange stillness in the storeroom, as the sunlight from a small window danced in the swirls of disturbed dust. Then through the rafters the wail of the *muezzin* from the lofty minarets of the Sultan Mosque called the faithful to their afternoon prayers.

Salleh hesitated; then, acting from a compulsion he had not experienced in years, dropped to his knees and touched his forehead to the dank floorboards.

37. The Betrayal of
Maggi Chancellor

"So what the hell is this?" emeritus professor of biology Arthur Strauss snarled, and the belligerence in his voice made Williard Howell, Jr., the attorney, wince and involuntarily draw back. A thick tape now protected Howell's nose, which had been broken in the brawl outside the doctor's office two days before; he never saw who threw the punch that smashed it.

"It's a contract," Howell said quietly, keeping his voice low so that the others in the dining room of the *Black Sea* could not overhear.

"Of course it's a contract," Strauss snapped irritably. "I can see the convoluted gibberish you lawyers use to justify your ball-breaking fees. What's this all about?"

Howell glanced nervously about the dining room. It was between meals, but the imprisoned passengers had taken to gathering here, as the ship's lounge had been commandeered by the pirate hierarchy. The jungle heat on the promenade decks was stifling during the day, and the hostages congregated at the unset tables in desultory groups to play cards, endlessly speculate with one another on their fate in aggrieved voices, write unmailed letters, or just read by themselves, but mainly to escape the oppressive cell-like confines of their staterooms, the loneliness, the fear.

Strauss, by himself at a corner table, was writing in what appeared to be a grade school composition book. "May I sit down?" Howell asked politely.

"Suit yourself."

Howell sat down and leaned forward in a confidential attitude, but his glasses slipped off his bandaged nose, and he grabbed at them. "I thought the Society's board of directors should draft an agreement, before we present it to the other passengers — "

"What's this legal mumbo jumbo about?" Strauss impatiently waved the papers the lawyer had handed him.

Howell took a breath. "Well, Professor Strauss, sooner or later we're going to be released, or rescued. And there will be a great deal of media interest in our ordeal here."

"It's not so bad. Believe me, it could be a lot worse."

"I absolutely agree." Howell nodded vigorously in agreement, but to keep his glasses from falling again he pressed his forefinger against the bridge in a gesture that looked as if he were shaking his finger at Strauss. "So I think it's important that any representation not be sensationalized or distorted."

"What the hell are you talking about, *representation?*"

Howell spoke in low, confiding tones. "There may be book offers, movie interest, certainly a TV drama."

"Books? Movies? TV?"

"There are certain rights to privacy in a situation like this, and we thought if the Society as a whole coordinated — "

"You want to tie up the rights!" Strauss suddenly exclaimed. "That's it! Am I right?" He stared at Howell with a mixture of curiosity and disgust.

"Well, we thought — "

"What *we?* It's so *you* the lawyer can negotiate the whole *schmeer,* jet back and forth to fancy hotels in Beverly Hills and New York, collect a fat fee and probably a very nice piece of the deal. I'm way ahead of you. Am I right or am I right?"

Howell did not say anything. He glanced down and tried to read whatever it was that Strauss was scribbling in the notebook, certainly not a letter but perhaps a journal.

"Lawyers," Strauss snorted in a mocking voice. "In my laboratory we're replacing all the rats with lawyers."

"I've heard the joke," Howell said. Several people in the room were staring at them, avidly eavesdropping.

"Yeah, well, there are a lot of things even rats won't do."

"We've all heard the joke, Professor Strauss," Howell repeated, hoping to check the litany of the sins of his profession.

Strauss jabbed the contract at him. "Mr. Howell, wipe your ass with this."

In the jungle an unseen gibbon shrieked, and Svetlana Fedorova cringed. The assistant purser of the *Black Sea* was terrified. The Russian woman had never spoken to any of the terrorists, let alone the pirate chieftain, the one they called Tengku Haji Azhar, the cutthroat who had mutilated Vladimir's face.

Vladimir had tried to shield the American woman, this whore who was undoubtedly sleeping with both Vladimir and that scum of the earth. She had all the men fooled, but not Svetlana. She knew exactly what this American divorcee was up to — pretending now to be the learned professor, then the helpless, frail married lady — dressing up like an Oriental *houri* for her filthy affairs with that savage, then prancing up into Vladimir's cabin.

The Russian woman nervously tiptoed up

the ladder to the lounge, not to be secretive but fearful that her normally heavy, truculent step might be offensive to the Malays. She was trembling. She had no idea how the terrorist might react when she told him about the lying American woman. The terrorists had not really harmed anyone, except for the American Mrs. Schneider, who had been running around the ship half naked and brought that attack on herself.

Vladimir had not touched Svetlana since Singapore, when that skinny American bitch in heat Margaret Chancellor had come aboard. And that beautiful face of his — like a boy's — now mutilated and scarred for life because of that woman. Even Captain Khromykh — who treated Svetlana like one of the waiters instead of the ship's acting purser, a department head — even Captain Khromykh was all smiles, the courtly gentleman, sputtering his incomprehensible English for the pretty professor.

Svetlana had dressed for the audience with Tengku Haji Azhar in her uniform — a tailored jacket over a ruffled white blouse and a skirt — and her brief, nerve-racking passage along the open promenade and up the ladder in the humid late-afternoon heat had her perspiring, as much in fear as from exertion.

She froze at the top of the ladder. In the verandah a terrorist in a filthy T-shirt and shorts stood guard with an assault rifle at the door of the lounge. He stared at Svetlana, apparently as startled to see her as she was frightened by him.

Some of the terrorists spoke pidgin English, although not a word of Russian. "I want to talk to Tengku Haji Azhar. I am Svetlana Fedorova, the purser of the ship," she blurted out.

The guard stared at her completely uncomprehending, but made no menacing moves.

With the practiced sign language of years of visiting foreign ports, she tapped a finger on her bosom. "Russian ship officer," she identified, then touched fingertips to her lips, "talk," and pointed into the lounge, "Tengku Haji Azhar."

The guard smiled broadly in comprehension. "Ah, Russia," he pointed to her. "Talk with Tengku."

She nodded eagerly. "Yes!"

He motioned with the rifle, "Here wait," then pushed through the door into the lounge.

Svetlana could see the pirate chieftain seated in one of the upholstered lounge chairs. Only one other terrorist was with him, standing before him, as if making a report. Svetlana had carefully watched and waited for the moment when Tengku came aboard, and she knew that Margaret Chancellor was in the dining room two decks below. The terrorist now glanced up at the door, studied Svetlana with interest through the window, then said something to the guard. The scrutiny of those dark, hooded eyes unnerved the Russian woman.

The guard, hoisting his AK-47 assault rifle as though it were a symbol of office rather than a weapon, escorted her into the lounge. She had the impression that half the furniture had been removed, making the space more airy; there were Oriental carpets about the floor now, layered over the geometric wall-to-wall carpeting, giving the chamber a Byzantine atmosphere.

The guard halted her before the pirate chieftain, and she noted, with a stab of fear, the long sword leaning against his chair. He sprawled back in the seat, something languid, even sensual in his posture, and continued to examine her with an enigmatic half-smile. Svetlana felt her face flush and her legs tremble. "I get Mrs. Chancellor to translate," he said finally.

"No," Svetlana protested. "She lies to you. We talk English."

Tengku cocked his head and studied her.

There was no anger in his eyes, but a gleaming curiosity. He said something in Malay to the guard and the other terrorist, dismissing them with a wave of his hand. He continued to stare at her until the two had left the lounge, then politely motioned her to sit down. "Please. Tell me Professor Chancellor lies."

The smile surprised Svetlana. The full, almost pouting lips exposing even white teeth, smooth, unblemished tawny skin, and glossy black hair. The man's beauty disoriented her. There was a pause before she declared, "I am the ship's purser."

"Ah, yes, you now ship's purser."

Svetlana wondered for a moment why he had said "now." Did this terrorist know that there had been another purser, who had missed the ship's sailing? "I hold all the passengers' passports and their personal data forms in case of accident or a medical emergency . . . if they get sick."

Tengku was silent, expressionless, waiting for her to get to the point.

"Mrs. Chancellor . . . Professor Chancellor says she is a married woman, and she wears a wedding ring. But she is really divorced. You know what *divorced* means?"

"Yes. Her husband no more wants her. The man is a fool. Why you tell me this?"

Svetlana was acutely embarrassed. The terrorist, for some unfathomable reason, seemed amused. But she must make him believe her. "The Russian officer you . . . the one whose face was cut. He was my . . . boyfriend."

"Boyfriend?"

"Lover."

"Lover? Ah, the gallant. Officer with blond hair, you fuck." He clapped his hands.

Svetlana could not raise her eyes. She nodded, then admitted, "but he not touch me since Mrs. . . . . *Miss* Chancellor come aboard." She continued to stare down into the interwoven Byzantine festoons of the carpet.

"His face wounded. Make pain. Also, he is prisoner. Perhaps he cannot fuck," Tengku said in a gentle voice, as if apologizing for Vladimir.

"No," Svetlana looked up at him. "This Chancellor woman goes to his cabin. I saw them."

Tengku stared at her, his eyes darkly brooding as a thundercloud, then lightning flashed. "Why you come to me with woman's talk? This means nothing to me," he snapped.

"No, I have something more important to tell you. Her cousins are not her cousins. They all lie to you to get off ship, because they are important people."

"What important people?"

"If I tell you what is valuable, you must do something." She rushed on now heedless, frantic to get it all out before he threw her out. "You give freedom to Vladimir and me."

"Her cousins? Who?"

"She said that to protect them. The man is Alan Schneider. He was the Secretary of State of America, the Foreign Minister. He is almost important like the American President."

Tengku's eyes were wide with surprise. "Foreign Minister of America. Ah, such big fish we catch!"

Svetlana bobbed her head, "Yes."

"The wife?" he suddenly questioned.

"Yes, that is his wife. But she is not Professor Chancellor's sister or cousin. They are not family. She said that to use her . . . influence with you for Mrs. Schneider's freedom from ship. And now Mr. Alan Schneider, who was Secretary of State, important same like Russian Foreign Minister."

Tengku was in anguish; his dark eyes reflected betrayal.

"This is very valuable for you, yes? You tell no one I tell you this, please."

For a long while Tengku just sat and stared at Svetlana. She became terrified in the long silence, hardly daring to breathe. She had gone too far. Finally he asked, "What you want?"

She let out her breath. "I ask you give freedom to Vladimir, then me. Like normal prisoners. No one know we are next, yes?" She had thought carefully about the sequence. If she were to be released first, Vladimir and Captain Khromykh might suspect something. And Vladimir would be alone with the Chancellor woman for two more days. If he were released from this prison ship first, he would be indebted to Svetlana for the rest of his life.

"This is God's will. I am His servant," Tengku said at last.

Svetlana did not know what he was talking about.

Then the terrorist smiled at her, but it was a baring of the teeth that was devoid of friendliness or warmth. "For information, we give all you ask. We give blond hair freedom. We give you freedom. Yes."

The "yes" sounded like the hiss of a snake, but Svetlana smiled back and nodded vigorously.

38. The Old Fisherman

"The rocket launcher looks like it has Russian markings on it, sir."

Stewart was not surprised. "You sure they're Russian?" he asked over the radio.

"No, sir, I don't read Russian. That's what it looks like," Nguyen reported. "There were a couple of loose rockets rolling around. Maybe we got him when he was trying to get another shot off. We put them back in their case — the loose rockets, I mean — and the gunner got the de-arming pins back in. We hope they're the de-arming pins."

"Take the boat in tow and pull it back to the ship. Anything else?"

"Yes, sir, we found an M16. Also a marine radio and some clothes."

"A radio! Is it on?"

"Yes, sir, but nothing's coming over except noise right now."

"Leave it where it is and don't touch the setting," Stewart ordered. "Keep one man aboard to monitor the radio, got that?"

"Roger, sir."

"Okay, Tram, tow it on back and take your time. Don't lose anything, but keep your eyes peeled for any other small boats."

"Roger, sir."

"*Decatur* out." Stewart stood staring at his hand mike as if it were the puzzle. A Russian rocket launcher, an M16, a lone attacker on a native fishing boat. It didn't add up. But the open radio . . . that might be the break.

"Bridge, this is the XO." The intercom barked at Stewart.

"Go ahead, XO."

"There's a flareup in the engine room, Captain. We've got to go down in to fight it."

"Hit it with everything we've got." His ship was in flames again, and Stewart cursed the dead man on the *perahu*.

As soon as the boarding party had secured the fishing boat, Robinson had raced below to take control of the fire fighting. Now the lead man flung open the fire door and stepped cautiously into the boiling hot and airless engine room. "Number One Nozzle Man entering space," he shouted, his voice muffled and otherworldly hollow through the breathing apparatus. The cry was repeated by the man right behind him and echoed by each man along the length of the fire hose. The thick high-pressure hose squirmed and throbbed as if it were alive.

Heavy, suffocating clouds of Halon enveloped the engine room, making the visibility zero, but the flames and the thick, black, oily smoke roiling up from the bilges stood out against the white mist. The lead man planted his feet, gripped the brass nozzle with hands that were sheathed in fire-resistant gloves up to his elbow, and leaned back. High-pressure saltwater and foam blasted out into the smoke. The water hit hot metal and flashed into steam, thickening the white mist so that now even the smoke and flames were hidden.

"NIFTI! We need the NIFTI!" the lead man shouted, and again the cry was taken up along the length of the hose.

"I got it!" Robinson grabbed the Navy Infrared Firefighters Thermal Imager and struggled down the ladder past the line of hose handlers into the engine room. The smoke and steam were opaque. "Stay in physical contact with me," he ordered the lead man. Through the face shield of his helmet he could hardly see the man whose shoulder he had grabbed.

"Moving into the engine room with the NIFTI!" the lead man shouted. Robinson heard the cry repeated behind him. The infrared scope was sensitive to the temperature of objects; in its sight the warm body of the sailor next to Robinson, the shape of the machinery, and the catwalk through the engine room stood out distinctly. Cold areas were black, red-hot metal and flames were white.

The Halon was rapidly dissipating and the oxygen was being replenished probably through the hole or holes in the ship's side. The superheated metal had reignited the fuel flooding the bilges. The drill was to move blindly through the engine room and inundate everything that showed up white on the scope, cooling it and pouring a layer of foam over the aviation gas and fuel oil before the fire roared out of control. A white patch flared in his scope almost beneath Robinson's feet. "Down there!" he shouted.

"Where? I can't see fuckin' nuttin'."

He covered the lead man's hands with his own and aimed them toward the hot spot. "There!"

The blast of the fire hose caught Robinson on the leg, spun him, and almost knocked him down. He recovered and peered through the scope. The white patch beneath him rapidly shrank, then cooled to a gray mass. "Okay, got it. Keep moving."

There was a right angle in the catwalk where it hit the after bulkhead. "More hose!"

the lead man commanded, and the order was shouted down the line.

Robinson refocused through the scope. There was a bright white patch to his right. No sooner had he spotted it than it enlarged, flaring up until it washed out the entire picture. Robinson was suddenly engulfed in flames. The red sheet blinded him, and the searing heat enveloped his body. He screamed.

The blast of the water caught him in the small of the back, lifted him right off his feet, and drove him down the length of the catwalk, slamming him into a bank of pipes and pinning him against the steel. He tried to shout, but there was no breath in him to cry out. The high-pressure stream dropped down and swept his feet from under him. He was thrown to the catwalk, where the blast of water now shoved his head and shoulders off the narrow walk, almost sweeping him down into the flaming pool of oil below. The steel upright of the railing crushed into his gut. He blindly wrapped his arms around the bar. But the agony in his arms was overwhelmed by the brute force of the high-pressure hose. Slowly the pounding water hammered him off the walk, down toward the flames.

Suddenly it stopped. The stream poured into the bilges beneath him, beating back the flames, smothering them, until the red glow faded. He crawled back onto the catwalk, gasping to regain his breath.

"XO, you all right?" The water had cleared the thick smoke about him, and he could see the fire crew a few feet away, now shooting the water under the port turbine. He still couldn't speak, but he waved. He wondered if he had been burned, but under the fire-fighter's suit his flesh was numb from the pounding, and he could feel nothing.

He sat up and moaned aloud with pain. With the movement, suddenly *everything* hurt. He felt as though he had been kicked half to death by a mule team. The NIFTI was still hanging from the strap about his neck. He peered through it. Miraculously it was still working, and he saw a white hot spot to his left under the lube oil storage tank. "There!" he shouted and pointed.

Through the scope Robinson watched the cold black stream of water pour on and the hot spot fade to a cooler gray.

Robinson staggered onto the bridge. The XO was sopping wet and in obvious pain, practically collapsing with each step on his right leg.

"What the hell happened to you?" Stewart demanded.

"Admittedly I fucked up, Captain," Robinson said and shook his head. "In all the smoke I got separated from the hose team for a second and walked right into a flareup. If they hadn't hit me immediately with the hose, I would have been toasted."

"You all right?"

Robinson nodded. "The hose was worse than the fire. It's like getting hit by the entire Notre Dame line at once." He gave a rich, deep-throated laugh and shook his head.

The joking football image annoyed Stewart. What the hell was the executive officer doing down in the engine room leading the fire-fighting team? The men were drilled to work together. But Stewart had not been on the scene, and he would not question Robinson's decision. "Everything under control?"

"Yes, sir, at least for now. We're pumping out the bilges now and blowing out the smoke so that we can get an assessment of the damage. But even in the smoke I could see a hole in the port turbine housing big enough for a man to crawl in."

"Any other good news?" Stewart asked sourly.

"A lot of the fire was aft, around the main reduction gear. If it got hot enough, it might be warped."

"Jesus!"

"Captain, the motor whale boat is alongside with its prize," the officer of the deck reported.

Stewart broke off with Robinson, strode out to the port bridge wing, and peered down. From his perspective the deck and top of the cabin of the thirty-foot *perahu* was a tangle of coiled lines of hemp, fishnets, wicker baskets, wooden crates, jugs, and floats. There was hardly space to move, let alone work. The big fish locker took up most of the deck forward of the cabin, and the pile of nets and floats the deck aft. The sight, even the smell of it stirred in Stewart a poignant sense of déjà vu that the mangled corpse sprawled across the nets only reinforced. "Something doesn't add up. I'm going down there, Robbie."

"Aye, aye, sir," Robinson responded, somewhat surprised.

Stewart stepped back into the bridge. "Officer of the deck, secure from General Quarters but reset Condition Three. Take your orders from the XO. I'm going aboard the fishing boat. Have Chief Ross report to me there immediately."

"Yes, sir."

Stewart was down the ladder.

"Captain's departed the bridge!" the boatswain's mate of the watch bellowed behind him.

★ ★ ★

Nguyen was astonished to see the lanky figure of the captain suddenly scrambling down the hastily rigged ladder from the *Decatur* to the boat. "Attention on deck — "

Stewart immediately silenced him with a gesture. He jumped the last few steps onto the boat, then stood still, studying the face of the dead man sprawled at his feet. "How old do you think he is, Tram?"

"My age. A few years older."

Stewart nodded, knelt, and gently picked up the dead man's hand. He carefully examined it, running his fingertips over the lifeless palm and fingers, then looked back at Nguyen. "Well, he's not a fisherman, that's for sure, in spite of the costume." He rose. "Did you search him for any identification?"

"No, sir, we haven't touched him." Nguyen's stomach quaked at the thought of searching the body. "But there are some other clothes in the cabin."

"Let's take a look." Stewart had to bend almost double to step into the deckhouse. The small marine radio immediately grabbed his attention.

"There've been no transmissions, sir."

There was a wristwatch lying alongside the radio. Stewart picked it up and peered at it. "Seiko," he pronounced. "Someone is probably scheduled to either call in or out."

Nguyen said nothing. The captain turned to the clothes that were neatly folded and stacked on the helmsman's chair. There was a pair of white Adidas running shoes, a cotton polo shirt, and pair of blue jeans. He held up the jeans. "Were these his real clothes or another costume for another operation?"

"It's what a guy his age from a big city like Singapore might wear."

Stewart nodded and went through the pockets. He pulled out a plastic comb and three separate wads of bills — Indonesian rupees and Singapore and Malaysian dollars — that converted to hundreds of American dollars. "But no I.D.," Stewart noted. "This guy traveled fast and light."

Nguyen shrugged. "If you're caught with any guns in this part of the world, it's a death sentence."

"Captain." Chief Ross crouched in sweat-soaked khakis by the opening.

"Chief Ross, good." Stewart pointed to the marine radio. "What's its range?"

The chief electronics technician picked up and examined the radio. "It's a standard VHF. The range is line of sight, about thirty miles, less without any antenna. It depends on the atmospherics. The ducting here in the tropics would increase the range, but it's hit or miss."

"What could you rely on?"

"Probably no more than twenty-five miles, unless they ran an antenna up the mast."

Stewart nodded. "Whatever frequency that radio's on, can we put a direction finder on it?"

Ross shook his head. "No, sir, we just don't have that kind of equipment on board. The SLQ-32 in Combat is for homing in on ultrahigh-frequency radar in the thousand-megahertz-and-above range. This VHF radio's in the 80-to-200 band."

"Can't you jury-rig something, like an old loop antenna? It doesn't have to be very accurate."

"We'd have to build it from scratch."

"We don't have time for that."

Ross stood, thinking hard, his eyes squinting up at the *Decatur,* searching through the thicket of EW, radio, and Tacan antennas, fire-control directors, and radar sensors. They swept to the fantail, then suddenly widened. "The fucking chopper."

"What?"

"Maybe we could rig something with their radio navigation gear. I'll have to check it out with their avionics."

"Do it. We'll need it fast. Something may break at any moment. Run a tape on it so that we record messages, times, and directions, if you can get it."

"Yes, sir, can I take the radio? It'll be quicker."

"Yes, but don't mess up the frequency. And don't broadcast on it. Just key the mike to check it out."

"Aye, aye, sir." Ross left, carrying the small marine portable as though it were a carton of eggs.

"It's a long shot," Stewart admitted to Nguyen. "They won't call him. He's supposed to call them at a scheduled time, but maybe they'll fuck up."

"Who are *they*, sir?"

Stewart twisted his head and glared at Nguyen. "I wish to hell I knew. But they sure as shooting have a ring in my nose and are yanking it." He started to stand up, banged his head on the low wooden overhead, and cursed softly. He stood bent forward almost double, rubbing the top of his head, then something outside caught his attention, and he stared through the forward window. "Tram, did you search the fish locker?"

"What, sir?"

"The hold there where they store the fish."

Nguyen followed the direction of Stewart's pointing finger. There was a raised section of the forward deck with a coil of line covering it. From this angle it looked as if a very large wooden chest had been recessed into the deck, and under the lines he now saw the hinged lid. In the excitement and tension of boarding the fishing boat, he had missed it. "No, sir. I'll do it now." The young Vietnamese felt his face flush with shame.

He started to bolt from the deckhouse, but Stewart grabbed his arm and moved outside with him. "Have two men cover you, ready to shoot if there's any sign of a weapon. Get the rest off the boat," he said in a low voice.

The captain climbed off the fishing boat, but then Nguyen saw him take an M14 and position himself on the rail directly over the locker. With hand signals he motioned the two shooters onto either side of the deckhouse, then indicated with a nod that Nguyen was to move in. He was grateful that the captain was allowing him to redeem himself.

Now that Nguyen studied the fish locker, he realized that it was big enough to hide a man, and with a sixth sense he was certain one was in there. He must have been in that airless box most of the day in the tropical sun, half crazed with heat and fear.

Nguyen's heart was in his mouth, but he stepped forward and banged on the lid with the butt of his 9-mm. *"Man in fish box come out. Give you water, food, money, bananas, chocolate ice cream. No come out. Shoot. Shoot."*

"I don't think he understands your Vietnamese, Tram," Stewart called with a note of impatience in his voice.

"That's my pidgin Malay, sir. I'm offering him food, water, and money if he comes out. Shoot him, if he doesn't."

"Your resources never cease to amaze me, Mr. Nguyen. Repeat your generous offer, then fire your gun near the box to let him know you're serious."

When there was no reply, Nguyen placed the butt of his 9-mm. on the lid and fired a shot off into the sea. There was a muffled cry from inside the locker, and the lid lifted up an inch or two, then dropped.

"Get away!" Stewart shouted in alarm.

Nguyen dropped into a firing crouch and pointed his automatic with both hands at the locker. The lid banged up and down again, as if whoever was inside was not strong enough to lift it. Then the lid came up slowly, agonizingly, and a pair of gnarled and scarred old hands came into view. "No shoot. No shoot," a voice croaked.

Terrified eyes, a weathered, deeply creased face rose up with a painstaking slowness and fearfulness out of the hold, as though at any instant the old man expected to be struck dead. The lid fell back onto the deck, and the old man, who was stark naked, kept his hands above his head in a gesture that was both a surrender and a beseeching.

39. Suliman Is Interrogated

Suliman, the Iranian carpet dealer from Arab Street, was slow to regain consciousness. He found himself strapped to a chair in a darkened, windowless room.

A young, bespectacled Chinese man in a white coat stepped into his field of vision and said, "I am Dr. Chen. How are you feeling?"

Suliman muttered that his head and neck hurt.

Chen nodded solicitously, then asked him his name and his business address.

"Why, you want to buy a carpet?"

The Chinese doctor did not respond. He peered into each eye with a small pen light, momentarily blinding the Iranian, listened to his heart, and took his blood pressure.

Suliman was badly frightened. That he was

manacled in some basement cell with a man in a white coat examining him was more terrifying than if there had been a couple of cops with bamboo canes to beat him.

"I'm going to give you something to ease the neck pain and headache," the doctor said.

Suliman barely felt the prick of the needle.

"Please count back from ten," the doctor requested.

Between "six" and "five" Suliman felt himself enveloped in dark, fleecy clouds, as though he were floating weightless in a starless sky. He drifted for a while. Then a foul, rotting odor assaulted him — a putrid, garbagy stench that made his heart tremble with memories — and he saw once again the corpses swelling up in the sun in the minefield outside Basra. Vultures circling overhead in the black clouds now swooped down to feed.

"Suliman."

Someone called his name. His eyes opened, and he saw disembodied faces peering at him out of the blackness. A woman and several men. They called out his name, yet he did not recognize them. No, as his eyes adjusted to the apparition, the dark-haired man directly in front of him became familiar, Iranian perhaps. It was . . . the purser from the *Black Sea*. The amber eyes that stared at Suliman were sightless, those of a dead man.

"*Suliman.*"

Suliman twisted violently in his chair, but his bonds held him fast. He peered at the other frightful faces surrounding him, each glaring accusingly at him. They, too, were all dead.

Suliman moaned in terror, and as he stared back at the ghastly bloodless faces, he perceived that it was only their heads, on butchered stumps, that pressed in about him, calling out his name, damning him.

"*Suliman.*"

He screamed and heaved at his straps, as unable to move an arm or leg as if he were paralyzed, and screamed again and again.

A true believer expects to die and awake in Paradise, and instead he opens his eyes in hell, surrounded by the screaming, stinking heads of the murdered. What physical torture exceeded that?

To Salleh bin Ali, the stench of the rotting pig offal from Ballinger's experiment had been sickening in itself. To the fanatic Iranian — his senses deranged by drugs — it had been the reeking corpses of the damned come to drag him into the bowels of hell. Suliman had shit and pissed in his pants in terror.

Salleh had to work fast before the sodium pentothal and hallucinogens wore off. It took four policemen to drag the cowering and whimpering Iranian from the cell, up a flight of stairs, and into the brightly lit interrogation room. "We will kick you back down into hell and let you rot there in your own shit if you lie to me," Salleh said in a low, firm voice, as though this were a routine procedure.

Suliman was trembling and drenched in sweat. At Salleh's orders his bonds had been removed.

"Do you understand?"

The Iranian nodded dully, but the black eyes glaring up at Salleh were wide and frantic with fear. Salleh had second thoughts about his own insistence that they be left alone. Police guards were right outside the door, but this huge, crazed assassin could snap his neck like a twig if he went berserk.

Salleh began slowly, as if he were continuing the conversation in Suliman's carpet shop. "When did you see Tengku Haji Azhar last?"

The dark, bearded head wagged back and forth like a dumb, brute animal trying to shake a halter. "I don't know what day it is." His voice was slow and sluggish with the drugs, despite the fear that galvanized his body. "It was the night they killed the purser."

"Who was with Tengku?"

"Ahmed and Mohammed."

"Who is Ahmed?"

"His cousin."

"Tell me about Ahmed."

"He is Tengku's cousin. He was not in Iran with Tengku and Mohammed, but he made all the arrangements for the weapons."

There were two sharp raps on the mirror behind Salleh. On the other side of the one-way window, Yee and other security agents were recording the interrogation.

"How many weapons did you smuggle to them?"

"There were two American Stingers, one Russian antitank rocket, an RPG-7, a total of eighteen AKA-47's and M16's, and three .45-caliber pistols."

Salleh was surprised at the exactness with which the rug merchant itemized the tally.

"Did Iran give the guns to them?"

"No, this was an honest business transaction."

"How did they pay?"

"In cash."

"Where did they get the money?"

"They are pirates. They had a *fatwa* to

steal money to buy guns for the holy war. Tengku Haji Azhar was very strict about this." A *fatwa* was an Islamic religious ruling, in this case from a conveniently militant *mullah*. "It is not a sin to rob infidels to finance a holy war," Suliman insisted, as if anxious to limit the sins of which he was truly guilty and clear his soul.

Salleh nodded, as though agreeing with him, but he felt a flush of shame at this perversion of the Faith. "Did they want more guns?"

"Yes, but I could not smuggle them. It is too dangerous now."

"What did they do?"

"They hijacked a ship to ransom the passengers for more guns."

"What ship?"

"The *Black Sea*."

"Did you help them?"

"I told them about the *Black Sea*."

"Where is the *Black Sea*."

"I don't know. They don't trust me. They treat me like a shopkeeper, not their brother. I was their teacher in Iran. I taught them what I had learned with my blood and my brothers' blood, and they treat me like a shopkeeper." Even in its drugged languor Suliman's voice was grieved and outraged.

"Who did you teach?"

"Tengku and Mohammed."

"When?"

Suliman's forehead screwed up, as if he were having difficulty separating past from present.

"What year?"

"Nineteen eighty-one."

"What about Ahmed?"

"He was not in Iran. He has never been out of Malaysia. And he trusts no one."

"Who gives the orders?"

"The *haji*."

"Where is he now?"

"I don't know. They don't trust me," Suliman said in the same aggrieved voice.

Salleh went back over the story again and again, each time extracting a new detail here, another there, until the drugs wore off, and Suliman fainted away into nightmares that made him whimper and the thick, powerful limbs twitch.

40. The Seduction of Maggi Chancellor

The nightjars circled overhead above the *Black Sea,* devouring the clouds of insects in midflight, and their plaintive mewing quavered in the air. The shriek of flying foxes, the nocturnal burr and croak of tree frogs clinging to the jungle canopy, and the pulsating buzz of the ground crickets all echoed through the hushed, haunted corridors of the ship.

Occasionally a guard with an AK-47 haphazardly slung over his shoulder wandered through the passageways, but most simply dozed through the night on deck chairs by the pool or on the promenade deck. It was several hours after sundown, and the curfew imposed on the passengers and crew by the pirates shrouded the ship in darkness and sinister sounds.

The rapping on Maggi's door was discreet, the knock of someone who did not want to be overheard by her neighbors. Maggi was not expecting anyone at that hour and wore only a light robe. She tiptoed to the door reluctantly, expecting to find a sweating, anxious passenger with a petition, bribe, or elaborate subterfuge to advance his or her name to the top of the list of those to be released.

She was astonished to see Tengku standing at her door. She rarely saw him below the Lido deck, and then only with his guards and pirate courtiers strolling about the ship like a Malay *tunku* inspecting his estates. He had never been to her cabin before, but he was apparently alone.

He quickly moved past her into the room. "Please shut the door," he said firmly in Malay. He gazed haughtily about the cabin. "This is very small," he declared. "No bigger than a whore's crib. You should have a bigger cabin." The dark, sensual eyes finally settled on her face, and she had the impression of something smoldering. The danger about him almost vibrated, a static electricity in the air that might, at any moment, leap a gap, spark, and explode.

"You have lied to me." His hand suddenly snapped out, seized her left wrist, and raised her fingers to eye level. Maggi was paralyzed by his quickness and power. With his other hand he snapped a fingernail against her wedding ring, the one that Liz Schneider had given her. "You are not the *memsahib* Chancellor. You are a divorced woman. Mr. Alan Schneider is not the husband of your cousin, or a very sick professor. He is the Foreign

Minister of the United States — a very important man," he said in a rush. "All these things are lies that you have told me, and I believed you. This is a terrible thing you have done."

His black eyes were so fiercely intent upon her that Maggi was terrified, and her immediate impulse was to deny everything. "Who told you all this?"

He dropped her hand, as if the pain of her betrayal had overcome him. "A terrible thing," he muttered in a whisper. "I had my guards beaten with bamboo because you told me that they had offended your sister."

Maggi was bewildered by the hurt and reproach she saw in his face. There was now no anger or threat in the dark, liquid eyes, only the anguish of her betrayal. She was touched by it. "No . . . I mean I'm sorry. I didn't want to lie to you. I had to protect Alan Schneider. We were all afraid . . . afraid — even the Russians thought so — that you might abuse . . . harm him, maybe, if you knew who he was," she pleaded.

"No, no, we would never do that. His great value to us is to keep him alive and healthy. Damaged goods have less value in trade," he said matter-of-factly.

Tengku brooded over her explanation for

a moment. "And Mr. Alan Schneider's wife, we would never . . ." He shook his head. "Perhaps this is God's will. It shows the Americans that we are very serious men — men to be treated with respect."

"Yes," Maggi agreed readily, but she bit her lip and restrained herself from asking what had happened to Liz.

Tengku stood in front of her and looked directly into her eyes. The only light was the filmy shaded lamp by the bed, and the room itself was, in fact, so small that it was almost impossible to stand in it without touching another person in the room. She could smell Tengku's body, and it gave off the fertile, earthy fragrance of the river water in which he bathed, Malay style, morning and evening.

"Why did you lie to me about your husband?" he asked in a soft, reproachful voice.

"I had to have your respect. You are a devout Muslim. A man of God. According to your faith, a divorced woman is little more than a whore." Maggi stood up straight, eye to eye with him. There was no point anymore in playing the respectful, virtuous, pseudo-Malay woman. "Even now you march into my cabin, look around, and insult me. 'This is no bigger than a whore's crib,' you say." Her voice gathered strength and authority. "But in my country it is different. I am a respected university professor. I earn my own living. My husband did not divorce me. I divorced him, when I found he was unfaithful to me."

"If your husband slept with another woman, and he lost you because of this, then he was a fool," Tengku declared passionately. "To have such a treasure and throw it away . . . ," he whispered, and did not finish.

Maggi was surprised by the emotion in his speech. But he was totally sincere. The pirate was an absolute romantic, she realized. His delusions of princely grandeur were nothing if not a romance; even the cruelty she had witnessed when he had cut Vladimir with his sword had been, however perverse, a romantic gesture. Only an obsessed romantic could conceive and instigate a revolution. And now he gazed at her with adoring eyes, accepting all her explanations of betrayal. It seemed he wasn't even breathing.

Tengku suddenly seized her hand and kissed her palm. He drew her to him, and she could not resist. The power in his hands was inexorable. He did not kiss her, not at first, but stared at her, fingered her long, unbraided hair, the skin of her cheek and neck with an awed, childlike sense of wonder that aroused Maggi. There was the faintly sweet, spicy smell of curry on his breath. He kissed her, lightly at first, as though tasting something unfamiliar, her lips, cheek, and neck, and then with a fiercer probing passion. Maggi felt weak in her knees.

He suddenly bent down, lifted her off her feet with a seemingly effortless sweep, and, like an ardent bridegroom, carried her off in his arms to the bed. Maggi was flat on her back on the mattress before she even entertained the first thought of resistance, and his mouth smothered any words of protest. "No, please stop," she finally muttered, but it came out in English.

He rose up and stared at her. Maggi felt his wild heat. It raged in his dark face and eyes, in the vein at his temple, about to explode, and the seething of it cowed and intimidated her. All her resistance melted.

He ripped open her robe and kissed her exposed white breasts as though they were a revelation. Then he seized her panties in both hands and fiercely yanked them off, as if the tearing itself were an act of passion.

His own skin was brown, smooth, and hairless as an adolescent boy's, his body slender and wiry, and the feel of it first intrigued, then excited her. His skin seared hers, inflamed hers with its heat. In her emotional chaos Maggi did not know how to react; she had a wild impulse to explore his lithe, brown body with her fingers, her mouth, to taste her lover's skin, but a thousand and one hesitations, cautions, inhibitions now stopped her.

She shyly traced the arch of his jaw with a fingertip and stared up into the moist, wild eyes. His flesh was so taut, she half expected his skin to burst, and he pressed her body into the yielding mattress. His lips, tongue were on her shoulders, the insides of her elbows, her breasts, his mouth closed about her nipples, his warm hands caressed her belly, her thighs, a gentle finger between her legs. There was no question she was warm, wet, ready — unfolding to him, totally vulnerable — and when he entered her, her body betrayed her thousand and one cautions, and she arched up against him, crooning, now suddenly forgetting everything, burying her face in his chest, her eyes closed, breath ragged.

Her hips moved with a will of their own, and her lips over his chest. She seized the thick black hair, inhaling the sweet, rank, spicy smell that was as palpable as the feverish heat that rose from his flesh, now gleaming with sweat. His breath came in gasps and whimpers, increasingly hurried, louder, until she became conscious of her own crooning deep in her throat, and she turned and pressed her mouth against his forearm braced next to her, baring her teeth against his wrist to stifle the cry at that last excruciating moment — her most intimate, vulnerable revelation — as his own cries burst out, and he shuddered.

He lay on her, breathing heavily, stroking her hair in an absent way, as though it were a reflex rather than a gesture of affection. He seemed defenseless, innocent, his dark eyes at once shiny and dazed. Maggi felt she was floating, languid, and somehow — for the moment at least — protected.

After a while he stood and dressed silently. Maggi did not look at him. "You have enchanted me," his voice came to her. It was an accusation, not a compliment, as if the seduction had been entirely her doing. There was a note of contrition in his voice.

She now turned her head to stare up at him. His wild eyes were glazed over, his smile now sheepish. She looked away again, and she did not hear his bare footsteps on the carpet, but his voice came from farther away, by the door. "Tomorrow I will 'release' the pretty, 'gallant' Russian officer with the yellow hair." He said both "release" and "gallant" in English.

"Why?" she asked.

Tengku watched her closely with hooded eyes, as if expecting a further reaction. "It is his time."

Then the cabin door opened and slammed shut, and he was gone.

41. The Hour of Darkness

After sunset, in the rapidly fading twilight, the sky was a deep violet, almost black. Then the darkness came down swiftly, as it does on the equator, enveloping the *Decatur*.

Stewart stared off into the night, absolutely enraged with frustration, then turned back to Chief Ross and Lieutenant Callahan. "I don't believe it. A half-billion dollars' worth of electronics and computers on this ship and the chopper, and we can't home in on a goddamn native fisherman's marine radio."

"That's just the point, sir. All our electronic surveillance gear is designed to hunt down and intercept high-tech Russian subs and missiles that work the ultrahigh frequencies, not a fisherman in the VHF band," the chief electronics technician explained.

"Jesus!" The irony of the situation would

591

be laughable if there were not so many lives at stake.

Callahan shrugged, "The only things that even operate at those frequencies are the disposable transmitters in our sonobuoys."

He and Chief Ross looked sharply at each other, as the same idea occurred to them in the same instant. "We'd have to reprogram the buoy locater, so that it thinks it's looking for a buoy on that frequency," the pilot explained.

"But will it pick up the signal if the chopper's tied down on the fantail?"

"It has an antenna system ten times that of the fisherman's radio." He turned back to Stewart. "It's worth a shot."

"Get to it!" Stewart ordered.

"Bridge, Central." It was the engineer officer, Marty Mitchell, calling on the intercom box.

"Give me some good news, Marty."

There was a long, foreboding pause, then, "Well, sir, the starboard engine looks undamaged. It doesn't appear that the fire affected it much. That's pretty much the good news."

"And now the bad news."

"The port engine is wiped out. We've taken it off the line." There was another ominous hesitation. "The rest we won't know until we start up. There was a lot of fire under the main reduction gear. The heat and sudden cooling might have warped it, or warped the shaft."

"Let me know as soon as you're ready to test it."

"We're ready now, Captain."

"Is the XO there?"

"Yes, sir."

"Tell him to get the hell off that leg before he permanently cripples himself."

"Captain, I've played Army on worse knees than this," Robinson's bass boomed over the speaker, but even Stewart heard the wince of pain in it.

The game's over, Robbie, Stewart thought. "Okay, let's light off," he ordered.

The accelerating whirl of the 25,000-horsepower turbine four decks below vibrated through the ship like the stirring of a monstrous creature. "Starboard engine at operating speed, sir," reported the operator seated at the ship's control console on the bridge.

"Central, Bridge. What does it look like down there?"

After a prolonged delay, Mitchell reported, "All the engine gauges are within normal operating range, sir."

"Very well." Stewart turned to the enlisted man seated before the control panel. "Now,

Johnson, very slowly bring it ahead one-third."

"Starboard engine ahead one-third, sir," he responded crisply.

"Very slowly!"

"Very slowly, aye, sir."

Stewart felt the tremor almost immediately, then the stronger vibration that went through the ship like a muscle spasm and grew more intense until the deck beneath was shaking like a freight train running on one square wheel.

"Starboard engine stop!" Stewart shouted over the noise.

"Starboard engine stopped, sir."

The *Decatur* was dead in the water.

Stewart bent over the intercom, "How did it feel down there?"

"A nine-point-oh on the Richter scale. The ship was shaking itself apart, Captain."

Stewart was silent. One fanatic with an RPG had crippled his ship. "We're out of it, gentlemen," he said in a soft, sad voice. "We have to creep back to Singapore on the auxiliaries."

"Yes, sir," Mitchell agreed, and the grief in his voice transcended the tinny speaker.

"XO?"

"Yes, Captain, I concur. There are no other options."

"Engineer, have ops prepare an operational readiness report for CincPacFleet. And XO, can you make it up to sick bay?"

"Doc's got his hands full with Novak and a few burn cases, Captain."

"Then I'll strap your leg personally."

The fisherman they had found hiding in the fish locker was being held in an after storage compartment. Nguyen and Chief Master-at-Arms Livingston, a Samoan built like a beer barrel, were with him.

"I haven't been able to get too much out of him, sir," Nguyen explained. "He doesn't speak any English, and my Bahasa is rusty, beach-survival Malay from when I was nine years old."

The fisherman was now wearing a T-shirt and a pair of khaki pants that almost fit him; judging from his diminutive size, Stewart judged that the trousers must have been Nguyen's own. The fisherman stared back and forth between Stewart and the Vietnamese officer with wide, frightened eyes. Stewart noted the gravy-puddled plate with a few grains of leftover rice, a water glass, and a coffee cup. Nguyen had been smart enough to feed the prisoner first and make sure he wasn't dehydrated.

"He doesn't understand our charts," Nguyen pointed to an open chart spread over one of the workbenches, "or at least pretends not to. As close as I can make out, they came aboard his boat somewhere between — "

"They?"

"There were three, and they threatened him with guns. I got this with a lot of finger counting and sign language."

"What happened to the others?"

"The other two went off in a speedboat and left the dead guy with a rifle pointing at the fisherman's head." As if he were simultaneously interpreting for the deaf, Nguyen held up two fingers, then his palm planed an unseen sea like a boat taking off, and he pointed a pistol finger at the fisherman's head.

The fisherman nodded vigorously, endorsing this mime show of events.

"This all happened in the islands to the northeast, *pulau* something-or-other, but I can't make out the name the way he says it."

"I thought he couldn't read the charts."

"No, sir, he doesn't. But I pointed to where the sun rises and sets, and we worked that out."

"*Very* good."

The fisherman's frightened, despairing eyes

darted from his Vietnamese interpreter up to the giant commanding officer to the awesome master-at-arms. Stewart had seen that terrified look before, a destitute fisherman caught between deadly forces, totally helpless, and used remorselessly by both sides.

In the close quarters of the after compartment they all oozed a rank, sour, unwashed smell. Like everyone else aboard, Livingston was filthy, sweat-soaked, and unshaven, but the beer-barrely chief looked particularly malevolent with a wiry black bristle covering his jaws, cheeks, and neck and a holstered 9-mm. on his hip.

"I think you and I are scaring this little fellow," Stewart said to Livingston.

"The Chief scares me," Nguyen said with a sly grin.

"Anything else?"

"No, sir. I think we've gotten what we can get out of him, at least for the time being. He's too frightened and disoriented. I think we might let him get some rest. Just put down a mattress here. And then I'll bring him some more food and coffee in a few hours, maybe some chocolate ice cream, take him to the head, be his friend. But I think you're right, sir. It would be less intimidating if Chief Livingston stood outside."

"The islands just to the northeast of us, huh?" Stewart asked.

"Yes, sir."

Engineman second class Washington, a hulking dark figure, sat on the deck outside sick bay, back against the bulkhead, shoulders hunched in a posture of dejection. Both his hands were swathed in white gauze bandages like a mummy's.

"How serious is it? You going to be okay?" Stewart asked with concern.

Washington had not seen the captain approach and now jumped to his feet to attention. Given the startled speed and agility of the move, apparently he had not been badly hurt. "Yessir, I just burn some skin. I be okay."

"Good," Stewart nodded.

The big, dark head craned forward anxiously. "You find out about Novak, sir?"

"I'll let you know how he is." Washington looked as if he had lost his best friend. Stewart was somewhat surprised, since he had not known the two were at all buddies.

"How's Novak doing?" Stewart asked, after he had entered sick bay and shut the door behind him.

"Bad concussion, loss of blood, burns from the deck plating that look like he was grilled on a waffle iron, some smoke inhalation," Doc Blowitz checked off. "But all his vital signs are strong. We've removed the shrapnel and stopped the bleeding."

"Do you want to med-evac him by helicopter?"

Blowitz shook his head. "Not with that concussion. I'd rather he stay quiet, at least tonight. I've already checked with the flight surgeons aboard the carrier heading here, and that's what they recommend. When will we be in Singapore, sir?"

"On our auxiliaries, at three, four knots, we'll be there tomorrow night, if we're lucky."

Robinson was sitting on the examination table, his trousers off and his legs stretched out in front of him. The thickly muscled thighs looked like fleshy fire plugs and the calves like hams. His right knee was encased in an ice pack.

"What about the XO? Are we going to have to shoot him?"

"No, sir, nothing's broken, but he's benched for a couple of Saturdays."

What was it about Robinson that made everyone suddenly talk like a play-by-play announcer? Even to Stewart's eye the knee looked painfully inflamed and swollen. It looked as if any movement at all would be agonizing. Stewart had read of football players' ability to perform with pain, but it was inconceivable to him that Robinson had climbed from the engine room to the bridge, back down to main control, and then back up to the sick bay with that knee.

"All things considered, Captain, I'm in better shape than the ship right now. I can hop around pretty good on one leg, but this ship can only creep like it's on hands and knees," Robinson said sorrowfully. He almost seemed to be reading Stewart's mind.

"What the hell were you doing down there in front of the fire crew?"

"I was engineer officer on my last ship. I knew the drill. Who would you have me delegate the job to?"

For the first time since he had been aboard ship, Stewart put his hand on the man's shoulder and squeezed the thick, hard muscle there. "Well, you knocked down the fire and saved the ship."

"No, it was the fire fighters."

Stewart was silent a moment. "And you were right about putting the ship in harm's way. One fanatic with an RPG . . ."

"Now we know they're really out there, or they would never have risked it. Tomorrow the fleet will be here on station, blanketing the area. They'll find them."

"It's nice to think so."

Washington was still sulking in the passageway when Stewart left sick bay. "Novak's going to be all right." He gave the sailor all the details Blowitz had given him, although he wasn't sure Washington was absorbing them.

The sailor bobbed his head with a hangdog expression. "I really fucked up this time, Captain, I know it."

"Fucked up?" Stewart was confused.

"I shoulda reported the fire right away, but I stopped to collect Novak first. Then I couldn't even get him outta the space. He's too heavy for me. I tried to put my mask on him, and I got that ass-backwards. Then I panicked and jerked off all the fire suppressant so there ain't no reserve to put out the fire. I fucked it all up at every step." The confession came out in one long rush. Washington raised his head, and his sorrowful eyes looked anxiously into Stewart's. "What's gonna happen to me now, Captain?"

Stewart listened to this admission with astonishment and all but laughed, but he said solemnly, "I know you'll get a medal. I'll recommend that. I can't guarantee Detroit will have a parade in your honor, but it's a good bet you'll at least have your picture

601

in the hometown paper and be on TV."

Washington blinked and regarded him warily.

"If you hadn't pulled Novak out when you did and got him on the other side of the fire door, he'd have been barbecued meat by the time the fire team got down there. He'd already inhaled a lot of smoke, and I don't think his lungs really cared that the hood was on backwards so long as they got pure oxygen when they did. If you hadn't released the reserve, the fire might not have gone out that first time, because the Halon was leaking fast out the holes the rocket made. That gave our fire team time to get their act together before it flared again. In short, you definitely saved Novak's life and helped save the ship. You're a hero, a big hero." He gently touched the bandaged hands. "A wounded hero at that."

"Yeah?" Washington asked in wonder.

"You've got a great future in the navy. The pick of your next duty."

"I can't even do no arithmetic for my First Class exam."

"I'll get Ensign Glover to personally tutor you. He's an MIT graduate."

"Yeah?"

"You married?"

"No, sir."

"Don't take the bandages off too soon. Women will wait on you hand and foot. After you're on TV, you'll probably get laid a lot."

"*Oh yeah!*"

He left Washington standing outside sick bay, staring at his bandaged hands with a whole new vision of life. Stewart knew how the navy operated. Both Washington and Robinson would undoubtedly be decorated as heroes, but the captain of the *Decatur* would be court-martialed.

42. The Cache in the Carpets

Salleh Bin Ali was lost, completely disoriented. At the sprawling docks to the south, cloud-scraping cranes worked through the night under blazing lights loading and unloading boxcar-sized containers from the ships in the harbor.

The *kampong* where Salleh was born had once stood here — clapboard shacks on piles along a palm-fringed estuary of the South China Sea. It had been drained and filled in, and now a thousand shipyards, crude rubber plants, and electronics factories congested the Jurong area.

A sulfurous stench hung in the humid night air, the belchings of the adjacent petroleum refinery, and it sickened Salleh. He stood very still, shut his eyes, and tried to sense where in this sprawl of factories, warehouses, and spewing smokestacks his *kampong* had once stood, hovering above the tide. He expected the ghost of his father — his father as he had been as a young man, bare-chested and leanly muscled in a bright batik sarong — to emerge from the mists and lead him to the spot where he had been born.

But his father's ghost did not appear, as if in death, as in life, he were overwhelmed by this holocaust of progress, and his soul had wandered away, lost and now forever homeless.

Sergeant Salleh checked on the policemen searching the outside grounds, then he stepped back into the small warehouse. Bins of rolled carpets, identical to those in Suliman's storeroom, crammed the building. A squad of policemen unstacked the rugs, searching, and two technicians scraped at the stained floor in a narrow aisle and meticulously placed the scrapings in plastic specimen envelopes. Yee and the CIA agent Blocker stood talking in a small office area containing a cheap metal desk and file cabinet.

They needed the Americans now.

Blocker turned to Salleh and said in honest admiration, "I was just telling Mr. Yee, that's one hell of a piece of undercover work you did."

As in the shop on Arab Street strips of paper identified the origins of the rugs. Salleh fingered an unevenly patterned Afghani tribal that had helped finance a revolution. "The RPG rocket and the Russian rifles were smuggled out of Afghanistan to Peshawar wrapped in carpets, the Stingers in Persians from the Iranian port of Abadan, then to Dubai."

The American stood with his shoulders hunched and head bowed in discouragement, then he said in a weary, disillusioned voice, "I damned near died of dysentery in those camps on the Northwest Frontier. Hot, dusty, the wind would choke a camel, and I thought I was a character out of a Kipling novel, playing the Grand Game. Crowbarring open crates of arms for the freedom fighters.

"The Stingers we originally gave to the *mujahedeen* to fight the Russians have already popped up in Iranian boats, pointing at our own planes in the Persian Gulf. And then they showed up on parade in Qatar, which bought them from the Iranians. And now *here*, where they shot down one of our helicopters." The big man looked chagrined.

After a long silence Blocker asked, "Who killed the Russian purser?"

"The pirates. The Iranian brought him here. Suliman told the purser he was going to give him an expensive rug for all the business of the wealthy American passengers the purser would steer to him. Ahmed, Mohammed, and this Tengku pretended to be warehouse workers. But the purser became suspicious about all the questions about the ship, the passengers, the departure time, and route. The pirates got the information they wanted by poking him with their knives." Salleh indicated the large rust-colored stains on the floor where the technicians were scraping samples. "Then they stabbed him. They told Suliman they would sink the body in the sea, and the Iranian left. He did not know about the heads. But he knew they were going to swap the hostages for arms. He was to get a cut of the arms to trade for cash. That was to be his part in the operation."

"It's all so straightforward, it's almost banal," Blocker said.

"Yes, the best plans are always the simplest."

Blocker was thoughtful. "All in all, they still haven't yet put together enough weapons for a revolution," he said finally. "Just enough to create a really ugly situation, if they have any military know-how at all."

"The rug merchant was in the Revolutionary Guard in Iran. He was this Tengku's and Mohammed's instructor in a commando school in Tehran."

"Ho, boy, it's scary how this all fits together. The think tankers in Santa Monica and Virginia are going to love it."

"Please, tell *me* how it all fits together," Yee prodded.

"It goes back to '79, when they overthrew the Shah in Iran and held the American embassy hostage for a year. It became a religious crusade to take over the world. The Revolutionary Guard set up what we called the Taleghani Center in downtown Tehran, as the headquarters for the, quote, Council for the Islamic Revolution. According to our intelligence, they had a war chest of a billion dollars annually — contributions from the faithful and a fat allocation from the government of Iran. They included groups from North Africa, the Middle East, this area; even the Moro Liberation Front of the Philippines had an office there. They recruited heavily, providing false visas, passports."

"The Singaporeans, the Malays, you have their names?"

Blocker shook his head. "All we know is

that in 1980 and '81, thousands of students all over the Muslim world heard the call; they dropped their books and headed for Tehran. Radicals, starving farm boys for whom any change was a step up, orthodox Muslims. They were smuggled across the Persian Gulf in *dhows* or drove over the mountain roads from Turkey or Pakistan. Idealistic students just jetted in. The traffic at Mehrabad Airport in Tehran was so heavy at one point the Revolutionary Guard set up a full-time office there to process the volunteers to training camps."

Salleh, of course, knew of this revolutionary hegira; he and counterparts in Kuala Lumpur had exchanged whatever intelligence they had, but now he was surprised by the magnitude. "What training camps?" he asked.

"Three in Tehran that we know of. The Revolutionary Guard took over the U.S. compound to train their 'foreign commandos.' The splendid villa of the Shah's ex-chief of secret police — who was summarily executed — was converted to an intelligence school. There were more than a half dozen all over Iran — Ahwaz, Esfahan, Shiraz, Mashad, Qum. The instructors were not just Iranians. They were Libyans, PLO guerrillas, South Yemenis, Pakistanis, all with combat experience. They trained the foreign commandos on both American and Russian weapons. That's where our analysts made the connection. The same weapons are on the shopping list the terrorists sent us."

"What happened to these foreign commandos?" Yee asked urgently.

Blocker made a sweeping gesture with his hand. "They're out there somewhere. They were sent back to their own countries as a cadre to set up local networks, train others. But Tehran now has the Islamic revolution on hold. After its war with Iraq, it needs Western help to rebuild its economy. Since the death of Ayatollah Khomeini, it's distanced itself from these terrorist groups it originally trained and financed."

"But why this . . . *incident* now?"

"We were hoping you could tell us. Apparently this is a local group with their own agenda. We can't penetrate cells like this. These bad guys are too secretive and tight, literally clans, made up of brothers, cousins, locals who grew up in the same village or went to school together." He looked admiringly at Salleh. "That's why you're a goddamn wizard to have found out what you did."

"*Sergeant Salleh!*"

They all turned at the excitement in the policeman's voice.

He held up a portable radio, the type carried by small boats. "It was wrapped in a carpet."

"Yes, very good," Salleh nodded, then turned back to Blocker. "The Iranian does not know where the ship is," he said in a quiet voice, "but he has a signal to call this Ahmed if he receives another shipment of weapons."

Blocker straightened up and stared at him in astonishment.

43. Escape

After Tengku left, Maggi did not move but sprawled motionless on the bed, a marionette whose strings had broken. She lay with eyes shut, not sleeping, breathing in the sweetly musky smells of sex and Tengku's spiced breaths that hung in the air like incense. She wanted to sleep, to luxuriantly allow her limbs and body to let go all will and strength and dissolve. She felt fragile.

But she couldn't sleep. A thought, then another, and another, buzzed like mosquitoes just at the edge of consciousness and kept her awake; then their gathering swarm

610

alarmed her, and she sat bolt upright and stared at them with frightened eyes.

Tengku had at first appeared so electrically attractive, admiring, passionate — or had that all been self-delusion on her part, a romantic illusion concocted in her loneliness? She was totally adrift, suspended in an exotic, and dangerous, never-never land where Tengku was the absolute ruler with power of life and death. *"You have enchanted me,"* he had accused her. But he had practically strutted out. Maggi trembled at the thought of what it boded for tomorrow.

She sat, hugging her knees to her chest, staring at the door.

"Tomorrow I will release the pretty, gallant Russian officer with the yellow hair."

"Why?"

"It is his time."

There had been something vindictive in Tengku's tone of voice, a viciousness in his eyes and posture that he had not even bothered to conceal, as though he were baiting her. Maggi suddenly shuddered. Something was terribly wrong. She had never seen that naked cruelty in his face before, or perhaps he had just hidden it. Without knowing how or why — with the telepathic intuition forged by their mating — Maggi knew with almost a certainty that Tengku was dispatching Vladimir Korsakov to his death.

But why? There had always been a strange morality, however twisted, to the "releases" before.

". . . *the pretty, gallant Russian officer with the yellow hair."* Tengku was, for some reason, jealous of Vladimir. *Jealous.* The word itself, the thought, immediately conjured up the image of that Bolshevik bitch Svetlana. It had been the purser who had betrayed Maggi to Tengku for some vindictive reason of her own — Maggi knew it intuitively. That's why Tengku had been suspicious about Maggi and Vladimir. In her jealousy and rage Svetlana Fedorova had, unwittingly, condemned her own lover.

Maggi had to warn Vladimir. She reluctantly forced herself to stand to clear the narcosis of sleep from her mind. But what could she possibly say to the Russian officer that was not in some way a betrayal of Tengku? Even then, what could Vladimir, or any of them for that matter, do? She nervously paced the cell of her cabin. By tomorrow morning it would be too late to do anything. Vladimir had to be warned tonight.

But she could not go straightaway to his cabin. She would have to pass by the lounge where Tengku might or might not be at this hour. What would he do now, if he found her in Vladimir's cabin in the middle of the night? He had already mutilated the gallant young officer on a whim. And with that question, its stir of tremulous excitement, Maggi had the terrible insight that Tengku aroused her precisely because he hovered at that edge of violence.

And for all Maggi knew, Vladimir was, at that moment, shacked up in his airless cubicle with that splay-assed communist cow. Jesus, Maggi's barging in on their sweaty screwing would be an imbroglio straight out of a French farce.

Maggi entered the bathroom, dropped her robe, douched, and showered quickly — an act of cleansing that declared her purpose, if not her still confused loyalties.

By the time she had dressed she had worked out a plan of action. She outfitted herself like a night commando in her darkest slacks, a long-sleeved blouse, a shawl, and silent-treading jogging shoes. She glanced at her watch. It was past midnight.

As quietly as possible Maggi opened the door and slipped noiselessly into the dark, empty corridor. The passengers and crew were by now asleep and the guards, she hoped, would be dozing. Maggi felt her way forward and through the black tunnel of a midships passageway to the port side. She was now familiar enough with the ship that she could maneuver through it in the dark, as she could through the maze of furniture in her own home, by a touch here and there, the occasional vague black outline of something familiar, an innate sense of the number of steps between things.

She touched the port ladder up to the promenade deck, stopped, and listened. There was only the telltale pant of her own breathing. She moved up the ladder, step by step, pausing with each movement, her ears straining for any alarming noise.

She reached the outside promenade deck, where she hugged the wall, a dark shadow slowly, silently moving forward. Her heart lurched. A glowing drag on a cigarette briefly flared on the face of a guard, and then he dissolved into the blackness of the jungle night. Maggi froze. From the guard's position by the rail on the forward deck, he would see her when she went up the stairs to the bridge.

Maggi stood motionless for several minutes, a quivering doe terrified of attracting a hunter's attention. She was about to retrace her steps when the cigarette flared up again. The guard coughed and sighed, then she heard him shuffle across the deck to the starboard railing, his rifle creaking on its strap, apparently to investigate the view of the black jungle from that side. The superstructure of the ship now hid her from him.

Maggi was at the point of greatest danger. She had to climb up to the veranda just outside the lounge, which was Tengku's quarters. It took her five minutes to move the dozen steps. Her nervous breath was so short she was certain that the gasping sound of it would give her away.

The lounge was dark, noiseless. Tengku was either dead asleep or ashore somewhere. She had no idea where he disappeared to at night. For the first time she wondered if he had another woman, perhaps his wife, at a camp ashore. But she was much too frightened to dwell on that thought.

She was on the opposite side of the ship from Vladimir's cabin. If she were discovered at this point, she could always plead — even with a certain sincerity — that she had only wanted to see Tengku again. It was the next step that was her infidelity, her betrayal.

Again the dozen steps took her an eternity — a step, pause, listen motionlessly, and then a second step — but finally she gained the bridge.

She had briefly considered warning Alan Schneider. But then she would have to confront all her own fears, and his alarm, possibly panic, concerning what had happened to Liz.

Captain Khromykh's cabin was in a brief passageway, an alcove actually, just aft of the bridge so that he could be on deck in seconds in the event of an emergency. Maggi timidly knocked on the door, fearful of alerting the guards, but to her own paranoid senses her knuckles exploded on the wood, booming and echoing in the corridor.

Khromykh, bless him, apparently slept the alert, light sleep of a mother, and the door opened at her second muffled rapping. He grumbled something incomprehensible in Russian.

"Please be quiet. Don't turn on a light," Maggi whispered urgently. "It's Maggi Chancellor."

The black shadow that was Khromykh silently absorbed this, then said, "Yes?"

"Please, I must talk to you. May I come in?"

"Yes."

The shadows seemed to shift. Maggi moved in, and the door closed behind her. She heard Khromykh fumbling about, then a red flashlight clicked on, shined on Maggi a moment, then clicked off.

"I must put on pants, please, Professor Chancellor," the captain whispered.

Despite the fear and the adrenalin rush

that made her legs tremble, Maggi almost laughed.

The flashlight again clicked on and off briefly, as Khromykh located his trousers and struggled into them in the dark. Maggi heard the hiss of a zipper.

"Yes, Professor Chancellor, you must talk to me?"

Maggi forced herself to speak slowly so that the Russian would understand her. She told of Tengku's sudden appearance in her cabin, the accusations of her lying about Schneider and of her having an affair with Vladimir, and the disclosure about Vladimir's release. Maggi did not tell Captain Khromykh about her having sex with Tengku.

Several times she paused in her narrative to ask if Khromykh understood her, and he answered, "Yes." The third time she asked, he said with an irritated snap, "Yes, yes, I understand English more better than I speak."

"I'm sorry, but I think Vladimir's life is in danger. The first sailor that Tengku said he 'released' was already dead. I saw him killed."

"Yes, Vladimir tells me this terrible thing today."

"You must believe me."

"I believe you, Professor Chancellor. I not

sleep when you come. I sit in dark, think, very afraid. I know this man, this . . . terrorist. The first day his knife is at my throat. All day. All day he has . . . crazy smile. I think he cut my throat like he cut Vladimir's face. He is crazy with . . . power. Of life and death. Crazy." Khromykh was silent. Apparently there were intimacies other than sex that gave insight into Tengku's soul.

"Please, you stay here, Professor Chancellor," he said suddenly.

"Where're you going?"

"Talk to Vladimir. You stay here." He flicked on the red beam of his flashlight briefly. "Bed there. Bathroom there. Maybe you sleep. No lights, please."

"Will you be gone long?"

"I do not know. Maybe two minutes. Maybe two hours." And then on bare, silent feet he slipped through the door, leaving Maggi in a strange, pitch-black compartment. She glanced at her watch, but without her reading glasses the dim luminescent green dots were not distinct enough to show the time. She groped timidly in the dark, fearful of knocking something over, felt an upholstered chair, and eased down into it.

Gradually, over a period of minutes, her anxiety relaxed, or rather it gave way to exhaustion. It was easier to shut her eyes than strain to see in the dark. A thousand worrying thoughts now tumbled through her mind and quickly ordered themselves into an ominous pattern. No one would understand her affair with Tengku. How could she possibly rationalize it? She could hardly explain it to herself. Her only possible defense was that she had been raped, and that was a lie. If she continued another day as his consort — and that was apparently Tengku's intention — she would be vilified as a collaborator with the terrorists. There were already those among both the crew, such as the insanely jealous purser, and the passengers — Mrs. Clarence Murdock of Houston, campaign contributor to the President — who were sticking needles in her. If she were sleeping with Tengku, not even Captain Khromykh or Alan Schneider would come to her defense. Tengku had done more than sweep her off her feet into a compromising position. He would get her hanged as an accomplice to piracy, terrorism, and murder.

The door suddenly opened, and Maggi gasped.

"It's me, Captain Khromykh," he whispered. Someone else was with him. Vladimir Korsakov.

"We must escape tonight," Maggi declared to Korsakov without preamble.

"You?" Vladimir exclaimed.

"I have to go with you. If they find you gone tomorrow, Tengku will know I warned you. Besides, I speak the language and know the country. You might walk right into the pirates and not know it until they cut your throat."

Vladimir and Khromykh conferred in whispered Russian. "It is very dangerous and too . . . *tough*," Vladimir said, groping for the English word.

"It's more dangerous for me to stay here. As for it's being too *tough*, I work out at a gym, jog, do aerobics. You won't be able to keep up with *me*," Maggi insisted truculently.

Again there was the whispered Russian. Khromykh flicked on the red light and in the glow of the lowered beam examined Maggi's face. The light was harsh, ghoulish, illuminating only the reddened chins, cheeks, foreheads, and shadowed eye sockets of both men, but Maggi had the sense that her measure was being taken in this uncompromising, ghastly beam.

Khromykh nodded, then nodded again to Vladimir. There was another rushed, whispered conference in Russian.

"Yes, you are right," the young officer said. "You will be in danger here, and together we will have a better chance to find help." Then Vladimir and Khromykh slipped out again.

Maggi sat down once more to wait. She was aware of Tengku somewhere about, either just below her, sleeping uneasily in the lounge, or encamped downriver amid his pirate pack. She felt wired to him, and knew that he was suddenly awake, tense, sensing the air around him like a panther, alert to danger. She wondered what he would make of it when he discovered both her and Vladimir gone. She imagined his rage, his feeling of being betrayed, his hurt, perhaps. He would assume, of course, that Maggi and Vladimir had indeed been lovers, her lovemaking with him a faithless act of deception. If he believed that, he might not take revenge on any of the passengers. If not in love, she had at least been sincere in her passion — whatever the hell that meant — and in the roiling confusion of her emotions, Maggi wept.

In a brief time Vladimir and Khromykh were back. Vladimir carried two small rucksacks, the type handed out to the passengers for their expeditions ashore. He unstrapped one. "There is a chart like the one I showed you, some rations for two, three days, some American money, a canteen of water, a flashlight, a flare pistol, flares."

"Where'd you get all this so quickly?"

"Much is in the lifeboats for emergencies. The gun is to signal search planes and boats. That is why we have good chance once we get to the sea or in the open land. They are searching for us." He quickly showed her how to load and fire the flare gun. "If we get separated."

Maggi gingerly touched the barrel of the gun and fingered a flare, a paper-covered firework that resembled a shotgun shell. The explosive power of it made her nervous.

"What about my passport?" she suddenly remembered. "The purser has it." Maggi felt a flash of alarm. "I think she was the one who . . . who betrayed me to Tengku." She saw Vladimir and Khromykh exchange a look.

"Yes," Vladimir acknowledged. "We think so. She is an emotional woman. But this is unforgivable. She will be denounced when we are free," he said in grim, angry tones. Apparently Maggi was not the only one aboard with a life-and-death sex life.

"How will we get off the ship?" she asked.

"I study the way they come and go, and I think there are many others that are camped down the river," Vladimir explained.

"With luck, we have only a few hours'

head start," Maggi interrupted.

"Yes, now listen carefully, because we cannot talk, not even whisper, once we leave this cabin," Vladimir said urgently. "This plan is very dangerous."

Maggi and Vladimir descended the ladders to the bridge, step by cautious step, like a pair of thieves in the night. Both wore flotation jackets, filched from the lifeboats. Vladimir, dressed in a dark shirt and pants — apparently a working uniform — carried a coil of rope over his shoulder.

He froze at each landing, listened intently, then tiptoed to the next ladder. On the main deck he stood motionless again, his head slowly swiveling about, eyes and ears searching. He wore a dark officer's cap but with the braid looped under his chin like a strap. Maggi thought that curious, until she realized that the cap effectively hid his shining blond hair and shadowed the pale skin of his face. He and Captain Khromykh had apparently planned this escape down to the minor details.

On the main deck he and Maggi inched forward to the raised bow, which pointed upriver. Vladimir led the way on the darkened deck. Maggi had a daylight memory of the bow as a platform of giant anchor chains and windlass machinery. The canopy of trees over the ship was a black awning that blotted out stars, moon, or any shading of light; the darkness of the open deck was so absolute it had a texture, a sooty, moist feel. Maggi bashed her shin on some metal protrusion and bit her lip so as not to cry out, emitting a stifled gasp of pain.

Vladimir took her hand. After a few steps she sensed, rather than saw, him stop and turn to her. She felt a rope being tightened under her arms in a halter, the bite of the line softened by the life jacket.

He looped the other end of the rope twice about a barrel-sized capstan. With a gentle nudge he guided her to the railing. "Now," he whispered. "You will not fall."

As if in reassurance, she felt the line tug taut, holding her to the ship. She climbed over the railing. Now hanging out over a black abyss with the river below, Maggi panicked and clung to the rail in desperate fear.

"Let go!"

She audibly sucked in a breath and unclenched her hands.

She did not fall but hung by the rope about her chest. Slowly, an inch at a time, then slightly quicker, she scraped down the side of the ship. As she was lowered, the ship's flank slanted in away from her until she dangled free, and a moment later she felt the water, sucking at her feet.

She floated at the end of her rope tether, the life jacket buoying her up to her shoulders. To her surprise the water was warm, a few degrees balmier than the night air.

The rope suddenly jerked violently. She looked up and barely made out a dark form directly above, dropping down on her. After lowering her, Vladimir had tied off the line and now was climbing down hand over hand.

His blindly lashing foot kicked her in the head, and the sudden weight of his body settling on her shoved her under water, stifling her cry. Then he was in the water, clutching at her jacket to keep from being swept away by the current.

She felt him fumbling about her shoulders, as if trying to tug off her jacket. In total darkness he was attempting to attach a cord from his jacket to hers so that they would not drift apart, but each time he released his grip, the current started to sweep him off. Maggi lifted her legs and wrapped them about his hips to hold him to her.

He untied the rope about her chest, and the pressure of the black water swirling by suddenly ceased, as though the river had stopped flowing. It was a moment before Maggi realized that the river had not stopped, but they were now flowing with it. They floated down the length of the ship, a ghostly white wall looming up out of the blackness of the water like a bank of mist rather than something solid. They quickly passed under the stern.

Maggi looked up anxiously and saw the glow of a cigarette. Her heart lurched, and she waited, chilled with fear, for a shout and then a blast of gunfire. She glanced at Vladimir, a silent dark shape a cord's length from her. Unless the guard shined a light directly down, he would not see them. Maggi strained to listen, but she heard only the gurgle of the rushing river, the screams of marauding night birds, the cacophony of tree frogs and insects that masked their passage. But Maggi nevertheless held her breath until they were well downstream, and the lighter hulk of the cruise ship faded into the surrounding blackness.

The current swirled by the bank and eddied, spinning her and Vladimir, joined by their short rope, around and around each other like two dancers caught in a turbulent waltz beyond their control. But then the tempo slackened, the black wall of the shore drew away, and the dark, impenetrable vault above split open, then widened to reveal a clear, star-spangled sky.

Maggi gasped. The sight of the stars and

a half-moon hovering at the edge of the trees and casting a pale silver light on the water was a deliverance. They drifted down-river in silence, making no attempt to swim to the river bank. Their plan was to ride in their flotation jackets until the high, se-cluding wall of jungle ended. According to Captain Khromykh, the river ran through a pestilent mangrove swamp before it de-bouched into a narrow strait. Navigating up-river, Tengku's knife at his throat, the Russian officer had had the presence of mind to note that where the mangroves ended, there was a stretch of higher, sandy open ground of scrub palms, before the jungle thickened and the giant trees of the tropical rain forest took over. Traveling in this open terrain would be much easier, and it might lead to a shore or beach more hospitable than the swamp, where they would have a good chance of finding a fishing settlement or hailing a passing boat.

"We shouldn't get too far from shore," Maggi whispered anxiously, as much to hear the reassurance of her own voice in the night as that of Vladimir.

"Yes," he whispered back, but he did not stroke. Apparently he somehow estimated that they were close enough.

To Maggi, the blackness on either side of

them had no dimension, neither beginning nor end. They were floating in warm, languid water, and despite their peril, it was lulling, comfortable. The open sky indicated a line of travel, but the constant equatorial stars overhead gave no sense of motion. They might not be moving at all, but turning to search fearfully behind her, Maggi saw no indication of the ship upriver, only the deeper blackness.

Downriver there was a bellow and a hissing cough, an animal sound that Maggi did not recognize but nevertheless galvanized her with fear. Every hair on her body suddenly bristled. Then there came a series of low bass grunts from a deep, leather-covered chest. Before her fear had a name, Maggi kicked and stroked wildly for the dark shore. Her legs and arms flailed and clawed at Vladimir, to whom she was still tied.

"What are you doing?" His whisper was almost a shout.

Maggi gasped a warning and swallowed mud-filthy river water, "Crocodiles!" The word was a choked cry.

"What?"

"Crocodiles!" Maggi shouted. She yanked at the cord, dragging Vladimir with her, thrashing the water in a blind panic.

Her feet struck something more solid than

water but still sank into it. Then her floundering hands smacked the mud bank. She grabbed at it, but the ooze came away in her clawing fingers. She grabbed again and again until her fingers clutched at a root, which snapped and pulled away. Then they caught another root that held, and she pulled herself from the river. The dead weight of Vladimir wrenched her back down.

She tugged at him, and somehow he grabbed his own hand- and footholds. They clawed up the black mud bank, the cord still tying them together, one time wrenching them backward, another seizing them up, as each slipped or hauled up the foul-smelling mud slope. In the shadow of the trees there was total darkness; they could see nothing and could hear only each other's panting, cursing struggle.

At the top of the river bank Vladimir collapsed, his air coming in strangled gasps.

"No, it's not safe here. They can still get us," Maggi cried, heaving at him. She crawled on her hands and knees, the unseen saw-edged grass slashing her palms, dragging Vladimir behind her by the life line. Twenty yards inland she too collapsed, exhausted, sobbing for breath.

44. Stewart's Last Night as Captain of the Decatur

"And the end of all our exploring will be to arrive where we started and know the place for the first time."

"Sir?" Callahan questioned.

"Just thinking aloud," Stewart said. He studied Defense Mapping Agency Chart 71241. A week before, returning from the Persian Gulf, Stewart had used the top section to navigate the final reach of the Strait of Malacca through the bottleneck of Phillip Channel, past Raffles Light into Singapore. Now the Decatur was threading up from the bottom of the chart through the Selat Durian. "The fisherman said the bad guys had kidnapped him in the islands east of us."

"Well, that narrows it to a couple of dozen islands, sir."

"Yeah, but most are probably flat, sandy rocks, no place to hide a ship. But look at the big ones." Stewart jabbed his finger at Pulau Kapaladjernih and Bulan. "And Tjombol and Sugi here just to the south. They all have mountains, a couple of peaks over a thousand feet. That indicates to me they probably have watersheds that are as wide and deep as rivers during the rains this time of year." He traced a shoreline with his finger. "Coral reefs, mangrove swamps, all shifting. Nothing is as it's indicated on the charts."

"You wouldn't want to take a ship there, Captain."

"No, you're right. *I* wouldn't. But a native who knows the area like you know your own backyard might do it. Especially if he didn't give a damn if the ship got out again."

"We'd never pick it up on radar. It'd be lost in all the land return. We'd have to fly right over it."

"Even then, they've now had time to camouflage it."

"If I had my MAD gear streamed, I might get lucky," Callahan said.

Stewart said nothing for a moment, then, "We'll be about *here,* approaching the Phillip Channel at first light."

Callahan stared at the chart, then his fingers moved over it tracing a ladder search pattern from that point. "It's our last shot," he said.

"You going to be all right?"

The pilot looked up at Stewart, held his eyes a beat, then nodded, "Yes, sir. It's amazing how clear things get when someone *really* shoots at you and sets your ship on fire. I'm ready for it now. Or at least I know what I'm *supposed* to do."

Stewart smiled. "At first light, then."

"Yes, sir."

Stewart spent the night in the bridge chair. It was not just to be there in case there were any problems with the auxiliary propulsion units. He knew it was going to be his last night as captain of the *Decatur,* his last night as the commanding officer of any ship.

It was in the dark hours of the midwatch that he heard Robinson hobble onto the bridge.

"The APU's holding up?"

"So far, but a fishing boat with two old ladies rowing passed us a mile back."

Robinson laughed, a low bass rumble that came up from the chest.

"There's hot coffee in the thermos," Stewart offered.

"Thanks, but I've got my leg to keep me awake."

"You're going to cripple that knee permanently if you don't get off it."

"I am off it, Captain. I'm using a crutch, and I'm an expert with it."

"This has happened before?"

"Oh, yeah. A running back my size has 1,500 foot-pounds of kinetic energy when he hits the line. That's like dropping a fifty-pound sandbag from thirty feet up. Something's going to give. On occasion it's been my knees."

"Is that why you didn't turn pro after Annapolis?"

It was absolutely dark on the bridge except for a faint red glow from the dials on the control panel. Robinson was just a shadow beside him, and neither man could see the other's face. Robinson was quiet, as though weighing his answer before he spoke. Stewart had the sixth sense that he had just touched a nerve in the man.

"No, sir, it was my father," Robinson said finally. "He'd been in the navy."

"Oh, really? So was my mine."

"Your father an officer?"

"Yes, in World War II."

"Yeah, well my old man might have served him. Literally. He was a steward."

Stewart remained quiet.

"When I had a shot at an appointment to Annapolis, he couldn't believe it. Problem was my grades, especially math. They wanted me to go to the prep school at Newport for a year. If I didn't, I wasn't going to make it through the academy. Hell, in my crowd I was a scholar. Half the guys I hung out with had trouble reading and writing. You know how it is when you're seventeen. Who needs this prep school shit? A couple of the Big Ten schools were rushing me. But my old man doesn't say a thing. He was a bus driver, working his way up to dispatcher. And one night he brings home another driver to dinner. This guy stands a whole head over me. I mean he's huge. And, of course, he'd played ball. At Ohio State. In his junior year he got hurt. No more football, no more scholarship, no pro career, and no more education or degree. He's just a bus driver who gets drunk and runs on at the mouth too much about what's wrong with Ohio State and the Bears. My old man doesn't say a word. He doesn't have to. I was a dumb kid, but I wasn't stupid."

"So you went to the prep school and then to Annapolis?"

"Yes, sir. It wasn't easy, but I made it. Because of football I got a few breaks. Special tutoring when I needed it — and I did. A higher class standing for leadership. But sure enough, I got hurt in my junior year."

"The knee?"

"Yes, sir, but at Annapolis the bottom line was that the navy doctors operated and gave me a chance to heal properly; the layoff only improved my grade-point average and class standing. When I hobbled home on Christmas leave, my old man, who's a great

634

one for statistics — point spreads, average yards per carry, that sort of thing — lays a beautiful one on me. The average pro gets fifty thousand hits in a four-and-a-half-year playing career. That's all he says, then gives my leg that deadpan stare of his.

"The day I graduated, I'm in my white uniform, and my mother puts on my gold ensign boards, and she's crying and carrying on. That's to be expected, because she cries at extra points. I look at my old man. He can't talk, and tears are streaming down his face. It's the first time I've ever seen him cry. Finally he shakes his head and says, 'Things are changing. They really are.'"

Robinson was silent for a long while. "You're right, Captain, when you say I'm concerned about watching my ass. I do. But it's not just my butt that's hanging out there. It's a *whole lot* of other people's butts."

"That's a lot of responsibility to take on yourself, Robbie."

"Yes, sir. But nowadays it comes with the job . . . if the guy in the job is black."

Robinson was being unusually talkative. At first Stewart thought that perhaps Doc Blowitz had given him something to ease the pain that had also loosened his tongue. The XO had, after all, been right. The commanding officer had brought his ship into harm's way.

Stewart stared out into the night. The rain clouds had broken, and the stars were amazingly bright. The next day he would be busy maneuvering into a shipyard in Singapore. Then Stewart would undoubtedly be ordered to fly back to Subic Bay or Yokosuka for court-martial. No, Robinson had opened up because he too knew that it was Stewart's last night as captain of the *Decatur*.

45. *The Nature of the Jihad*

"The flashing light *there* is Raffles Lighthouse," the captain of the Republic of Singapore corvette pointed out. "When it's off our starboard beam, we'll be in the main channel, and in Indonesian territorial waters."

Salleh stared at the light that dissolved away into total darkness then suddenly flashed on in a dazzling glare every few seconds. He had only a vague sense of what the navy officer was saying. He had never before been aboard one of the new guided-missile corvettes. At 190 feet long, the RSS *Valour* was the size of a small tramp freighter, but sleek and fast as a speedboat. A half dozen of the corvettes, originally based on a West German prototype, were now being built in the Singapore yards. It was astonishing to Salleh that his little country now had such ships of war.

"This has guided missiles?" he asked.

"We carry eight American Harpoons," the captain said with great pride.

"*Aaah.*" Salleh had little idea what that meant. "You can shoot another ship without seeing it?"

"Seventy miles away," the captain nodded. "The computer guides it to the target, and then the homing radar takes over for the final phase."

"Can it find pirates?"

The captain, a Chinese, glared at him and said nothing.

"But that is our problem," Salleh insisted.

"The Indonesians have the Dutch frigates with Exocet missiles," the captain said testily.

"Then we must have West German ships with American Harpoons, *lah.*"

The captain regarded Salleh with suspicion. From the moment Salleh stepped aboard, the naval officer had bristled at every order the hippie-haired, scruffily dressed Malay had given him.

A sailor came onto the bridge and saluted

smartly. "The radio is rigged to our antenna, Captain."

The captain turned to Salleh. "You may make your transmission." He was eager to get this strange business over with.

Salleh shook his head. "No, we must wait until the sun rises," he said. It was an order.

Yee's assistant brought him the radio message from Salleh.

"Our corvette is in position in the channel."

The CIA man Blocker grunted an acknowledgment, but sat studying the map on the wall. Then, as if it were a casual afterthought, he called after the departing messenger, "Make sure they establish communications with the American aircraft before they transmit."

The assistant looked to Yee, who nodded.

"Your commando teams?" Yee asked.

"The SEALs are mounting up now. They'll be ready." Blocker continued to stare at the wall map as though divining another meaning from the patchwork of nations, multicolored rags randomly sewn on the blue quilt of the sea. "Middle Eastern conspiracies are the fashion in paranoia in Washington now," he drawled. "They've replaced the Soviet's Evil Empire since *glasnost*."

"And what's in fashion in Moscow?" Yee questioned.

What is the KGB's paranoia? Blocker asked himself. They're sitting on a powder keg of almost fifty million Muslims — more than any Arab country — within the borders of the Soviet Union. The Christian Armenians and the Muslim Azerbaijanis are already cutting each other's throats. The Soviets will kiss away the *Black Sea,* the passengers, and the entire crew before they give up one rusty AK-47, he reasoned. But to Yee he said, "I'm sorry you persona non grata-fied Yevshenko. He saw how the arms worked out. A guerrilla battalion, equipped to fight with any weapons it picked up."

"Where?"

Blocker suddenly rose and walked to the chart. "What's the local joke? Indonesia is the country of tomorrow . . . and always will be."

"Jakarta?"

"I wouldn't start there, and I have a little experience in these matters. I'd start *here.*" He jabbed at Sumatra. "In the countryside, the jungles, the hill country with a battalion of well-equipped fanatics, full of revolutionary zeal. The trick — and this is the Gospel According to Mao Tse Tung, who literally wrote the book — is to let the revolution build slowly in the countryside and city slums. Then the army of the people marches into the capital without firing a shot, except in celebration, one step behind the corrupt old regime — which flees on a chartered jet to London or Los Angeles carrying everything it can loot or liquidate. Of course, this isn't a Marxist revolution but a Muslim fundamentalist one, but the tactics are the same. And the passion."

Yee nodded. "An interesting speculation. Then Indonesia is the goal of this *jihad*."

"For openers," Blocker said cryptically. Historically, a revolution of this nature seeks to erase the old colonial boundaries and unite the people of the same race, language, and religion. A pan-Malay movement. A quarter of a century earlier, Sukarno had had that vision. Again Blocker kept his analysis a state secret.

"Then it would include Malaysia?" Yee probed.

"And Brunei, with its hoard of oil; possibly the southern Philippines. But, as I said, I'm just speculating," Blocker said easily.

Yee was not taken in. "And Singapore?"

Blocker shrugged. "An island of prosperous Chinese entrepreneurs with a significant Muslim minority."

"Sukarno once tried it. His 'army of liberation' was defeated," Yee spat out the words.

"By British troops in Singapore, Malaya,

and Brunei." Blocker's voice was matter-of-fact, affable, not at all contentious. He silently studied the map. All the oil and natural resources of Brunei, Indonesia, and Malaysia. Singapore's banking and trading power. Both sides of all the strategic sea routes between Europe, the Middle East, and Japan, China, and the west coast of the United States. Where the hell were the tankers and container ships going to go — by way of Australia? It was the most powerful package in the world. And the populations were overwhelmingly Malay and Muslim.

Blocker glanced at Yee. They wouldn't kill *all* the Chinese. Just enough to keep them terrified and in line. They were needed to keep the trade and technology humming. What could the tens of millions of overseas Chinese do? Flee back to China? China couldn't feed them and didn't have jobs for them. Besides, they were all independent capitalists. Beijing didn't want them starting all that shit again in Tian An Men Square. No, they were exactly where Beijing wanted them to be: a dangerous subversive element out of the country. Prosperous but isolated and surrounded by other people who despise them, Blocker regretted to say. So they were nostalgic for old China, even loyal in an ethnic way, and they kept the trade and

641

money flowing back in. But the fact was that Singapore and the overseas Chinese were totally on their own.

"The United States would not help us now?" Yee asked, almost as if he had been following Blocker's chain of thought.

Blocker shrugged. "The political reality is that if you kill one American, we'll send in the Sixth or Seventh Fleet. But a million Chinese gets profound regrets from the White House."

Yee said nothing.

"Look, I don't mean to be callous or insensitive," Blocker said apologetically. "These are the stakes we're playing for." He threw up his hands. "But I don't think any of this is getting through to the White House."

"I am grateful for your honest counsel."

"There's one other absolute requirement for such a revolution."

"Yes?"

"A charismatic, almost mythic leader."

"The one who reincarnates the ghost of Parameswara," Yee whispered.

"We must find out who he is, at any cost, and before the population knows he even exists . . ."

"Yes."

"And terminate him — totally erase every memory of him."

46. Endangered Species

In the rain forest all life conspires to flow to the sea. In the high, dark umbrella of the jungle, evolution has designed leaves with long, pointed drip-tips that rapidly shed the water of the tropical downpours. But the forest itself can absorb only a fraction of the massive rainfall, and the cascading water cuts a web of downhill waterways through the soil and rocks, channeling into ten thousand rivulets, streams, tumbling waterfalls, swirling jungle pools, muddy tributaries, all shadowed under the canopy of great trees, until the currents converge in an ever-widening river that bursts into the sunlight in its final rush toward the sea.

In the lush herbage at the sunlit water's edge life quickens, and the shy creatures of the forest come at night to eat and drink. The sambur deer graze on ferns, the huge-eyed tarsiers stalk crickets, the bearded pigs root for earthworms. And along the paths to the sea, the meat-eaters wait.

Maggi and Vladimir sprawled on the river bank, gasping for air. Once Vladimir started to speak, but the words were strangled by his breath, and he fell silent.

They lay for what seemed to Maggi a quarter of an hour, although it may have been shorter, recovering their strength. And when her panic subsided and her breathing settled, Maggi lay there simply savoring the wonder of it, that they had actually pulled off the escape from the ship in that daredevil way. "We did it!" she said in a hushed voice. She felt like giggling.

Vladimir did not answer at first, then said, "Captain Khromykh saw no crocodiles."

"They probably didn't sit up on the bank, waving, as a three-hundred-foot ship sailed by," Maggi snapped. "But I heard them. That's what they sound like."

Vladimir was silent. He didn't challenge her, but she sensed he didn't believe her either. "We're still in the jungle," he said after a while.

"No, the trees are thinner. Look, you can see the sky between them," she pointed out. She could also see Vladimir's outline, if not the features of his face. He had apparently lost his cap in the scramble to shore.

"Yes, the stars," he said, and there was a laugh in his voice.

"We're going to make it," Maggi said.

"We must still follow the river until there is more light, or we will get lost."

There was a sudden scurrying sound in the bushes next to them, and both started.

"What's that?"

"I don't know."

Vladimir rummaged frantically in his knapsack, and then a flashlight clicked on. Its strong yellow beam exposed a jumble of low bushes, then suddenly illuminated a small fawnlike creature no more than twelve inches high. Large, gentle black eyes shined back at them.

"It's a mouse deer," Maggi exclaimed.

The animal seemed dazzled by the light and did not move.

Vladimir stood up, and at the movement the mouse deer trotted off, disappearing into the undergrowth on tiny, frantic hoofs.

With Vladimir in the lead, they now stumbled along the high bank following the river. Every step was a struggle. The tangle of tough ferns tripped them, sharp pandanus leaves slashed at their legs, and they got tangled in barbed rattan tendrils. Maggi took a few steps away from the river to catch her breath, and the basic botanical error of their way struck her. The shrubbery and thick undergrowth crowded the open river bank, the palms, ferns, and vines competing for the unobstructed sunlight during the day. But under the trees, where little sunlight penetrated, the ground vegetation was sparse, the walking considerably easier.

They hiked among the black pillars of trees, the river indicated by a lighter glow of sky on their left. The night forest was a chattering place of unseen, scurrying creatures only feet away and the deep, purring mating call of frogs; across the river the throaty roar of a croc suddenly resounded. Vladimir ignored it, nosing through the low trees, branches lashing his face and arms. Every fifty yards or so he suddenly veered off to struggle through the undergrowth to make visual contact with the moon-bright river, as though fearing that they were lost, or perhaps simply panicked by the darkness of the clamorous jungle about them.

They had trekked in this manner for perhaps a half hour when Maggi noticed they were walking fairly easily along the outer edge of the trees, paralleling the river on a natural path through the brush. She flicked on her flashlight for a second to confirm her suspicion. "This is a trail," she exclaimed.

Vladimir stopped. "What?"

"This is a trail," Maggi repeated. She switched on her light again, pointing it low on the ground at the parted bushes ahead of them.

"There are people here?"

646

"Not necessarily. Deer or the wild cattle, the *tembadau,* make paths like this through the bush."

"Oh!"

Vladimir was short of breath, and in the brief flash of light she had seen his face, gleaming and oily with dripping sweat.

"Do you want me to lead for a while?" she asked.

"No, I will lead," he said, as though offended by the suggestion. To their left, beyond the low wall of bush, there was a splash in the water like a large fish jumping.

They followed the path for a few hundred yards, and it suddenly opened into a brief clearing, a soggy mud flat on the river. Maggi instinctively shined her light onto the area. Vladimir grabbed her and hissed, "The terrorists will see it."

Maggi shook off Vladimir's hand and kept the light on the water. She backed away, grabbed Vladimir's belt and pulled him after her. No more than a dozen feet away the beast lay, looking like a sunken log, except for the two glowing coal-red eyes that reflected the light back to them, afire like the eyes of a devil rising out of hell. Maggi made out nostrils barely raised above the water, an elongated triangle of yellow and black scales, and the bumps of ears directly behind the demon eyes, and that was all. But it smelled them, saw them, heard them.

"That's what Captain Khromykh didn't see from the ship."

The crocodile suddenly submerged, simply slipped under the black water with hardly a ripple, and disappeared.

Maggi whirled and bolted up the path into the high bush, yanking Vladimir along.

"What is it? Will it come out of the water . . . after us?"

"I don't know. You want to wait and find out?"

"I didn't see anything, maybe eyes or something."

"If you see any more at this range, you're in big trouble."

"How big was this thing?"

"I don't know. Judging from the spread of the eyes, it's a lot bigger than me or you. A lot bigger."

"It had terrible eyes," Vladimir admitted.

"The better to see you, my dear. You ought to see its teeth."

"How do you know such things?"

"I'm an expert on the local natives, remember?"

Vladimir silently trudged on ahead, up the trail, pushing through the pandanus scrubs along a higher bank above the river. Once again Maggi felt that he did not entirely believe her, that he thought she was hysterically exaggerating what she saw and heard. Vladimir's greatest fear was getting lost, losing his way in the trackless jungle, and he was obsessed with keeping the river in sight.

Maggi looked nervously behind her, quickly flashing the light down the path. Despite her brave authority with Vladimir, she had never really seen an estuarine crocodile in the wild before. On her field trips with Bryce the monstrous reptiles had always been rumored to be there, lurking just below the surface or in the weeds at the water's edge, and sightings inspired fear and nervous jokes among the natives. The saltwater crocodiles of South Asia — the world's largest — were notorious man-eaters, primeval nightmare creatures that predated the dinosaur. Since the Second World War they had been hunted almost to extinction for the soft cream-colored leather of their underbellies, but now they were partially protected as an endangered species. In recent years their numbers had increased in backwater mangrove swamps, estuaries, and tidal rivers.

A mile farther downriver, or maybe only a half mile — it was difficult for Maggi to estimate the distance they had slogged —

the path dipped down again to the water's edge. Vladimir strode on steadfastly, but Maggi flicked her light onto the black surface. The eyeshine of two red embers glowed back at her. From the size and visible scale markings, Maggi was sure it was the same animal. It was following them, silently stalking their path.

"The crocodile is following us!" she exclaimed.

"What?"

Maggi turned to shine her light, but in the space she had scurried to catch up to Vladimir, thick bushes concealed the river.

"If you shine that light again, I will take it away from you," he snapped harshly, as if she were an exasperating brat. "You will betray us." He turned and trudged on, as though it were Maggi's fault they were now fighting their way along a soggy footpath through lacerating vines instead of effortlessly drifting down the balmy stream. Red-eyed demons lurking beneath the dark waters were a myth to the Russian officer. The terrorists encamped on the river, perhaps now somewhere about them, were the real danger.

He was right, of course. They were exposed here on the game trail, and any light was reflected and magnified by the water. The trees were now smaller, less dense, the gaps

650

of sky against which they might be silhouetted more frequent. The jungle was thinning. Ahead a low overhanging branch framed the trail. *It moved!*

Maggi instinctively flashed her light on it. A black-and-yellow-banded snake hung down, almost within striking distance from Vladimir's face.

He screamed, recoiled back, and crashed into Maggi. She dropped the light, frantically groped about in the bushes for it, retrieved it, and shined it back up into the tree.

The snake slithered away into the leafy branches and disappeared, its distinctive bands now melding into the black shadows and yellow-green foliage.

"It is poison?" Vladimir asked, and there was the pitch of hysteria in his voice.

"I don't know. I think so. I think it was a krait. Like a cobra."

In that brief flash of light, Maggi saw his white, bloodless face and the wide, frightened eyes. Vladimir stood still now, and she heard his panting breath.

"It's gone now," she said, but her own words did not reassure her. She was as terrified as Vladimir was. But she had the sense that he was consciously trying to calm himself.

He started off again, then stopped after a

few steps and turned back to her. She felt his hands on her arms. "Thank you, Maggi," he said in a voice still slightly breathless but calmer. Then he led on again.

They marched for another ten or fifteen minutes. The land about them suddenly seemed to flatten out, the trees ended, and low palms and bushes stood out in the bright, unobstructed moonlight. Maggi felt sand underfoot.

"This is maybe the dry land before the swamps Captain Khromykh saw," Vladimir whispered, the delight and relief at being out of the jungle animating his voice.

But another fifty feet brought them to a sandy beach where a tributary debouched into the river, blocking their way. Vladimir switched on his light to examine how wide and deep it was. It was no more than twenty yards across, but the joining waters created a wider pool. The searching beam of light illuminated a tangle of weeds and logs, a high mud bank, and a carved-out wallow in which two crocodiles, each about ten feet long, lay half in and half out of the water.

In a reflex, Maggi and Vladimir both stepped back from the water. He cursed in Russian, then wailed, "We're trapped here!" in a voice that broke with despair.

Maggi desperately looked about. She explored a few yards up the beach. The tributary, like the river itself, flowed out of the jungle behind them, but it immediately narrowed. It was little more than a good-sized stream.

"I'm sure if we work upstream a little way, we can find a safe place to cross," she said.

She walked back to Vladimir, who paced the beach in distracted frustration. In the shining surface at the water's edge a dark shape moved.

"Vladimir!"

Two glowing, red-coal eyes rose up out of the water. The crocodile was enormous, almost twice the size of the two across the stream. It did not waddle on its belly but lifted itself up out of the water on its four legs, holding its body straight and high off the ground like any land animal. It dashed up the beach right at Vladimir and seized his leg in its long, demonic jaw. Vladimir screamed and was thrown to the ground by the power of the snap.

Maggi was paralyzed.

The croc now dropped down on its belly and, tail thrashing wildly, crawled backward toward the water, dragging Vladimir. He screamed again and clawed at the ground.

Maggi ran forward and grabbed his arms,

trying to pull him away from the crocodile. His sweaty hands slipped out of her grip, and she grabbed him about the arms. It was a terrible tug of war for Vladimir's limbs and life.

The croc's strength was inexorable, and it dragged both Vladimir and Maggi toward the water.

She let go of his arms and snatched at the straps of his backpack for a better grip. It ripped open, spilling their survival gear along the beach — packets of food, canteen, flares, gun.

Without a calculated thought, Maggi seized the gun, snapped a flare into it, and fired.

The explosion was blinding, searing her face and hands with its heat. Vladimir's and her cries were both lost in the roar.

Still blind, she groped for Vladimir. She felt him rise up on his hands and knees and scrabble frantically up the beach to the high ground away from the water. Maggi, still on her feet, yanked him along by the straps of his knapsack.

At the tree line they stopped. Maggi looked back, her eyes still dazzled by the flash. A myriad of little streams of red smoke rose up from the beach and swirled away in the night sky. The crocodile was nowhere in sight.

"Oh my God! Oh my God!" Maggi was hysterical, laughing and sobbing at the same time. "I don't believe this."

"What happened?"

"I shot it with a flare. I don't believe this."

Vladimir started to rise to his feet, howled, and collapsed to the ground, as if he had been shot.

"Vladimir, what is it?"

He writhed and moaned in terrible pain. "My leg."

Maggi dropped to her knees to examine it with the flashlight. The trousers were only slightly torn, where the crocodile had seized him. There was no blood that she could see.

Propping the light in the sand, she pulled up the trouser leg as gently as she could, but even that slight movement made Vladimir cringe and cry out again in pain. There were two lines of deep, raw puncture wounds from the croc's teeth about midcalf; they oozed but did not bleed very much. Despite the power and ferocity of the crocodile, the bite was astonishingly neat.

Maggi raised the leg slightly for a better look. Vladimir shrieked. The way the calf bent unnaturally at the middle of the shank, Maggi knew that the bone had been shattered by the croc's bite.

She lay the leg back down, delicately, as though the slightest movement might cause it to disintegrate.

Vladimir's eyes were extraordinarily bright, glistening not only with the pain but with the terrible realization that they were trapped on this beach.

Part IX
The Assault on the *Black Sea*

47. The Hunters

It was the hour when the night trembles, the morning stars still blaze like beacons, and a line perfect and straight appears in the east dividing the black sea from sky. Stewart had spent the night in his bridge chair, and now he watched Betelgeuse and Rigel fade away, the two stars marking the shoulder and foot of the giant hunter Orion as he chased the Pleiades, the daughters of Atlas, across the heavens.

To the ancient astronomers who first charted their fixed passage, the constellations and brightest stars were gods. At a given moment the angle between those celestial pinpoints of light and the horizon — that true line separating heaven and earth — would tell a navigator exactly where he was, how far he had traveled, and how much farther he had to sail to reach his destination.

Stewart had first learned celestial navigation on an NROTC training cruise in the North Atlantic between his junior and senior years in college. In those northern latitudes sunset and sunrise were only a few hours apart in summer, and they had to shoot the evening stars after sundown and the morning stars before dawn. In his delirium of sleeplessness, Midshipman Stewart had perceived the wonder of celestial navigation, not in man's cleverness to decode it, but in the order of a universe in which a man could find his exact place in a tractless sea. Any storm, even a sky-shattering typhoon, might throw a sailor completely off course; but if he survived, he could still navigate by the stars right to his destination. The old pagan gods were obviously the messengers of a higher divinity.

Sailors no longer made this mystical communion at sunrise and sunset. They now had gadgets — satellites, radio signals, computers — to pinpoint their position.

Commander Henry Stewart sat in his bridge chair and contemplated the fading constellation of the hunter Orion, and then gazed at the spreading glory of the dawn. He lowered his head and whispered, "God help me. Amen."

A few minutes later Lieutenant j.g. Gerling, the officer of the deck, checked the night orders and the time. "Permission to call away Flight Quarters, Captain?"

"Permission granted."

Six nautical miles from the *Decatur,* where the eastbound Phillip Channel joined the Singapore Strait, Salleh watched the sunrise from the bridge of the RSS *Valour*.

"It is time," he declared to the captain.

The Singapore navy officer quickly led the way into a cramped, dark compartment eerily glowing with radar scopes, target-acquisition instruments, and sonar readouts. That sailors on a tropical sea worked in this dark cave, walled in by buzzing steel cabinets, was a great paradox to the Malay.

"We have communications with the American aircraft. They are E-2C Hawkeyes," a young officer announced self-importantly.

"We have Hawkeyes. Why do we need the Americans?" the captain asked Salleh. His initial resistance to having the civilian agent aboard, directing operations, had slowly given way to a consuming curiosity.

"They will have to fly into Indonesia. If Singapore air force planes do it, it will be viewed as an act of aggression. If it is the Americans, they will express their gratitude to Jakarta, give them a fat foreign aid loan and a few Harpoon missiles, and everyone will be happy, *lah*."

The captain grunted and nodded knowingly.

Salleh checked the radio. "Is the direction-finding equipment set on this frequency?"

"Yes, sir."

Salleh took a deep breath. He raised the

mike and keyed the transmit button. "The winds of Paradise are blowing," he said in Malay. He repeated the call twice more, then waited, listening intently to the hum of the speaker.

"The message is in Bahasa?" the captain asked.

"Quiet," Salleh ordered.

The Chinese captain was offended, but before he could say anything, the crackle of a responding transmission came over the speaker. "The winds of Paradise blow like a typhoon."

"Did you get the direction?" Salleh snapped.

The operator looked confused and stuttered. "It looked to the south, but it was too short. I didn't understand what they said."

"You don't need to understand. Just get the direction. Are you ready now?"

"Yes, sir."

Salleh took another breath to calm himself. Again he spoke in Bahasa. "This is the ship chandler. We have the supplies you ordered. We have one shark hook and a crate of hooks for small fish. Repeat. We have one shark hook and a crate of hooks for small fish. Over." Salleh turned anxiously to the operator, who was tuning the direction finder.

"The ship's chandler has one shark hook

and a crate of hooks for small fish for us. Over."

Salleh glared at the operator, who tuned a dial, then announced, "Steady at one-six-seven degrees." He looked up at Salleh with a frightened expression.

Salleh nodded with a grim smile. "This is the ship chandler. *Selamat*. May your actions be blessed. Out." He turned to the young officer. "One-six-seven. Tell the Americans."

"Sea Hunter, this is *Valour*. Vector one-six-seven. Over."

"Roger, *Valour*. This is Sea Hunter, steering one-six-seven." The American pilot's voice was easy, confident.

Salleh was amazed at such confidence. He lowered his head and let out a deep, audible breath. He felt completely exhausted.

"That is it?" the captain demanded, incredulous.

"Pray to God, that is it," Salleh bin Ali whispered.

In the operations room of the Republic of Singapore Navy, Blocker stared down at the chart and traced the thin, neat pencil line heading one-six-seven degrees that the Chinese officer had drawn from the corvette's position in the strait, south through the reefs, across small islands that were little more than rocks and sandbars, isolated *kampongs,* Pulau Kapaladjernih, *selats,* shallows, and over the steepening contour lines indicating a mountain.

"Goddamn it all to hell!" Blocker exploded.

Yee was taken aback. "What is the matter?"

"This is a wild goose chase," Blocker snorted. "Damn, I should have known this was too easy." He turned to the American navy captain. "Jack, you might as well tell the SEAL team to stand down. Those planes aren't going to find shit."

"What the hell's going on, Block?"

"Yes, Mr. Blocker, please. I do not understand you." What had gone wrong? They had monitored the messages between Salleh and the pirate radio. They had established communications exactly as the arms smuggler Suliman had instructed them. The "hooks" they offered were a missile launcher and a crate of rifles. "What is wrong?"

Blocker jabbed his finger at the chart in frustration. "Look where we're pointing. Straight to a mountaintop. One thousand and four feet. That ain't high, grant you, but it tops everything else in the area."

"Yes?" It was a question. Yee still did not understand.

"It's a radio relay point. They receive messages and relay them to wherever the bad guys are *really* camped out. It's probably just one or two guys with the same Japanese portable Suliman had. But because of their height, they have fantastic range. As soon as our planes fly right at them, they'll damn well know we've got a bead on them. They'll be long gone before that SEAL team drops down. Damn!"

He looked at Yee and shook his head in disheartened resignation. "Baiyu, my friend, I'm afraid we're back to square one."

"Blue Knight, this is Eagle Claw Seven, over."

Stewart followed the helicopter's search on radio from the bridge of the *Decatur*. The ship's combat information center on the deck below was controlling the helo.

"Notify the captain we just picked up two transmissions on that VHF channel we're monitoring."

Stewart leaped for his microphone. "Eagle Claw, this is the captain. Did you get the messages and bearings?"

"Negative on the messages, Captain. They were in a foreign language. But we got *two* real good bearing indications. It sounded like messages back and forth. The first was bearing three-three-one from my present position. I can see out in that direction, and I'm looking right out into the Singapore Strait. It either came from a ship out there or downtown Singapore."

"That's interesting," Stewart commented to no one in particular, then ordered Chief Quartermaster Fields, "Plot these lines. Get the chopper's position from Combat."

"Yes, sir, I'm already on it."

"Eagle Claw, Blue Knight. Where's the second transmission you intercepted?"

"The second bears due south at one-eight-two degrees."

"Roger, one-eight-two degrees."

"I can't see anything in that direction. The morning mist is still thick, limiting visibility, and . . . wait one second, sir. I'm getting another shot. Out." The chopper's transmission broke off.

Stewart stretched his mike cord to the chart table.

"The chopper's right here, over this mess of islands, rocks, and reefs just south of the strait." Chief Fields pointed. "The first transmission is, like the pilot says, out of the strait from the direction of Raffles Lighthouse here. Now the second one runs due south along to this mountain peak *here*."

"With a VHF set, they sure as hell aren't transmitting from the other side of the mountain."

"No, sir, technically it's a line-of-sight transmission. But that peak is surveyed at 1,004 feet. When you figure a good height for a shore station antenna is 350 feet, that would give them a hell of a range with just a store-bought, off-the-shelf transceiver. When you add the freaky radio ducting we get out here in the tropics, they could probably send and receive to hell and back." The quartermaster was a medium-height but broad-shouldered man in his early thirties, now sporting a salty beard and mustache grown on the long cruise in the Persian Gulf. "Yes, sir, I'll bet a month's pay that's where they're set up." He tapped the chart with his pencil and nodded.

"They really know their playing field, don't they? Taking messages from all over. Dogging our ass with just fishing boats."

"We've been bushwhacked three times now, Captain, one way or another. Three times is no coincidence. They know exactly where we are and where we're heading." For some reason Fields's beard made not just his face but his eyes seem older, the crow's-feet at the corners deeper.

"Washington and Seventh Fleet think I'm paranoid when I suggest just that."

"Seventh Fleet ain't here, Captain."

"Blue Knight, this is Eagle Claw Seven,"

the overhead speaker boomed.

"This is Blue Knight. Go ahead."

"That was another transmission bearing one-eight-two. But then we had another brief transmission, a third one, bearing about twenty, twenty-five degrees east of the second one. Make that bearing one-five-five. It wasn't on long enough to get a clear fix. And it was weaker, like there was some interference."

"Roger, one-five-five. Anything else?"

"Yes, sir. I didn't understand the language, but it sounded like someone was answering, 'Roger, wilco,' and briefly repeating part of the message. I mean, it all sounded like chop suey to me, but that was the rhythm of it. Over."

"Roger, Eagle Claw. Hold your present position while we take a look at this. Over."

"Eagle Claw holding. Out."

Stewart studied the trace of that third transmission. Nothing stood out. The line crossed deserted islands, narrow channels, swamps.

"You couldn't get a ship in there, sir," Chief Fields commented, as if anticipating Stewart's speculation.

"No, you're right, Chief. I couldn't; but they might." He keyed his mike. "Eagle Claw Seven, this is Blue Knight. Vector one-five-five. Run down that last transmission."

"Roger, Eagle Claw vectoring one-five-five."

"Tom, be very careful."

"Roger, Captain, you don't have to say that twice, sir."

48. The Return of Liz Schneider

There was a subtle shift in the noises and buzzings from the dark forest and swamp — a gradual quieting of the crickets, burping frogs, screams of night birds, and the sonar shriek of the great black fruit bats. Different birds and insects were now stirring, tentatively calling, and then, quite suddenly, there was a sharp, plaintive hooting from a nearby treetop, the call of a lone male gibbon announcing the morning.

Maggi shivered and hugged her knees. When they had been hiking, she had been warm, actually sweating with the exertion. But now huddled, soaking wet, on the high bank above the beach in the blackness of predawn, she was thoroughly chilled, as much from fear as from the temperature. She stared into the shadows next to her, but she could not see Vladimir's face. She sensed that his eyes were wide and bright with the same panic and desperation she felt. And the pain. She could not imagine the agony of the shattered bones, but she had winced at every groan as Vladimir had excruciatingly guided her to build a cushion of palm fronds for his legs. Raising the legs, she hoped, would relieve some of the pressure and keep down the swelling. The position would also help prevent his slipping into shock.

The gibbon hooted again, a sad whistling song to the dawn.

"It will be light soon," Maggi whispered.

Vladimir was silent.

"Please talk to me."

"Yes, it will be light soon." His voice was strained, as if even the effort to talk was painful, but at least he was not in shock. They had already discussed — while Vladimir was still lucid — what Maggi must do, and now they waited silently for the first gray-pink streaks of sky to brighten into morning. A steamy mist overhung the water, veiling the canopy of trees across the stream and the swamp downriver, and the vapors now rose up to filter the rising tropical sun.

At the water's edge a sudden eruption of splashing, hissing, and growling exploded — crocodiles at some terrible rending of prey. Maggi could see nothing through the mist,

670

but she shuddered at whatever nightmarish confrontation had taken place.

The chorus of cicadas, birds, and monkeys rose with the light. The clamoring *kera* calls of a troop of long-tailed macaques raced through the trees like wildfire, and all at once a horde was shaking the branches right above her. Maggi sprang to her feet. She startled the macaques — small, skinny monkeys who glared at her and screamed threats, then leaped away through the trees as swiftly as they had arrived.

Maggi rummaged through the knapsacks for a fish knife and a small, red-handled utility knife. The first thing she had to do was splint Vladimir's leg. In the gray light she found a climbing rattan palm and bent to work sawing at it, first with the larger fish knife and then the smaller blade. The tough, fibrous stems did not cut easily, and Maggi was sweating heavily, her arms aching and both palms raw and bloodied by the time she finally hacked down four lengths. She dragged them back to Vladimir.

"You must leave me," he insisted in a pained whisper. "It is the only chance."

Maggi said nothing. It was a terrible decision, and it would have to be made in a little while. But it was unthinkable to leave him totally helpless. Using the line Vladimir had carried, she fashioned a brace for his leg. Any movement or pressure on the shattered calf brought forth an anguished groan from him. Perhaps the elaborate splint did nothing for his injury, but the labor of cutting the rattan and now constructing it about the tortured leg made Maggi feel, for the moment at least, less helpless. It drew her out of the paralysis of her terror.

Along the tributary bank Maggi could make out a few pole-sized trees, perhaps saplings. If she found one that forked, creating a natural shoulder rest, she could fashion some sort of crutch for Vladimir.

He had not moved but sat staring out at the beach below, his face dreadfully pale, his eyes hooded, as if mesmerized by the pain.

"If you can manage — "

The motion of his hand and his look silenced her. Then Maggi heard the whine of an outboard motor on the river piercing through the hush of the morning forest.

They were hidden from the river by a hummock of sand and scrub palms. Maggi crawled forward, and through the blades of pandanus she saw one of the pirates' motorized *perahus* churning upriver. She could not make out who was in it, and in a moment it passed around a bend where she could not follow it without betraying herself.

She started to crawl back to Vladimir when a sudden thrashing in the river directly below startled her. A big croc, half in and half out of the water, ripped at some sort of brown sack. A flash of silver-bordered cloth sent a paralyzing chill through Maggi with its familiarity. The big croc powerfully shook its head back and forth, lifting its prey for an instant entirely out of the water, the lifeless legs and one delicate white arm flapping, the shawl of silver-bordered Kelantan silk flashing in the morning sun.

Maggi screamed and screamed and could not stop screaming.

From an altitude of five thousand feet the jungle and mangrove swamps below appeared to be literally steaming. The mists and low clouds cloaking the rain forest frightened Callahan, piloting the Seahawk helicopter. He would not be able to see the white plume of an antiaircraft missile against that fleece, and he had to see it in order to evade it.

The sun, now a hot yellow and well up in the sky, had burned off most of the morning mist from the sea, but the heavily dew-drenched canopy seethed, as the dark leaves absorbed the heat and the moisture boiled off. Callahan's hand flicked down to the switch activating the flare dispenser, then to the infrared jammer. There was no groping in that movement. His fingers located each switch in a split second. But he had to see the missile coming. Eddie DiLorenzo had not seen it coming.

"Think it's an ambush setup, like Di-Lorenzo?" the copilot Henshaw asked, as if he had been reading Callahan's mind.

"You're paranoid," Callahan said, then added, "I like that in a copilot."

The Seahawk soared across a narrow strait between two large islands.

"They couldn't have known we'd pick up and follow the third signal. It was too weak," Henshaw said, as if reassuring himself.

Ahead of them the terrain dropped sharply, as the cloud-cloaked jungle hills descended into a misty swamp.

In a corner of her consciousness Maggi knew she was hysterical, but she could not stop sobbing uncontrollably.

Vladimir was at a total loss, unable to rise. He kept saying over and over, "What is the matter? Please be quiet."

Maggi cried and hiccupped, unable to catch her breath. "It's . . . Liz . . . Liz. The crocodiles . . . they . . . they are eating her."

"What are you saying? Liz? Liz who?"

Maggi gasped for breath, now trying to make sense of it. "Liz Schneider. Alan Schneider's wife. The pirates didn't release her. They murdered her. Fed her to the goddamn crocodiles." The horror of it walloped Maggi in the stomach. She retched and threw up, dropping to her knees, gagging. She again gasped for air. She could not catch her breath, and she stayed on her knees, head bent, until her breathing became less tortured and a measure of sanity returned.

"Why? Why would they do that?" Vladimir asked, when she finally seemed to have recovered. "Did you see her?"

Maggi shook her head, denying the thought. "I didn't see her face, her hair even." The image of the flailing body was elusive. "I saw . . . only one arm," she said in wonder rather than horror. Maggi felt numb, as though horror had an anesthetic element that would not allow its victim to feel its full sting. "Maybe the crocs ripped it off. Only her clothes . . . the silk shawl I'd given her."

Through the numbness came a terrible burning resolution. "I'm not going to let those fucking monsters get the rest of her." She fell on the knapsack, rummaged frantically through it, and grabbed the flare gun, a red shotgun-sized shell.

When Vladimir realized what she was doing, he cried out, "No, Maggi, you can't!" He reached out to grab her, but the movement jammed his leg, and he fell back writhing in pain.

In her rage Maggi ignored him, broke open the gun, loaded the flare, then leaped up to charge the crocodiles at the water's edge, and froze.

Ahmed and two pirates with assault rifles stood not fifteen feet from her. Ahmed stared at her with his dark, malevolent eyes, glanced at the crippled Russian, then smiled at Maggi, his eyes flashing with a terrible triumph.

Maggi swung up the flare gun and fired point blank at Ahmed's face.

There was a blinding red explosion, and the three pirates disappeared in the flash of scarlet flames. Maggi had a glimpse of the small man blasted right off his feet and hurled down the slope.

As the cloud of choking red smoke thinned, Maggi first saw Ahmed lying on his back, covered with a hundred match-head flames of burning magnesium and sulfur. He did not move. The other two pirates fled down the beach, staggering, but moving blindly as though their lives depended on reaching the trees. In his panic, one dropped his rifle, but he did not stop to recover it.

Maggi stared at the still flaming figure on his back, not really aware that it was she who had shot him but as though he were the victim of a spectacular accident in her vicinity. She wondered vaguely if she ought to try to beat out the little fires still flaring on his chest and legs.

She turned back to Vladimir, who stared at her with astonished eyes, then cried, "Look out!" and pointed. At the far end of the beach, one of the fleeing pirates crouched down in the bush and stared at the rifle he had dropped.

Maggi aimed her flare pistol at him, and the pirate scurried back into the trees.

There was a burst of gunfire from the bushes. Bullets slashed through the tree behind Maggi, shredding leaves and branches. "Get down!" Vladimir shouted.

Maggi dropped to the sand and crawled back to Vladimir. She was not at all frightened, but possessed by a terrific clarity of thought. She swiftly reloaded the flare gun with another shell, a white cartridge. From her low crouching position behind the dune she could not see the bushes where the two pirates were concealed. There was another burst, the bullets smacking into the tree branches to her right, splintering a branch, which tumbled slowly, leaves and twigs flurrying down. The pirates could not see her; they were firing at random.

Maggi squirmed on her stomach up to the crest of the dune, where she could just make out the trees that sheltered the pirates. She aimed and fired. The shot was high, a streamer of white smoke that streaked over the beach, arching up, and exploded high in the trees. The foliage erupted with a fantastic shrapnel of squawking multicolored jungle birds; smoking phosphorus fragments poured down onto the bushes. Maggi heard panicked cries and glimpsed two figures thrashing deeper into the woods.

For several moments an eerie silence prevailed; neither birds, monkeys, nor cicadas screeched.

"What now?" Maggi said.

Ahmed was lying very still, scorched and smoking. She wondered if he were dead or only knocked unconscious by the explosion, but rejected the thought of crawling over to him to check.

"They'll go back and get the others," Vladimir said. "You have to go now."

"I can't leave you here."

"It is not your choice. There are over two hundred other people on the boat. You must get help to them. What will happen to me will happen, whether you stay or leave."

"You can lean on me."

"*No!*" The word snapped out like a slap across Maggi's face. The pale blue eyes glared at her, shining with a terrible intensity.

It was then that she heard the helicopter. It was so far overhead that at first its distant engine drone and rotor slap seemed just another ratcheting, insectoid jungle call, another hard-shelled, whirring bug declaring its territory.

Vladimir's head twisted up. "Quick, fire a flare."

Maggi groped for a cartridge.

"No, a red one. Run out onto the beach and fire straight up."

Maggi fired one, then another red flare. They rocketed up into the air several hundred feet, leaving white contrails, then burst into blossoms of scarlet smoke.

She searched the sky, squinting into the bright glare of the sun. She spotted the helicopter and waved frantically. But the aircraft was so high it seemed impossible for its crewmen to see her, a slight, dark-clad figure on a muddy beach. It was more likely that any pirates in the area would see the red smoke flares.

She thrashed about in a panic searching for something she could wave to attract the helicopter's attention but spotted nothing except the bright-colored shirt Ahmed wore. She loathed to touch him.

She ran back to Vladimir for more flares. "We have to attract their attention. They can't see me out there."

"Wear the life jacket." One of the bright orange jackets cushioned his back, the other propped up his leg. The movement to release each of the jackets made Vladimir blanch, and a cry of pain hissed through his clenched teeth.

Maggi seized the bulky kapok vests and ran down to the beach, holding up and waving both jackets. In a few moments the helicopter would fly out of sight.

She loaded the pistol from the box of cartridges and fired a third and fourth directly at the chopper.

The aircraft did not turn but looked as though it were now meandering toward them, as if drifting on an upper wind that would carry it overhead.

Maggi again frantically waved both jackets, but their heaviness quickly exhausted her arms. She donned one of the orange vests and then flagged the other overhead with both hands.

The helicopter abruptly banked and swooped off, disappearing beyond the trees.

"*No!* Oh, my God, don't leave us," Maggi

screamed. "Don't leave us." She dropped to her knees, utterly desolated, and wept.

"What's happened?" Vladimir shouted.

Maggi could not answer.

The helicopter suddenly burst from a parting in the trees, no more than a hundred feet off the ground. It spewed bright white flares like a Fourth of July sparkler.

Maggi sprang to her feet, screaming crazily, jumping up and down, waving both orange jackets overhead, like a pompom girl whose team had just scored on a freak play.

The helicopter circled the beach once, then flew out over the river, banked, and dropped down, hovering at water's edge. A man, faceless in a bright helmet, crouched in the open doorway pointing a machine gun directly at her. There was a white star in a blue circle, a red, white, and blue bar, and the letters NAVY on the aircraft's gray flank.

Maggi dropped her life jackets and ran toward it. "Don't shoot. I'm an American. I'm an American. Don't shoot." She could not hear her own cry above the deafening whine of the turbines, but then, as if somehow recognizing her, the truck-size aircraft settled down onto the sand. The door gunner pushed aside his machine gun and reached out his hand to Maggi.

49. *Maggi Aboard the* Decatur

To port a steep wall of rock erupted from the water, and to starboard there was a gentler slope of nipah palms, but Robinson could make out the milky line of a submerged coral reef. Ahead the channel — if the passage could be given that navigable a name — took a dogleg to the right around a rocky island that thrust up in midstream. The officer of the deck held the *Decatur* in position in the strait by jockeying the ship's two auxiliary propulsion units.

"Yes, sir, we estimate we'll be at the river's mouth in about fifty-five minutes," Stewart said into the radio mike.

"I don't understand, Captain Stewart. I have a report here that your ship is disabled and is supposed to be en route to a yard in Singapore." The voice of ComSeventhFleet in Yokosuka boomed over the bridge speaker.

"Yes, Admiral, we're on the auxiliary power units now. This strait we're navigating is very narrow, and I wouldn't proceed faster even if we had the power. But if we run into trouble, we'll need a tug from Singapore to pull us out."

"Is it prudent to take your ship into that

area, Captain, especially in its condition?"

"No, sir, it is *not* prudent. But there are 135 American lives at stake and another hundred Soviet civilians. We've been trying to get through on the Command Net for an hour now, sir. And we've sent messages asking for instructions since our chopper first picked up the two hostages."

Robinson heard the fury and frustration in Stewart's voice, and for once he shared it. But he was grateful that computerizing, digitizing, encoding, and decoding the voice would strip it of that emotional charge.

"Yes, Captain, we've been busy today. The carrier task force has moved into the area to launch its search for the *Black Sea,* and in addition we've had a special operation under way with the Republic of Singapore."

"Admiral, we *know* where the *Black Sea* is. According to Mrs. Chancellor, it's just a few miles up a narrow, uncharted river, the one on which we picked her and the other hostage up. It's camouflaged under a primary jungle canopy. Our planes may not be able to see it from the air unless we stick a helicopter right on top of it."

"The other hostage you've recovered is the *Black Sea*'s first officer, Vladimir Korsakov?"

"Yes, sir, but he's not in very good shape.

His leg is apparently shattered, and they had a rough time getting him in and out of the chopper. The pain sent him into shock. He's heavily sedated in sick bay. We also captured one of the terrorists. According to Mrs. Chancellor, he's sort of the second in command, the cousin of the leader. He appears to lapse in and out of consciousness. He may be faking it — we have guards on him — or he may have a concussion. He's also suffering from bad burns. Mrs. Chancellor said she shot him with a flare gun, apparently at point-blank range. I would recommend med-evacking them both out as soon as possible, sir."

There was a long pause, as though someone on the other end was discussing this information. "Anyone else, Captain Stewart?"

"Possibly, sir. Mrs. Chancellor says she saw the remains of Mrs. Alan Schneider on the beach. A crocodile was feeding on them."

"Mrs. Alan Schneider — that's not possible. She was one of the victims in Singapore." There was another break in communications. "Maybe it is possible that she saw some remains. What kind of shape is Mrs. Chancellor in? We might want to evacuate her to Singapore to debrief her ASAP."

"She's shaky and exhausted, but she's unhurt, sir. We've already anticipated her evacuation and discussed it with her. She's very insistent that she'll be more useful on the scene. She's the only one who really knows where the ship is who's conscious at the moment."

Stewart paced back and forth across the bridge to the limits of the phone's line as he talked. "We've examined a chart that the *Black Sea*'s captain sent out with her, and it's wrong. He's got the wrong island. So even the ship's crew and passengers don't really know where they are. But we've got a fix on exactly where the helo picked them up, and Mrs. Chancellor's information tells us where the ship is in relation to that point. Apparently she's fluent in the language and was the liaison with the terrorist leader. That's why she was chosen to escape with the first officer."

"Captain, let us have the coordinates of your ship's present position and your estimate of the *Black Sea*'s position."

Stewart read off the latitude and longitude, and the robotic voice read them back to him.

"Admiral, these terrorists may not know yet that we've picked up the two and their man. We may still have the element of surprise, if we move quickly, sir."

"Yes, thank you, Captain Stewart, we'll

take that into account. We'll be back to you shortly with a plan of action. Seventh Fleet out."

Stewart replaced the radio telephone.

"You get the feeling that they just forgot we were out here?" Robinson said. "Sort of misplaced this little model of a Perry-Class FFG on their strategic game board. Someone in the Pentagon accidentally knocked us off it reaching for a cup of coffee."

Stewart shook his head and made a sweep of his hand. "On the other side of this archipelago, in the safe, deep waters of the South China Sea, there's a magnificent carrier task force steaming around, launching jets right and left."

"And they can't find their dicks with either hand," Chief Fields snorted.

"God help us," Stewart whispered. "The Pentagon is still searching for a high-tech version of World War II to fight." But Stewart's eyes were gleaming now, not from frustration or anger but a fierce pride that all but shouted out. He had confounded the navy at its highest level. He suddenly straightened and peered down the channel.

"This is the captain. I have the conn. Mr. Balletto, please resume forward lookout."

"Aye, aye, sir."

The *Decatur*, its main gear crippled, should

have been creeping into a shipyard at that moment. Instead, the frigate was burning up its auxiliaries, threading among razor-edged reefs and rocks at a reckless four knots, to the rescue. And under the circumstances, no one dared to order Stewart back.

The captain prowled the bridge, hanging from the port wing and then the starboard, intently studying the water and the shore, noting the continuous readings of the fathometer that the quartermaster sang out, rechecking his position on the chart while constantly muttering that the chart was worthless. Balletto, the ship control officer, was stationed on the bow with a walkie-talkie as lookout.

If Stewart was mad, there was a skilled seamanship to his madness that held Robinson in awe. The executive officer felt worthless. His knee had become swollen, and even hobbling about on a crutch was excruciating; he was now propped up in the captain's bridge chair with an ice pack on his leg.

With a sharp thrust of shame, what Robinson now saw clearly was not Stewart's recklessness but his own caution. The executive officer was a competent, prudent professional; he never would have sailed the *Decatur* into the dangerous straits where it had been ambushed. In football Robinson had known quarterbacks, linebackers, safeties who played with a secret intuition he had never had, constantly positioning themselves for the big bomb pass, the interception, or the fumble, even when the game was lost. Robinson recognized that sixth sense in football. He had just never seen it before in the navy, and he wondered on what terrible gridiron Stewart had honed such instincts.

"What are we going to do when we get there, XO?"

It was Callahan, the helicopter pilot.

"That's for higher authority to decide. The mission is to get there. To be there when whatever's going to happen happens."

"*Yes, sir,*" Callahan responded enthusiastically, as if it made unquestionable sense to him.

The woman looked fragile, like a child who had witnessed horrors children should never see. But at that she looked considerably better than when she had tumbled from the helicopter a few hours before, near collapse and hysteria, desperately holding herself together by sheer force of will to answer Stewart's groping questions as rationally as possible, because she knew others' lives, hundreds of them, depended on the acuity of her answers. This desperate knowledge she had borne out of the jungle. Stewart had been tremendously impressed by her strength.

"I'm sorry to have to disturb you. I know you're exhausted," he apologized. "But there are several people flying out by helicopter to talk to you. They'll be here in a few minutes."

She smiled wanly, but said nothing at first. Stewart had given her his cabin, and she had evidently washed and brushed her hair. She had had an hour or two to rest, although he doubted she had slept, but the edge of hysteria — the threat that any moment she might shatter — was gone. She was still clearly exhausted, her eyes puffy and shadowed purple with fatigue, yet something about her deeply moved and touched Stewart.

"Who are they?" she asked finally.

"I only know one of them. He's from the embassy in Singapore. Harold Blocker. Another is a naval officer, a Lieutenant Commander Hamilton, and the third is from the Singapore government. I don't know them."

"How is Vladimir?"

"He's unconscious right now, but stable, according to the corpsmen. There's also a navy doctor flying out to take care of him and the prisoner."

"The prisoner?"

"The man you identified as second in command of the terrorists. He is, isn't he?"

"Terrorists," she repeated, as though questioning the word. "I think so. Yes." She gazed about the bridge and through the windscreen. "Where are we?" she wondered vaguely.

"We're anchored in a strait not very far from where we picked you up.

She continued to search about the bridge, staring not at the high-tech panel of instruments but at the men about her. Just a few hours before, Stewart had taken a perverse pride in their salty appearance after six months of continuous operations. Suddenly *personages* were descending on the *Decatur*, and he was acutely conscious of the crew's rumpled, sweat-stained uniforms, dark, unshaven jowls, and his own bristling three-day stubble and rank odor. The sailors in their filthy dungarees and the officers and chiefs in khakis with murky stains at their armpits, waists, and crotches looked as mangy and unwashed as any pirates they were hunting.

"I have to apologize for our appearance," Stewart stammered. "Our evaporators broke down, and we don't have water to spare for washing and shaving."

"You all look beautiful to me," she said.

"The air conditioners also — "

She shook her head, stopping his apology. She was dressed in one of the junior officer's khakis, much too big for her, with the sleeves and legs rolled up, the waist scrunched by a belt. Like his wife, Charlotte, she made the oversized men's clothing somehow feminine, cute. *Charlotte!* That's what so touched and disturbed Stewart about Maggi Chancellor. She had the same lush, thick auburn hair as his wife, the delicate features and high, smooth brow that would forever give her a look of girlishness.

"I'm sorry we didn't have anything more appropriate for you to wear." This time he smiled broadly at her.

She touched her sleeves with pleasure, as if hugging herself. "These clothes make me feel safe. I'd forgotten what a wonderful feeling it is just to feel safe." She looked directly at Stewart, and her eyes were bright with tears.

"Captain, the helicopter from Singapore has the ship in sight and requests permission to land," the officer of the deck sang out.

To Stewart's surprise, Blocker, Lieutenant Commander Hamilton, and the Oriental man with them were all dressed for combat in dark camouflage-patterned jump suits, the two Americans hoisting sawed-off Colt Com-

691

mando 5.6-mm. rifles. There were also two marines with them.

Blocker grinned broadly and held out his hand as he came off the flight deck. "You just can't seem to stay out of trouble, Captain Stewart," the CIA man greeted him with hearty informality.

"Jumps to me like fleas to a hound dog."

They moved into the hangar, where the piercing whine of the chopper's turbines were muffled and they could speak in a normal voice. "This here is Sam Hamilton," Blocker continued in his offhand, gregarious way. "It goes without saying, he's one of your SEALs."

Stewart looked into the lean, tanned face and squeezed back the fierce grip that was offered.

"And this is Mr. Salleh bin Ali, of the Republic of Singapore government." Salleh was a small, dark, wirily built man with a mustache, shaggy hair, and almost theatrically handsome features that somehow made his appearance all the more sinister. "It was Salleh's message that you first picked up this morning. It was designed to flush out the bad guys."

"And we got lucky."

"How were you listening on that channel?" Salleh's question was intense, probing.

"We were monitoring it. We captured one of their radios yesterday, when one of them ambushed my ship."

"Ah, then it was not luck," Salleh smiled.

"The two marines are Sergeant Johnson and Corporal Martinez from our embassy. They'll take over the security for your prisoner."

The marines' neatly pressed, starched fatigues and the SEAL's clean-shaven cheeks and short haircut again made Stewart painfully self-conscious about his grubby, back-from-jungle-patrol appearance, but this time he offered no apology.

A master-at-arms led the marines off to the sick bay, where Ahmed lay hovering in a fitful coma.

"You won't get much out of him, or the Russian for that matter," Stewart offered.

"What about Professor Chancellor?"

It was the first time Stewart had heard her title. "She's had it very rough. She's unhurt, but at the edge of collapse. But she's anxious to tell you everything she can. She's waiting in my cabin. If you'll please follow me, gentlemen." Stewart led the way forward through the narrow passageways.

"I'd like you to sit in on the debriefing, Captain," Hamilton said earnestly. "You're the only asset we have in place. The fleet

693

and Singapore are too far. We'll need you for backup, communications, a helo pad, emergency medical. God knows what'll go down."

Stewart nodded. "Who's in charge?"

"My orders come direct from the National Command Center."

Stewart opened the door to his cabin. The woman half rose from her chair, obviously startled by the appearance of the three men outfitted to storm a guerrilla base.

"Professor Chancellor, I'm Harold Blocker from the embassy in Singapore. I've read and admired several of your papers on Malaysia and Indonesia; I wish we were meeting under less drastic circumstances," he said persuasively.

"You're going to assault the ship? That's why you're all dressed like that?"

"Under the circumstances, I'm afraid our options are limited."

Maggi Chancellor's eyes pressed shut, and she took a deep breath and let it out slowly. Then in a shaken voice she said, "The ones they said they were releasing — the passengers and crewmen — the pirates killed them all, didn't they? That's why you're not negotiating."

"How many were released?"

"There were three passengers. I saw two

Russians that left the ship, bartenders, but there was another one, a sailor they said they also released. But I know they killed him the first night. Tengku said they were going to release Vladimir today. That's why we escaped."

Blocker frowned. "I'm afraid they were all killed," he said in a soft voice. Stewart was surprised by the gentleness in the big man's manner.

"I saw Liz Schneider's body in the river."

Blocker glanced at Salleh. "How did you know it was Mrs. Schneider?"

"She was wearing a shawl I gave her when she left the ship. To protect her from the sun." There was no irony in the comment, just a flatness, a lack of inflection that refused to acknowledge the horror it was describing.

The woman now looked directly at Blocker, and her eyes were wide and frightened. "What happened to them?"

"I'll be happy to answer all your questions, Mrs. Chancellor. But first there is information we must have as quickly as possible to save lives."

The woman nodded. She seemed almost relieved that Blocker had put off her question.

Without the air conditioning, the cabin was hot, fetid, and the air the blower circulated had a sour, swampy smell.

"Is the ship wired for explosives?" Hamilton asked suddenly.

"I don't think so. I never saw anything like that. I had fairly good access about the ship."

"Gasoline drums?"

"Nothing like that. Unless, of course, they rigged it all this morning when they found Vladimir and me gone. And, oh — wait. There might be something in the engine rooms. I never went down *there*."

"But they don't know you were picked up?"

"I'm sure they do. The man Ahmed you captured, there were two others with him. I frightened them off with the flare gun. It was just before your helicopter came. It was shooting off fireworks like the Fourth of July."

"It's an antimissile defense," Stewart interjected. "We've lost one of our helicopters to a Stinger."

"But they probably saw it. I think they had a base camp downriver. That's what Vladimir and Captain Khromykh thought. That was the pattern of their coming and going."

"My helicopter didn't spot it," Stewart said.

"Hell, these guys have hidden a 333-foot

ship," Blocker commented. "They're not going to fly battle flags at their base camp."

The woman stared at Salleh, as if recognizing his presence for the first time. She spoke to him in a foreign language. He answered, and there was a brief exchange. The woman seemed satisfied and gave the Singapore agent a faint smile.

"It's good that Salleh is with you," she said. "The pirates don't speak much English. Just speaking to them in their own language may prevent bloodshed. That's why I was the go-between."

"How many are there?"

"I don't really know. There were never more than a half dozen around at one time, but they kept shifting around. The first night about a dozen boarded the ship. But when we pulled into the river, there were about two dozen more on the banks, waving guns, screaming, *'Allah akbar!'* That really intimidated the hell out of us. We never really saw that number again, but we felt they were around somewhere, downriver or in the jungle."

"How well armed were they?"

"The guards on board always had M16's or Russian AK-47's. The ones I saw on the banks weren't that well armed. They had shotguns, old American M-1's, even old

British Enfields."

"That's *very good!*" Blocker exclaimed, surprised, as Stewart was, by the completeness of the description.

"In our field work, my ex- . . . I mean, we learned to identify the arms of the army men, the militia. It tells us a lot about foreign aid, other connections, et cetera."

Blocker regarded Maggi admiringly. "It certainly does." He, Hamilton, and Salleh all seemed to lean forward at once, as they realized that this woman was going to be more valuable than they had anticipated.

"The leader, Tengku Haji Azhar, carried a .45 the first night, but I never saw it again. But he always carried a sword, a Malay *parang,* as if he disdained to carry a gun; *he* was the sword of Islam."

Again Blocker and Salleh exchanged a sharp look.

"What about their military training?" the SEAL officer Hamilton persisted.

"I don't know. When they first came aboard — I saw them climb aboard — I thought, my God, these are commandos. But after that everything was very sloppy, haphazard, not very military."

"Yes, that is what they do very well," Salleh said, with a nod of appreciation at the point. "They board ships."

"There was one — Mohammed. I heard Tengku refer to him as a professional. I think he had something to do with the missiles."

"A man with long hair and a pocked face?" Stewart asked.

"Yes." Maggi was surprised.

"He's in a body bag in my meat locker," Stewart explained. "He bushwhacked us with a Russian RPG."

"Maybe he's their only trained shooter."

"Don't count on it," Blocker shook his head. "Remember this Tengku Haji Azhar."

"No, I don't think so," Maggi said, a mild protest in her voice. "I mean he's dangerous, but he's a romantic."

"Yeah, a romantic and fanatic who's trained in terrorist camps in Tehran," Blocker snarled.

"You know that?"

"Yes, we know that." And Salleh nodded, as if to confirm this intelligence personally.

It seemed to Stewart that Maggi Chancellor was unusually disturbed by the disclosure.

Then the SEAL commander took over the debriefing. He had Maggi sketch the ship's position in the river, the height of the banks, the surrounding jungle. They worked out an estimate of the ship's distance upriver from the time she and the Russian had floated downstream, then hiked, until they had reached the beach where they were picked up. But it was a terribly rough estimate, miles off either way, on which to plan an assault.

"We can pinpoint the ship with the MAD gear on our chopper once we're within a half mile," Stewart volunteered.

Hamilton looked up at Stewart and nodded, then frowned down at the crude sketch and cursed, "It's a bitch. They know we're coming. It's like assaulting a fort with a moat around it."

Stewart studied the SEAL, the lean face with knotty jaw muscles, the flat-bellied, wiry body. He was not a big man or powerfully built; in fact, next to the huge, chesty Blocker, he seemed almost puny. People thought that SEAL training was about physical fitness, but that was merely the preparation for a test that football players and marathon runners often failed. Exhaustion, cold water, sleeplessness, constant harassment eventually reduced all the candidates to the point where their physical strength was totally spent; only the raw will, still burning in a chilled, wet, quivering body — the mind numbed in its misery and pain — pushed a man on, crawling like a primordial creature through the sand of a cold, dank beach in the blackest midnight of each man's soul. In Vietnam the SEALs had been the only people crazier than Stewart's river-boat crews.

Hamilton, Blocker, and Salleh rose to leave.

"I want to know what happened to the hostages who were released," Maggi said in a quiet voice. "You promised you'd tell me." She took a deep breath, as if to steel herself, both hands pressed against the table top.

Blocker leaned forward and gripped both her hands in his. "I'm sorry," he said in a gentle voice. "They were murdered . . . beheaded, and their . . . heads have been delivered to Singapore, one each day the ransom has not been paid."

Maggi did not make a sound but sat mute as tears flooded her eyes and streamed down her face.

"I must ask you this." Salleh's voice was thick with apology. "This *romantic,* Tengku Haji Azhar, this sword of Islam, would *he* do such a thing?"

The answer was a strangled whisper, a hardly audible "Yes."

Hamilton and Salleh bent into the wind churned up by the whirling helicopter blades, but Blocker hung back in the hangar for a word.

"Are you going to med-evac the Russian out?" Stewart asked.

"Not just yet. The doctor says he's in no medical danger. And we'd just as soon not notify our Russian friends until we've got this operation buttoned up. It keeps it infinitely simpler."

"Is he a prisoner?"

"No, sir, he is an honored guest."

"And the terrorist?"

"You apprehended him while rescuing hostages. A United States Navy vessel on the high seas. It's humanitarian, legal, and diplomatically above reproach. That is, until we start transferring bodies around. For instance, our slightly singed terrorist is a Malaysian national wanted in Singapore for the murder of a Russian maritime officer for openers. Not to mention piracy on the high seas, the murder of U.S. and Russian nationals both on a Russian-flag vessel and on the sovereign territory of the Republic of Indonesia."

"It's out of my league."

"Hell, we're not exactly sure what the game is. We'll keep you posted." He started for the helicopter, then turned back to Stewart. "Your old friend Jack Campbell told me a week ago that the good Lord had put the right man in the right spot. I'm proud to know you, Captain Stewart." Blocker threw Stewart a mock salute.

The navy officer hesitated, then smiled and saluted back. "We'll be out here, if you need us."

Blocker grinned. "Where the hell else would you be?"

50. The Assault on the Black Sea

Callahan swept in, pressing the Seahawk low over the treetops, just high enough so that he could make out the black concourse of the silt-thick river a quarter mile off to his right.

The bright red and yellow dart of the MAD "bird" streamed behind the chopper like a lure on a troll line. The Magnetic Anomaly Detector was sensitive to the deviations in the earth's magnetic field caused by a large, hidden metal body — specifically a submarine deep beneath the ocean's surface or, in this instance, the steel hull and machinery of a liner under the dense jungle canopy below.

The black band of the river visibly narrowed, then twisted and abruptly closed, as the terrain ahead climbed into the rolling foothills of the mountain that formed the island's brief cordillera.

Callahan rolled into a bank, still following the river, now marked by a barely discernible cleft in the canopy where the trees on either side meet.

The copilot Henshaw pointed to the changing patterns on the MAD display, "Oh, yeah, there's something definitely down there."

"Stand by," Callahan said into his mike. He waited a beat, then another. "Madman. Madman. Madman," he signaled.

"Your position is marked," the controller's voice came back.

The electronic images on the helicopter's sensors were transmitted back to the combat-information center on the *Decatur* and reproduced on video displays there.

"We're outta here," Callahan said. He banked steeply away from the river and dropped low to hug the treetops, the downwash of his rotors creating a visible wake in the sea of green leaves behind the fleeing Seahawk.

Four Huey helicopters now swept in from the sea, flying the nap of the earth, their landing skids barely clearing the trees.

Two flew a mile to the right of the river, two a mile to the left. Their modified 1,400-horsepower turbines were muffled almost to silence, so that the only sound was an eerie *whoosh* of the rotor blades.

In the lead chopper Blocker sat at the end of the bench, his guts rumbling, and studied the line of faces across from him. Each, like his own, was made up in green with streaks of russet brown and black, the men camouflaged like their jump suits to blend into the foliage and shadows of the jungle. With the exception of Hamilton, Blocker did not know any of the men in the Naval Special Warfare Task Unit, and that made him even more edgy. If the shit started flying, the SEALs would cover one another's ass, not the strange spook's. He was as expendable as the new replacement in an old combat unit.

But what now had Blocker's bowels fluttering was the approaching jump through the trees. He had not dropped from a chopper since his field training, and that had been over ten years and thousands of too damn rich meals ago. There had been time in Singapore for only one quick dry run, hooking up and dropping from the Huey while it was still on the ground. Even then he had felt as heavy, bloated, and middle-aged as a thirty-year bureaucrat next to the younger, rock-hard SEALs.

Keep your feet together and stay as small as possible, he reminded himself. He consciously squeezed his thighs and ankles together. He was determined not to freeze at the door, but he was terrified of breaking a leg or, worse yet, his pelvic bone or back. It was a long drop to the ground, longer than any he had made years ago in training.

The helicopter suddenly went into a hover. The SEAL commander Hamilton, standing behind the pilot, pointed out something, and the helicopter sideslipped into position, making Blocker's queasy stomach lurch. Hamilton turned and signaled to the men stationed at the right and left doors. Simultaneously they heaved out a coil of thin nylon rope, over one hundred feet of it. Then they disappeared out the doors. Two more SEALs followed, then another pair, and another — the entire squad out of the aircraft in seconds — and then it was Blocker's turn.

He heaved up and clipped the harness of his Swiss seat to the half-inch nylon line. He wrapped the rope over his right shoulder and down under his left thigh, then awkwardly backed out the door, paying the line out gradually, his gloved left hand gripping it in front, his right hand behind him, keeping the rope clear of the sawed-off assault rifle strapped low on his butt. He backed into the blasting downwash of the rotor, his feet groping blindly for the narrow rail of the helo's landing skids. He braced his legs and leaned back, way back, gripping the rope tightly until he was hanging almost horizontal, then jumped.

In his nervousness he was clutching the line much too tightly, and he almost slammed right back into the helo, just missing the skids. He dangled there a moment, eased his grip, dropped a few feet, panicked, squeezed again, jerked to a stop. He dropped, jerking to a stop three or four times, before he worked out a smooth rhythm of descent. Branches slapped at him. *Stay small as possible.* He brought his legs and arms in. Then he was through the canopy, and he watched the ground come up fast. He jerked to a stop, let go, and hit the ground hard and heavy but kept his feet.

Hamilton was beside him and gave him a thumbs up. Blocker looked about for Salleh, who had been in the other helo. The Malay was already on the ground, packing away his harness. He looked up and beamed at Blocker, a giddy, triumphant ear-to-ear grin. Blocker nodded and grinned back at him.

The two squads of SEALs were already

deploying through the trees in a skirmish line. No one said a word. Hamilton gave silent hand signals, and the few SEALs Blocker had in sight seemed to disappear, blending into the vines and dark bark in the dusky twilight of the forest floor.

This was primeval jungle, where little sunlight penetrated the layers of red belian and dipterocarp leaves. The underbrush was meager, and the two squads traveled quickly through the rain forest. There was something almost hallucinatory about their movement, the silence of the warriors, momentarily materializing as they darted quickly ahead through the dark cathedral columns of tree trunks, then froze and dissolved away into a tangle of climbing lianas.

The *Decatur* cast about on its anchor in midchannel, south of the river mouth, where Stewart had a clear field of fire upstream; the two .50-calibers mounted on the starboard side could rake the mangrove swamps off his bow and quarter. Helmeted sailors manned each of the guns, broiling in the sweltering afternoon heat. Whatever breeze stirred in the narrow strait was cut off by the guns' steel shields, the steel heated by the sun now hot enough to sizzle bacon. Stewart wondered how long he could keep his crew at battle quarters.

He searched the shoreline, making a low sweep with his binoculars, but he saw nothing but nipah pines and mangroves. The breather roots of the Sonneratia mangroves which normally poked up through the mud like a field of spikes were now covered by a rising tide, giving the dangerous illusion of a wider channel. A fish eagle rose from the stark branches of a dead tree and soared up effortlessly on the heated air currents, now wheeling out over the *Decatur*'s masts as if searching its leafless metal limbs for whatever strange, hapless creatures might live there.

Stewart was keenly aware that somewhere nearby the terrorists had their base camp, and he wondered what, or *who*, had disturbed the eagle. The *Decatur* — all 453 broadside feet of it — was anchored motionless in the glaring sunlight, a sitting duck, and that made him very jumpy.

To the south he spied two white masts perhaps a mile away and intently studied them through the binoculars, trying to reckon what they were. The masts moved slowly from east to west, and with the movement he recognized them as the rigging of a trading schooner, its sails furled, hull down behind an outcrop of rocks. Without enough wind for safe steerage, the sailing ship was apparently picking its way through the islands on an auxiliary diesel engine.

"Is it all right for me to be up here?" a soft feminine voice at his elbow inquired. Maggi Chancellor looked wan, her eyes swollen and red.

Stewart smiled, nodded, then added, "But if you hear anything that remotely sounds like gunfire, drop down behind the bulwarks."

"Is that likely?"

"I've had a man killed on this spot by a sniper. And I've had a missile shot into our engine room, and the explosion started a major fire. So this is as safe, or rather as dangerous a place, as any on the ship." He was not going to send her back below.

"It all appears so lovely. A cruise along a tropical shore. And what horrors those mangroves are hiding — " Her voice broke off, and she stood peering into the black and green shadows of the stand of Sonneratia that formed the seaward wall of the swamp.

"Are you going to be all right?"

She looked up at Stewart, shading her eyes against the low, glaring sun with her palm. "Thank you for sending the doctor, but I just need some time alone. All he could do was give me a sedative, and I don't want to sleep. I won't sleep until I know the others are safe." There was an amazing timbre to her voice, a vibrancy that declared her will more than any words. "I looked in on Vladimir. The doctor said he's in no danger. Was he able to tell you anything more?"

"Not much. He was able to confirm a few things about the ship and the terrain that you already told us."

"What about Ahmed?"

"His concussion is real, but he'll live."

"No, I mean what will you do with him?" she persisted.

"I don't know. It's not my decision; it's the State Department's. From what Blocker said, I think Singapore will get him." Stewart saw no reason not to tell her whatever he knew.

"Good. They'll hang him." She said it with a quiet fierceness. "After they find out what they want. They have the British system of justice, except where their national security is involved. And they don't hesitate to use the death penalty."

It was not just concern for the hostages that was keeping her going; there was a rage now fueling her, a rage that had not been there earlier. Stewart recognized it in her, as he recognized it in himself. It was a healthy thing — he knew that now, despite the sermons to the contrary — because the alternative was despair, the yawning black desperation that led, ultimately, to self-destruction.

He said, "Here, let me show you something beautiful out there," handed her the binoculars, and pointed to the distant schooner. It had apparently worked its way out of the narrows and found a wind blowing between the islands. The black trapezoidal sails unfurled from the gaff booms like night herons taking flight.

"What is it?"

"A Bugis schooner. They still use them to trade in the islands."

"It's *elegant.*" There was a lilt to her voice.

"That's my fantasy for when the navy throws me out for wrecking my ship. Sell the home I have in Alexandria — one I haven't lived in in years — and buy a schooner. *They're* still making a living at it down here. Why not a real Yankee trader?"

She cocked her head and smiled up at him, a brief, fleeting smile that, for the moment, seized the fantasy. "Take me with you. I can do great things with fish and a handful of rice, and I speak the language," she cajoled.

He laughed. And just for that moment the horror, and the rage, dispelled for both of them. He noticed the toss of auburn hair, the flushed cheeks, the pretty, eternally girlish features that again reminded him, achingly, of Charlotte, and he was suddenly very grateful that this woman had survived.

"Captain," Robinson shouted from inside the wheelhouse, "the SEAL teams are at the boat."

The SEALs silently crept into positions along the river bank, their black and green grease-painted faces invisible amid the giant ferns and roots, except for the whites of their darting eyes; they crouched behind shielding buttresses that anchored the giant trees in the shallow, moist soil, their rifle sights scanning the *Black Sea*'s decks.

The ship's gangway was down, leading from water level up to the promenade deck, as though inviting them on board. There was no boat at the foot of the gangway, but the lifeboats and launch still hung undisturbed from their davits. The decks *looked* empty, but a hundred armed men might be hiding behind the bulwarks.

Blocker's bowels knotted in spasms again, and he consciously sucked up his guts, fighting the urge to urinate and relieve himself that preceded any fire fight. He took a deep breath and smelled the rank, sour taint of fear in the sweat that now drenched him.

It was very spooky, surreal — the luxurious liner, sleek as a yacht and gleaming white as vanilla ice cream, crammed into the turbid jungle river. It looked completely deserted, not a soul on deck and not a sound, except for the distant hum of an auxiliary generator deep within the holds of the ship, and that sound was drummed out by a cicada in the trees behind Blocker.

Hamilton glanced nervously at him, took the headset from the radioman at his side, and whispered into the mouthpiece. He listened to the report from the SEAL teams deployed on the other side of the river. He looked back at Blocker and shrugged in bewilderment. *Nothing.*

A troop of monkeys suddenly crashed through the trees about them, and everyone started. In the deep silence that followed the monkeys' branch-shaking, squabbling passage, Blocker heard a loud, savage buzzing of flies from somewhere aboard the ship.

Hamilton swept the deck foot by foot with his binoculars. He peered at the head of the gangway, licked his lips nervously, as though his mouth had suddenly gone dry, then lowered the glasses and turned to stare at Blocker. Underneath the grotesque green camouflage makeup, Blocker could not make out his

714

expression. The SEAL commander handed Blocker the glasses and pointed to the top of the gangway.

Blocker focused the binoculars. To his surprise he saw two people, white men, apparently kneeling on either side of the gangway. No, a man and a woman. They were utterly still, staring straight out. It took a few moments for Blocker's eyes to adjust and recognize exactly what he was looking at. The buzzing of the flies sounded almost deafening in his ears, as he identified their source.

The two heads — eyes open in a frozen terror, mouths agape in a scream that pierced and echoed silently through the jungle — were mounted on either side of the threshold, like hideous sideboys to welcome them aboard.

Blocker lowered the glasses. The miasmic heat, the stench of the river mud all but overwhelmed him, and he had to clench down and swallow hard to keep from throwing up.

Hamilton stared at him, his eyes shadowed by the floppy brim of his jungle hat, only the grim set of his mouth readable. He made a pumping motion with his arm, and Blocker nodded in agreement. There was no question of negotiations. The assault was on. God only knew if any of the hostages were still alive.

By the bow of the *Black Sea,* where the deck flared out almost touching the narrowing river banks, four men — one after the other — slipped noiselessly through the foliage and mud into the water. Ferns sprouted from their floppy hats, and they wore flotation devices to minimize swimming so that only the camouflaged patch of their heads, no wider than a lily pad, floated on the water. In a moment they were alongside the hull under the overhang of the deck, and the current carried them right to the gangway.

When all four were gathered there, Hamilton gave a hand signal and whispered the order into his mike. On both sides of the river concussion grenades were lobbed onto the open decks. There were deafening explosions, blinding flashes, eruptions of smothering smoke. From both banks a dozen lightweight scaling ladders suddenly thrust out; the hooks on their ends seized the railing of the promenade deck. The four men in the water leaped onto the gangway and raced up it. But at the top they froze, transfixed by the horrors that flanked them. Then one broke and sprang onto the deck to the right, the other jumped left. The next two followed.

There was no gunfire, only the distant,

rumbling echo somewhere of the "flash-bang" grenades. The four men now on board were hidden, crouched down behind the bulwarks. For an instant Blocker saw their bobbing, camouflaged heads and the probing dark muzzles of their Colt Commandos against the white bulkhead of the ship.

Then one stood up and signaled. Half a dozen SEALs crawled across the scaling ladders, totally exposed, one hand clutching the rungs and the other an assault rifle by its pistol grip. A dozen guns covered them from each bank as they scampered across the moat. Then another group crossed, a third wave, and a fourth.

Blocker waited impatiently. He had to remain on the bank with the backup group. He was not trained for the search and assault work aboard. There was the strong possibility that the ship was booby trapped, that the whole thing might blow up. The SEALs on the bank kept their guns pointed, but none moved from behind the thick protective buttresses of ironwood trees.

Blocker watched with a terrible premonition growing, as the dark, incongruous figures crept along the promenade and disappeared into corridors, and green-painted faces appeared in the portholes of the main deck.

One of the SEAL officers, a lieutenant

named Garcia, stepped out onto the Lido deck, not crouching or bothering to conceal himself. He held both hands out wide, palms up, in a gesture of frustration and shouted across to Hamilton, "Sam, there's nothing here. *Nada*. There's nobody aboard."

51. The Sea Chase

Stewart listened to the radio communications between Hamilton and the National Military Command Center in Fort Ritchie, Maryland, with amazement.

"They must have herded them all into the jungle. We found the bodies, or rather the remains, about fifty yards in. And there's a pile of luggage deeper in, as though the passengers started out with some belongings and then were forced to ditch them," the SEAL commander reported. The *Decatur* was the radio relay, and Hamilton's voice had not yet been digitized and encoded. His excitement and revulsion, the hurried impatience of his report, were palpable, a tremolo that shuddered from the overhead speakers on the bridge.

"Was there any identification on the victims?" The computer-reconstructed voice from Maryland recognized neither the horror nor the urgency.

"Yes, sir, they were very precise about that. A passport and a sea book were hanging around their . . . from the posts. The American was Williard Howell, Jr." Hamilton spelled out the name. "And the woman was one of the Russian crew members, a Svetlana Fedorova."

Stewart looked at Maggi Chancellor. Her eyes were shut, and she was trembling. "Did you know them?"

"Yes, both," she whispered.

"I suggest, sir, that we immediately take off after them. They can't get too far too fast herding over two hundred hostages. It'll be nightfall in an hour, and they'll have to stop."

"Yes, pursue them, and report as soon as you make contact."

"Yes, sir, this is Golden Retriever. Out." The radio relay ended.

"My God, this could turn into a disaster," Stewart said.

"They're not in the jungle," Maggi said quietly. "That's not Tengku's element. He and his men simply are *not* going to herd 225 hostages through the jungles and swamps. This man envisions himself as an Oriental potentate. He always had as little as possible to do with the passengers and crew."

"But he was trained as a terrorist in Iran, according to Blocker."

"Who is Blocker exactly?"

"CIA."

Maggi nodded. "Figures. They loved the jungle. So did that SEAL officer in his camouflage uniform. But Tengku's a pirate, a smuggler, a man of the sea." She shook her head vehemently. "The bodies, the luggage, I mean it's all so damn obvious. Why not throw the bodies into the river for the crocodiles? That's what they did with the others."

"Then where the hell are they?"

"I don't know."

"Did you see any other boats?"

"Just *perahus,* dugout canoes with outboard motors."

Stewart turned to Callahan, who had been monitoring the radio with them. "Is there another outlet to the sea?"

"Where I picked up Mrs. Chancellor, it's sort of a delta. The river branches."

Stewart stared off, as if trying to see farther upriver, beyond the bend and the wall of mangroves. "But we're talking over two hundred people. It would take a whole fleet of small boats to move them."

"They've had all day to do it."

"You never saw anything bigger?" he interrogated Maggi.

"No, nothing but the canoes."

"That's not going to work," Stewart insisted, "even if they had dozens of them. Hamilton's right. They had to take the hostages into the jungle."

"It doesn't make sense."

"It does if you're going to massacre them," Callahan blurted out, then gnawed his lip and glanced away, immediately regretting he had said it in front of the woman.

She looked startled, then shocked.

"I'm afraid he's right," Stewart said softly.

"No, he isn't," Maggi insisted. "Why not just kill them all aboard the ship?" The woman was not letting go of it. She looked at him evenly, all the hysteria gone now.

"You can bury a lot of bodies in the swamp. We might never find them. This Tengku Haji Azhar could still hold on to some of the hostages. And we'd never be sure how many."

She frowned, like a schoolgirl puzzling out a problem, but Stewart noticed the trembling, a slight fluttering of the oversized khaki trousers that betrayed her. She was not as tough as she was trying so hard to be. Maggi suddenly whirled on him.

"That sailing ship we saw, what did you call it?"

"A Bugis schooner."

"Why that specifically?"

"That's the design. The Bugis make and sail those windjammers through the islands."

Maggi started to say something, then stopped, as if grasping for connections. "The Bugis are traders — I mean, that's their reputation now. But they used to be feared as pirates. Historically, it's all mixed up."

"You could say the same thing about this ship's namesake. Decatur's father was a pirate, a privateer."

"But he wasn't a religious fanatic. That's how the other Indonesians regard the Bugis. Am I making any sense? Or am I spouting — I don't know — a lot of academic nonsense?"

Stewart frowned, his brow knitting in thought. "Under the circumstances, you're making some crazy sense, yeah."

"But how could they get a schooner like that upriver?"

"Tow it with any broken-down scow. That's all they do to pick up cargo," Stewart explained. "But that kind of schooner can't hold over two hundred people."

"Yes, it can." Robinson's voice boomed across the bridge. He had not spoken until then, but had sat silently in the bridge chair, his dark face grim and set, his leg immobilized in its ice pack, following the radio report.

722

Stewart was startled by the authority in the executive officer's voice. "How do you know that?"

"A racial memory," Robinson said. "But you have to allow for a heavy loss of cargo over a long voyage, maybe all of it if disease breaks out. That's why I don't share your romantic view of eighteenth-century schooners, Captain."

Stewart looked from Robinson to Maggi for confirmation. "Yes, that's exactly what Tengku would do. He'd revel in it."

Outside the sun was rapidly setting, shooting out great spokes of red light, transforming the banks of rain clouds to the west into ragged rose and magenta billows. "He's got a head start, and a ship like that can make eight or nine knots with a good wind. We'll never catch it!" Stewart exclaimed.

"I can check it out, Captain," Callahan volunteered. "Maybe I can even slow it down."

"Do it." Stewart gave orders for weighing anchor, hesitated, then commanded, "Light off the starboard main engine." He looked at Robinson. "How much can we get out of it?"

"I don't know. It's a gamble. The gear's warped. If it throws, it might blow a hole in the ship that'll make the missile look minor. Are you going to check with National Command?"

"How would you explain this?"

"I can't. And I don't understand everything that Professor Chancellor is saying." Robinson took a deep breath, as if he were about to plunge into water over his head. "But I've got a gut instinct that she's right."

Stewart stared at his executive officer.

Robinson's mouth twisted into an ironic smile. "Or maybe I've just been hanging around you too long, Captain."

"Captain, engineering reports starboard engine is lit off."

"Very well." Stewart felt the ship trembling. He used the two electrical auxiliary propulsion units under the bridge and a hard rudder to twist the frigate around in the narrow channel, then ordered the two APUs retracted. They could be used only for maneuvering if the ship was traveling slower than seven knots. Otherwise they would be damaged.

"Captain."

Stewart turned to his executive officer.

"The main engine is controlled by computer if you operate it from up here." Robinson pointed to the throttle on the helmsman's right. "If we switch control below, they can bypass the computer."

"What'll that do?"

"They can throw the prop to maximum

pitch. It'll keep the shaft r.p.m.'s down and still give us a few more knots of speed. It's not efficient, but it's easier on the reduction gear until we get up to speed."

"A hell of an idea. Pass the word to Central Control."

"Captain, the helo is airborne."

The Seahawk banked to the left, then soared swiftly down the channel ahead of the ship.

The ship's speed increased with a frustrating timidity. The shaft r.p.m. dropped slightly as the propeller shifted to maximum pitch. Stewart could hear the change in the gas turbine five decks below the bridge. It was like shifting a sports car into high gear too soon.

"Rudder amidships, engine ahead one-third. Indicate five knots."

"Rudder is amidships. Engine ahead one-third, sir," the helmsman responded.

Stewart felt the shudder, like an old train moving out, but it was not quite as bad as before. As Robinson had predicted, there was less vibration now. He nodded to his executive officer. "Okay, now everything more we get out of it is at least faster than the APUs."

"If we don't tear a hole in the ship."

Stewart studied the wind speed and direction indicator. "Mr. Balletto, call down to the flight deck and have them open both hangar doors. I want a man on the phones, and a crewman standing by to shut them on a moment's notice."

"Aye, aye, sir."

He caught Robinson's questioning expression. "There's a good wind on our stern coming down the channel. This ship has a lot of sail area, and even a five-knot crosswind will give you a noticeable set. An open hangar really catches the wind and pushes the stern."

Robinson shook his head. "The engineering plant I know, but the art of ship handling . . ."

"Always remember this class of ship's pivot point is right behind the bridge, but you've a whole football field of ship behind you, swinging the stern opposite to the way the bow is pointing."

"Christ, this channel's not that wide!"

"That's why it's an art," Stewart commented, then ordered, "Helmsman, indicate seven knots."

"Indicating seven knots, sir." The ship clattered and shook like an old freight train.

"Come right to one-seven-eight."

"Coming right to one-seven-eight, sir."

Stewart strode onto the port wing and

leaned out perilously to peer aft to see how the *Decatur*'s stern was positioning itself in the narrowing channel.

"The open hangars are acting like a spanker sail, but they sure whip the stem around," Stewart announced to the bridge. "Mr. Balletto, take the starboard wing."

"Aye, aye, sir."

Robinson started to move out of the bridge chair, but Stewart stopped him with a sharp wave. "You're not going to be there when I need you, Robbie, if you're crippled or doped up in pain."

Robinson nodded glumly.

"Okay, let's see what happens now when we push it. Helmsman, engine ahead two-thirds."

"Engine ahead two-thirds, sir."

The freight train was now running on dented and chipped wheels, and the shuddering of the ship set up a clatter that was deafening.

Robinson had to shout, "I don't know if we can hold this speed very long, Captain."

"If we don't, we can't catch them."

"Blue Knight, this is Eagle Claw Seven, over."

"Go ahead, Eagle Claw."

"I have the schooner in sight, sir, in my binoculars. And it is definitely unfriendly.

There are a lot of guys on deck with guns pointing at me."

Suddenly Maggi Chancellor was beside Stewart. In the controlled crisis of getting under way, Stewart had forgotten she was on the bridge; she had apparently retreated back into a corner.

"Does he see anyone who looks like American civilians, or Russians in uniforms?"

Stewart repeated the question.

"That's a negative, Captain. Just a dozen or more natives on deck. But it's riding pretty low in the water. Damn low. It's got a full load of something."

"Is it out of the strait yet?" Stewart leaped to the chart table.

"Just about. A half mile more, and they'll be in open water. They're under full sail, and you're right, Captain, they're moving faster than the *Decatur*. I hate to say it, but it's a pretty sight."

"I'll bet it is," Stewart said to no one in particular, then into the radio mike, "Stand off and let me know when they're about a mile into the open sea." He turned to Maggi. "You saw only M16's and AK-47's?"

She nodded. "But you said they had missiles."

"You're convinced that Tengku would take the hostages aboard?"

"I'll swear to it."

"You may have to at my court-martial. XO, get on the horn to the Command Center. Detail the situation . . . and request permission to fire."

"No!" Maggi shouted. "You'll kill the hostages."

"We'll avoid the hull. Just tear up the sails and rigging, but we have to stop them. We're not going to catch them otherwise."

Then everyone on the bridge fell silent, the clattering, rattling clamor of the ship tearing itself apart to make eight knots punctuating Stewart's every word. The pandemonium and the close proximity of jungle and rocks on either side gave the sense that the *Decatur* was racing hellbent through the strait.

Stewart strode back and forth across the bridge, bolted onto the wings to check the set of the frigate's stern as a cross-wind caught, and shouted commands to the helmsman.

"Captain, I can't get through on the satellite. There's a lot of traffic," Robinson yelled above the din.

"Goddamn it, there's a whole carrier battle group out there trying to figure out what to do next with themselves."

"Blue Knight, Eagle Claw Seven. Over."

"Go ahead, Eagle Claw."

"The schooner's about a mile into open water now, sir, and it's racing away."

The setting sun, magnified by the sweltering tropical air, was a hallucination — an enormous disc of red fire that inflamed the sea to the west like a torch put to a pool of oil. The Seahawk dove straight out of the fire, zooming just above the waves toward the schooner.

A sudden cotton ball of smoke rose just beyond the sailing ship, and from it a steamy white plume headed for the helicopter.

"Stinger!" the copilot Henshaw screamed.

Callahan jabbed the release button that spewed flares from the cartridge dispenser under the fuselage.

But the straight white contrail never deviated. The heat-seeking missile ignored the explosion of decoys. It shot straight for the helo and passed a hundred feet directly overhead, fixed on the hotter fiery target ninety-three million miles behind them.

Henshaw turned and stared at Callahan, his eyes unnaturally wide with fear and astonishment. "Jesus, I didn't even have time to shit in my pants!" he shouted exuberantly.

"Goddamn right," Callahan shouted back. He glanced behind, but the Stinger's trail was lost in the blinding glare of the sun off the water. The low sun and the glare were the Seahawk's shield. The pilot keyed his mike. "Blue Knight, this is Eagle Claw Seven. The schooner fired what appeared to be a Stinger at us, but we faked it out. The Afghan Zoom worked. I dove in low out of the sun, under the level that the missile's programmed for, and it just took off over us."

"Don't get cocky. They might get lucky," Stewart advised. "Their assault rifles only have an effective range of a quarter mile. So hang outside that and rip their sails to shreds."

"Rip their sails to shreds, yes, sir." Callahan hit the intercom. "Jimenez, you heard the man. Keep it high."

"Aye, aye, sir."

The first blast from the M60 machine gun sprayed the trapezoidal black sails midway up their masts. The armed men in firing stances on the schooner's deck were blasting away with their rifles at the helicopter. But at the first burst of the M60 they all dropped to the deck, scurrying behind hatch covers, coils of rope, the two thick masts, the deck cabin, whatever flimsy protection the sailing ship offered.

Callahan hovered just out of range of the M16's and AK-47's, but he was a target for anything bigger. Even a light machine gun like the M60 could kill him from over a mile away. At the door gun Jimenez poured fire into the huge black sails, but the pilot could not make out any damage. "Are we getting anything?"

Henshaw studied the schooner through his binoculars. "Nothing serious, just rips and tears in the sails. We're not slowing them down any. It's like shooting into a mountain of shit. It just absorbs it."

A small topsail on the mainmast collapsed as a bullet severed a line. But it was obvious to Callahan that it was going to take more of the small 7.62-mm. bullets than they had to cut those huge sails down. "Cease fire," he ordered.

He banked away and circled at a safe distance to study the schooner. Its half dozen sails full of wind, the ship plunged through the wave crests, the long blue blades of its twin tillers slicing the water aft.

"Jimenez, do you see the ship's stern? The way it hangs out over the water like a junk's?"

"Yes, sir."

"That means there's no cargo hold with hostages back aft. Can you concentrate all your fire there? That'll shoot up their tiller. They'll still have power, but they'll only be able to sail in a circle."

"We'll have to get closer, but I can walk the tracers right there and just hold it there."

"Are you sure of this?" Henshaw asked.

"Hell, no, what am I, a sailor? You have a better idea?"

"No, sir."

"I'm going to have to fly within range of their guns to give you a shot," the pilot briefed Jimenez. "So keep cutting up the sails to keep their heads down as we come in. Whatever you do, don't hit the hull or you'll kill hostages. If you don't have a shot, don't take it. You got that?"

"Yes, sir."

Callahan set up carefully, with the low sun again directly behind him, blinding the shooters on the sailing ship. He swooped in at an angle, cutting from bow to stern. The M60 tracers raked the sails just over the cabin level. The men on deck, who had got to their feet again, sprawled for their lives.

The Seahawk was only a few hundred yards from the schooner when Callahan pulled into a hover. Jimenez's tracers wove a white line that sliced across the stern into the wake, then bounced up again into the overhanging tiller and held there.

At that range Callahan saw wood shattering, and two men either jumped into the sea or were blasted off.

There was a pause in the M60 fire, and in the silence Callahan heard the ping of bullets hitting the chopper. The hovering sixty-five-foot broadside of fuselage and blades were now a pot shot from the ship. "We're getting out of here."

Jimenez sent a final burst into the stern, then sprayed the sails again.

Callahan fled back into the sun.

"We got it! We got it!" Henshaw cried out.

The pilot looked back at the schooner, now out of rifle range. The sailing ship was veering sharply to the right, and as it lurched, stern to the wind, the billowing black sails first fluttered, then luffed, then appeared to collapse against their masts.

A cheer went up on the bridge when Callahan radioed that he had disabled the schooner.

"Where'd they hit you?" Stewart interrogated him.

"I don't know, and I don't want to find out out here, sir."

"Head in immediately."

"Coming home. Eagle Claw Seven, out."

Stewart stood, hands on hips, smiling.

It was Maggi Chancellor who put a damper on his triumph. "They may repair it before you get there. It's only wood and rope.

They're low-tech sailors, and their lives depend on making quick repairs at sea."

Stewart stared hard at her, then turned to the bosun of the watch. "Pass the word for Powder Keg to report to the bridge on the double."

Master Chief Gunner's Mate Maggio's nickname was a natural, bestowed by his craft, the gunpowder black hair and mustache that bristled like a fuse atop his chunky, keglike body, and his explosive temper when anyone, even junior officers, handled weapons and munitions with anything less than absolute reverence.

"Can you demast the schooner?" Stewart questioned him.

Maggio's dark brows, which met over his blunt nose, contracted. "We'll have to take the gun off the Mark-92 fire-control radar and use the backup optical sight. Manually load the ammo."

"No explosives. We can't start a fire."

"BL and P nonexplosive warheads, yes, sir."

"You can do it?"

"Yes, sir, if we can get close enough, and I have a clear line of sight. I've hit target balloons on manual."

"There are American hostages in this target balloon."

"No, sir, there are American hostages fifty feet *right below* the target."

The *Decatur* burst out of the narrow strait into a broad reach of the east bank, its surface placid with light twilight winds. The sunlight was nearly gone. To Stewart's surprise he spotted the schooner almost immediately, sailing toward him. Or rather it was still circling about with its crippled tiller, its port bow facing him.

The windjammer had hauled in the after sail, but the mainsail and the three flying jibs were still furled.

"Why haven't they pulled in their sails?" Robinson asked.

Stewart glanced at Maggi. "Because they don't want to be dead in the water when they get the tiller repaired." Stewart had to make a difficult decision. The *Decatur*'s 76-mm. gun was in the middle of the ship behind the bridge. If he headed straight for the schooner, Maggio did not have a shot. But if the schooner got under full sail in the next few minutes, he would never catch it. And a shot at the narrow sail area from astern would be impossible.

"Helmsman, right full rudder. Come right to two-one-zero."

"Coming right, to new course two-one-zero, sir." Then, several heartbeats later, the helmsman announced, "Steady on two-one-zero, sir."

"Very well." Maggio now had the best shot Stewart could set up.

The retort of the 76-mm. was a sharp crack. Stewart could follow the contrail of the shell through the thick, moist air with his naked eye. The shot was high, a whole mast length above the sails and ahead of the schooner.

"Mind your helm."

"Yes, sir, steady on two-one-zero."

"Keep it there."

Bam!

The second shot headed straight for the schooner — but it was too low. Stewart's heart lurched. The condensation trail cleared the schooner's deck and disappeared into the black expanse of the mainsail.

Nothing happened. The nonexplosive steel-jacket warhead simply ripped through the cloth, as Callahan's bullets had done. *Bam!* Maggio, now zeroed in on the target, quickly fired a third round, then a fourth.

The high gaff boom yanked away and, as if viewed in slow motion, dropped down, collapsing the mainsail, which was hoisted on it.

"Cease fire!" Stewart shouted through his telephone talker. "Helmsman, hard left rudder to — " he estimated the course to cut off the schooner " — to one-six-five."

"Hard left, sir. New course, one-six-five."

"Mr. Balletto."

"Sir."

"You're relieved from the bridge. Take charge of the boarding party."

"Which side, Captain?"

"Starboard."

Balletto saluted and leaped for the ladder.

"Tengku and his men won't let you aboard," Maggi protested in an anguished voice. "They'll fight to the death. It martyrs them."

"We're happy to oblige them," Stewart said.

"No! The hostages will be killed."

"My men have been briefed. They will be very careful."

"They can't be once the shooting starts. Maybe Tengku plans to blow us all up, I don't know. But please let me try and talk to him in his own language," Maggi pleaded. "Maybe it won't do any good, but we've got to try."

Stewart shook his head. "He'll kill you."

"Then you kill him," she said simply. "But I must try."

Stewart studied her a moment, then turned to Robinson. "I've got to lead the boarding party."

"Why? Balletto's capable," the XO objected.

"No, Mrs. Chancellor's right about one thing. We're dealing with fanatics who are ready to die and take everyone along with them. They've probably got that schooner rigged to blow as soon as we step aboard. Balletto and the others wouldn't know a booby trap until it blew in their faces."

"Do you?"

Rather than seeming offended, Stewart smiled grimly. "I wouldn't have gotten to my twenty-fifth birthday if I didn't."

The schooner was now practically dead in the water, only the three small flying jibs along the bowsprit giving it a slight headway. As the *Decatur* approached, Stewart paced the bridge, leaning over the bulwarks to look at the sailing ship and then at the sea, peering astern at the pennant, estimating the wind. He issued brief orders in a firm, confident tone, as if chasing down and demasting pirate schooners were a somewhat unusual, demanding, but perfectly natural part of his job. For a few fleeting seconds Maggi had the sense that she was witnessing something extraordinary — a man totally in command in the midst of chaos.

She could now see the pirates crowded

on the port side firing at them. They were still out of range. The sun had set, and the light was dropping quickly, the darkness encroaching from the east like a malignant overcast.

"Bosun, pass the word that we'll soon be under small-arms fire. Everyone on deck take cover." In an aside to Robinson he added, "The shooters are down at water level, so just lying flat will cover the boarding party."

On the bow directly below sailors were rigging a cargo net that draped over the sides like a wide ladder.

"But what happens when they climb down?" Maggi asked in a frightened voice.

"We have a surprise," Stewart said. He immediately turned to the lieutenant who had relieved Balletto. "Mr. Nielson, you'll have the conn during the boarding. Take your orders from the XO. I'll reverse the main engine during the approach, then stop it. Drop the APUs and use them to keep us pressed against the schooner." He turned to Robinson and said, as if apologizing, "Nielson is the best ship handler in the squadron."

"I know — " The sudden ping and ricochet of bullets against the bridge interrupted Robinson. The windscreen fractured into a spider web of breaks but did not shatter.

"They're firing right at the bridge. We're the target."

"Raise the missile," Stewart ordered.

A warning clangor blasted on the deck below, and just forward of the bridge a raised hatch slid open. The missile launcher, a huge cantilever of gray steel, swiveled about, and a gleaming blue pointed missile rose up out of the magazine directly below and automatically coupled to the launcher. The hatch closed, the launcher swiveled about and deflected, pointing the missile like a giant spearhead at the schooner.

"You're not going to fire it!" Maggi shouted in alarm.

"Naw, I just want to scare them to death," Stewart said.

Almost immediately the gunfire silenced, as if in awe. Then it erupted again in a sudden volley that pinged and banged against the bulkhead directly below.

"They're shooting at the missile! Trying to blow it up!" Maggi exclaimed.

"Good! That's what they're supposed to do."

Maggi stared at Stewart as though he were a lunatic.

"It's a dummy. It's only for system testing and show."

Maggi let out a wild laugh. "My God, you're wily."

Stewart barked out a series of commands. "Hard left rudder . . . Engine back one-third . . . Lower the APUs . . . Engine stop . . . Train port and starboard APUs to zero-six-zero."

With the frigate's turbine stopped, the jarring vibrations and clatter of the ship suddenly ended, and there was an eerie stillness on the bridge, punctured by the sharp cracks and bursts of the gunfire from the schooner.

The light had dropped fast, and the sailing ship was a black silhouette against the darkening eastern sky, red bursts flickering on and off along its length.

Stewart again shouted commands, but in the chaos Maggi made out only the word *searchlights*.

Two white beams snapped out from the *Decatur* in an incandescent blaze. The pirates were frozen, blinking at the blinding light like wild animals caught and momentarily paralyzed in the headlights of an automobile.

The *Decatur* swung behind the schooner and eased up its port side. The pirates were now all crowded on its stern or hanging precariously over the sides trying to shoot up at the bow and bridge of the ship looming forty feet above them.

"Open fire!" Stewart shouted. The .50-caliber machine guns, all concentrated on the starboard side and silent until that moment, now exploded at once. The effect was an eruption of fire. The gunners' aim was high, well above the deck of the schooner, but the heavy wooden masts and booms splintered, the sails ripped and shredded, lines and ladders burst, all collapsing on the stunned, cowering men below as if a hurricane had burst on the boat.

Under this storm the *Decatur* pulled right alongside, taking the schooner under its starboard quarter.

"Cease fire!" Stewart ordered. The shattering barrage stopped as abruptly as it had detonated.

"Mr. Nielson, you have the conn." Stewart rushed out onto the wing of the bridge, then dropped down a ladder. The deck of the schooner was littered with debris, with men lying about, moaning, struggling to free themselves, crawling out from underneath piles of canvas, broken wood, and ropes. Maggi did not see anyone who looked like Tengku.

For the first time she noticed the long fire hoses snaking across the *Decatur*'s deck, sailors crouched or sprawled clutching them, as if they were wrestling giant pythons to the ground. Just below her Stewart emerged from a hatch onto the bow.

On the schooner one of the pirates struggled to his feet and groped for his rifle.

"Hoses!" Stewart bellowed. "Clean sweep down fore and aft."

The sailors visibly tensed, bracing themselves as high-velocity streams of water spewed down on the schooner. The violence of the water was, if anything, greater than that of the machine guns. The pirate regaining his feet was abruptly swept off, his rifle ripped from his grasp and hurled overboard, and he was smashed against a mast. A blast of water caught another in the chest and hurled him bodily across the deck and over the side. Men, guns, boxes, jumbles of rope and debris were tumbled over the wooden deck and off the ship like insects, twigs, and leaves before a garden hose.

The hoses suddenly stopped, and Stewart and several of the sailors carrying guns crawled over the side and vanished, for the moment, from Maggi's view.

She ran to the ladder down which Stewart had disappeared and came out on a narrow walkway. Stewart, pistol in hand, and a few men were just below her on the schooner deck. The pirates she could see lay pummeled senseless amid the debris or were struggling in the inky water beyond the boat.

There was a low cabin on the stern, and

in the middle of the deck between the fore and aft masts was a raised, covered hatch. Stewart signaled his men to move onto the bow, forward of the hatch, and then he stepped toward it. He knelt, examining it very carefully, gingerly running his fingers about the edge. He dropped to his knees and slowly lifted the hatch cover up a fraction of an inch at a time, peering under it.

The door to the stern cabin flew open, and a man stumbled out, a white man, his hands tied behind him, his legs hobbled by a short rope. He almost fell forward, but another man, directly behind, held him up with a cruel yank on his pinioned arms.

Before he spoke, Maggi saw it was Schneider and Tengku. "You go back. I kill Secretary of State Schneider." Tengku gestured with a .45 in his right hand. The other hand, around Schneider's neck, held a grenade.

Stewart did not budge from the opened hatch, despite the pirate's threatening gestures. Tengku suddenly shoved Schneider at him and at the same instant fired at Stewart.

Stewart cried out, clutched at his chest, and fell back across the hatch, his own pistol dropping and bouncing on the deck.

Tengku again seized the dazed Schneider as his shield and advanced toward the hatch and the fallen Stewart. No one on the schooner or the *Decatur* could fire without killing Schneider and, perhaps, the people in the hold below.

From her angle Maggi saw a belt about Tengku's waist from which dangled another half dozen grenades. Tengku himself was the detonator for whatever bomb Stewart had been searching.

"Tengku, my darling, my beloved!" Maggi cried out in Malay. "It's me, *Maggi Chancellor!*" She crawled over the side. "Please wait for me, my beloved, sun of my mornings." Maggi babbled out any absurd thing that leaped to her mind to grab his attention.

Tengku stopped and looked up in confusion toward the familiar voice calling endearments to him out of the blinding light.

She struggled down the heavy, sagging rope rungs of the cargo net. "They made me go with them. I didn't want to leave you, my love." Stewart was sprawled, face down, bleeding from a wound in his chest, struggling to reach his gun. Maggi leaped the last few feet, sprawled on her hands and knees, her hands groping about the wet wooden deck. Through the open hatch she had a glimpse of faces in the hold, almost unrecognizable in their terror, crammed body against body like cattle in a slaughterhouse boxcar.

Maggi looked up. Tengku stared at her, bewildered by her sudden appearance. He shoved Schneider, who lurched forward, tripped over his own hobbled feet, and dropped to his knees.

Maggi stood and stretched out both arms to Tengku, the oversized man's shirt she wore now undone and flopping ridiculously over her hands. "Beloved, the light of the East, the winds of Paradise are blowing."

Tengku's lips pulled back, and he smiled, his eyes shining in recognition.

Through the sodden cuff of her shirt, Maggi fired Stewart's pistol into the pirate's heart.

She fired again and again, each blast of the 9-mm. hurling Tengku back. His legs caught on the low wooden plank rail, and he tripped and tumbled backward, his hands, still clutching the grenade, flailing. He sprawled full length on the dark water, then, dragged down by the weight of the grenades about his waist, disappeared.

There was a flash and a muffled explosion beneath the surface. Then an instant later a much larger explosion blew up a geyser of spray, and in its midst Tengku Haji Azhar rose up, his arms and legs splayed out, his eyes frozen open. He hovered a moment in the incandescent spotlights, then dropped back and was swallowed by the black sea.

Epilogue

A Debriefing over Spicy Pomfret

The old East Coast Road no longer paralleled the coast, and the concentration of seafood restaurants in Bedok, a half hour's drive from downtown Singapore, was no longer lapped by the waves of the South China Sea. A flat stretch of landfill and the traffic on the new East Coast Parkway racing for jets at Changi Airport now cut off any sight or scent of the ocean.

Still, a pleasant breeze stirred the palms in the open forecourt of the restaurant as Yee and Blocker were seated. Two months had passed since the *Black Sea* incident. The northeast monsoons had long since ended, and no threat of rain veiled the bright tropical stars overhead.

"The best chili crab in Singapore?" Blocker questioned.

"My nephew, who is an expert in such matters, assures me," Yee said.

The waiter stood silently between them, waiting for the order. "Please, since it is your last night in Singapore, you are my guest," Yee said with an imperious wave of his hand. He ordered in Chinese.

The table was large, round, wooden, and bare, and in fact the courtyard and the restaurant itself were notably devoid of decor, reflecting the Chinese suspicion that the purpose of decoration in a restaurant was to distract the diners from badly prepared food. The surrounding tables were packed with large, chattering families ranging from aged grandmothers to babies-in-arms.

As the waiter scurried off, Yee shrugged in an apologetic manner. "Unfortunately, my stomach objects to chili crab no matter how much my palate enjoys it, and its loud complaints would keep my wife, even my neighbors, up all night with its grumbling."

Blocker laughed. "But it's practically the national dish of Singapore."

"A curious paradox of American history."

"Oh, how's that?"

"Columbus sailed west to find a new route to these Spice Islands, and instead he discovered the Caribbean and its chili peppers. The Spanish brought them here as an item of trade. Now, throughout all South Asia — Szechuan, Thailand, from Java to India — it is the main spice of our food. And since food is so important to us, nothing else from the West is so common in Asia as the chili pepper. Yet, I understand it is not that popular in Europe or America, a curiosity only. That is the paradox."

"You take only what you want from us, even if we ourselves don't appreciate it."

Yee smiled. "That is a paradox for you to contemplate in your new job in Washington."

"What peppers are we now unwittingly unloading on the docks of Asia?"

The waiter brought two large bottles of Anker beer and a dish of tiny squid, fried crisp and golden and garnished with pineapple.

"*Sotong goreng,*" Yee identified. "After the chili crab you will not be able to appreciate other flavors." They poured their beers. "You will miss being in the field?" Yee asked.

Blocker sipped his beer, then bit into a piece of squid and winked appreciatively before answering. "Baiyu, my friend, to be honest with you, there came a moment in this last operation — what my old grandmother would call an *epiphany*. I was hanging out on the skid of that Huey, dangling on a very stretchy quarter-inch nylon cord a hundred feet above a slimy jungle floor I couldn't even see. Head-chopping terrorists, crocodiles, cobras — I don't know what in hell is waiting down there. And the good

Lord whispers in my ear, and He says, 'Harold Blocker, you're getting too old and too fat for this sort of shit.' "

Yee laughed delightedly.

"No, a promotion and a desk job in the Directorate of Operations in Virginia suit me just fine. Hell, I may even pick up a Ph.D. at Georgetown. That's the ticket to a bureaucratic career these days, I hear. Take the onus off my reputation as a cowboy."

In a totally unexpected gesture, Yee reached forward and patted Blocker's hand. "I am sorry that we've not had the opportunity to be friends longer."

"It's not the length of the friendship that's important, but the heat that tempers its metal."

"Yes, yes."

"But bring me up to speed. I've been bopping back and forth to Washington with briefings and debriefings. What kind of flak are your chaps getting from Kuala Lumpur and Jakarta?"

"Nothing, actually. The murder, kidnapping, and piracy of American and Russian nationals are criminal matters. However, we have taken pains to privately point out that our . . . *punishment* has been in accordance with the *Sharia*, the Islamic law. There was recently a similar case in Sudan, which has a Muslim fundamentalist government. In two bombing attacks seven British citizens were killed by terrorists from Lebanon. When they were caught, they insisted they were *mujahedeen*, holy warriors from a group named the Arab Revolutionary Cells, and should not be tried as common murderers. The Islamic court in Khartoum rejected this. And, in fact, they even went so far as to ask the blood heirs of the victims — who were English — to approve the death sentence, all in accordance with the *Sharia*."

"And you pointed this out to K.L. and Jakarta?"

"Very discreetly, yes." Yee looked over at the adjacent, noisy table where a smiling, coaxing young mother lifted a morsel with her chopsticks to her baby's open mouth. "Singapore is a prosperous oasis, a link between Europe, Asia, and America. We've always been that kind of place. But we are still a small island, a fragile city-state, precariously set in the middle of a volatile, violent, and impoverished region. Even with our wealth, we cannot afford your great country's luxury of military arrogance."

"But you used us to your own purposes."

"We stay at the center of the circle and let things take their course. For every force there is a counterforce, and violence always rebounds upon itself."

A small smile played on Blocker's lips, but he said nothing.

"And how is Commander Stewart?"

"His wound was not disabling, and he's already been reassigned to the navy's surface warfare school in San Diego. Our naval attaché here, an old friend of his, says it's a good career post. The navy brass are not comfortable with him — Stewart's something of a loose cannon — but now that he's been personally decorated by the President on the White House lawn, he's got friends in high places. He's made captain and is in line for command of a cruiser. And my agency's watching him. They've always been partial to navy officers."

"Ah, yes, indeed. And the redoubtable Professor Chancellor?"

"Coincidentally, she's also in San Diego. On the faculty of the University of California's Graduate School of Pacific Studies. Something of a star now, a consultant for the Rand Corporation." He sipped his beer and then asked casually, "And my friend Salleh?"

"Ah, Salleh," Yee exclaimed. "That's very interesting."

The way he said it made Blocker alert.

"He asked for a leave."

"What's that about?"

"He is studying with the old *mullah* in Kuala Selatan, I think." Yee contemplated a tiny fried squid on his chopsticks. "This has been a very disturbing business for him. He needs to find his center. I understand that." He looked up and smiled slyly at Blocker. "But he will return to a very important promotion. He is — as you yourself commented — an exceptional man. Singapore cannot afford to lose him. *Aaah!*"

Yee's exclamation was for the dish the beaming waiter now presented, a whole pomfret in a steaming, fragrant, spicy broth. The waiter set it down with a flourish.

"Please," Yee gestured, inviting his guest to take the first piece out of the fish's unmarred silver side.

Blocker poked with his chopsticks in one hand and the serving spoon in the other; a large piece of tender meat lifted easily from the pomfret's plump flank.

"I'm afraid the pirates would throw you back into the water," Yee said. "You would not bring them very much of a ransom." He shook his head glumly, as though he had just pronounced a death sentence.

Blocker looked at him bewildered.

"You see, in the early days of Singapore, when the pirates captured a prisoner they knew nothing about but *suspected* might be wealthy, they served him a whole fish like this, a pomfret or garoupa. If he took the head or the tender, sweet underbelly, they knew this was a man who ate only the very best. He would bring a fat ransom. If he took his portion from the back, along the fin, this was a merchant who automatically accepted second best, but there was still a small ransom to be had. But if he took the side meat, as you just did, then they would throw him to the fish before he ate any more of their food."

Blocker leaned back and laughed uproariously, drumming his chopsticks on the wooden table top. "What a way to tell me this is a very old business. Baiyu, my friend, you have a wicked black humor."

Until he heard the American's rich laughter, Yee had not realized what a dark and elaborate joke, given the circumstances, it was. "Black humor," Yee repeated. He found the term curious.

"The darkest."

"Darkness within darkness, the gateway to all understanding," Yee quoted.

Blocker wiped his lips with a napkin and looked at Yee quizzically.

"But I sometimes talk like a fortune cookie. Isn't that what you once said?"

Blocker did not laugh. "No, what is that really?"

"It is a verse from the *Tao Te Ching*. The Book of the Way."

Blocker nodded respectfully.

"It might also be translated, 'The mystery of mysteries is the door to all essence.' Translations of the ancient Chinese classics are very . . . difficult. Our language and writing are very old. They evolved differently from English or French. A written character is not just a word. It is a pictograph *and* a sound that suggest many images, many emotions. The symbol *hsuan,* for instance, may translate as dark, mystery, deep, profound, secret, abstruse, or abyss — according to its context. And a single brief sentence is enormously rich in its ideas, its meanings. Yet boiled down to simple English, it indeed sounds like a foolish scrap from a fortune cookie. The *Tao Te Ching* is a very small book, yet it has been translated more than any book other than the Bible. It is said it will take all the translations already made and others yet to come to convey its full meaning."

"Why do I have the feeling, Baiyu, you're not talking about ancient books and translations?"

"I am talking about Asia, my friend."

Blocker said nothing for several moments, then, "Let's eat this fish before it gets cold and greasy."

It was Yee's turn to rear back, laugh, and slap the table. "Yes, yes, now you understand."

Above the diners the palms in the courtyard stirred, as the wind from the South China Sea shifted, an augury of the southwest monsoons to come later. In the clear, relatively dry air, the stars were unusually bright, magnified, once again outlining, as they had for eons, the figure of the hunter Orion as he pursued the Pleiades across the black vault of heaven.

Acknowledgments

I am indebted to H. Elliott McClure, Ph.D., the old Asia hand who first guided me into the jungles of Malaysia, Sumatra, and Borneo, was a constant consultant, and reviewed the manuscript.

The officers and men of the USS *Crommelin* shared their lives at sea, their experiences, and their hospitality with me during several embarkations. Captain Paul K. Vosseler, USN, and Commander Martin J. Leghart, Sr., USN, at that time the *Crommelin*'s commanding officer and executive officer, respectively, and Lieutenant David Lemek, USN, of squadron HSL-47, were extraordinarily professional and unstinting in their counsel beyond any call of public relations duty, and in reading and correcting the manuscript.

Other academics and professionals from Singapore and Malaysia assisted me in my research and critiqued drafts of this novel, but because of the sensitivity of their positions, they asked that their names not be published. I am no less grateful to them.

The employees of THORNDIKE PRESS hope you have enjoyed this Large Print book. All our Large Print titles are designed for easy reading, and all our books are made to last. Other Thorndike Large Print books are available at your library, through selected bookstores, or directly from us. For more information about current and upcoming titles, please call or mail your name and address to:

THORNDIKE PRESS
PO Box 159
Thorndike, Maine 04986
800/223-6121
207/948-2962